Touched by Magic

a magical, mysterious shapeshifter/vampire romance

Château Nocturne
Book 3

Anna Lowe

Contents

Other books in this series

Château Nocturne

Brushed by Moonlight (Book 1)

Marked by Moonlight (Book 2)

Touched by Magic (Book 3)

Touched by Starlight (Book 4)

Bound by Midnight (Book 5)

www.annalowebooks.com

Free Books

Get your free e-books now!

Sign up for my newsletter at *annalowebooks.com* to get three free books!

- *Desert Wolf*: Friend or Foe (Book 1.1 in the Twin Moon Ranch series)

- *Off the Charts* (the prequel to the Serendipity Adventure series)

- *Perfection* (the prequel to the Blue Moon Saloon series)

Chapter One

GENEVIÈVE

I put my hand on the door of the *boulangerie*, bracing myself for what awaited me. Then I mustered a friendly smile and stepped inside.

Ding-ding! The bell above the door chimed as I stepped from chilly November air into the warm, welcoming bakery.

Madame Martin, the baker, looked up from her conversation with Madame Fontaine, the retired schoolmistress. When they spotted me, they practically clapped with excitement, exactly as they had when I'd first arrived in town two weeks ago and every time in between.

Now I knew how endangered species felt.

"Oh *bonjour*, Geneviève! Look, Gérard. It's Geneviève!" Madame Martin gushed to her husband.

Subtext: *It's her — the one who finally showed up after months of procrastinating.*

I hadn't been procrastinating, though. I'd been finishing my contract at the Children's Theater of New England. . . and disentangling myself from another disastrous romance.

My shoulders sagged at the thought of all the head- and heartache Brandon had put me through. Correction — all the head- and heartache I had put *myself* through. Again.

But that was my past, and I'd learned from it. No more men. No more reckless flings. No more trusting my notoriously poor judgment.

I sighed. No more fun?

"Geneviève!" Madame Fontaine echoed Madame Martin's surprise. "So good to see you again!"

Subtext: *Good to see you haven't abandoned us...yet.*

"*Bonjour,*" I replied as sweetly as I could. I leaned left and waved to Monsieur Martin, who was pulling a rack of buns out of an oven in the back. "*Bonjour,* Monsieur Martin."

He was just as surprised as the others. "Geneviève! You're still in Auberre?"

"Why would anyone leave when the best éclairs in France are right here?"

He grinned proudly, while Madame Martin held her hand out for my shopping list, like she had ever since I was a kid. I'd spent every summer visiting my grandmother in France, and now, my sister, my cousin, and I had inherited her place.

A very big, very run-down place. Château Nocturne.

"I can't get over how much you look like your sister," Madame Martin said, though Madame Fontaine's expression said, *She sure doesn't act like her.*

I heaved an inner sigh. Similar packaging, very different interiors.

We shared the same blue eyes (our father's) and the same long brown hair (our mother's), though mine had a natural auburn tint. But while Mina was reserved and responsible, I was... Well, me. More outgoing. Slightly more reckless — er, spontaneous. And equally inconsistent when it came to using the little bit of magic that had trickled down to us through a very mixed family tree. *Brushed by moonlight,* some called it, though I preferred *touched by magic.* Either way, it showed up in the weirdest way and at the damnedest times.

Not that we let on about that. Our human neighbors didn't know about magic, and it was better to keep things that way.

"How is work going on the château?" Madame Martin asked while assembling my order. "I know your sister is delighted to have your help."

Subtext: *Finally helping her after months of shirking family duty.*

"It's going well, thank you," I said, embellishing a bit.

We were all busting our asses to renovate the place on a shoestring budget — a very frayed shoestring — but sometimes, I felt we were rolling boulders uphill.

"We're still looking for an electrician. Do you know any?" I asked.

That was the one job we weren't willing to try ourselves, lest we made an amateur mistake and burned the entire place to the ground.

They shook their heads. "None around here. Not since Jules Delmont retired."

"Didn't his son take over the business?" I tried.

Madame Martin huffed. "He took it, all right — all the way to Dijon, where the high-paying customers are. It's the same with anyone else in the business — their fees are too high or they're impossible to book."

Darn. That was what my sister had said, but I'd been hoping she was wrong. We were on Jules Jr.'s waiting list, but we'd be lucky if we got new wiring before the first Starbucks opened on Mars.

"And how are your sister and that beau of hers?" Madame Martin went on with a knowing grin.

The subtext on *that* comment was X-rated.

"Mina and Marius are fine. They send their regards," I fibbed, giving the wholemeal loaf a significant look. Couldn't she hurry up and give me my order?

"*Very* fine, no doubt," Madame Fontaine insinuated, totally missing my hint.

The two women chuckled. I sighed. As happy as I was for my sister, it was hard to be around blissfully mated lovebirds — especially when those lovebirds were dragons who were constantly touching, kissing, and cooing, not to mention soaring side by side over the château.

Only slightly jealous, I swear.

On the bright side, *beau* was an upgrade for Marius, who'd gone from *dangerous bad boy* to *enchanting new citizen* of Auberre. All it took was marrying my sister and staying mostly out of sight.

"Isn't Jules's grandson getting married?" Madame Martin asked Madame Fontaine.

She nodded. "Yes. He's just praying the bride doesn't invite too many guests."

"Oh? I'd love to get in touch with her," I said, sensing an opportunity.

But Madame Martin took off on a totally different subject.

"How are those houseguests of yours?" She practically waggled her eyebrows.

Subtext: *Those four hot men you're scandalously living with, doing who knows what with.*

The floor creaked as Madame Fontaine leaned in to listen.

I nearly laughed. Yes, we lived together, but in a château — hardly the kind of tight quarters that made hanky-panky inevitable. The guys were all the way over in the west wing, while I lived in the east wing, making for a very, very long walk of shame if one were so inclined.

Which I absolutely wasn't, because I'd sworn off men. Those men, especially.

And if I were to eye anyone, it would be a totally different man. A man I'd secretly loved since I was a kid.

The bell over the door chimed, and six feet of magnificent man-flesh stepped in.

"Clement!" the women cried in happy greeting.

He doffed his hat to each of them. "Madame Martin. Madame Fontaine." Then he turned to me and added, "Geneviève."

My ears strained for a drop in pitch that signaled powerful emotions, but if there were any, they were hidden — and hidden deep.

"*Bonjour,*" I said a little breathlessly.

In my defense, Clem had that effect on a lot of people. He was that effortlessly gorgeous. So effortlessly, he even made a police uniform look good. Not a given, as his portly colleague, Monsieur Blanchet, proved. Hell, Clem even made that boxy police minivan they drove around in look cool.

An image of being handcuffed and hauled away zipped through my mind, and not in a bad way.

I tried very, very hard to recall why I was not in the market for another relationship.

Instead, I found myself rationalizing why Clement was a worthy exception to my new rule. The man was a cop and a family-oriented wolf shifter. That made him highly loyal and protective. Even my sister approved of him, though she had warned me that he took *protective* to a whole new level.

One look at his caramel-colored eyes, and I decided I would be up for a whole lot of protecting. Especially if I got to run my hands over his sculpted body and weave my fingers through his neatly trimmed, blondish-brown hair.

I inhaled his sage-and-lavender scent, picturing him running through woods and fields in wolf form.

As it so happened, I had a fair bit of wolf-shifter blood in me. (As well as bear and dragon, not to mention witch and warlock, but that didn't seem pertinent at the moment.) We were practically made for each other, he and I!

Madame Martin had been one croissant away from assembling my order, but she stopped to serve Clem.

"What can I get you, dear?" she asked sweetly.

One baguette, one raisin bun, and a brioche, went through my mind.

"One baguette, one raisin bun, and a brioche," he said.

I flashed a smug grin, picturing future marital bliss.

"Oh! Geneviève ordered a baguette too!" Madame Martin exclaimed.

So did half of Auberre, but I loved her for trying. The woman had gone straight from trying to fix Clem up with my sister to fixing Clem up with me.

God bless meddling, small-town matrons.

Clem turned to me slowly, "Let me guess. For your *guests.*"

Then his tone dropped, and not in a good way. One of those guests had stolen the love of his life — Mina. Which was terrible and everything, but here I was, ready and willing to help him back aboard the love train.

I wanted to jump up and down, wave my arms, and holler, *Here I am! Can't you see me?*

But I'd been doing that since I was six, and Clem had never noticed. He didn't notice now either.

"Well, our guests do have to eat." I tried a joke.

Clem's sour expression suggested I could use starvation as a tactic to get rid of them.

Sadly for him, I didn't intend to. They made an excellent work force, and my godfather was paying good money for them to board with us, at least for the last few weeks of their contract with him. After that... Well, everyone avoided the subject for the time being. Marius had a plan for what to do next (renovating the château and living happily ever after with my sister), but the others had been pretty vague about their plans. My guess? They didn't have any.

We had a lot in common that way.

"How have you been?" I asked, trying to change the subject.

Sleepless. Suffering. Heartbroken, the dark lines under Clem's eyes said.

"Fine," he grunted. "Work keeps me busy."

I couldn't imagine what with, since the majority of Auberre's 200-plus residents were law-abiding senior citizens.

His nostrils flared, and he whirled as someone walked past the shop window.

"Claudette," he murmured.

I sighed. I could wave pom-poms in front of his face and Clem wouldn't notice, but Claudette got a full head whirl.

"Claudette?" Madame Martin's tone oozed concern.

Claudette was Auberre's pierced, tattooed wild child who flitted in and out of town, providing townsfolk with a constant stream of gossip — when they weren't speculating about me, my sister, and the goings-on at Château Nocturne.

Claudette must have spotted Clem, because a split second after walking past, she U-turned and entered the bakery.

"Claudette!" Madame Martin called in a sweet, *I swear I wasn't just talking about you* tone.

Claudette barely nodded back, making a beeline for Clem, whom she kissed three times in the standard French greeting.

Well, standard was air-kisses. Her lips grazed hungrily over Clem's cheeks.

"Back in town, I see," he said warily.

"Paris isn't what it used to be." Claudette shrugged, oozing antiestablishment attitude. Then she turned to me. "Geneviève. You finally made it."

Zero subtext, all straight talk. Kind of refreshing.

"I did." I held her arms as we traded air-kisses.

And, oh. Her studded faux-leather jacket didn't hide that she'd gone from lean to thin. Too thin.

"Good to see you," I said.

As a kid, I'd spent every summer in Auberre, and Claudette and I had been steady playmates. We'd grown apart in our teens, when Claudette started smoking, dressing Goth style, and hanging out with the wrong crowd, but I still counted her as a friend.

"That's new," I said, picking one of a dozen new piercings to point to.

She flicked her tongue, revealing the studs there. "This too."

"Nice," I said, going for tact.

Mesdames Martin and Fontaine exchanged horrified looks.

"What are your plans?" Clem asked.

She shrugged, exuding exaggerated, *I go where the wind takes me* vibes. "We'll see." She studied me for a moment before hinting, "Could stay a while if I had a job. You still need help with those guests?"

I froze, tongue-tied. My sister had filled me in on Claudette's brief interlude working at the château. Claudette hadn't been all too punctual or reliable, and she'd put more effort into flirting with the guys than into serving breakfast or cleaning. When she'd quit abruptly, my sister had been relieved.

Claudette was trouble, as everyone in Auberre knew. Me too.

And while most of Auberre knew Claudette hung out with the wrong crowd in Paris, they didn't know that crowd was *vampires.*

I did my best to look past the tattoos and attitude to the little girl I'd climbed trees and turned cartwheels with. I'd had many lucky twists of fate in my life. Claudette hadn't. Didn't she deserve a break?

Yes, but not with us. Not again, I could already hear my sister protest.

Claudette would distract the men and antagonize Madame Picard, our reliable housekeeper of fifty years. My sister would kill me for not consulting with her before opening my big mouth and for dangling a hot-blooded temptress in front of Henrik, our resident vampire.

Claudette's aloof expression said she couldn't care less, but I sensed her inner plea for just one more chance.

My magic didn't stir, but it didn't take superpowers to help a person in need. Plain old human compassion was enough.

"We can use all the help we can get," I heard myself say.

Clem's brow furrowed. Mesdames Martin and Fontaine exchanged looks that said *Disaster on the way.* But Claudette's hollow cheeks lifted a little, and her eyes lit up.

Even the danger Henrik posed, I figured, was better than her heading back to an entire coven of vampires in Paris.

"Can you come by tomorrow at eight in the morning? We can discuss details with my sister then," I said.

That would give Mina almost twenty-three hours to holler at me, I calculated. Enough for her to get everything out of her system before Claudette turned up for work. . . if she turned up.

I feverishly hoped that would be the case.

"Nine would be better," Claudette said, already pushing the boundaries.

Behind her, Clem shook his head in warning.

How sad was it that I barely existed in his world, and only my proximity to Claudette put me on his radar. And, *duh.* Did he think I was a complete moron?

"Eight. Do you need a ride?" I told Claudette, channeling my sister's firm-but-friendly teacher vibes.

Claudette scowled a little, then shook her head. "Nah. I have my own."

I pictured her roaring up on the back of a leather-clad vampire's motorcycle. Or, wait. Did vampires do leather and motorcycles? I wasn't sure.

"Perfect. See you then," I said, half in hope, half in challenge.

"See you then," she echoed, leaving with barely a glance at the others.

The bell chimed as she exited, and five pairs of eyes followed. Clem grabbed his purchases, paid, and jogged out the door after her.

Yes, *jogged*, because he couldn't risk *not* catching up to her.

I sighed. Would anyone jog after me one day?

"Bye," I whispered, watching him go.

Chapter Two

GENEVIÈVE

Madame Martin rang up my purchases, and I exited the *boulangerie* to a chorus of goodbyes. I'd parked down the street on the left, but my eyes went right, where Clem stood in earnest discussion with Claudette. It stood to reason that Clement's interest in her was purely professional, but I couldn't help feeling jealous.

With some effort, I tore my eyes from them, turned, and walked into a brick wall.

Oof.

"Watch it," a deep voice grumbled.

"*Pardon*—" I started, then glared. "You. Again."

I should have been happy to bump into one of Auberre's few eligible, under-forty bachelors, but this one was beyond annoying.

"A pleasure to see you too." His voice was low and growly, as usual. Maybe he'd missed his morning coffee?

"*Bonjour*, Roux," I muttered, stepping around him.

"*Bonjour*," the tiger shifter growled.

The man was best described as *David Beckham meets Bollywood and GI Joe*. His hair and skin were light brown, and his amber eyes would have been beautiful if they hadn't been so intense.

"Why is it that everywhere I go, I find you?" I groused, though I'd already figured it out.

My sister had assigned him to protect me from lurking, evil forces. Which seemed pretty unlikely in this forgotten little corner of Burgundy, but not impossible, given everything Mina had been through.

"It's a small town and a free country," he grunted.

"Not when you're being stalked," I muttered, opening the car door.

His expression told me I'd wounded his honor. And there was a *lot* of that in him to wound. I didn't know enough tiger shifters to know whether that was a general characteristic or something particular to him. But boy, was the guy touchy.

"Stalking is what the enemy does," he grumbled.

"I don't have enemies." When he snorted, I grimaced. "Ex-boyfriends don't count."

He rolled his eyes, distracting me momentarily. They were the color of sunset — all those colors, in fact — and downright beautiful. But brooding, too, like every problem in the world was packed behind them.

"I mean real dangers," he said.

"Like tigers?" I tossed my purchases in the back seat.

He gestured curtly, changing the subject. "You shouldn't leave your car unlocked."

I waved around. "This is Auberre, not Paris. And even in Paris, no thief would bother with this car."

The battered little Citroën had been built long, long before I graduated from high school. In my mind, that wasn't too long ago, but our fifteen-year reunion was right around the corner.

I slammed the door and walked to the driver's side.

But Roux blocked the way, arms crossed, legs braced. Did he think I was going to shove my way past him? And what the hell did he schlepp around in all those cargo pockets?

"What did the cop want?" he demanded.

"A baguette, a raisin bun, and a brioche."

He glared down at me as only 180 pounds of muscled tiger shifter could.

"I mean, what information did he want?"

"No, you mean, what information was I dumb enough to give him?"

From the day I'd arrived at the château, I'd had secrecy drilled into me. I wasn't to share any details about our houseguests (all supernaturals), their true professions (mercenaries), or what they suspected my beloved godfather of (all kinds of bad stuff). And I certainly wasn't to mention any long-lost artworks.

Roux jutted his jaw. "Well, did you?"

"Of course not." I huffed and walked around the back of the car.

Roux walked around the front and thrust a hand against the driver's side door before I could open it.

"What did Claudette want?" he barked next.

"A job."

He scoffed, then caught my expression and stared. "Tell me you didn't."

"I didn't."

We glared at each other for ten full seconds before I gave in.

"Okay, I did. And as much as I hate to pull the *I inherited the château, not you* card, I will. That's my decision, not yours."

"And your sister's. She'll be furious."

I reached for the door handle, but he smacked his hand over it. I wasn't as fast to react, so my hand landed on his, and a little zing went through me.

I whipped my hand back and shook it in the air.

"Yeesh. Attack me with static electricity, why don't you," I complained, then motioned to where Clement and Claudette stood talking, just down the street. "Do I need to call my police officer friend for help?"

Roux twisted to look over his shoulder, and my dirty mind pictured rows of rippling abdominal muscles. The guy was a real pain, but damn, did he keep his body sculpted.

Roux looked at Clem, then back at me. *Down* at me, in fact, making the most of his eight-inch height advantage.

"He's not a friend," he warned.

Sad, but true. Clem was Mina's friend, but not mine.

"He's a cop." Roux's voice dropped to a gravelly whisper.

"A harmless, small-town cop."

"Recently transferred from the special crimes unit in Marseille." He leaned in, and my nostrils filled with his fresh scent. "A transfer he made when we arrived here. Funny coincidence, don't you think?"

"Wouldn't he have launched a raid or busted you all by now?"

"Maybe he's still gathering intel."

"Maybe you're paranoid."

His eyes flashed. "I prefer cautious."

He also preferred *security consultant* to *mercenary*, I knew, but I let it slide.

"Seriously, Roux. If you guys are such bad news, my sister would have long since kicked you out of the château."

"We're not the problem. Gordon is."

Gordon, my generous godfather, was a rich and successful businessman. But not all his businesses were legit, as my sister had learned. I trusted her, but I'd also trusted Gordon my whole life. Which of them should I believe in now?

"Are you implying Clem is using us to gather information on Gordon?"

"I'm saying we need to be careful. You, especially."

"Wow. You really think I'm stupid, don't you?"

He snorted. "You're sharp as a scalpel, but you've spent the last few years in...New Hampshire?"

"Maine," I grumbled. "With lots of trips to Boston," I added defensively.

"Working for a children's theater, right?"

I did a double take. Roux, who made a point of ignoring me when he wasn't forced to follow me around like an unwanted bodyguard, actually paid attention to such things?

"Not *a* children's theater. *The* Children's Theater of New England," I corrected, lest he think we were an amateur operation that threw together the occasional puppet show. "We've won awards, you know."

He nodded. "Two Community Theatre Spotlight Awards for set design. I know."

My mouth hung open. He did?

"My point is, you've left that world," he said. "And no matter how competitive community theaters might be, I guarantee, you're in an entirely different level of *cutthroat* here."

I gulped, then tried a joke. "You mean, in Auberre?"

He shook his head, dead serious. "I mean, in the world your godfather has dragged you into."

A little chill went down my spine.

"You have to be careful about who you invite to the château," he concluded.

"Well, that will be hard since the plan is to rent the place out for events."

He made a face. "I mean, until then, when we'll hopefully have this all sorted out."

I wanted to ask what *all this* was, but I wasn't sure I wanted to know.

"So, having Claudette around is a no-go. Especially given her background," he whispered.

Anger flared in me, and I stuck a finger at his chest.

Zing! More static electricity. Did the man rub himself with balloons or something?

"Her *background?*" I nearly shrieked. He meant consorting with vampires, but I doubted he knew the rest of the story.

Roux patted the air with his hands, telling me to quiet down.

I jerked my head to the passenger side and growled, "Get in. Now."

He hesitated. Did he think I was going to kidnap him?

"Get in, dammit, and I'll tell you a thing or two about her *background.*"

His eyes narrowed, but he did as he was told, slamming his door in tandem with me.

Clem, I noticed, didn't so much as glance our way. I could be abducted by a tiger shifter, and he would never know.

My mood plunged, and it showed in my snippy tone.

"The summer my father died, everyone said how sorry they were. You know what Claudette said?"

Roux waited, lips tight, his knees practically to his chin in the confines of the compact car.

"She said, 'I wish mine died too.' And for the first time, I put it all together," I said.

Roux paled, indicating he had too.

"I finally realized why she put off going home after play-times," I said. "Why she never invited me to her house, and why my grandmother strictly forbade me from ever going there. Why hanging out with a wild crowd was better than spending time at home, and why she ran away again and again..."

Roux's expression went hard, and a muscle ticked in his cheek.

I gazed off into the distance. "I used to feel sorry for myself for losing my father at a young age, but Claudette taught me how lucky I was to have a good dad instead of... Well, instead of the monster she had."

Roux flexed his fingers, and the points of his tiger claws showed.

"No one ever did anything?"

"Madame Fontaine contacted the authorities several times, but nothing ever came of it." I took a deep breath. "But Claudette got her wish eventually. Her father died in a work accident."

Roux's eyebrows jumped. "Accident?"

I shrugged. "Something with heavy machinery. So maybe someone *did* do something. I never asked, and no one ever said. But I figure Claudette deserves a lucky break from time to time. Like now."

We both watched as she and Clem walked toward the end of the street.

"What about Clement?" he asked, a little less harshly than before.

I snorted. "You can't possibly blame him. He was just a kid then too."

"Not blaming. Maybe looking for something positive about the guy."

I raised an eyebrow. "Says the mercenary about the police officer?"

He closed his eyes briefly, then flashed a bitter smile. "Touché."

For the briefest of moments, he looked older, sadder. Then he ran a hand over his three-day shadow, blew out a long, slow breath, and opened the door.

"I'll be going, then," he said, so quietly, I ached.

"No!" I blurted, then caught myself. "I mean, wait."

He looked at me, confused.

"I mean, that came out too harsh," I finally managed.

Roux had spent years in the military, including several tours in war zones, and he was damn proud of it. But he'd been forced to accept an honorable discharge after questioning one too many orders. Another example of principles getting the best of him.

So, shoot. My comment had definitely touched a raw nerve. I didn't like the guy, but that didn't mean I couldn't be civil.

"Sorry. What is that called...? Displaced anger? From thinking about Claudette, I mean. I didn't intend to take that out on you."

I had many character flaws, but I could be humble when I had to.

He nodded, then pushed the door open and slid out, murmuring, "All good, Geneviève."

But it wasn't, I sensed, feeling awfully small.

"*Au revoir*," he murmured, closing, not slamming, the door.

I waggled my fingers less obnoxiously than usual, then started the engine and drove off. Seconds later, I reached the end of the block, where Clem stood, back turned to me, watching Claudette walk away.

He barely glanced up when I passed. But when Roux — already in his vehicle and following me — passed, Clem's head whipped around.

I couldn't be sure, but I thought I heard two mutually resentful growls. Clem's wolf-shifter side growling at Roux, and Roux's tiger snarling back.

Boys, boys, I wanted to say. *Let's keep the peace in Auberre, all right?*

Then I remembered this was no joke. Auberre might be a sleepy little town, but evil forces lurked, even here.

I tapped my fingers on the steering wheel. Was Clement's job transfer merely a coincidence or the harbinger of trouble? Was my generous godfather the *worst* kind of godfather, as my sister warned? And what about Claudette? Was I doing the right thing by offering her a chance, or was I stirring fuel into a simmering cauldron?

Then there was Roux. What would it take to get him off my case?

I sighed, did my best to clear my head, and drove on.

Chapter Three

GENEVIÈVE

Roux was right. My sister was furious, and hiring Claudette was a bad idea. But even Mina had reluctantly agreed that we had to give her a chance.

"This is the thing, Claudette," Mina said in her fair but firm way. "We're happy to have you back, but we need you to be punctual. Reliable. And to...um...well..." Mina stirred the air with her hands, looking to me for help.

Keep your hands off the men? was the best I could come up with.

Mina grimaced. "You need to be discreet. Professional."

Claudette's eyebrows knitted together.

"Mindful of boundaries," Mina tried next.

"No flirting," I finally blurted.

Claudette's mouth formed an *Oh*. Then she grinned. "I'll be a nun."

Hard to imagine, given her tattoos and piercings, but hey. One shouldn't judge a book by its cover.

Then her grin stretched, and she added, "I'll even take a vow." She hooted. "You get it?"

She and I laughed ourselves silly, and for a moment, it was just like old times, when we were kids and life seemed so simple.

"Excellent," Mina murmured, though she looked doubtful.

Claudette, to her credit, managed to stick to those guidelines for a full week. Her only flaw was a few batches of burned toast.

Mina caught me on my way to another efficiently served breakfast days later, whispering, "Wow. Claudette really seems to be turning over a new leaf."

Bene wasn't making it easy for her, though.

"*Bonjour*, everyone." Bene entered cheerfully, as he did each morning. The main difference was that he was no longer the last to appear, as he'd been B.C. — *Before Claudette.*

"*Bonjour*, Benedict." Claudette's voice dropped suggestively, and she stopped to drink the man in.

We let that slide, because even a nun would stop to ogle his cover boy good looks. His unruly blond hair and fluid stride hinted at his lion side, and his sunny disposition was infectious — er, in a good way.

"Best eggs ever," he announced, then winked. "Eggs Benedict. Get it?"

Everyone groaned, including Claudette, though I caught her winking back.

Mina met my eyes, sending worried thoughts into my mind.

As for me, I calculated the probability of those two hooking up at ninety-five percent — and rising fast.

"Oh! Let me help with the dishes." Bene jumped up eagerly.

Roux grabbed him before he made it two steps, though. "Too bad you have other work to do."

And off he hauled poor Bene to work at eight thirty on the dot.

The man was definitely a stickler for the rules, and not just because they were counting down the last few weeks of their contract with Gordon. I didn't know the details, but apparently, the guys had gotten themselves into hot water and had been forced to work for Gordon to clear their records of past indiscretions, as Mina put it.

They all seemed plenty reformed to me, though. Especially now that they were keeping busy with renovation work until Gordon assigned them a new mission. He hadn't since I'd arrived, but everyone expected him to squeeze in another assignment or two before their contracts ended in a few weeks.

"Thanks, Claudette," Mina said, then turned to assign the rest of us jobs.

"Henrik, can you please continue helping Bene and Roux with the upstairs bathrooms?"

His expression suggested such things were beneath him, but he didn't actually complain.

I found him creepy as hell, as did Mina. Still, there was merit to the old adage, *keep your friends close and your enemies closer.*

"Marius and I will continue plastering the corner room." Heart emojis practically fluttered between them as they locked eyes, as was the case ever since they'd gotten married a week ago.

Yes, married. I was still getting over my surprise at my sensible sister's spontaneity. We'd staged a fake wedding to snap promotional photos of the château, but my sister and her hot dragon shifter had gone all out and decided to tie the knot for real.

Only because we've gone to all the trouble, Mina had explained a little defensively.

She'd tried to play it cool, but inside, she'd been squealing with glee. I could hear it. I could hear a lot of things, actually. More and more, ever since I'd moved in to the château.

Ten long seconds later, I nudged Mina, and she blinked. "Oh. Sorry. Are you good to continue in the ballroom?"

"Yes, but it's bigger than two theater stages combined, and I usually have an intern or two helping me. Can't we spare someone?"

She pursed her lips. "We'll see how it goes, but finishing the guest rooms is the priority."

She was right, but that didn't make renovating the vast ballroom any easier.

Everyone split up, and their voices receded down corridors and stairwells, while I made the shorter "commute" to the ballroom. Huge double doors led to it from the dining room, though we kept those closed against the cold. I used the adjoining hallway instead and paused at the first of five arched doorways opening onto the ballroom. Yes, five. The ballroom was that long.

My grandmother had been legendary for hosting huge parties for a mix of supernatural guests — shifters, witches, warlocks, and so on. Once, a dazzling mermaid/merman couple had attended, or so my mother claimed. My sister, cousin, and I had only witnessed my grandmother's last few gatherings, but even those had been amazing. There'd been string quartets. Glamorous dresses. Dancing. Champagne. Fireworks.

Now, a bird chirped outside one of the floor-to-ceiling windows, and that was it.

Then a faint sound reached me from the left. I glanced at the artwork hanging there — an oil painting my father had made after one of my grandmother's grand parties. He'd used quick brushstrokes to echo the motion of dancers, waiters, and ladies fluttering fans, resulting in a work straight out of Monet. My grandmother had loved that piece.

Me too.

Listen. Listen carefully, and you will hear, my grandmother used to say. *Especially when the artist has poured emotion into their work.*

I closed my eyes and held my breath, hoping to hear more.

The magic at Château Nocturne must really have been flowing, because the faint notes of a violin reached my ears, growing gradually more distinct. A cello joined in, along with background sounds. Laughter. The clink of champagne glasses. Shoes scuffing over the floor.

All that seeped out of the painting and into the vast, empty ballroom, bringing the entire scene to life, not just the fraction captured within the limits of the frame.

A dozen couples stepped and twirled. Waiters made their rounds, offering drinks and hors d'oeuvres. Candles flickered, and logs crackled in the massive fireplaces.

I found myself humming the bright, swirling melody of Emile Waldteufel's "Les Patineurs" and swaying in place.

More details waltzed out of the fog of my memory as the scene continued to play out. The jangle of my grandmother's bracelets. The tuba-honk of my great-uncle Toby blowing his nose. The creak of the parquet floor, and my mother's chuckle — the special one reserved for my father.

A tear slipped over the contours of my smile.

The music rose, swelled, and drew to a close. So did the scene playing out in my mind. Guests showered my grandmother with *mercis* and *au revoirs* before heading home. Then, one by one, the lights in the ballroom were extinguished.

Slowly, I opened my eyes on the empty ballroom.

Mina was right when she'd said, *The walls may have been stripped of wallpaper, but the memories are still there. They always will be.*

But, whoa. Those weren't just memories. That was an entire scene replayed to me by a painting.

I turned to it, whispering, "Thank you, Dad."

Another tear slipped down my cheek.

Then real footsteps sounded and I whirled.

"Reporting for duty," Roux announced, not all too enthusiastically. Then he cocked his head. "Everything all right?"

I tossed my hair, using the motion to dry my cheeks.

"Of course. I guess Mina decided she could spare you?"

He nodded glumly.

Well, yay to you too, I nearly said. *And thanks for chasing away the most magic I've felt in years.*

Not much of my ancestral magic had worked its way down to me, but it did pop out from time to time — especially since I'd moved here a few weeks ago.

Mina said the longer she stayed at the château, the more magic she felt — and the more she mastered. Was that happening to me too?

I chewed the thought over while explaining the task at hand to Roux.

"We need to clean the grime off the molded plaster on the ceiling." I pointed up.

Goodie, his glum expression said.

I jutted my jaw. Next time I asked Mina for help, I would be more specific. Couldn't she have sent Bene instead?

Roux was a good worker but taciturn as hell, and he didn't have an artistic bone in his body, let alone a funny bone. I found myself overcompensating on his behalf, cracking jokes and singing along with whatever song came on the radio. I picked a station that played upbeat music because it was hard to listen to mopey breakup songs around a guy like Roux.

He didn't so much as hum a note of any song, though. Not even the Caribbean tune of Sting's "Every Little Thing She Does Is Magic," for Pete's sake!

On the plus side... those eyes were beautiful. Arresting, even. Every time I caught sight of them, it was hard to tear myself away.

"So glad to be putting my college education to work," I joked at one point. "But I guess cleaning ceilings beats cleaning toilets."

"Have you ever actually cleaned toilets?" Roux muttered.

I rolled my eyes. "It's a figure of speech. Have you?"

He nodded. "Latrines."

I snorted. "Let me guess. Your drill sergeant didn't appreciate it when you caught him miscounting the number of sit-ups your unit was supposed to do."

His mouth cracked open, proving my hunch correct.

I shook my head, chuckling. "Oh, Roux. Honesty isn't always the best policy."

"Honesty is the *only* policy," he grunted, going back to cleaning. "And sticking to your principles."

We were fifteen feet up on a wheeled scaffold, our necks and backs aching. Well, *my* neck and back ached. The platform was barely big enough for two, and we kept bumping in the most arousing — er, *annoying* — way possible.

"Principles are for big things. Other things, you can let slide," I told him. "You know. Pick your battles."

His only reply was a dark look. Then he turned on the vacuum and swept it over the next portion of sculpted ceiling.

I followed him with a brush and damp cloth. Thank goodness the artisans who'd designed the place had limited themselves to a single oval of molding and small, sculpted wreaths in the corners. Otherwise, cleaning and painting it all would take years.

One thing was for sure — many hands made light work. Especially Roux's. Time flew, and it seemed like only a matter of minutes before we had to climb down and reposition the scaffold. Progress was that swift.

Agreeing on things, on the other hand...

"This way." I angled my head to the right.

He shook his head, pointing left. "That way."

I jutted my jaw. "This way makes more sense."

He snorted. "How?"

"Because we follow the wall."

He pointed. "Yes — *that* wall."

"No, *that* wall," I shot back.

He made a face, and I did too. Boy, oh boy. Talk about obstinate tigers.

"Are you the helper or the mastermind here?" I finally snipped.

He grimaced. "Helper."

"Then help, please, by moving the scaffold this way."

He did, though he wasn't all that pleased. Neither was I. Next time, I would ask for a different helper. Maybe even Henrik.

At some point, a bell in the old-fashioned call system jingled, and Bene cheered from upstairs.

"Lunch! Finally!"

I climbed down the scaffold, then checked over our work. We'd finished a much bigger section than I'd imagined, and while there was still a lot to be done, it was starting to feel manageable.

Obstinate tigers definitely had their plus sides.

Roux sighed, though, as if he'd expected us to have finished by now. "That's going to take at least another week."

"It's going to look stunning when we're done, though."

We took in our handiwork for another few seconds, then turned to put away our brushes. And dammit — even in the vast emptiness of the ballroom, we managed to bump butts again.

"Would you cut that out?" I muttered.

Quite unnecessarily, because he jumped away faster than I did.

"*You* cut it out," he said, all offended.

Which went to prove I *definitely* wasn't his type — if he had one. The man would probably have been happiest married to the military. But the poor guy hadn't seen that nasty divorce coming, and now, he had to reinvent himself. Hard to do when you weren't all that creative.

I, on the other hand, was a master at creating. Briefly, I even considering helping him. Then I decided Roux was a big boy, and I had already done my good deed of the month by helping Claudette.

However, that became increasingly challenging, especially when she turned up to breakfast the next morning acting strangely. Giddy, on the one hand, but lethargic on the other.

Henrik, meanwhile, looked rosier than ever.

Seconds later, the terrible truth dawned on me. They'd spent the night together, indulging in more than just sex, hadn't they?

A closer look revealed the light bruise on Claudette's neck, along with a faint pair of bite marks.

"*Bonjour*," Mina greeted everyone cheerily on her way in. Then she froze. Her cheeks went from pink to furious burgundy, and her hands curled into fists.

Marius was right on her heels, and he stopped too, instantly alert to his mate's change in mood.

I towed my sister into the adjoining ballroom before either of them exploded.

"I'll kill Henrik," she fumed.

Well, she would have to grab her wooden stake and get in line behind me.

"I can't believe he would do this to her," Mina ranted.

Her was Delphine, Henrik's mistress. The woman was incredibly sweet and hopelessly in love with him. *Hopeless* because he was a vampire and she a mere human. Also because she was a prostitute, and he treated her like one. Well, sometimes. Occasionally, he showed a quieter, more indulgent, and — dare I say — human side. For example, during Delphine's recent visit for Mina's wedding. Delphine sang beautifully, and when Henrik accompanied her on piano... Well, the results were heavenly, if such a word could be used in the context of a vampire.

But once Henrik had drunk his fill and tired of her company, he'd sent her away, leaving Auberre a little less sunny — and Henrik even more irritable than usual.

"I hate it too, but there's another angle to this," I said, trying to calm my sister.

"You mean, the angle I ram a stake into Henrik's heart from?"

"No, I mean for Claudette."

Mina looked shocked. "Are you suggesting there's an upside to this?"

Not the wording I would choose, no.

"I'm saying Claudette can hold down a steady job here and let one vampire suck her blood, or she can head back to Paris and become a sex toy and drinking fountain for an entire coven."

Mina blanched. I felt sick to my stomach. But that was the ugly truth, and we stood there, wrestling with our emotions.

"God, this sucks," Mina muttered.

I grimaced. "Please tell me that pun wasn't intended."

She winced. "Correction. This stinks."

Slightly better, but that didn't change things.

It also didn't change another consideration we left unspoken, too ashamed to even admit to. Having Claudette giving blood freely to Henrik put us at less risk.

So, there it was: Real Life, with all its complications and contradictions. Did we protect Claudette or ourselves — and stand by Delphine? Did we turn a blind eye and consider this an act of Claudette's free will, or did we intervene, knowing that circumstances didn't offer her a wealth of good choices?

I found myself thinking of Roux and his hard-nosed, black-and-white approach to life. What would he do?

Drown defending his principles in a sea of nuances, the back of my mind muttered.

I ended up hugging my sister and grasping at slippery slivers of positivity.

Maybe I was overdramatizing. Maybe everything would be okay. I had found my way into several bad relationships, and I had found my way back out of them. So could Claudette. So could Delphine.

I hoped so anyway.

"So, what do we do?" I finally asked, defaulting to my younger sister role.

Mina thought it over, then swallowed hard. "I'll talk to Claudette — and to Henrik."

"He'll be leaving soon, right?" I asked.

Mina frowned. "I can only hope. But until then, well... We're safer keeping a snake in our sights than having one lurking around in the garden."

True. But boy, would I prefer a reptile-free garden.

Chapter Four

GENEVIÈVE

A week passed without incident — as long as swooping dragons, outbursts of magic, and the guys' constant bickering didn't count as *incidents*. But otherwise... a normal week at Château Nocturne. Projects progressed, some faster, some slower, and the guys quietly celebrated the milestone of only two weeks left in their contracts with Gordon.

Henrik and Claudette seemed to have gotten enough (or too much) of each other, because they no longer shacked up at night, at least as far as I could tell. I wasn't sure how they felt about it, but Mina and I were relieved, to say the least.

All in all, we'd all achieved enough of a routine that Mina finally allowed herself and Marius a four-day, belated honeymoon/getaway.

"Bye!" We all waved from the front steps to see them off that Friday morning.

Marius revved the motorcycle he'd borrowed from a friend, Mina hopped on the back in a leather getup that was about as far from her teacher persona as she could get, and off they roared, heading who knew where.

"Have fun!" I called.

"Oh, they'll have fun, all right." Bene smirked.

I elbowed him in the ribs. "Grow up."

He laughed. "I'll grow up when the boss returns." He meant Mina, of course. "Until then—"

Roux growled under his breath. "Until then, we work. Mina left a list."

He showed us a sheaf of pages covered with detailed notes. Lots and lots of notes.

Bene sighed. "Of course she did."

Slowly, everyone headed off to work, and did indeed work, as we did six days a week. Yes, we even worked Saturdays, though only to midafternoon. Sunday was a day off, and I had a plan for mine. One that didn't involve paint, ladders, or any type of renovation work.

Oh, and no tigers. But that was the tricky part.

I woke extra early that morning — well, early for a Sunday — and snuck out a side door. I tiptoed to Mina's battered little Citroën and closed the door quietly, determined to sneak off unnoticed.

I winced as the engine coughed to life and at the loud crunch of tires over gravel. Gripping the steering wheel tightly, I turned the corner to the front of the château and—

Thump! Roux stepped in front of the car, bracing both hands against the hood.

I hit the brakes. Jeez. Was he planning to hold me back with sheer muscle power?

"Where are you going?" he growled, ignoring my curses.

I beeped. Hard.

"Where. Are. You. Going?" he gritted out, word by word.

I rolled down the window. Yes, by hand. The car was that old.

"I have some errands, if you must know."

"Errands." His tone was flat.

I nodded. "Errands."

"What errands?"

I threw up both hands. "How is that any of your business?"

"What errands?" he growled.

"Small, unimportant errands not too far away," I snipped.

He snorted, then pointed to the garden. "Mina was attacked right over there. She was attacked in London too."

I rolled my eyes. "Good thing I'm not going to London."

He crossed his arms, trying to look big and intimidating. Mostly succeeding.

I beeped again. "I can go anywhere I want, dammit!"

He walked around to the passenger side and got in. Which was quite the process, given his size versus the space in the compact car. Then he pointed down the driveway.

"Fine. Go anywhere you want."

"*Alone*," I emphasized. "I can go anywhere I want *alone*."

He buckled his seat belt. "Just pretend I'm not here."

Ha. Having a herd of antelope in the car would be less distracting than Roux.

"I'll be out all day," I warned.

He jutted his jaw. "Great."

I tried a new tack. "Roux, it's Sunday. Your only day off. Why don't you enjoy it?" I motioned toward the stables, where he devoted every free moment to repairing our vintage Jaguar. "You could spend your day there."

He socked me with a dark look. "Yes. I could."

"So, go. I promise, I won't tell Mina." When he gave me a strange look, I snorted. "I know she's making you follow me for protection, but it really isn't necessary."

He opened his mouth, then closed it and thought a while.

"It's not safe out there. Anything could happen."

I dropped my head against the steering wheel and kept it there.

Roux didn't say a word. Nor did he exit the car.

"Fine." I straightened in a huff. If he was so dedicated to making my life miserable, he would have to deal.

I sped down the driveway and swung onto the village road. The force of the turn threw Roux my way, and our shoulders brushed.

Zing! More static electricity.

I shot him an angry look and raced on.

Roux glanced around as we passed Auberre's bakery, church, and war memorial, but he didn't say a word. He didn't say anything when we passed the next two villages either, but he did look perplexed when we passed the local *hypermarché* without stopping.

"Where exactly is this small errand?" he finally asked.

I kept my eyes straight ahead. "Paris."

He whipped around. "Paris?"

I nodded firmly.

"How is that a small errand?"

"It is small," I reasoned. "It's just far away."

He stared at me suspiciously. "And what exactly do you plan to do in Paris?"

"Oh, you know. Walk along the Seine. Check out a few bookshops. Pop in to see Gordon..."

"Oh no. Absolutely not. Out of the question." He motioned for me to pull over.

I did not.

"I have to go. I've been promising him for weeks."

"Promise a little longer."

I shook my head. "Why put it off?"

He snorted. "You mean, why wait for a time when your sister could talk some sense into you?"

"That too," I muttered.

He huffed. "Your logic is faulty, and that's putting it politely."

A fair point, and I knew it. Still, I shook my head. "Gordon is my godfather. He's looked out for us for years. I can't just ghost him."

"He's a crook and a liar, and he's used you."

"He's used *Mina*, and that's terrible. But he also helped us when we needed it most. He paid most of my college tuition, for goodness' sake! The least I can do is drop in for tea. Then he'll get off my case."

Roux's nostrils flared. "He's been on your case? What does he want?"

Boy, the guy really did suspect everyone.

"He just wants to chat." I cut off his retort. "I know, I know. I have to be careful what I say. But I owe it to him to at least say hello."

Roux grimaced. "Safest not to say anything."

"Don't you think it looks suspicious if we completely avoid him?"

His grimace told me I'd scored a point.

"Just two hours on the train in, an hour at Gordon's, and two hours back," I said.

Roux grimaced. "Just how I like to spend my Sundays."

I jerked a thumb behind me. "I could put you on the next bus home, and you could enjoy your Sunday with the Jaguar."

He shook his head firmly.

Which was how I found myself on the train to Paris with Roux a short time later. Parking in Paris was a bitch, so we always drove to our nearest station and took the train from there.

It wasn't a holiday weekend, nor were the personnel on strike, nor had any demonstrations been called, so the train was on time — hallelujah — and relatively uncrowded.

Well, most of the train was uncrowded. Roux kept me boxed in at my window seat like I was the Hope Diamond aboard a train full of jewel thieves. And boy, did the guy take up a lot of space. Him and those bulging cargo pockets of his.

"What do you even have in there?" I demanded when his thigh brushed against mine for the third time.

He shrugged. "Just the bare necessities."

My mind filled in the blanks. Grenades? A rocket launcher? A Swiss Army Knife and bolts of every possible size? Or did he carry a nail clipper in case his claws grew a little too long?

He spent the first hour staring ahead furiously, like this was my fault and not his. I took out my sketchbook, drew our 1936 Jaguar, and showed it to him.

He grimaced. "Rub it in, why don't you."

"I'm not rubbing it in. I'm reminding you you have choices."

He looked away, muttering, "Not as many as you think."

I frowned. What did that mean?

I turned a page and sketched an angry tiger.

Roux huffed. "The stripes are all wrong."

He didn't correct me on the beast's expression, though.

I turned another page, thought a while, and started sketching again.

Roux peeked from time to time, and I sensed his curiosity mount.

"What's that?" he finally asked.

"I'm working on a design for the ballroom, but I can't decide on one."

Roux, Bene, and my sister had come up with the idea of painting every room in the château with the theme of a different artist. She had already painted a replica of Franz Marc's *The Tower of Blue Horses* in the corner of one room, with the idea to do the remaining walls in complementary colors. We had plans for a Van Gogh room too, with sunflowers painted on the walls, and furniture and bedding that matched the scene in his *Bedroom in Arles*. But the ballroom was huge, so I had to find a theme that would work over a large area without becoming totally unmanageable.

I pointed to my doodles. "I was thinking Picasso, but *Guernica* is just too depressing."

He rubbed his chin, and I braced myself for a suggestion along the lines of Napoleon at *The Battle of Waterloo*. Something big, bold, and military. At best, I expected *Liberty Leading the People* or Rembrandt's *The Night Watch*.

"What about Chagall?" Roux tried. "He made those big canvases, didn't he?"

Wow. A military man who knew art. Who would have guessed?

"True, but I'm not a big fan of Chagall."

"I guess *The Raft of the Medusa* also counts as depressing." He thought it over some more. "What's that really big one in the Louvre? *The Feast. . .* or wait, *The Wedding. . .*"

"*The Wedding Feast at Cana,*" I filled in, impressed. "Do you hang out at the Louvre in your spare time or something?"

He looked away. "Maybe. Sometimes."

Definitely, I decided.

"It gets too crowded, though. Same with the Musée d'Orsay," he muttered.

It was no surprise that this tiger didn't like crowds. But that he knew art. . . Well, that was a revelation. Were hushed galleries his way of compensating for the noise and chaos of war zones he'd been deployed to?

He gazed out the window, eyes hard, expression inscrutable.

And just like that, I felt terribly guilty for ruining his day.

"Musée Rodin is nice too," I murmured, hoping that was a safer topic.

He nodded. "Nice garden."

I chuckled. "Especially the ice cream they sell. The pistachio is divine."

The corner of his mouth flicked up. "Not as good as the strawberry."

For once, I didn't argue the point.

"Not a lot of space for a tiger to prowl around in, though," I murmured.

He shook his head. "No. You have it good at the château."

"We do — very good — and I love having the space. It's kind of wasted on me, though, since I can't shift."

When he cocked his head at me, I ticked a list off my fingers. "We have wolf shifters in the family. Bears. A dragon or two, if you go far enough back. But did any of that trickle through to me? No." I shook my head sadly. "I'm useless."

He shook his head. "You're far from useless, Geneviève."

As flat as his tone was, my soul buoyed a little bit.

"Yes, well. You can shift into tiger form. I would be happy to be able to shift into anything. A mouse. A flea, even."

He raised one slash of an eyebrow. "A flea?"

I shot him a look. "You get the idea. But I can't. No shifting, no magic..."

"No magic at all?"

I shrugged. "Not much anyway."

Which left both of us gazing pensively out the window.

Eventually, the train flashed through a station on the outskirts of Paris.

"Not long now," Roux murmured, indicating for me to turn to a new page in my sketchbook. "Time for a battle plan."

Yikes. He made it sound like we were storming the Normandy beaches on D-Day.

Forty-five minutes later, I had my sketchbook buried in the bottom of my backpack and Roux's words etched deep in my mind.

No details. No promises. No confidential information.

Clearly, this was not going to be your average teatime. But, yikes. Gordon couldn't possibly be devious enough to warrant all this. Could he?

∞∞∞∞

"Geneviève!" my godfather greeted me warmly.

Gordon looked like any other well-to-do businessman — medium build, buffed leather shoes, self-satisfied expression. My grandmother always said he reminded her of 1960s heart-throb Alain Delon.

After an internet search for pictures of Alain Delon in his prime, I'd decided James Dean was a closer match. Either way, Gordon must have been quite the catch in his day. He'd never found someone to settle down with, but that was common with warlocks, apparently.

"So nice to see you." I hugged him, and it was just like old times.

Mina and Roux had to be exaggerating. Gordon was my father's dear friend and confidant. A man who had generously supported us for years.

Then he spotted Roux, and his voice dropped to a growl.

"Mr. Anand."

I'd never heard a tone quite that vicious, or one that promised so much retribution. So, yikes. Maybe Mina and Roux hadn't been exaggerating.

"*Bonjour*," Roux said evenly.

"Roux was kind enough to accompany me today," I explained.

"Ah. Sensible," Gordon said, though he still looked displeased. "Paris isn't as safe as it used to be."

Did he mean vampires? Shady art dealers? Himself?

"Please come in, my dear. Have a seat." He ushered me into the living room that overlooked the Canal Saint-Martin below and Sacré-Cœur in the distance. I paused at the threshold to take it all in.

I'd always known Gordon made a lot of money. According to Mina, though, he made even more than we realized. Dirty money.

I looked around at the antiques and paintings in his penthouse, wondering.

The moment I'd walked into the apartment, I'd sensed magic tingling all around. Not the warm, comforting embrace of the château's magic — an edgier kind of magic. Edgier than on previous visits. Had something changed here, or had Roux made me hypervigilant?

Gordon, I noticed, didn't invite him past the entrance hall. The tiger stood there stoically, gazing at nothing in particular. The perfect, discreet bodyguard, in other words. Not that I needed one.

Or did I?

Gordon settled down on the couch opposite my armchair. "So good of you to stop by."

"Sorry not to have made it sooner. We've been so busy."

"I can't wait to hear about the progress you've made."

Roux didn't look, gesture, or comment, but I could sense him growling into my mind.

No details. No promises.

Gordon's housekeeper brought us tea and apple tarts. Poor Roux wasn't offered a thing.

I frowned. Not very nice of my godfather.

Gordon raised his teacup. "To progress at the château."

I touched my cup to his.

"And to your future plans. May they all come true."

I sipped my tea happily.

"And to the next group of boarders I send over to stay with you," Gordon added.

I almost sputtered tea all over the rug. The next *what*?

"Oh. Too hot," I bluffed, taking another bite of tart to buy time to think.

A warm, itchy feeling set in on the back of my neck, and I scratched it. But it only increased.

I forced down the apple tart. Gordon was trying to read my mind, wasn't he?

I knew he was capable of that and much, much more. Powerful warlocks had all kinds of tricks up their sleeves. But he'd never tried any on me.

Until now.

I sipped my tea, thinking fast. Raising mental defenses was easy. Raising them subtly, so the other person didn't realize you were onto them, wasn't.

I unlocked the part of my mind that obsessed about food, my appearance, and my future love life — all the usual issues for a woman my age. Meanwhile, the hidden part of my mind spun. Why new boarders? The current group was okay. Well, Bene was. Roux was annoying, but even he was better than someone new.

Henrik, on the other hand, I would be happy to trade in.

"Mina didn't tell me you planned to send us more boarders," I said as casually as I could.

"Well, with the current group reaching the end of their contracts soon..." Gordon's eyes flashed unhappily. "I'll compensate you according to the same terms, of course."

Very favorable terms, I knew. But Roux's warning flashed in my mind. *No promises.*

"That's very generous. I'll make sure to discuss it with Mina when she gets back."

Gordon went still, like a predator spotting prey in the distance.

"Oh? Is she away?"

Oops.

I wiped my mouth. "I mean, when *I* get back."

"I see." Gordon took a bite of his tart, though he didn't seem to savor it. "And the current crew... What are their plans?"

More warning lights flashed in my mind.

"I haven't asked. I've been so busy working on the ballroom. We've made good progress on the ceiling." I pulled out my phone and came over to sit beside Gordon. Bad idea, because the itch in my mind became a pounding.

I briskly stirred the thoughts in the open part of my mind. Things like how delicious the tart was and how much more I could eat of it. What colors I might choose for the ballroom ceiling. How far our savings might stretch, and how soon we might generate sorely needed income...

"Doesn't the ceiling look so much better now? Those flourishes in the corners take forever to clean, but they're coming along well."

"Wonderful, wonderful." Gordon was his usual polite, supportive self, but I sensed an unusual level of disconnect. Was he simply regretting that his relationship with Mina had cooled, or was he busy plotting a rival crime boss's downfall?

I retreated to my original spot and dug back into my tart.

"And how about you?" I asked between bites. "Have you found a new assistant?"

Mina had filled me in on the previous one — Celeste, a succubus who had plotted to steal parts of Gordon's business empire.

He grimaced. "No. But such positions are always difficult to fill."

"I can only imagine," I murmured.

His phone rang, and he stood to take it. "Sorry, my dear. It will just be a minute."

"Of course."

I finished my tart and tea, then stood to take in the view. Roux, meanwhile, might have been one of those unblinking guards at Buckingham Palace.

I turned to the paintings decorating the walls next. There were dozens, but I went straight to my favorite.

My father hadn't named that particular artwork of his, but I'd always thought of it as *Easter at the Château*. Blurred figures moved over the croquet lawn, and the patio table was piled high with food.

The closer I stepped, the more the painting reached out to me. I heard the clack of croquet mallets. Wind whispering through the trees. The laughter of children...

My chest rose in a deep sigh, remembering that gloriously sunny Easter at the château.

It was all so clear — in my memory, and in the painting. So clear, I could hear individual voices.

You've outdone yourself with this pie, my aunt said to my grandmother.

No, not that way, I heard Mina chide Dora. *You have to do the gates in order.*

Ha. I could hear the teacher in her, even back then.

Then another voice, fainter than the rest, wormed its way out of the painting and to me.

Maman, maman, ça va encore durer longtemps? a little boy complained. *How much longer will this take?*

I tilted my head, wondering who that was and how he fit in. We didn't have any boy cousins.

Clement could have been there since his grandparents were friends with mine. But Clem didn't whine. Even as a kid, he'd been tough and tight-lipped.

I frowned. He'd barely noticed me then. He barely noticed me now. Boy, did I have bad luck with men.

I pushed the thought aside, focusing on the mystery before me. I'd caught a few whispers emanating from it in the past, but never anything as distinctly as now. I'd always assumed I was more likely to be touched by magic at the château, but maybe it worked in other places too.

But who was that boy?

I studied the painting, but there was no other figure there. He could have been off-camera, so to speak — in earshot of my father at the time, but not painted into that particular view.

Touching the frame didn't bring any clues, but I noticed it was thick. Really thick, as if the canvas had been mounted on a solid panel of wood.

Gordon appeared at my elbow, making me jolt.

"Ah. One of my favorite paintings," he said, sounding bittersweet.

"Mine too. Do you mind if I take a picture?"

"Of course not," he said.

I took one, then went back to contemplating the scene — and those voices.

"Were you there that day? I don't remember."

Gordon shook his head. "No, I wasn't. Your mother gave me the painting, after..." He cleared his throat. "After your father passed."

There wasn't much to say, so I stood quietly remembering. Wishing. Wondering.

"If I could go back in time and change things..." Gordon whispered, so full of emotion, his voice trembled.

I touched his arm. "It's like Mom says. We can't, so all we can do is remember."

"I remember," Gordon murmured, as solemnly as a man at a war memorial.

I made a mental note to chide my sister. Gordon might have his faults, but he'd been a steadfast friend to our father and our family. We couldn't ever lose sight of that.

Silence stretched, and I'd never felt as close to Gordon.

When the clock over the fireplace struck the full hour, I checked my watch.

"I'll have to catch the train home soon. Would you be up for a walk?"

"Regrettably, no. I have a few things to prepare for tomorrow. It's been wonderful seeing you, though."

He saw me to the door, helped me with my jacket, and hugged me goodbye.

"Please come again," he said. "Any time."

"I will." I waved and stepped toward the lift, where Roux waited.

Gordon didn't ruin the moment by glaring at him, and Roux didn't ruin the moment by glaring back. The apartment door closed, and that was it.

So, whew. No confrontation. No crimes. Mina had definitely been exaggerating things.

We rode the elevator down in silence, then walked along the canal. I had no idea what Roux thought about, but my mind stuck on one thing — the mystery of the boy in the painting.

Chapter Five

GENEVIÈVE

Neither Roux nor I said much on the train ride back to Burgundy. I was worn out, and the gentle rocking of the train soon lulled me to sleep.

At some point, it lurched, and I opened my eyes, then closed them again. No reason to break off such a nice, comfy nap.

Wait. Nice? Comfy?

My eyes snapped open, and I was mortified to discover I had fallen asleep with my head on Roux's shoulder. But damn, did the man smell good.

And, oh. He was asleep too, with his head tipped against mine.

When the train lurched again, we broke apart, both awake. I stared out the window as if nothing had happened. And it hadn't. Had it?

My cheeks heated as I blinked at the landscape.

Luckily, my phone rang, giving me something else to focus on.

"*Oui, c'est moi,*" I said when the woman on the line asked for Geneviève.

It was Lily, fiancée of Georges Delmont, grandson of electrician Jules Delmont.

"Madame Fontaine said you wanted to speak to me," Lily said.

Boy, did I, because I had a great idea.

An idea I outlined in some detail, pausing only to send photos through.

My heart raced as Lily looked them over. Then she came back on the line.

"Let me get this right," she asked. "You would let Georges and me hold our wedding at the château for nothing more than a cleaning fee of a few hundred euros."

I nodded. "It's all yours — the chapel, the beautifully converted stable, the ballroom..."

Technically, the chapel didn't have a roof — yet — and the ballroom was months away from being presentable. But, hey. Everyone worked better under a deadline, right?

"You can even spend the night in the honeymoon suite," I promised.

Once again, I congratulated myself on the genius move of talking my sister and Marius into a wedding, where we'd snapped hundreds of pictures to use in advertising. Hosting Lily's wedding wouldn't generate any revenue, but it would get the wiring done, if this genius plot of mine worked. We also stood to gain a good review and a chance to test all those newly developed areas of the château.

Once we actually developed them, that was.

"It looks amazing. What's the catch?"

"No catch," I assured her. "It will help our marketing efforts, and we're happy to help someone with roots in Auberre, so it's a win-win. But I would appreciate it if you could get your future father-in-law to move us up his waiting list and complete all the wiring before then. We'll pay his regular rates, of course." I paused a little breathlessly. "Do you think he'll agree?" I paused, then threw in, "Did I mention we have a vintage roadster from 1936?"

Roux's eyebrows jumped up.

"A real classic," I went on. "Your father-in-law can take it for a spin. Here's a picture..."

I sent it through, and a moment later, a whistle of appreciation came over the line.

"Oh, I'm sure he can be convinced," Lily said.

"You can choose any date you want. I mean, sometime after the wiring is done."

My hinting knew no shame, but heck. That wiring was crucial.

"I have to say, that sounds a hundred times better than renting the local *salle des fêtes*," she said.

I laughed. Better than the average community center? "I guarantee, it will be. No squeezing yourself in between scout meetings and senior bridge night. The whole place will be yours — and you can make things as grand or as intimate as you like."

"I'll talk to Georges and get back to you. Soon," she promised.

Her giddy tone suggested that wouldn't be long. I said goodbye, hung up, and did a little fist pump.

Roux didn't look impressed, though.

"What?" I demanded.

"Is there another vintage car I don't know about? One that runs, perhaps?"

I patted his shoulder. "I have faith in you."

"I'm a tiger, not a magician. Getting parts has been impossible."

I snorted, taking out my notepad. "What do you need?"

"Forget it. Those parts are impossible to find."

I patted my chest. "I work in theater. We specialize in the impossible."

He scoffed. "Even car parts?"

"Anything," I assured him.

Men were hunters. Women were gatherers. And I was a *champion* gatherer.

"Theater is about illusions," he pointed out.

"Tell that to the actor I had suspended from the ceiling on wires."

"It's one thing to put on *Peter Pan*. It's another to meet road safety standards."

"Try me," I said flatly.

His look suggested I was wasting his time. I countered by pointing to the overhead display that said we were stuck on the train for another forty minutes.

Roux checked that against his watch — one of those massive devices that could double as a dive watch, if it didn't drag him to the bottom of the ocean first.

With a sigh, he finally indulged me. "I need pistons, for starters. From *1936*."

I made a note. "What else?"

"I've been trying to track down a Wrigley carburetor for weeks. I'm telling you, it's impossible."

I shook my head. "If I can track down a vintage jack-in-the-box or parts to make a flying elephant, I can find a Wiggly carburetor."

"Wrigley," he muttered.

I handed him the notepad.

"One of the best directors I ever worked with had a saying. You want to hear it?" I asked as he noted the correct spelling.

"No."

I plowed ahead. *"Can-do energy is more productive than can't-do energy."*

He gave me a hard look and underlined *1936* on the notepad.

"What about the chapel? The ballroom? Oh, and the honeymoon suite?" he challenged.

"What about them?"

"You can't promise things that aren't ready."

"They'll be ready. I know I've been busting my ass. How about you?"

"We've all been busting our asses," he growled.

I glanced down at the body part in question. It was hard to appreciate from this angle, but I knew his to be magnificent. On par with Clem's, not that I'd gotten up close and personal with either.

My body warmed at the thought, so much that I couldn't help conducting a quick reassessment when we filed off the train at our destination. And when I did...

Truly *magnifique*.

The car was parked what seemed like miles away. Given that walk and the ensuing drive, it was pitch-dark when we approached Auberre. My phone beeped with an incoming text, and I motioned for Roux to read it to me.

"It's from Lily."

I rolled my hand impatiently. "What does it say?"

He scowled. "Heart emoji, heart emoji, heart emoji. Thumbs-up."

I grinned and did another fist pump.

When the phone beeped again, he squinted at it. "It says, *Maybe early June?*"

"Tell her yes."

He typed three letters, then looked at me. "Send?"

I shook my head. "Add a smiley face. The kind with hearts for eyes."

His expression said that was beneath his dignity.

I pointed firmly at the phone. "Do it. We could wait years for an electrician if this doesn't come through."

He grimaced and hit a few keys. I swear, the man would have been more comfortable firing off live weapons than a few emojis.

"Okay?" He held out my phone.

I glanced at the screen, then nodded. "Perfect. Send it."

My mood soared...for about thirty seconds. Then the car coughed and sputtered. I'd barely coasted to the side of the road before the engine died completely.

I cursed, trying to restart it. No go.

Roux leaned over to peer at the instruments. And, oh. He smelled nice, even after a long day of train rides and traipsing around Paris.

"Lights. Many lights. But not a single red one," I pointed out defensively.

He muttered, exited the car, and motioned for me to release the hood. I did, then joined him.

Give me a theater stage to design, and I could do it — from an underwater set for *The Little Mermaid* to outer space for an adaptation of *The Magic School Bus*. Making sense of a car engine, on the other hand...

Roux poked around while I held my phone light. Then he pulled out a rubbery thing.

"Snapped fan belt. When was the last time you had this thing inspected?"

Probably during Jacques Chirac's presidency, but I didn't volunteer that. I just shrugged. "Can you fix it?"

"If I had tools and a replacement belt."

I gave his cargo pockets a significant look.

"But I don't," he grumbled.

"Pity." I grabbed my things, zipped my jacket, and set out for home, less than a mile away.

Roux muttered and joined me.

My breath showed in the dim light of the quarter moon, and my shoes crunched over dry leaves. My ears were freezing. Still, it was invigorating in other ways. Pleasant, even. Especially when I turned the corner to the long drive to the château and spotted lights at the end of the tree tunnel.

My heart warmed. The château called to me, as it always had. I could be blindfolded and turned until I was dizzy, and I would still be able to find the place.

I smiled. Soon, I would be home with a warm mug of tea and the delicious meal Madame Picard had left for us. In the meantime, I would take this as a sign to get out more often to enjoy the crisp, quiet nights.

Too quiet, hard-wired instinct warned.

I shook off the feeling. No need to get creeped out. Bad things happened in big cities, not out in the countryside.

Still, I walked a little faster, focusing on the château lights.

Faster, they seemed to whisper.

Roux fell behind, then caught up. "In a hurry?"

A twig snapped in the forest, and we froze, listening.

Leaves stirred ever so slightly. Too quiet for a normal sense of hearing, but not for someone with my shifter ancestry.

Somewhere behind me, something was moving through the forest.

My heart rate tripled, and I broke out in a cold sweat.

"Keep walking. Slowly," Roux whispered.

I did, sniffing the air. Unfortunately, the wind was blowing from the wrong direction, giving me no hint of what that might be.

But whoever — or whatever — it was, they continued stalking us.

"If that's Bene, I'll kill him," I whispered.

"If that's Bene, *I'll* kill him," Roux grunted. "But it isn't."

"Who, then?" I whispered.

He shook his head. "No idea."

I pulled out my phone as I speed walked, thinking to call Bene.

"Already alerted him," Roux rumbled, pushing me along.

Oh. Right. Those two had worked together long enough to mentally communicate. In the few weeks I'd spent around them, I'd consciously blocked them out, but maybe it was time to rethink that.

Another twig snapped — on the opposite side of the driveway this time.

Shit. That meant we had two stalkers — or more.

Hurry, the magic woven into the stonework of the château urged.

"Roux..." I murmured nervously.

He kept my arm in a vise grip. "Don't run. Not until I say so."

Branches snapped as our stalkers picked up their pace.

Roux pushed me forward. "Run. Run!"

I sprinted, with Roux half a step behind, but our stalkers were faster.

I glanced back just as one broke out of the woods directly behind us. A man with long, glistening fangs and eyes that glowed red with the thrill of the hunt.

Vampire! my instincts screamed.

Then I caught a glimpse of a forked tongue and a weird, flaring neck.

"What the hell is that?" I whisper-yelled, running for my life.

"Naga," Roux grunted.

I had no idea what a naga was, but if Roux was concerned, I was concerned.

He pushed me forward. "Run. Run!"

"What about you?" I slowed when he did.

He didn't answer. He was too busy shifting.

My eyes went wide. Oh, right. Tiger.

"I'll catch up," he said in a choked voice. "Run!"

I jogged backward, watching as he hunched and dropped to all fours.

He held his jaws painfully wide while his teeth extended, making a terrifying sight. His back stretched, and his shoulder blades went from flat on his back to sharp, vertical ridges. A thin, silky coat of fur broke out, covering his skin.

He lashed his tail and snarled at the naga. *I dare you.*

The naga hit the brakes, then advanced when two more emerged from the forest.

"Come on!" I yelled. "Run!"

I ran, worried that he wouldn't follow. But soft footfalls sounded a moment later, and a huge, dark body glided into view beside me.

And I mean, *glided.* Muscles rippled, and his motion was more a flow than a series of steps. The stripes probably enhanced the effect, but boy, was I impressed.

Faster, Roux's low huff ordered.

I was trying, dammit, but we had no hope of beating them to the front door. Still, reaching the château wasn't our only option. A pair of small pavilions flanked the driveway, just a few hundred yards from the main building, the sole features punctuating that long, straight road. But they weren't just there for decorative purposes, according to my grandmother.

Safe harbor, I remembered her saying.

I'd never had occasion to test them, but it sure looked like the time had come.

Light flared ahead as the front door of the château flew open. Growls split the night, and a shadow blurred through the doorway.

Bene! I nearly cried in relief, though he was a good quarter mile away.

I raced down the middle of the road, counting down the distance to the pavilions. Twenty steps…ten…

When Roux disappeared from my side, I glanced back in alarm. He spun to attack the nearest naga. Snarls and cries pierced the night as they tussled.

Run! I sensed him hollering.

I ran, covering the last five steps...three...

The pavilion had four arched, open entryways, one for every cardinal direction. I veered across the road, leaped into the structure, and whirled, gesturing wildly in the shape of an X.

"Close!" I yelled. "Close, dammit!"

Fangs flashed as a man raced up. Then, *bam!* He crashed into an invisible barrier and staggered backward.

"*Mais qu'est-ce que...*" he muttered. *What the hell?*

I stood with my hands raised, not sure what I'd done, but desperate for it to keep working, especially when a second naga appeared beside him.

Roux broke away from the first stalker to charge them with a blood-curdling snarl. At the same time, another feline hurtled in from the direction of the château.

"Bene!" I cried when the tawny lion sailed in to tackle one of the nagas.

The night exploded into earsplitting screams and thunderous growls — so many and so loud, I wanted to slap my hands over my ears and wish this all away.

Not an option, however. Especially when leaves crunched nearby. I whirled, spotting the third naga, who had slipped by Roux and Bene as they fought with the other two.

"Close! Close!" I yelled, gesturing frantically at the east entryway.

With a grunt, the naga bounced off an invisible barrier. A cloud of something like fairy dust glittered in the entrance, briefly highlighting his features before fading away.

I gaped at the horrible sight — a cross between a man and a snake — and sent quiet thanks to whichever ancestor had woven magic into this structure.

The naga reached cautiously for the archway. Then he yanked his hand back, and more fairy dust twinkled.

His forked tongue flicked, and the sides of his neck flared like a cobra's as he cursed me.

"Garce!"

How was I the bitch here?

I shot him the finger. "Get the hell off my property!"

He smirked. "Not yours for long, honey."

What the hell did that mean?

When he circled the pavilion, I yanked magic over the next entryway to block it. But the air wobbled, telling me the protective force was overtaxed.

The naga must have sensed the same thing, because he slammed against the invisible barrier. It held — barely — and swirls of magic dust flew at me. Not good.

I raised my left hand in front of that space, desperately keeping those threads of magic together. With my right, I waved at the west door, releasing the magic and redirecting it here. The next time the naga slammed against it, he jerked back in pain, and sparks flew outward, following him.

I didn't know whether to cheer or cry. Why build a pavilion with four entrances when there was only enough magic to protect one at a time?

The naga circled back to the east side, and I repeated the procedure, only to have him dart around and try another arch. We were playing a deadly cross between chess and basketball — minus the board, the court, and a ball, and with an angry, fork-tongued opponent.

Well, I was angry too, dammit! This was my home. My property. Furthermore, I was a nice person. (Okay, mostly.) I certainly didn't go picking fights. Why were these monsters picking a fight with me?

Meanwhile, Roux and Bene battled on. I caught flashes of fangs, fur, and lashing tails.

The cats had a size and power advantage — not to mention those terrifying roars they made. But the nagas moved lightning-fast, dodging and slicing with their fangs and long, sharp fingernails.

Roux wrestled one to the ground, going for the throat. The naga fought back savagely, raking Roux with his teeth and nails.

Roux grunted in pain. Extraordinary healing powers allowed shifters to bounce back quickly, but certain supernaturals carried venom that could kill even the mightiest shifter. I prayed nagas weren't among them, but judging by Roux's grunts...

Stop! I wanted to scream. *Stop!*

Bene fought more cautiously, standing on his back legs to batter the second naga with his front claws, then retreating to a safe distance. But Roux was going all out for a kill, taking all kinds of crazy risks. Why?

I whirled to seal off yet a different entryway as my stalker changed directions. Then cold air sliced through the night, and I cried in relief.

"Henrik!"

Yes, relief. Not an emotion one normally associated with a vampire's arrival, but hey. The circumstances were far from normal.

Bene's foe took one look at Henrik and made for the woods. Roux snarled as his opponent slipped out of his grasp and sprinted after his comrade. Seeing them flee, "my" naga joined them.

Henrik followed, cursing in...Polish? Lithuanian? The man spoke so many languages, I couldn't keep track, but his tone made it clear he wasn't asking nicely. Bene bounded after him, while Roux circled the pavilion, snarling ferociously, as if someone had threatened his most prized possession.

Which was...what? Pride? Honor? I doubted it was a physical thing since tigers, unlike dragons, weren't hoarders.

He glanced over to check on me, then snarled twice as loudly into the night, hell-bent on defending his territory.

And, yikes. What if that territory was *me*?

I dismissed the thought immediately. My sister had probably made him swear to protect me, her baby sister. As far as he was concerned, this was just another mission. No reason to flatter myself.

But boy, did that tiger snarl as he circled me.

Chapter Six

ROUX

"You're limping," Gen said once we'd regrouped and headed back to the château.

I huffed. No, I wasn't. I was conserving energy with my right rear leg. There was a difference, dammit.

I kept my eyes on the lights ahead and did my best to strut, not shuffle. But naga wounds — even small ones — were a bitch. I could feel icy venom trickling through my veins with every shaky beat of my heart. Not enough to kill me, maybe, but enough to make my eyesight blur and throw off my balance. If we didn't get inside soon, I might be reduced to flopping over — or accepting help.

Which might just kill me, because tigers didn't flop, and we certainly didn't need help. Especially not from lions, vampires, or their boss's kid sister, no matter how beguiling — er, exasperating — she might be.

"Any idea who they were?" Gen asked Henrik.

He and Bene had followed the intruders and seen them race off in a dark car parked behind the Citroën Gen and I had left at the side of the road.

That meant they hadn't stumbled across us. We'd been followed.

"Stéphane, Nicolas, and a third naga I don't know," Henrik said, leading us inside like he owned the place.

I snorted. All vampires were snobs, but Henrik took the cake. Still, he'd made himself useful, and I couldn't fault that.

I could, however, fault his track record. For every time Henrik raced in to the rescue, there was another occasion when he let us down, big-time. The man made *wild card* his *modus operandi* because it was useful. He got the privileges of warm-blooded company, and every time we vowed to banish him, he would make himself indispensable.

Like now.

"Who the hell are Stéphane and Nicolas?" Gen demanded.

She and her sister might not have a lot in common, but they'd both gotten the *bossy* gene.

Henrik made a dismissive gesture. "A couple of young up-starts."

I rolled my eyes. Anyone born after 1910 counted as young in Henrik's book.

My joints creaked as much as the staircase. It didn't creak under Henrik, though. Something I found creepy as hell, even after all these months working together.

"Either they're fools, or they hired out to someone — again." He sighed.

"Again?" Gen yelped.

At the top of the stairs, I intended to veer off for my room in the west wing. But I wasn't sure I would make it, so I followed Gen into the drawing room instead.

She turned to me, then gasped. "Oh my gosh. You look terrible."

I mustered the energy to glare at her, but she was right. I felt terrible.

"Shoo." Henrik waved to me. "Go to your room and sleep it off, won't you?"

I would if I could, dammit, but I was close to swaying.

"Sleep it off?" Gen admonished. "We have to check those wounds."

Bene gave an exaggerated whimper and stuck out a paw.

"Bene's too," Gen added.

The lion hid a grin.

Henrik pointed. "He'll drip blood on the parquet floor."

Gen snorted. "That's rich, coming from a vampire. If you're so worried about it, get me that old blanket. Quickly."

Henrik made a face. "Must I?"

"Yes, you must. Now, move it."

The woman could issue orders better than some commanding officers I'd known. I pictured her backstage at a theater, marshaling extras and stage crew into position for a quick scene change.

She shoved the couch back, making space in front of the fireplace, then spread the blanket on the floor.

"Over here." She patted the blanket.

I flicked my tail irritably. I was a tiger, not a puppy. But given the choice between keeling over on the bare floor and keeling over on a blanket, I did as I was told.

Bene tried to muscle his way in, but I shoved him aside and stretched out, claiming as much space as possible.

He whined and looked at Gen.

Most lions had a sense of pride — no pun intended — but not Bene. Not when he stood to gain female attention.

I snarled at the idea of Gen bent close, gently tending his wounds. If anyone would get gently tended to, it would be me, dammit!

"You have plenty of space," Gen told him firmly.

Not fair, he grumbled in my mind.

I was the one actually putting myself on the line out there, I shot back.

Yes, you were. The question is why? he asked.

I'd been wondering the same thing. What had possessed me to go for a kill rather than simply chase the nagas out of our territory?

Bene tilted his head toward Gen, chuckling. *Unless you were trying to impress her.* Then he stopped. *Wait. You were.*

I was not. I was just, er...totally overreacting in the face of a threat to a woman I had absolutely no feelings for.

That was my story, and I was sticking to it.

Bene chuckled in a way that said, *Well, well.*

I flicked my tail, whipping him across the muzzle.

"Can you two behave for five minutes?" Gen complained.

"No, they can't." Henrik's tone was as dry as the gin he poured for himself.

Gen hovered over me for a moment, clearly intimidated by my size, ferocity, and battle wounds.

Sure, Bene scoffed. *Just don't let her find out how tiny your brain — or other parts — are.*

Overcoming her fear, Gen leaned over me, clucking in concern. "So much blood."

"Yes, so much," Henrik murmured dreamily.

I flashed him an inch of fang.

Gen didn't notice, thank goodness. She did step away to check Bene, which annoyed the hell out of me — until she declared his wounds less serious and sent him off to shower.

Bene gazed at her with wide, imploring eyes that said, *Shower? I could bleed to death in there.*

"You'll live," she muttered.

I shot him a smug look, then eased painfully onto my side.

"Oh, you poor thing..." Gen murmured.

I flexed my claws. Tigers were neither *poor* nor *things.*

You fucking love it, Bene grumbled on his way out the door.

A little, yes.

Maybe I was getting old. Or maybe it was after all those years in the military, where no one fussed over anyone. Everyone cared, of course. It was just that you weren't allowed to show it.

"I'll be right back," Gen said, heading out the door.

As if I were going anywhere.

"Oh, Henrik. Could you please make a fire?" she called from the threshold.

He held out his right arm, indicating a torn sleeve. "I'm injured too."

"I'll check you next. Now, make that fire. *Please.*"

Henrik huffed, clearly wishing for the good old days when a woman wouldn't dare boss him around. He did as he was told, however.

Within minutes, my eyes drooped, and I listened to the soothing crackle of the fire. Meanwhile, my feline entertained foolish ideas that went way, way out on a thin limb in a strong breeze and swayed around dangerously.

Maybe Gen and I... the beast started.

I stifled the thought with a snarl that Henrik misinterpreted.

"Yes, I find her insufferable too."

I frowned. Gen wasn't insufferable. She was chatty, tempestuous, and impulsive. She had terrible taste in music. She ate in tiny, annoying bites and slurped her coffee — black with a splash of milk. But insufferable?

Less and less, recently. In fact, I missed working beside her. More than I liked to admit.

She bustled in with a steaming bowl of water, an old towel, and a first aid kit.

Henrik snorted. "Shifters heal on their own, you know."

"They heal more quickly with help. And it's less painful."

God, I liked the sound of that. The gash on my left shoulder was killing me, and the slash across my nose stung. I licked it miserably.

I tensed as she brought the wet towel closer to the gash. She tensed too, and the brows over her blue eyes creased. Eyes as blue as an ocean, and just as deep.

She smoothed her hair back and chose a smaller scratch to start with.

And, oh. *Gentle* wasn't the word for it. My eyes slid shut, and my tail softly tapped the floor.

Heavenly, my tiger murmured.

She tended my smaller wounds first, which took a while. Not that I was in a rush. In fact, I discovered a whole new upside to being injured. Her touch was gentle, and whenever she leaned in, silky hair tickled my body, carrying her floral scent with it.

Bene eventually waltzed back into the drawing room, freshly showered and in human form.

"I'm back," he announced.

"Joy to the world," Henrik muttered.

"Look. I have all these wounds." Bene stuck his arm toward Gen.

She barely glanced over.

"They're very painful," he went on.

She rolled her eyes, then did a double take, because Bene had taken the opportunity to saunter over in a pair of low-slung sweatpants…and nothing else.

Gen's eyes snagged on his abs and stayed there for a full five seconds.

Sneaky bastard, I rumbled into his mind.

Desperate times call for desperate measures, Henrik muttered dryly.

I snorted. Easy for him to say. He'd enjoyed the company of Delphine for a full week and moved right on to Claudette. A total shit move, but what could you expect from a vampire?

Luckily, he and Claudette seemed to have cooled it…for the time being. For her sake, I hoped that would last.

"Take a seat. You're next." Gen motioned Bene to a chair, focusing on my gash.

Bene made a drama out of lowering himself into the chair, wincing and groaning. Then he sat, rubbing his shoulder tenderly.

Gen shuffled around, turning her back to him.

Not sure the young lady is interested, Henrik snickered.

They're always interested, Bene declared, extending a bare foot into her field of vision.

Gen inspected my wound then dabbed gently with the washcloth.

"What did they want?" she asked as she worked.

"You, clearly," Henrik said much too casually.

Her throat bobbed. "Because…?"

Henrik shrugged irritably. "I don't know." Then he gestured to her with his gin. "My turn for a question. What did you do back there?" He swung the half-empty glass in the direction of the driveway. "In the pavilion, I mean."

I flicked an ear, and Bene leaned closer.

"You mean, other than shitting my pants?" Gen grumbled.

Bene cackled. "Other than that."

I winced as her dabbing grew more aggressive.

"Sorry," she mumbled, backing away, then continuing more gently. "The château grounds are full of spelled corners."

"Spelled, how?" Henrik asked.

Gen shrugged. "I don't know. Magic is not my strong suit."

Bene snorted. "You could have fooled me."

Gen shook her head. "It comes and goes. I can barely control it."

"Well, you're a great artist," Bene pointed out, upbeat as ever. "There's that."

She sighed. "Not super helpful when I'm attacked."

"What other areas are spelled here?" Henrik's casual tone didn't conceal his interest, making my inner alarms clang.

"Oh, they appear here and there from time to time," Gen said, keeping it vague.

Smart woman. Maybe even cunning. A woman I had definitely underestimated.

"Anyway, the magic is wearing out in places," she finished.

"Maybe you could learn enough to revive it," Bene said helpfully.

Damn the man. Always saying the right thing at the right time. *Not* my strong suit.

Gen laughed outright. "Don't hold your breath. I'm more likely to sprout wings and fly."

The sorrow in her voice went right to my heart, as did her comment. Did she mean *dragon*?

I think she would make a better tiger, my beast whispered hopefully.

I thought so too. Then I winced at a sudden burn on my shoulder.

"Antiseptic," Gen explained apologetically. Then she stopped. "Wait. Does antiseptic even work against naga venom?"

It had better, part of me growled. Still, the sting was worth it for the rest.

She looked expectantly at Henrik.

He shrugged. "Why would I know?"

Ah, vampires. So fucking helpful.

She worked a while longer, then patted my back. "All done now."

I frowned. So soon?

When I looked up, our eyes locked. *Really* locked, like two sides of a lifting bridge snapping together, clearing the way for a sudden rush of magic. Everything else faded away, leaving just me, her, and an inexplicable sense of belonging. An alien sensation, because tigers didn't belong. We prowled around the edges of the action, keeping a safe distance — physically and emotionally. We avoided trouble. And, like soldiers, we protected ourselves.

Our hearts most of all.

"Are those nagas based around here?" Bene asked Henrik, yanking us both back to a world of harsh realities.

Henrik scoffed, as if no self-respecting supernatural would settle in such a remote region.

And yet, here he was. But that was the least of the mysteries that shrouded the guy.

"No," he finished. "They're based in Paris."

"They followed us all the way from Paris?" Gen yelped.

My tail went from tapping softly to lashing in anger. Raising my head, I caught Bene's eye.

He nodded and relayed my thoughts. "Roux would have noticed if they had. More likely, they had orders to lurk around here."

"Whose orders? And why would they be after me?" Gen asked.

A thought struck me, and I looked at Henrik. What about Celeste?

He frowned, thinking. "Celeste can never be discounted, and I wouldn't put it past her to hire nagas."

"Celeste — again," Gen said bitterly. She hadn't met the succubus in person, but obviously, her sister had filled her in. "Why does she hate you guys so much?"

"She hates Mina too," Bene pointed out cheerily.

I frowned. What if Celeste hated Gen for the same reasons? Greed, resentment, jealousy...

Gen's frown said she was wondering the same thing.

"If Mina or Marius calls, please don't tell them about this. Not until they come home, I mean. I don't want to ruin their honeymoon."

“Three nagas are grounds enough to break off a honeymoon,” Bene countered.

“Maybe, but it’s just one more day. Please,” she tried.

Bene looked at Henrik, then me.

I was torn. Bene was right — this was serious. But recalling Mina or Marius suggested we couldn’t handle this on our own, and that didn’t sit well with me.

You two take turns patrolling tonight, I ordered. *I’ll scour the grounds for any signs of naga — or anything else   in the morning*

Bene made a face, but neither he nor Henrik protested — a sign of how earnestly they took this.

“God, I could use a drink,” Gen muttered.

Henrik stepped to the drinks trolley and raised his hands expectantly. Old habits must die hard, because that was one of the few gentlemanly things he did.

“A little red wine, please,” she said. “Whatever is open.”

He poured a glass and brought it over.

“Thanks,” she said, taking it absently.

Henrik looked about to turn away, but something stopped him. Dangerous vibes filled the room, and pinpoints of red shone in his eyes, fixated on a speck of blood on Gen’s arm. My blood, probably, but it mixed with her rosy scent, making for a unique bouquet.

The vampire flared his nostrils greedily.

“Oh no, you don’t.” Bene yanked him back just as I was gathering myself to pounce.

Henrik stalked to his favorite corner of the room — something only a vampire would have — where he straightened his collar and muttered, as if Bene were the unreasonable one.

Painful as it was, I maneuvered myself into sphinx position to keep an eye on him.

Where is Claudette when you need her? Bene half joked in my mind. *Henrik could quench his thirst with her.*

My mouth went sour. I felt for Claudette — truly — but I was also wary. Why give an outsider free run of the château — especially a vulnerable human susceptible to manipulation by our enemies?

I really doubt Claudette is passing information to Clement, Bene said, reading my mind.

Well, I didn't. The wolf shifter would give his right arm for information that incriminated us or Gordon. That would bump his furry ass up the career ladder *and* potentially clear the way for him to have another chance at Mina.

Marius would fight to his last breath for Mina, but I had the feeling Clement would too.

A snarl built in my throat. Claudette meant trouble, and so did Officer Clement Dulaire.

A phone rang, breaking the silence of the room. Everyone tensed as Gen pulled out her phone and looked at the display.

"If that's Gordon, I'll shit," Bene muttered.

Me too, because the big boss had a way of calling at the most inopportune — and suspicious — moments.

"Not a word about this if that's him," Henrik warned.

My sentiment exactly.

"Not a word if that's Officer Dulaire either," Henrik added.

That ass, I couldn't help thinking.

"In fact," Bene threw in, "it's probably best if you don't answer at all."

Gen stared. "Aren't you overreacting a little?"

"No," Henrik and Bene said in unison.

She looked at me, and I lashed my tail. Definitely not overreacting.

Another ring. Then another. Finally, she answered, turning on the speaker.

We fell silent, listening.

"Oh hello, *Mina,*" she said, giving Henrik a look that said, *See? You always find the worst in things.*

Yes, but that had kept him alive through several tumultuous centuries.

"Are you all right?" Mina demanded, clearly anxious.

"Yep. Great," Gen chirped.

"I felt something," Mina persisted. "Like you were scared or something."

"Bene surprised me when he was prowling around in lion form," Gen lied.

He put a hand on his heart, making it clear his pride was wounded.

Gen winced, mouthing, *Sorry.*

Mina sighed. "Bene again."

He frowned. *What the hell does that mean?*

I chuckled. *That's what you get for being class clown, asshole.*

"Everything else is okay?" Mina asked.

"Yep. Great. Oh, well, except the car. It's... er, acting up. I have to bring it to the shop."

Ha. A minor understatement.

"But I have a lead on an electrician," Gen said and explained her farfetched plan. So farfetched, it might actually work.

Mina, of course, *loved* it.

They chatted for a while, then said their goodbyes.

"Say hello to everyone for me," Mina said.

Gen waved at each of us. "I will."

Marius piped up from the background. "Tell those assholes they'd better be on their best behavior."

"Marius sends hugs," Mina said cheerfully.

I barely bit back a snort.

Bene blew a kiss at the phone, and Gen relayed, "Big hugs from everyone here too."

Henrik looked ill. I didn't relish the thought either. Mina had hugged me once, at her wedding, and that was okay. But anything more than a thump on the arm from Marius, Bene, or Henrik would cross a red line.

"Okay, good night. Thanks for calling... Take care..." Gen went on and on.

Bene stirred the air with his hand and mouthed, *Women!*

"You too. And Marius. Oh, and don't forget to bring us something!" Gen continued.

I had a sister too, and we got along well, but Christ. We could have held an entire conversation in the time it took Gen and Mina to say goodbye.

Henrik stalked out of the room, mouthing *See you in the morning* as they went on and on.

"Okay. You too. Be good..."

I lowered my head and closed my eyes, listening to the crackle of the fire — and to Gen's voice, which was just as soothing, for reasons I couldn't explain. My body ached, but the fire was warm, and now that everything was okay...

"Love you," Gen said, though her voice seemed a hundred miles away.

A bleary corner of my mind captured those words and held them close.

Then I drifted off into a deep, peaceful sleep.

Chapter Seven

GENEVIÈVE

Needless to say, I didn't sleep well. In fact, I didn't sleep at all. I just stared at the ceiling, thinking about Roux.

Was he all right? Had I missed a venom-filled wound? And did all tigers have such beautiful eyes or just him?

At some point, I glanced at the clock. Two a.m.

I stared at the ceiling, then threw back the blankets. A minute later, I was padding down the long hallway in my robe and my grandmother's fluffy pink house shoes. I went all the way through the central section of the house then to the west wing, where Roux and Bene lived.

I quietly thanked the shifter ancestors I inherited my night vision from — and cursed them for not passing down much else. Fur would be nice. Wings, even.

Stripes, the back of my mind threw in. *Claws. Impressive teeth.*

But, no. I was just plain old me.

The door to Roux's room was open, and I paused, listening.

And, whew. I heard soft, steady, peaceful breathing.

I glanced around, identifying the main points of the room — the bed, a chair, and a pile of blankets on the bed. A human-shaped pile, thank goodness.

My heart rate settled, but a sense of sorrow replaced my concern. No curtains on the windows. No family photos, no mementos. Nothing to make the space feel homey.

Not much time remaining in his contract with Gordon, I realized.

What are their plans? Gordon had asked.

I wondered too. I even worried about it. And not just because of the convenient, in-house workforce.

The floor creaked as I crept forward, telling myself it was perfectly legitimate to check on my patient.

A patient who'd fought for me — ferociously. A man who'd followed me all the way to Paris and back out of a sense of duty.

Philip, one of my many regrettable mistakes, would have followed me too — but only to ensure I wasn't seeing anyone he didn't approve of.

Brandon would have as well, on the grounds that he couldn't live a minute without me.

So would Nate, in hopes of scoring a few freebies on my tab — a meal here, a drink there, all while dropping hints at leather jackets or shoes he would look good in. The man had been sure I had secretly inherited millions.

Yes, my track record was pretty dismal when it came to men. Still, I was resilient, and I was damn proud of that.

Roux probably had much better judgment, and thus had zero interest in me.

The notion cut deeper than a naga wound.

Roux lay on his side with one arm over the blanket. That favored his injured side, though the gash was already healing. I pulled the blanket gently over his shoulders, then stood there, wondering why my heart felt a size or two bigger than yesterday.

Then I padded out and made the long trek over to my room in the east wing.

A single light glowed in the drawing room, and I nearly went in to flip the switch. Then I spied Henrik in a chair by the windows, reading so intently, he didn't hear me.

Instinctively, I made a clutching motion, and darkness closed in, forming a cloak around me.

I backed away, quiet as a mouse. I had no idea why Henrik was there, but I knew better than to disturb a vampire.

"Someone there?" he called, looking right at me.

I froze, but somehow, he didn't see me.

Holding my breath, I retreated quietly. Then, a few steps down the hallway, I stopped and looked around.

Everything was different. I saw the world as if through a bottle — a little blurred, colorless, and even dimmer than a moment before.

When I drew my fingers together, darkness tightened around me like a cape. When I opened my palms, the darkness inched away.

I grew a little bolder, stirring the air with one hand. Shadows rippled, mirroring the motion.

Shadow-weaving. My grandmother's voice echoed in my mind. *A handy trick, making you impossible to see.*

She'd attempted to give Mina, Dora, and me lessons in various types of magic, but none of us had shown much talent. Mina could shadow-walk, which involved erasing your image from one spot and casting it to another. A trick way, way out of my league.

But shadow-weaving was easier. You "just" collected darkness that was already there and melted in with the shadows.

I'd never pulled it off before, but now...

I stared down at my body — perfectly clear — then my surroundings, which were dark and blurred. Then, poof! I flicked my fingers out, and the shadows flew back from whence they came.

Wow. I'd done it — shadow-weaving. For real!

"Hello?" Henrik called suspiciously.

My breath caught, and I inched away. Slowly at first, then faster. When I made it to my room, I turned the lock and stood, listening. Slowly, I backed away, thinking back over the past few hours. The intruders. The chase. The magic that had saved me at the pavilion.

Something was definitely afoot at Château Nocturne. Magic was stirring. Evil forces too.

And forces for good, the back of my mind whispered.

Like a certain tiger who'd fought fiercely — not to save his own skin, but to protect me. For the tenth time, I thanked my lucky stars he was all right.

I shivered, then slipped into bed, pulling the blankets over my head. I'd never spent a night in the château without a family member around before this weekend. Now, I was on my own with three strangers. A laid-back lion, a snippy vampire, and a testy tiger.

I closed my eyes and tried to clear my mind, but those strangers kept revisiting me.

One, especially.

∞∞∞

I awoke at sunrise, bleary-eyed and cranky. Then I did a double take at the clock. Eight-twenty already?

Pulling on a robe, I rushed to the drawing room, but all I found was a blanket on the floor and ashes in the fireplace. I glanced out the window as I folded the blanket. When had Henrik left? How were Roux's wounds? Where was Bene?

The clatter of dishes drew me downstairs, where I pulled up short at the sight of Bene clearing away breakfast.

"Where's Claudette?" I asked.

"Good morning to you too," he said cheerily, though the dark lines around his eyes suggested he hadn't gotten much sleep.

"Good morning. All healed up?" I looked at his arm.

"Pretty much." He pulled up his sleeve to show off his biceps then went back to clearing platters. "Claudette didn't show up, so I helped myself. You want some?"

He held out the last of the bacon.

I took a crispy strip and munched, thinking about last night. Roux. Henrik. Shadow-weaving. Had that really been me, or had I dreamed that part?

"I see you slept in," he observed, moving to the kitchen.

I followed, grumbling, "It doesn't count as sleeping in if you had a shitty night."

"Call me next time." He grinned and put the plates in the sink.

I rolled my eyes. "I've sworn off men. Also, you're not my type." When he cocked his head, I went on. "You're too nice. On the other hand, you would make for a disastrous relationship, which I seem to specialize in."

"Nah. You just haven't found the right guy yet," he said, more like a brother than a flirty bachelor for a change.

I sighed. "Maybe I need a new strategy. Using the process of elimination hasn't proven all too efficient."

He laughed. "Ever think of going after guys you have no interest in?"

I snorted. "You mean like you — or Henrik?"

He chuckled. "I was thinking Roux."

I went perfectly still.

"The guy is too principled to break hearts," Bene continued as he moved around the kitchen. "But you'd have to put up with the world's most annoying tiger and endure a lifetime of boredom."

I pursed my lips. Principled, yes. Annoying. . . sometimes. But boring? Every time I looked into his eyes, I saw a universe of longing and mystery.

"I guess he's still in bed?" I asked as casually as I could.

Bene snorted. "Are you kidding? He still lives by five a.m. reverie." He jerked an elbow toward the side of the building. "He's out in the stables, sneaking in a little work before work."

He pointed to the clock. Mina had established a strict schedule, with an eight thirty start time every morning.

I grabbed a piece of toast, ready to head to the stables to see for myself. Then I peeked out the window, remembering the intruders.

"No sign of trouble?" I asked.

Bene shook his head. "Nothing. We took turns patrolling last night, but there was no sign of them or anyone else."

My mouth fell open. "You. . . what?"

"We took turns patrolling. Standard procedure," he explained.

I'd never felt more ashamed.

"I'm so sorry. Here I am, complaining about sleep when you guys were up all night."

"No worries. Happy to help."

A sweet sentiment, but I still felt terrible. "I owe you. All of you."

He shook his head. "Not an issue, Gen."

It was, and I resolved to make up for it as soon as I could.

With a last, inadequate *Thank you*, I left and did my best to walk, not run, to the stables. I did dash across the lawn, but that was because it was freezing, and because I was still creeped out from last night...and maybe also in a rush to check on someone.

Roux looked up, alarmed, when I burst through the double doors.

"Everything all right?"

"Sorry. Yes. Just checking on my patient."

A tiny smile formed on his lips, and he nodded. "Much better. Thank you."

"Even that?" I pointed to one shoulder, then the other one, trying to get my bearings. But heck. The guy had been a tiger last night. I could be excused for being a little confused.

The eyes were the same, though — the richest, most vibrant amber.

He rolled his shoulders slowly. "Just a bit sore." Then he frowned, looking at me. "You sure everything is all right?"

I looked down at myself. Oops. I was in my pajamas, a robe, and the mud boots I'd yanked on over bare feet. Was my hair a disaster too?

"I guess I'm a little...distracted. Last night was kind of scary." I swallowed hard. "Thank you. For everything. Bene said you were patrolling all night."

He shook his head. "He and Henrik patrolled. I took the early morning shift. Everything looks okay."

"Well, thank you. Again. Truly." I said, still ashamed. Still, he seemed uncomfortable with praise, so I motioned toward the 1936 Jaguar, changing the subject. "How's it coming?"

"You mean, will it be ready for Lily's wedding?" he challenged.

I touched the perfectly polished hood of the car. "No, I mean, will you get to enjoy it sometime soon? You deserve it."

The corners of his mouth curled up. "Depends on you hunting down those parts."

I grinned. "That's the first thing on my agenda." Then I groaned. "Make that, the second thing. I have to call Jacques to ask if he can tow the car to the shop with his tractor." When I thought that through, I groaned again.

"What?" Roux tilted his head.

"That means I have to walk out to meet him there." I hesitated, then came out with it. "You wouldn't want to walk with me, would you?"

"I thought you hated me following you."

"That was before the nagas."

He looked outside. "Bene and Henrik chased them off."

I snorted. "So did you."

He scratched his chest, leaving another smudge of grease on his shirt. My eyes stuck there for a moment, and my imagination went into overdrive.

"Maybe *you* scared them off," he joked.

"Very funny." I thumped his arm, then cringed when he grimaced. "Oh! I'm so sorry! I wasn't thinking."

"Obviously," he muttered, rubbing it gingerly.

I hung my head. "I'm really sorry."

"It's fine," he said.

Ha. I was pretty sure a *ten* on my pain scale was only about a *two* on his.

"I should leave you in peace. Sorry again."

God, why was I so flustered all of a sudden?

"Wait. You don't have to."

"I do," I said, moving toward the door. No wonder I had such a bad track record with men. I gravitated toward jerks, and I was a jerk to the good ones.

Roux reached out, whispering, "Don't go, Geneviève."

I halted. God, I loved the way my name rolled off his tongue.

And, oh. Maybe he didn't hate me.

"You could stay and...uh..." He looked around, suddenly shy.

"Note down any other parts you need?"

A tiny smile formed on his lips, starting from the right side, then stretching all the way over to the left.

"Yes. In addition to the wiggly carburetor."

I chuckled, then checked my watch. "I'll see what I can do, but unfortunately, work on the ballroom comes first."

He gestured. "Wearing that?"

I looked down at myself, then sighed. "I'll squeeze in a wardrobe change first."

Which meant I had to tear myself away from the stables. A new sensation, because I'd never felt particularly drawn to the place before. But now, that classic car had jumped to the top of my list. That, and its mechanic.

I cleared my throat and hurried back to my room. Ten minutes later, I was hurrying down the stairs in my work overalls, doing my hair as I went. Opening the front door, I spotted Roux on his way in from the stables.

Bene came up behind me with a sigh. "What page are we on on Mina's job list? Thirteen?"

I laughed. "Thereabouts. I'm sure Roux knows."

The man loved lists. It was a wonder my sister had hooked up with Marius instead of Roux.

Every beast in the Noah's Ark of my shifter ancestry growled jealously.

Roux made his way toward us, wiping his hands on a rag. Then he slowed, stopped, and turned back toward the stables.

My first thought was, *Did he forget something?*

My second thought was, *Great ass. Maybe even better than Clement's.*

"What's that?" Bene pointed into the distance.

I adjusted my focus, spotting the flash of red and blue lights over by the caretaker's cottage.

"Uh-oh," Bene murmured.

Roux jogged a few steps toward them, then broke into an all-out sprint. Bene and I followed. Several long minutes later, we reached the caretaker's house where Henrik lived. Decades ago, that building had been carved out of the grounds and sold to raise funds to maintain the rest of the estate, a decision my grandmother had quickly regretted. Now it was owned by a stranger — the absentee landlord who rented the neglected place to Henrik.

I caught a whiff of Clement's scent and assumed he was inside. But why?

"What's going on?" I blurted to the police officer standing guard by the door. Not Clem's usual partner, Monsieur Blanchet.

This guy was slimmer. Bigger. Tougher. A bear shifter, judging by the scent.

"Keep back, please." He motioned briskly.

I stepped back and repeated myself. "What's going on?"

My breath swirled in the frigid morning air.

"Police investigation, ma'am. Keep back. You too," the guy growled at Bene.

Roux pulled him back, and Bene whispered in alarm. "Looks like they called out the big guns."

They, who? And what big guns?

The two vehicles parked outside were both sleeker and sportier than Clement's boxy patrol car. Both were marked with the logo of the DGSI — the French equivalent of the FBI, though the color scheme appeared reversed.

"Supernatural unit," Roux whispered.

Bene retreated another step.

"I told you Clement isn't regular law enforcement," Roux hissed.

My heart nearly stopped. If so, this was bad. Very bad. For all of us, not just Henrik.

Voices carried down the stairs, one angry, one steady.

"This is ridiculous," Henrik protested.

"Keep moving," Clement grunted, sounding grimmer than I'd ever heard him.

"And keep those fangs retracted," a third man ordered — another DGSI agent, I saw when they all emerged.

Not a bear shifter, I decided. A low-level warlock, judging by the shimmer around his shoulders.

"What's happening, Clem?" I asked, though the handcuffs locking Henrik's hands behind his back made that obvious.

"Not now, Geneviève." Clem barely glanced at me, the way one ignored a pest or a child.

Every illusion I'd ever entertained about Clement shattered and rained down around me like shards of broken glass. Hurt — a lot of it — bubbled up in my soul. Then anger muscled in and took over.

Bene pulled me back, but I lunged forward. And, oh. A fit of magic must have given me a little boost, because I found myself standing firmly between the bear shifter, Henrik, and the door of the squad car.

"This is my property, dammit. I have a right to know what's going on." My voice rang out, silencing everyone.

So, yikes. I'd definitely had a *Mina* moment.

Then Clement looked at me.

"Monsieur Velchynsky is under arrest," he gritted out.

"For what crime?" When I gestured, sparks jumped from my fingers. Whoa. Definitely a *touched by magic* moment.

The bear shifter glanced uneasily at the warlock.

Clement heaved a deep breath, then grunted, "For the murder of Claudette Villard."

Chapter Eight

GENEVIÈVE

The first thing I did was call my sister.

The second thing I did was chase the police car into town — on foot, because my car had broken down.

A kilometer or so down the road, a van beeped, passed me, and stopped. Roux jumped out and jogged to me, but I didn't stop. I just swiped away the half-frozen tears stuck to my face and hurried on.

"Gen, wait. Stop." Roux jogged alongside me, his breaths crystallizing in the crisp morning air.

I shook my head. "I have to get to Claudette. I have to help."

That made no sense, and I knew it. But my mind wasn't too clear, and all I could think of was reaching Claudette.

Roux put a hand on my arm, but I shook it off.

"There was some mistake. She can't be dead," I voiced the mantra that kept circling through my head.

Roux hurried a few steps ahead and opened both arms, blocking me.

"Gen. Stop. We'll give you a ride."

I jogged right into him. A smaller man might have been bowled over, but Roux braced himself and locked his arms around me. That shielded me from the chilly air and the slanting fall sun, but not the cold, hard truth. I sagged against him, sobbing.

"It's a mistake. It has to be..."

He held me, not saying a word.

"Claudette has left suddenly before. She always comes back. Always..." I tried, but I wasn't fooling anyone. Not even myself.

Roux helped me into the back of the van, slid in beside me, and motioned to Bene, who drove on.

Good. They were taking me to Claudette's house. Soon, we would get this all cleared up.

But Bene, I realized, was going the wrong way.

I pointed over the front seat. "Claudette doesn't live in town. It's that way. *That* way!"

Roux quietly took my hand and held it in his. Using his free hand, he started wiping my cheek. Then he cupped it instead, warming my skin.

"You're freezing," he muttered.

So? What was a little frostbite? I was alive.

Claudette was dead. Murdered. Forever gone.

"That way," I tried again, but Bene continued into town.

Roux caught me in a bear hug, closing out the light. "Breathe, Gen."

I was. It was Claudette who wasn't. Or so Clement claimed. But he was wrong. Terribly wrong. He had to be.

The vehicle stopped at some point, but Roux didn't release me. I heard Bene exit, then return a minute later, reporting, "He's not here."

He, who? Henrik? Clement? Those agents?

Popping my head up, I recognized the compact headquarters of the local *gendarme.*

Bene twisted around in the driver's seat, facing Roux and me. His trademark smile was gone, his mouth hard, his eyes full of pity.

"They took Henrik to the nearest DGSI office, just outside Dijon," he reported.

I pointed down the road. "Henrik doesn't matter. We have to get to Claudette."

Bene bit his lip, looking at Roux.

A painfully long silence stretched before Roux nodded. Even then, Bene took a long time getting the van back on the road.

"Faster," I urged, pointing the way.

His eyes flicked to Roux's in the rearview mirror, then back to the road.

Five minutes later, he pulled over. I leaped out of the car and ran for the police tape around Claudette's house.

Roux caught me before I broke through the barrier.

"Claudette..." I called miserably.

The neighbors were out, looking ashen — among them, Madame Fontaine, the retired schoolmistress. She walked straight over and hugged me. And hugged me and hugged me...

"It's too late," she whispered. "No one can help."

It ought to have sounded harsh, but Madame Fontaine was a teacher, and she knew how to hit exactly the right tone. Soft. Sad. Clear. Above all, steady, promising me as bad as this was, we would find a way through.

Slowly, I pulled myself together, asked a few questions, and returned to Bene and Roux.

I hung my head. "Sorry."

Bene shook his head gently. "No reason to be."

Easy for him to say. *His* shirt wasn't stained with my tears — or worse, snot, like Roux's.

I curled my hands inside my sleeves and wiped the front of Roux's shirt. "I'm really sorry."

He caught my hands and waited until I met his eyes. I didn't want to, but I was glad when I did, because they were as soothing as Madame Fontaine's gentle tone.

"All good, Geneviève," he murmured.

I closed my eyes, savoring that tiny moment of calm in a truly terrible world.

Then I swallowed hard, straightened, and looked at the car. "Next stop, Dijon?"

∞∞∞∞

An hour of driving brought us to the outskirts of Dijon, but it took another three-quarters of an hour to find the DGSI office. Which, I supposed, was the point. Feds didn't exactly set up shop between the local hairdresser and *boulangerie* with a large, bright sign that spelled F-B-I — or, in this case, D-G-S-I. The supernatural branch was even more secretive, though we eventually hunted them down in a narrow alley in an industrial part of town.

"What about the Guardians of Paris?" I whispered on the way. "Don't they take charge of supernatural crimes?"

I didn't know much about them, but I knew such a group existed, headed up by a few old-timers along with a dedicated young couple.

"They do their best to keep the peace between supernatural groups — vampires, shifters, gargoyles, and so on," Roux explained. "But they have their hands full in Paris."

"We try to operate under their radar as much as possible," Bene chimed in.

"Why?" I asked.

He snorted. "Because we work for Gordon."

Which said a lot about the kind of *business* my godfather really ran.

Roux nodded grimly. "We're dealing with a secret, nationwide layer of law enforcement — the supernatural unit of the DGSI."

Letters that only appeared in size twelve font on the door, they were that secretive.

We stormed in, only to be stopped by the bear-shifter agent.

"We're here to see Henrik," I said. "And Officer Dulaire."

I couldn't think of him as Clement any more. I doubted I ever would again. Not after the way he'd cold-shouldered me.

Not now, Geneviève, he'd said, like I was a child.

"This facility is not open to the public," Agent Bear replied.

I glared. "We're not the public, and you know it. Now, get me Officer Dulaire, dammit."

Beside me, Bene and Roux exchanged surprised glances. Did they think I was a pushover just because I'd soaked Roux's shirt with tears and snot?

Well, I wasn't. Unfortunately, I also wasn't my cousin Dora, who would handle this much more diplomatically than I ever could.

"Wait here," the agent finally conceded, heading down a narrow hallway to the back. When he returned, he pointed to four folding chairs set against the far wall. "Have a seat. He'll get to you when he can."

We waited. For *hours*. Literally. We huddled together, speculating in low tones. Where was Henrik? Why him? What had happened to Claudette?

I shivered, thinking of the nagas. But why would they go after Claudette?

Finally, Clement appeared and pointed to Roux. "You. Come with me. Now."

Every word was clipped and angry.

Roux looked at Bene, then tilted his head at me before following Clem into a side office.

Bene shuffled a little closer, giving Agent Bear the evil eye. The guy immediately pretended to be busy with papers on his desk.

"I know Mina put Roux up to watching over me, but you don't have to do it too," I complained.

Bene's eyebrows knitted. "Mina didn't put Roux up to anything. But if he wants me to look out for you, I will. You don't cross a tiger when he's that worked up."

My mouth fell open. All this time, Roux had been watching out for me of his own volition?

I stared at the door he'd disappeared behind, reexamining all our interactions. That day in Auberre... That long trip to Paris that had robbed him of his day off...

He'd done all that... for me?

Tears slid down my cheeks. A whole different flavor from the ones I'd shed for Claudette.

Whatever Clement was doing to Roux — Interrogation? Torture? — he did it for nearly an hour. When the door finally creaked open, Roux stepped out, looking much calmer and cooler than Clem. Inside, though, he seethed. I could tell.

"You're next," Clem barked, pointing to Bene.

"Yes, sir." Bene forced a wide smile.

Roux gave him a sharp look, and I remembered what he'd said at Gordon's. *No details. No promises. No confidential information.*

Yikes. Did that apply here too?

Clem slammed the office door, and Roux sat down beside me. Hard.

I leaned in, whispering. "What's going on?"

Roux ran a hand through his hair — the calm, composed tiger equivalent to throwing a tantrum.

"Are you sure you're ready to hear this?"

I gulped. That bad, huh?

"Yes. And sorry about before. I've got my armor back on now." I tapped my chest in a weak joke.

His lips curled slightly, but it faded fast.

"He's not giving much away, but it sounds like a vampire attack. Sometime last night."

"Did you tell him about last night? The intruders, I mean?"

Roux nodded. "He listened and took notes, but he didn't see a connection. Hell, I can't see a connection between the nagas and Claudette either. Unless..."

The furrow in his brow deepened.

"Unless what?" I whispered.

"Unless Claudette was selling information to someone who is out to get us."

"Someone who sent three nagas after us and a vampire to kill Claudette?" I shook my head. "Why?"

He shook his head slowly. "I don't know."

We chewed that over in silence.

"Well, one thing's for sure," I finally muttered. "You don't deserve to be treated like a criminal."

And he doesn't deserve all the grief I've given him, I reminded myself, ashamed.

He shook his head. "Claudette deserves a thorough investigation. I can't fault the guy for that."

Most folks pulled out their principles when it was convenient. Roux carried his front and center like scripture.

A good man, I decided. Too good for a girl like me.

"Well, Henrik doesn't deserve it either," I grumbled.

We both glanced down the back hallway, where the warlock agent stood guard over what I presumed to be Henrik's cell.

Roux pursed his lips.

"What?" I finally asked.

"Maybe he does deserve it."

My mouth fell open. "You don't believe Henrik did it, do you?"

When he didn't answer, I stared. "Wait. You think Henrik killed her?"

He executed the world's slowest, most insinuating shrug. "He is a vampire."

I opened my mouth, ready to bawl him out for even suggesting something so unthinkable. Then again, so was the fact that Claudette was dead.

"I thought you said he was patrolling the grounds last night," I tried.

He made a face. "He was supposed to be."

I gaped. Surely he didn't suspect Henrik.

"Don't forget, Henrik went after Mina once," Roux said. "He's impossible to predict."

I sat, reeling.

Eventually, the office door opened, and Bene sauntered out, though the spark had gone out of his eyes, replaced by edgy anger more characteristic of Roux.

I stood slowly, bracing myself to be called next.

Clem didn't so much as look at me, however. He just motioned to the bear shifter at the front desk. "Get me Haddad on the line."

Then he disappeared back inside the office.

I sat down, not sure whether to be relieved or outraged.

"What did he say?" Roux asked Bene.

The lion shifter dropped into his chair. "More like, what did he *demand.* Where was I, when. When and where did I last see Claudette..."

His voice hitched, and he studied his hands for a long time. Then he cleared his throat and went on.

"When and where did I last see Henrik..."

"Clem is hell-bent on blaming Henrik, isn't he?" I complained.

Bene looked at me in surprise. "Wouldn't you?"

I looked at Roux, but he didn't relent.

"I can't believe you two," I chided as quietly as I could. "You work with Henrik. You know him."

"Yes. We do," Roux said with a heavy note.

Chapter Nine

GENEVIÈVE

I felt sick. "But Henrik and Claudette..."

I trailed off, because it seemed like poor form to say *screwed each other senseless for a few days then broke up faster than you can say "get me a clove of garlic."*

"Exactly," Roux grunted. "He and Claudette."

I wanted to stomp and say, *Just because Henrik spent three nights sucking her blood doesn't mean he killed her,* but I petered out, studying my own words.

But, wait. I'd seen Henrik last night.

"What time did it happen — the murder, I mean?" I forced out that ugly word.

Bene snorted. "Officer Dulaire might be a tight-ass, but he's a smart tight-ass. He didn't let any details slip."

"Well, I saw Henrik in the drawing room at two in the morning."

"What was he doing in the drawing room at two in the morning?" Roux asked. "Hang on. What were *you* doing in the drawing room at two in the morning?"

I thought fast, not ready to fess up to the nature of my mission last night.

"I couldn't sleep. I went to the drawing room for a magazine, and I saw Henrik. He didn't see me, though."

They stared at me, then each other.

"Henrik stopped patrolling at around that time, and I took over," Bene said. "So, that fits."

Roux rubbed his chin, and Bene looked at the floor.

I cocked my head. "What?"

"Let's say that's actually the time of the crime," Bene ventured slowly.

I waited.

"Then Henrik has an alibi."

I nodded eagerly.

Bene spent a long time thinking that over, then shook his head. "Okay, I'll admit it. I'll shed a lot more tears for Claudette than I ever will over Henrik getting locked up."

Me too, but—

Then it hit me. "Are you suggesting we let him get locked up?"

The time it took for Bene to reply spoke volumes. "Just wondering if we should let karma run its course."

I looked at Roux for support, but he was staring into the distance.

I opened my mouth to protest, but Bene spoke quickly. "Nah. Probably not right."

Still, now that he'd planted the thought...

Bene sighed and rubbed his belly. "Would it be rude and insensitive to suggest getting lunch?"

Roux grimaced, but his stomach rumbled. Up to that point, I'd had zero appetite. But now that Bene had raised the topic...

We waited another half hour, then asked Agent Bear if we could step out.

He snorted. "No one asked you to be here."

"You know, I'm pretty sure I've never met a rude bear — until now," I told him, point-blank. I was that hangry.

He looked down, a little ashamed, and we stalked out.

We kept our break to a quick half hour, then stomped back in.

"We're back," I said, a lot more sweetly now that I'd had lunch.

The agent sighed and went back to his paperwork.

I almost felt bad for not offering to pick up something for him. These agents were doing their best to investigate Claudette's death, which was the least she deserved.

Then I spotted the last bite of a sandwich on the man's desk. Peanut butter with honey, judging by the smell. I wondered if he'd packed it himself or whether his mom had. Or maybe there was a nice, comely Mrs. Agent Bear who'd lovingly packed his lunch?

A wave of sorrow hit me so hard, I sat down.

Love. Kindness. Two things Claudette had experienced far too little of in her life.

I clenched my fists and stomped up to the desk, seized by the need to act.

"Uh, Gen?" Roux jumped to his feet to follow.

"When can I talk to Officer Dulaire?" I demanded at the desk.

"*Mademoiselle,* this is an ongoing investigation. These things take time. If you'd like to leave your number, Officer Dulaire will call in due course."

"Not sure talking to Clement is a good idea," Roux whispered, pulling me back.

I pushed his arm away. "Because you don't trust me not to say something stupid?"

"You, I trust," he said firmly.

I stopped. Oh. Well, that was refreshing.

Still whispering, Roux jerked a thumb toward the office. "But I don't trust *him.*"

"I have to tell him what I saw." Then I mouthed, *No details. No promises.*

Roux didn't look happy, but he stepped back, relenting.

For weeks, everyone had treated me like a child, at least when it came to guarding our supernatural secrets. Now, at least one person respected me. So, doubly refreshing.

I turned back to the agent and gestured to Bene and Roux. "Officer Dulaire took their statements. Doesn't he want one from me?"

"No."

One little word, but I might as well have been slapped.

"No? No?" My voice rose. "He doesn't want to hear what I have to say?"

"Now, don't get excited, miss," the bear tried.

"Oh, I'm not excited. I'm pissed off."

With that, I started hammering on Clement's door.

"Now, wait a second," the bear said.

"Clement!" I hollered. "Open up right now! I want to make a statement."

The longer I knocked, the madder I became. It was one thing for Clem to ignore me for most of my life. It was another for him to ignore me now, when Claudette's killer was on the loose.

Finally, he opened the door — so suddenly, I nearly smacked his face. I caught myself just in time and used the momentum to stumble in.

"Finally," I muttered, taking the chair facing the desk.

Clem closed the door and sat down wearily.

"I appreciate your concern, but—"

I snorted. The man appreciated nothing about me, but that wasn't the point now.

I tapped his notepad. "Just take my statement already."

He kept his hands folded. "I believe I have all the information I need."

"Claudette is dead, and you're refusing to hear a witness?"

"A witness?" he asked in the same bored, disbelieving tone he'd used when I was six.

A rock? Uh, nice, I remembered him saying. Or, *A drawing, for me? Thanks,* he'd said before turning his full attention back to my sister — and leaving the drawing behind, forgotten, when he'd left.

For years, I'd secretly loved Clement. Only now did I recognize it for what it was: my first toxic relationship.

"Yes. A witness," I growled.

"You witnessed the murder?"

"No. I witnessed Henrik. He was at the château in the middle of the night. Is that when the murder occurred?"

"What would he have been doing in the château?" Clem asked. "He lives in the caretaker's cottage, correct?"

I nearly smacked my hand on his desk. "He was reading in the drawing room. I saw him."

"You saw him," he said flatly.

I barely bit back a scream. "You don't believe me?"

"Well, it is quite the coincidence — you wander off to lunch with your friends, come back, and suddenly the vampire has an alibi."

If my heart were a castle tower, it would have wobbled, then crumbled into ruins. The man I'd secretly loved for years thought I wasn't trustworthy?

If I ever needed evidence of my own poor judgment, there it was.

I trust you, Roux's words echoed in my mind, offering some comfort. A lot more than Clement's hard expression, that was for sure.

"I left because you didn't call me in for questioning," I snipped. "You didn't even think to ask."

He jutted his jaw, clearly impatient to get on with his day, his week, his life. A life I had never really factored into and never would.

"Claudette was killed by a vampire," he said, as if that explained everything.

"How do you know?" I demanded.

He gave me a hard look. "I'll spare you the crime scene photos, shall I?" He touched the veins of his wrist. "She had puncture marks here..."

His voice cracked a little, reminding me he cared about Claudette too.

He motioned to the other wrist, then his neck. "And here, and here."

The taste of bile filled my mouth.

Finally, he drew a finger across his neck. "Then she was slashed, here. Which ought to have left a bloodbath, but she was sucked dry by then."

I stared at the desk.

"No one does that, Geneviève. No one but a vampire," he finished more gently.

But I didn't want *gentle*, dammit. I was an intelligent adult, not a child.

"When?" I demanded.

He frowned. "What?"

"What time did it happen? Do you have an estimate?"

He smirked. "How about you tell me when you claim to have seen him."

"I'm not *claiming* anything. I saw Henrik. Are you saying you don't believe me?"

He let a few seconds tick by, probably to let me cool off.

Well, he'd be waiting a long time, dammit.

Finally, he replied. "I'm saying I have a chance to put away a vampire with a criminal record longer than the Loire. One who could turn on you or your sister at any time," he added.

I sucked in a sharp breath. Maybe Clem was right. Maybe I should use my chance to rid us all of Henrik. No more serving huge amounts of red meat at every meal. No more snide remarks. More importantly, no fear for our lives.

Then I caught myself. That was so, so wrong. Henrik should be accused of any crimes he'd committed if evidence sufficed. But bending the law was a dangerous game.

"He was in the drawing room at two a.m. When was Claudette killed?" I barked.

Clement glanced down at what I assumed was the coroner's preliminary report.

I watched his eyes move over the text, then snag. The storm in his eyes raged, and I could practically hear thunder clap.

Estimated time of death, two a.m. I would bet good money those words appeared in the report.

He stared at the report for a long time, then leveled a hard gaze at me. "Why are you so eager to protect him?"

I thumped both my hands on the desk and raised my voice — enough that even Officer Dulaire couldn't forget I existed.

"Because he's innocent!" I gestured angrily at the door. "Because another vampire is roaming free right now. The one who killed Claudette."

I'd grown loud enough to make the ensuing silence deafening, but I refused to release Clement's hard stare.

Let him look at me. Let him take notice. Just this one time, if nothing else.

A muscle in his cheek twitched. A moment later, his eyes dropped back to the report.

"Thank you for the information, Mademoiselle Durand. That will be all." He motioned to the door.

I glared for another ten seconds — the slowest of my life — then stomped out.

Bang! I slammed the door, making Agent Bear jump.

I stalked over to Roux and Bene and sat with my arms crossed. Neither said a word, nor did I — until an hour later, when my sister and Marius charged through the door. Then there were *lots* of words, not all of them polite.

"Fucking Clement," Marius muttered exactly as Clement opened the office door.

Their eyes locked, and the tension in the room skyrocketed.

Handy rule of thumb: never put a dragon and a wolf shifter in a small space with the woman one had stolen from the other.

Mina put her hand on Marius's arm and shot his nemesis a weak smile. "Hello, Clement."

Shakespeare could have written a tragedy on the expression that drifted over Clem's face.

"Hello, Mina," he whispered, gazing at her for a little too long. Then he motioned to Agent Bear. "Report the following to HQ. New evidence has arisen that may exonerate the initial suspect."

The bear typed a few letters, then stopped and went back several spaces.

Clement huffed. "Ex-on-er-ate."

The agent typed slowly along.

"Suspect will be held for additional questioning, but is expected to be released shortly," Clem said, then paused for the bear shifter to catch up.

I was tempted to shove the guy aside and go for the keyboard myself, just to speed things along.

"However, Monsieur Velchynsky remains a person of interest and can expect to be contacted again as the investigation progresses."

Clement leaned in to check the message, then nodded to his colleague to hit *send.* After a glance at his watch, he turned to us with a sour expression. His eyes wandered slowly from Mina to Marius, to Roux, then Bene...

I shuffled, expecting them to return to Mina from there.

But they didn't. They continued over to me and stayed there when he spoke.

"Monsieur Velchynsky will be available in approximately two hours. Then he will be free. . . for the time being."

I gritted my teeth at the not-so-subtle warning. A warning with several layers of meaning, I realized, because any crime Henrik committed in the future would be on me.

My knees wobbled, and I looked around for a chair. But a strong hand gripped my shoulder, guiding me to the door.

It was Roux, of course. The man specialized in saving me from myself.

I shot him a grateful look, and warm amber eyes told me, *You did good.*

God, I hoped so. But Henrik plus Claudette's murderer added up to *two* vampires — two more than I wanted lurking around my neighborhood, not to mention those three nagas.

I stepped out into the night and shivered in the cool fall air.

"Mina," Clement called urgently.

She hesitated, then stepped back inside, listening intently.

I didn't catch what he said, but she nodded hesitantly, then rejoined us. Marius shot Clement the evil eye and slung an arm around her shoulders.

Bene was the last to leave, having held the door for Mina.

"We'll be back," he called, Terminator-style, to Clement and his fellow agents.

I grimaced. Something told me the opposite was more likely.

Chapter Ten

ROUX

We held a quick powwow, then reached a decision. Bene and Marius would stay with one vehicle to await Henrik's release, while Mina, Gen, and I drove home in the van.

Throughout the long, quiet drive, Gen stared out the passenger-side window, hugging herself.

Should be us doing that, my tiger snarled silently.

I stared out the window from the back seat, while Mina stared straight ahead from behind the steering wheel.

It was the worst possible time to bring up what had happened the previous night, but it seemed pertinent, so I did.

"You went to Paris?" Mina's shriek pierced my ears.

Gen winced, then admitted to everything. Seeing Gordon in Paris... The car breaking down... Fighting off the shifters who'd attacked us...

Yes, it was pretty clear which sister was the impulsive one. But the strength of their bond was just as obvious, along with something else. Gen meant what she'd said about principles. She certainly stuck to them, at least for the *big things*, as she'd put it.

A woman after my own heart.

I gulped, because that wasn't the only way she'd been worming her way into that off-limits space.

When we reached the driveway to the château, I had Mina drop me off. Gen obviously needed space, and I would go crazy if I sat around waiting for Bene, Marius, and Henrik. Instead, I checked the area for any trace of the previous night's intruders, as I had that morning.

God, what a day. A long and perilous one.

An hour of searching in tiger form brought no new insights, and I eventually headed back to the château in human form. I didn't mind cold, dark nights, but something in me yearned for the comfort of a crackling fire and the company of others.

Or rather, the company of one person in particular.

I paused at the pavilions, reliving the previous night's attack and marveling at what Gen had done. I even reached gingerly through one of the entryways. Nothing happened.

Hoo. Hoo, an owl hooted.

I trudged on, then stopped. The lights were on in the central part of the château, but something flickered to my right, and I detoured to the chapel, a separate building a few hundred yards away from the west wing.

Time had turned the beautiful structure into a near-wreck with gaps in the roof and birds nesting in the beams. We'd put in just enough work to tidy and stabilize the structure, so the pews were clean, and you could walk right in. But I paused at the threshold, peering inside.

A dozen candles flickered at the altar, casting a soft glow over a lone figure seated in the front pew. Gen?

I stepped forward, scuffing through leaves carried in by autumn winds. Slate slabs lined the floor, and carved columns rose on both sides of the aisle. The darkness and candlelight heightened the timeless feel of the place, and I imagined my steps carrying me back through the centuries.

But I wasn't. It was a cold November night in Auberre, less than twenty-four hours after a young woman's murder.

Hence the candles, I realized.

I walked past Gen, found an unlit candle, and held the wick over one of its neighbors. When it flickered to life, I found a spot for it and watched it quietly for a while.

My throat went all thick, and I rounded one hand into a fist.

Whoever had killed Claudette and whoever had threatened Gen had a very limited time to live. Because I was coming after them, and soon.

Not the most appropriate mind-set for inside a church, maybe, but that's how I felt.

"Mind if I join you?" I asked Gen, my voice raw and hushed.

She nodded quietly, and I took a seat beside her. Together, we gazed at the candles.

"It's so sad," she whispered, her cheeks glistening in the dim light.

I hated seeing her like that, but boy, did the tears illuminate those amazing blue eyes.

"The worst is, people will remember Claudette as the girl who lived dangerously," she continued. "Like she brought this upon herself or something."

I focused on a single candle, watching the flames twist and twirl.

"What will you remember?" I asked quietly.

She sniffled a little. "The girl I climbed trees with. The woman with the guts to live life on her own terms."

I thought it over, then added, "I'll remember her toughness. Her strength. That batch of toast she burned."

Gen chuckled. "I remember that." Then she sobered. "Will it be enough, though?"

"Enough for what?"

Gen knotted her fingers together. "Enough that she won't be forgotten — or worse, that she'll only be remembered as a person with a lot of... troubles in her life."

That was putting it delicately, but a fair point.

I thought it over. "She won't be forgotten. Not by us. That's guaranteed. And as for the rest..." I cleared my throat and gave myself a moment to put my thoughts together... and rein in a few emotions.

"My unit lost a few guys over the years, and not all of them were angels," I finally said. "That was part of who they were, so no, that doesn't disappear. But mostly, you remember the little things. What food they liked and hated. Their best — and worst — jokes. The times you spent together, making a mission that much more bearable or more successful. That's what creates a memory."

Gen nodded, keeping her eyes on the candles. A fact I was glad for, because talking wasn't a tiger's strong suit. Especially when it came to the tough stuff.

"Do you think Clement will find the vampire who did it?" she asked softly.

"I know he'll put everything into it. His heart is in the right place, at least when it comes to getting justice for Claudette."

"That's the only time his heart is in the right place," she muttered bitterly.

I wasn't sure what that meant, but I knew better than to push it.

"What will happen if they do catch that vampire? It's not like they can put him through a public trial."

"No, they'll keep this hushed up. And the vampire — if they catch him — will be turned over to his home coven for punishment."

Gen snorted. "Severe enough to make up for murder?"

I nodded solemnly. "More severe than any human court would, I guarantee."

"As in. . . ?" Gen asked.

I shrugged. "Death. A very slow, painful one. Vampires don't tolerate their kind attracting attention."

Gen shivered, and I resisted the urge to wrap an arm around her shoulders.

Then she sighed. "I'm glad Henrik isn't falsely accused, but I'm not exactly looking forward to his return."

Tires crunched over gravel as a vehicle came down the drive. Neither of us looked, but then, we didn't have to.

"Speak of the devil," I murmured.

Gen let out a dry chuckle. "Well put."

It was time to check in with the others, but neither of us budged. We just sat there, giving Claudette her due.

I was about to suggest joining the others when cold air sliced into the chapel. The candles flickered, struggling to stay lit, and we both whirled.

"Henrik," Gen whispered, not too cheerfully.

He stood, barely a shadow in the doorway, for a few seconds before speaking. "May I join you?"

No, I nearly barked, for a number of different reasons. But Gen beat me to it.

"Sure." Her voice wobbled nervously.

He walked down the aisle and gazed at the candles for a while.

"A fitting tribute to Claudette," he finally murmured.

Gen nodded quietly.

"I will find the guilty vampire and ensure he is brought to justice," he said.

I sensed Gen pale, but she nodded. "That would be good."

Sometimes, I wondered if the military had made me too hard. It was reassuring to know that even sunny souls could have a taste for revenge.

"I would like to speak to you," Henrik said, facing Gen.

She motioned, looking weary as hell. "Go ahead."

He gave me a pointed look.

As if I was going anywhere.

"Privately," Henrik growled, more to me than her.

"I'd rather he stayed," Gen said firmly.

Warmth trickled through my veins.

Henrik frowned and stepped closer, pulling something from inside his jacket. I tensed, keeping my hands at my sides.

But it was only a wooden box, roughly the size of a cigar case. A fancy one, inlaid with ivory and mother-of-pearl. It seemed familiar.

"I wish to express my gratitude." Henrik's gritty tone suggested how difficult he found that.

Either Bene and Marius had filled him in on what Gen had done for him, or he'd heard her long, insistent "conversation" with Clement as clearly as we had.

"I only did what's right," she insisted.

"Doing the right thing can get you killed, you know," he murmured.

I stepped closer with a quiet snarl, but Gen shrugged off his comment.

"Maybe I sensed an opportunity."

He hooted. "You? Not a chance."

"What does that mean?" she grumbled. Then she caught herself, muttering, "My morals must be slipping if I'm mad at being called out for doing the right thing."

That didn't reflect well on the company she'd been keeping. Namely, us.

I swallowed hard. Gen was a positive, cheery soul and innocent when it came to the evils of the world. She would be better off without us. Mina too.

My inner beast growled. *She belongs right where she is, and we do too.*

"I won't pretend to speak to morals," Henrik said. "But I vow to honor my debt to you. Any time, anywhere, anything within my power to do, I will do when you require it."

Quite the speech, until he ruined it with, "Just once, you understand. One favor."

Gen stuck up her hands. "I hope never to have to ask, believe me."

Henrik handed her the small wooden box. "Until that day, I give you this for safekeeping."

Typical Henrik — making a loan sound like a generous gift.

"Oh. Thank you." Gen accepted it uncertainly.

Henrik tensed when she touched the lid and asked, "May I open it?"

The time he took to answer spoke volumes.

"Yes," he finally said.

Only then did I realize where I'd seen it. That was the box Mina had retrieved for him from a burning villa in Mallorca.

Gen opened it slowly, revealing a worn black velvet interior. Clearly, that box had seen a lot of use over the years — and a lot of care, because the outside didn't show so much as a scratch.

"Oh. It's beautiful," she breathed, carefully holding up the necklace within.

An obsidian pendant hung from a silver chain, held in place by intricately worked silver settings.

"It is my most precious possession. A reminder of someone very dear to me," Henrik murmured.

A woman, obviously. And I had a good bet who that might be.

Katarina. It had to be.

Gen looked at him in surprise, then quickly turned away.

"I entrust it to you as a token of my gratitude," he said, then fished for words. "And as a...guarantee of my trust. I will never harm you or your sister, and I will do everything in my power to protect you from others of my kind."

I nearly snarled, because protecting Gen was *my* job.

Gen carefully put the pendant away, keeping her eyes down. "That's very..."

Dark, I nearly filled in the blank. And that was just the first of several adjectives that jumped to mind.

Limited was another, because he was offering one lousy favor, not eternal gratitude.

Unsettling was yet another. Would Gen be fair game if she hadn't saved his ass?

"Generous," she finally said. "That's very generous." Then she paused, carefully formulating her next words. "How long do I have the honor of keeping this for?"

I could hear the snark between the lines, but Henrik was tone-deaf.

"Until you feel the need to invoke a favor," Henrik said with his usual arrogant air.

"I see." She shut the box. "Well, I'll let you know."

Not anytime soon, I hoped.

Henrik gave a little bow and quietly left. *Creepily* quietly, to be precise. The dry leaves in the aisles barely stirred under his feet, but the candles shone a little brighter for every step he took.

When I was sure Henrik was a safe distance away, I exhaled and slid closer to Gen.

"What a ray of sunshine that man is." She blew out her cheeks, then shook her head. "Wait, I take that back. He has every excuse to be grouchy after getting locked up for a crime he didn't commit."

Once again, she was more generous than I would have been.

"Anyway, thank you," she whispered. "For saving me yesterday. Thank you for today. For everything."

"Not necessary. Really."

She shook her head. "On the contrary. You went out on a limb for me again and again, and I'm really grateful." Then she sighed. "Also, thank you for not telling my sister I was going to go to Paris without you."

I held back a grin. I'd been close to flipping out at the time, but now, I recognized it for what it was: the spontaneity that made this woman so fascinating — and the admirable capacity to admit to her mistakes.

"Thank you for following me around to protect me, too," she went on, then whispered, "I'm really, truly grateful."

The shine in her eyes said she knew I'd done it of my own volition, and I searched for plausible excuses. But all I had was, *I've been following you because I care. Because I hate when we're apart. Because I lo—*

I cut off the thought and ran a hand through my hair. I would come off like a goddamned stalker if I said that. And as for the L-word... That was ridiculous... right?

She blew out a deep breath.

Then she jerked her head up, listening. A moment later, she sighed.

"Mina's calling a meeting — now, in the drawing room."

I nodded, having just received the mental message from Bene. Crappy timing in some ways, great timing in others.

When it came to life-and-death situations, I was as courageous as hell. Also when it came to upholding my principles. But when it came to matters of the heart... Denial was a tempting option — or running.

Gen stepped to the candles, hesitated, then blew them out. It took a few puffs, but soon, they were all transformed into fragrant threads of smoke.

Gen transformed, too, from a woman racked by grief to one intent on revenge. Then she strode out with a frighteningly cool, calm demeanor that said, *Vampires, watch out.*

Chapter Eleven

GENEVIÈVE

That evening, we all gathered in the drawing room. Mina paced restlessly until everyone filed in. I lit another candle for Claudette. Marius served drinks...the hard stuff.

Henrik stood brooding in a corner of the drawing room, gazing out over the night. Bene entered from the kitchen with a platter and crackers, looking uncharacteristically downcast. Roux was the last to join us — freshly showered, I noticed, and wearing a clean shirt.

He shot me a thin smile, which I returned.

I didn't think such a shitty day could have a silver lining, but it did. I'd learned that touchy tigers had their lovable sides, and I'd gained a true friend.

When he indicated the drinks trolley, I shook my head. After a detour there, he sat beside me on the couch, placing a glass before me.

"Water," he murmured. "Just in case you change your mind."

No pressure, just a kind gesture. The man was a gem. I nearly touched his thigh by way of thanks, then whipped my hand away. Oops.

"All right. Let's get started," Mina said, looking grim.

Everyone looked up. Clearly, this wasn't their first crisis meeting.

She opened her mouth to continue, then choked up and looked at her feet.

Marius put a hand on her shoulder, and she forced a smile.

I knew how she felt. *Could have, should have, would have* weighed heavily on me too. We'd had the best intentions in hiring Claudette, but had that inadvertently led to her death?

"I know I have to put my emotions aside and think analytically, but it's hard," she admitted.

She wasn't the only one, as a long silence proved.

"We'll get the bastards who did this," Marius snarled.

"Hear, hear," Bene agreed, as did Roux.

Mina patted Marius's leg, like he'd made a sweet gesture instead of a murderous threat. But brutal, bloody vengeance appealed to me too.

"Would a really bad joke help?" Bene ventured quietly.

"No," Marius muttered.

Mina smiled. "Yes, please."

"A dragon, a tiger, and a lion walk into a bar..."

Mina and I smiled, while Roux and Marius groaned. Henrik shook his head in disgust.

"The lion asks for a Johnnie Walker," Bene started. "The dragon orders a vodka. The tiger only wants water, and the bartender says, 'Don't you want something with more bite?'"

Everyone groaned, and Roux swirled the liquid in his glass. "This is rum, for the record."

"Okay, okay. Second try," Bene announced.

I couldn't wait, but Marius made a cutting motion with his hands.

"No need to make a bad day worse," Henrik sniffed.

But Bene plowed on. "A dragon, a tiger, and a lion walk into a bar..."

"No vampire?" Henrik grumbled.

"No, because this is funny. Now, listen," Bene chided. "The bartender is a witch, and she says, 'I'll add a little something to your drinks. As a result, you,' she says to the dragon, 'get a brain.'"

Marius shot Bene a dangerous look, but he went on, unperturbed.

"'You,' she tells the tiger, 'get a sense of humor.'"

Roux rolled his eyes as Bene plowed on.

"'And you,' she says to the lion, 'get drinks on the house. You're gonna need it with this crew.'"

I chuckled. It didn't take a brilliant joke to lift my spirits at this point.

Marius rolled his eyes. "I'm the one who needs the free drinks."

Bene shook his head. "Greedy, greedy. You already have Mina."

Huh. Did I sense a touch of yearning there? Not for Mina, perhaps, but for someone to call his own?

Marius grinned from ear to ear. "True."

"I deserve the free drinks," Roux insisted.

"No, I do," Bene shot back.

Mina stuck up her hands, cutting them off. "Oh no. No fighting. Not tonight."

They quieted instantly. Obviously, Mina's experience in disciplining unruly middle schoolers applied here too. A parallel I didn't think the guys would appreciate, so I kept it to myself.

I opened my sketchbook and gripped my pencil, ready to take notes. Notes and doodles always helped me focus. And boy, did I need that now.

"We have to try to make sense of what's happened," Mina went on. "Who killed Claudette? Why? Is that related to the attack on Gen and Roux?"

Everyone mulled that over, sipping drinks or staring into the crackling fire.

"I can't see how, but they must be related," Roux said.

"I say we start with the nagas who attacked us," I suggested, mostly because it seemed like the easier place — emotionally — to begin.

Which said a lot, because those beasts had scared the hell out of me.

"Nasty things, those nagas," Bene said.

I replayed the incident in my mind. "When I yelled at one to get off my property, he said, 'Not yours for long.'"

Mina frowned. "Implying...what? They're after the château?"

Bene scratched his chin. "Well, considering you can't make off with an entire building, and assuming no one has made a cash offer for this place..." He looked at Mina.

"Sometimes, I wish someone would." She sighed, then shook her head. "Just kidding. And, no. No one has expressed interest in buying the château."

"I guess that means scaring you two off to clear the way for someone else," Bene concluded.

Killing us off was more like it, I feared.

"That would never work," Marius declared. "No one scares Mina, and anyone stupid enough to try would never get past us."

"No one scares Gen either," Roux murmured.

Or, wait. Was I picking up on an unspoken thought?

I glanced over a moment too late to see whether his lips had moved or not.

Either way, my heart fluttered a little.

"Oh, I get scared, all right," Mina muttered.

"Well, you can be pretty scary yourself," Bene said agreeably. "Especially when you do that frowning thing."

"What frowning thing?" Mina protested.

He pointed at her face. "That." Then he pointed at me. "Gen does it too. It's scary as hell."

"I'll take that as a compliment," I decided.

Mina gave me a long-suffering look that said, *How little you know.*

"In any case, the nagas took off," Roux said, keeping the discussion on track. "And a few hours later, Claudette was murdered."

I folded my hands tightly. I'd had Roux to help me, plus Bene and Henrik. Claudette had had no one.

Roux nudged me, indicating my glass, then his.

I gave a weak chuckle and took a sip of his. Rum beat water at this point.

"So, we're back to how — or if — those two things are related," Mina said.

"Anything new about the murder?" Roux asked.

Mina nodded glumly. "Clement called me about twenty minutes ago."

I jutted my jaw. Of course he had. Why call me, the pertinent eyewitness?

Deep down, I knew Clement was a good man. He cared about justice, and he mourned for Claudette. He'd been snippy with me, but that showed how hard he'd been hit by Claudette's death. So I could forgive the way he'd treated me today.

But I would never, ever forget.

And one thing was for sure. I was forever cured of my childhood crush.

"Apparently, evidence at the crime scene suggests Claudette was collecting information on us. For whom or for what purpose, I can't begin to fathom." Mina bit her lip, then looked at Roux. "So, you were right."

"He's smarter than he looks." Bene patted him on the back.

Roux stared into the fireplace. "I wish I were wrong."

"Even so, I don't have it in me to blame Claudette," I said quietly.

"Me neither," Mina agreed. "I can only imagine that someone bribed or blackmailed her into doing it. Maybe the same someone who has their eye on the château."

"Someone?" Marius scoffed.

"Yeah, I can think of someone," Bene agreed.

Mina and I stared at him. Who, then?

"Let's see..." Bene began sarcastically. "There are hundreds of châteaux in France, but someone is interested in this particular one. A *supernatural* someone with the connections, money, and ruthless willpower to send nagas and vampires our way."

I looked around, stumped.

"Celeste," Henrik growled. "It has to be."

"Makes sense," Marius agreed, pointing to Mina. "She hates you..."

Mina grimaced. "Not even my toughest students hate me."

"Well, they're not driven by jealousy," Bene pointed out.

"Jealous of what — this?" Mina gestured around. "The leaky roof, the endless repairs..."

The hot dragon shifter at her side, I thought.

Roux snorted, and I whipped around.

Did you hear that? I tried mind-speak.

He made a face. *Hot? Please.*

Oh. My. I would definitely have to watch what I thought from now on. But it did prove we'd broken through that barrier in our minds.

I gulped. It felt weirdly intimate. Was I ready for that?

My gut warmed. Yes. Yes, I was.

"Celeste was trying to maneuver her way into taking over Gordon's business," Bene said. "So losing her job before she was ready to execute her plan must have been the last straw. And from her perspective, that was our fault."

"Her own damn fault," Marius growled.

Anger energized the room, and I wouldn't have been surprised if the men set off to lynch Celeste that night. But we needed to think things through.

"Sounds plausible, but we need more to go on than that," I said, then faced Henrik. "I hate to ask, but I must. Did Claudette ever mention anything to you in the time you...uh..."

I faded out, unable to find a delicate way to say *during your brief, bloody fling.*

Vampires were usually as pale and pasty as your average librarian, but Henrik went crimson with indignation.

"I would have said something if I had any reason to suspect her motives."

Kind of rich, considering his motives — *easy sex* and *freely offered blood.* Yuck.

"Any idea who she'd been with in Paris before coming here?" Mina asked.

Henrik shook his head, slowly returning to a vampire's normal, "healthy" hue. Another yuck.

"I don't know, and I didn't ask. But I can travel to Paris and make some inquiries." His eyes glowed red, hinting at how final those *inquiries* might be.

I couldn't bring myself to be appalled. Anyone who had used or abused Claudette deserved the worst.

"Okay, that's one theory — Celeste masterminding all this. But it's iffy, at best," I decided. "Any other possibilities?"

Everyone looked at Henrik, then Marius, and both growled.

"No...uh...enemies who might be after you?" I asked Marius carefully.

Marius looked pained. From what I'd heard, he'd managed to make quite a few. Enough to have put a major monkey wrench in his recent trip to London with Mina — the deadliest kind.

"Enemies, yes. But no one organized enough to pull all this off. No one but Celeste."

"What about you? Any lovely lady vampires who might take offense to you being here?" Bene asked Henrik.

I thought of poor Delphine, his human lover, and the woman whose pendant he'd given me for safekeeping.

Henrik scoffed, then went very, very still.

"Uh-oh," Bene murmured.

My heart rate spiked. Now what? Was it not enough to have a conniving succubus like Celeste after us? Was there someone else? A ruthless siren, maybe? A vampire-naga cross?

"Leonora," Henrik whispered.

I pictured a shape shifting Catwoman-lookalike in a tight leather outfit and a lot of feline sass.

Roux groaned. "Leonora? Let's hope not."

"Who?" I demanded. God, I hated being the newest kid on the block.

"A woman Henrik turned without coven permission," Bene supplied.

When Henrik gave him an icy look, Bene backpedaled. "I mean, *unauthorized conversion*."

"She begged me to." Henrik shrugged.

I stared.

Mina sighed into my mind. *Told you we have to watch ourselves around these guys.*

Yes, I was catching on to that. Fast.

But if Leonora begged him, why would she be his enemy? I asked Mina privately.

She shot me a look. *I don't know, and I don't want to know. And whatever you do, don't ask.*

I didn't plan to.

Henrik mulled over the possibilities a while longer, suggesting a very long list of candidates. Finally, he shook his head. "Celeste is the most likely culprit."

The room was so quiet, I could hear the splash as he topped up on the hard stuff — eighty-proof Żubrówka.

Bene was the first to speak up. "Hey, Mina. Do you have your phone on?"

"Yes," she said. "Why?"

"I'm half expecting Gordon to call. He always seems to when bad things go down."

Mina pulled her phone out of her pocket, then shook her head. No calls, apparently. Or, not *yet*?

When she laid it gingerly on the coffee table, everyone stared at it in anticipation.

"What are you implying?" I demanded, taking offense.

Gordon was my caring and generous godfather. He might be involved in a few off-the-books deals, but I couldn't believe things were as dire as Mina made them sound.

Bene shrugged. "Just observing that Gordon calls at the damnedest times."

Roux rubbed this chin. "Apropos Gordon... When Gen visited him, he mentioned sending a replacement crew here."

"Yeah — the guys he brings in to bump us off because we know too much," Bene joked.

I huffed. These guys saw conspiracies everywhere.

Struck by a brilliant thought, I pulled out my phone and hit speed dial.

"Why not take the initiative and call him, then?" I put my phone on speaker setting, letting the beeps of Gordon's number echo through the room.

Mina practically jumped off the couch. "Don't!"

"Why not?" I demanded. "Let's get it straight from the horse's mouth."

"But—" she started.

"*Allô?*" Gordon came on the line.

Everyone leaned back like it was a grenade instead of a phone.

"Hello. It's me, Gen," I said cheerily, ready to disprove their unfounded paranoia once and for all.

"Oh, Gen. What a coincidence. I was about to call you."

My jaw dropped, and Mina shot me a look that screamed, *I told you so!*

"Oh? What about?" I managed, hoping it would be something innocent. An offer to host Thanksgiving dinner, maybe, or questions about what I wanted for Christmas.

"Unfortunately, it's a rather urgent and perplexing matter," he said.

As urgent and perplexing as Claudette's death? Mina's dubious look asked.

"I have just returned home from an evening out to find my home broken in to."

I gasped. Gordon was a powerful and respected warlock. Maybe even powerful and *feared.* He also had a bear-shifter doorman to watch over things.

So, who would be audacious — or crazy — enough to break in to his apartment? Who had even a remote chance of succeeding?

Celeste, Marius mouthed to Mina.

"That's terrible," was all I could say. "What about Fabian?"

"It was his night off, and the power to my alarm system was cut," Gordon grumbled.

Two obstacles Celeste would have known how to circumvent, I realized.

"Was anything taken?" I asked.

"Part of my art collection is missing. Perhaps more."

First, the nagas. Then, Claudette. Now, this?

"I will need Messieurs Anand, Aecher, Velchynsky, and Bembridge to travel to Paris immediately to investigate," Gordon continued.

Everyone tensed. We'd been expecting Gordon to assign them one last task, but yikes. No one had imagined a case regarding Gordon personally.

I looked nervously at Roux. "I'll pass on the message. Any way I can help?"

Everyone in the room shook their heads vehemently.

Don't even think about it! Mina hollered in my mind.

"As a matter of fact, I was going to request your help, and your sister's," Gordon said.

Everyone stared in shock.

"Oh?" I peeped.

"I'm afraid so. Something very precious to me has been taken. Something precious to you as well."

Mina shook her head. *No way. No matter what it is, you and I are not getting involved.*

But I was definitely hooked. Precious? To me?

"Your father's painting of the château," Gordon finally said.

Mina's jaw dropped. Mine too.

"The one painted that Easter?" I squeaked.

"I'm afraid so."

His second *afraid.* Well, I was afraid too, because Gordon's fury was obvious, even over the phone. Fury and...something else. Deep concern — too deep to be warranted by the painting's sentimental value. What, then?

On the periphery of my vision, I saw Roux, Bene, Marius, and Henrik shaking their heads. *No. Do not risk getting mixed up with Gordon again.*

But I kept my eyes locked on Mina's, and a moment later, she nodded, resolute.

Marius groaned, and Roux muttered.

"What did you say?" Gordon asked.

I gulped and spoke up. "We'll leave for Paris first thing in the morning."

Chapter Twelve

GENEVIÈVE

Our discussion dragged on for a good hour. Correction — there wasn't much *good* about it, least of all the arguing over who should — or shouldn't — travel to Paris and why.

The guys were all for charging over to Paris and leaving us womenfolk back at our little home on the prairie.

Well, that wasn't happening.

Mina argued that she should go with the men, leaving me at home with Madame Picard.

Also not happening.

After a hell of a lot of arguing, they gave in.

"Fine," Mina grumbled. "We'll all go, first thing in the morning."

Henrik stuck up his hand. "I'll depart immediately in order to begin my inquiries."

One less vampire in the neighborhood was the only part of the plan everyone enthusiastically agreed to, and off he went.

Mina stood, stretched, and extended a hand to Marius.

"Time to turn in. Goodnight, everyone."

Bene executed one of those huge, lion yawns that was practically performance art, then drifted off to the west wing.

"*Bonne nuit.*" He waved wearily.

"*Bonne nuit,*" I echoed.

That left Roux, me, and the last embers of the fire.

I stood to go, then stopped. I was exhausted, but I couldn't face going to bed. The real-life nightmares of a truly crappy day were sure to find me there. Maybe if I hid here, I could evade them.

I added two logs to the fire and settled back on the couch, watching them burn.

Roux looked up. "Not going to bed?"

The château was drafty as hell, so Mina and I had continued our grandmother's practice of keeping shawls and knitted throws handy. I pulled one over my shoulders and another over my lap, then leaned back and closed my eyes.

"Yes. I mean, no. I guess you'd call this *going to couch*."

Roux didn't say a word, and he didn't budge from his spot in the middle of the couch. I was on the left end, with a narrow no-man's-land separating us.

Leaning my upper body against the left armrest of the couch, I drew my legs up in the space between us and rearranged the blanket, my eyes still closed.

"Hang on." Roux tucked the blanket around my feet. "How's that?"

"Perfect," I murmured. Especially with my feet now resting against his leg. It felt nice, safe, and cozy.

Really cozy, I quickly decided. My toes hadn't been this warm in weeks. A new central heating system was on our work list, but way, way down in the *wish list* section. Roofing and wiring came first, and we barely had the funds to cover those major projects. The only good news was, the château hadn't been upgraded enough in the past for us to have to deal with asbestos.

The fire crackled. Roux sipped the last of his rum, then downed the last of my water. I heard his swallow and the hollow tap as he placed the glass on the coffee table.

"Thank you," I whispered.

He chuckled softly. "Pretty sure you already covered that."

I shook my head. "Second-worst day in my life, and you made it slightly more bearable."

He didn't ask. He just put a hand on my shoulder.

The day of my father's car accident was number one on the list, and I hoped to hell it would never get pushed to number two. But the violent murder of a childhood friend came pretty close.

I frowned. As awful as this day was, I doubted it would make Roux's five-worst list. He'd spent over a decade in the military, and mankind had done enough warring in that time to make even peacekeeping missions deadly.

I tucked my toes under his thigh, sending a little warmth his way.

"Tell me something good," I mumbled.

"Like what?"

I shrugged, making my blanket move. "Something that will help me sleep."

"We could ask Henrik to read some poetry."

I laughed. "Not that desperate... yet."

Just that little laugh buoyed my mood slightly.

"Something about baby Roux, maybe?" I suggested.

"State secret, sorry."

I tried again. "Anand is an Indian name, I think."

"*Oui*," he murmured.

I thought that would be it, but a moment later, he went on quietly.

"My mother was backpacking through India when she met my father. It didn't last, though. A few years later, she returned to France with my sister and me."

His tone suggested a warm relationship with those two, but not his father. Which was strange, because shifters were great believers in destiny. On the other hand, destiny didn't instantly serve up one's perfect partner, as I'd learned the hard way.

"Do you ever visit him there?" I asked.

"No."

One short syllable. A crystal-clear message. Papa Anand was not in the picture. I changed the subject.

"Is your mother a tiger?"

He shook his head. "Lynx, like my sister."

"Oh. Cool."

He shrugged, then tapped my shoulder. "What happened to going to sleep?"

"Still trying," I admitted.

"So, something boring..." He thought it over, then chuckled. "Croquet."

I shook a finger at him. "Don't knock croquet, man."

"Not knocking it. Just trying to think of something nice."

The firelight reflected on his face, making his amber eyes glow. Gorgeous.

"You and Mina played croquet here as kids, right?" he asked.

I marveled at the tiny wonders taciturn tigers revealed at times. I didn't think he knew that, let alone cared or appreciated the value of such a silly pastime.

I nodded.

"So, think of that. All the details. Starting with a misty morning and dewdrops on the lawn."

A smile stretched over my cheeks. Nothing said *peace* more than mornings at the château. We were miles away from town, the main road, and anything remotely resembling industry. All we heard were the sounds of the forest and homey things, like the bubble of a tea kettle or the low sizzle of pancakes on a Sunday morning.

"Picture the sun breaking through the mist and illuminating everything," Roux went on in a hushed voice.

"You would make a great painter," I mumbled.

He snorted. "I can barely draw a stick figure. *Allez, chut,*" he ordered softly. *Now, hush.*

I did as I was told, waiting for more.

"Then you walk around, setting up the croquet gates..."

I grinned, because that usually entailed a fair amount of arguing — the kind you came to cherish as time went by.

"Then you pick your mallet." He paused. "Let me guess. Yellow for you. Or red."

Huh. Yellow was my favorite. How did he guess?

He snorted like it was so obvious.

I wondered what color he would choose. Something dark and serious, no doubt. Blue. Black. Gray. The man definitely had the Batman vibe down.

"Where did you grow up?" I asked.

"Near Bordeaux. Stop changing the subject."

"Yes, sir." It came out in a sleepy murmur rather than clipped army style.

"Then the game starts. The mallets click..."

I loved how the imagery mirrored my father's painting. The thought of it ought to have made me fret — Who had stolen it? Why? Could we recover it? — but somehow, I remained in my peaceful little bubble.

"The ball rolls..." Roux continued.

I pictured the spin of the yellow line painted through the middle of the ball... The glint of dew kicked up in its wake...

"You aim for the first gate, then the second gate..."

Either Roux missed a few, or I'd nodded off momentarily, because the fifth gate came next. Then the sixth, then the...tenth? Eleventh?

Somewhere in the double digits, I drifted off to sleep for good.

∞∞∞∞

I woke the same way — without even realizing it. Then I blinked, getting my bearings.

The fire was down to embers, the house quiet. Every window was a rectangle of darkness draped by dim curtains.

I was still curled up in a corner of the couch, and Roux was still beside me, keeping my feet warm. He was asleep, angled toward me with his head resting on the arm he'd stretched over the back of the couch.

Now that didn't look comfortable.

I lifted my feet, wiggling quietly in search of more space. But there wasn't any, and frankly, my heart wasn't in it.

I nudged him. "Roux."

No response. Surprising, since he was the *I have eyes in the back of my head* type.

"Roux." I tried again.

He stirred, grumbling.

"Move a little," I murmured, trying not to wake him fully. Heck, I didn't want to wake either. I just wanted to get more comfortable and drop right back into that same, deep sleep.

I stretched out, nudging him and rearranging blankets as I went. Then, *ah.* I found exactly the right position and drifted back into sleep. No dreams. No nightmares. Nothing. Just the profound, comforting nothingness I desperately needed.

At some point, I grew vaguely aware of Roux nudging and rearranging, much as I'd done. But I fell asleep without thinking about what we were doing. It was only hours later, when the first hint of dawn colored the windows, that my brain switched back on.

And, oh. No wonder I'd been so comfy. We were both stretched out on the couch, nestled up against each other under a heap of shawls and throws that crisscrossed our bodies.

My eyes drifted from Roux's chest to his face. There, my breath caught, because he'd opened his eyes too. Gorgeous, multifaceted eyes that shone like orange-tinted diamonds.

I froze. My cheeks heated in a blush, and my mind started working out how to ease away as gracefully as possible.

But this was Roux, dammit. The guy who never stopped me from setting off on an ill-founded venture but always stuck around to make sure I was safe. A man who'd joined me in the candlelight of the chapel and seen me through a miserable night. The man who didn't respect me any less, even after I'd sobbed all over his shirt and dragged him into several tricky situations.

Instead of wiggling away, I angled my chin up. He tilted his head down at exactly the same time, and our lips grazed.

I gulped, gazing into those kaleidoscope eyes. They spun and blazed, indicating a battle within.

And oh, did I want to charge out onto that battlefield and make bold demands. But I'd made terrible decisions at exactly this juncture in a half dozen doomed relationships.

I'd made terrible decisions about lots of things.

I spent a moment absorbing that truth. I had lots to be proud of, but I had my weak points too. And, as my mother always said, if you wanted to own your successes, you also had to own your failures and learn from them.

So, there I lay, owning the pain and regret. Learning. Hoping.

Roux, on the other hand, was the reliable one. The one who considered pros, cons, and the consequences of his actions. Maybe I would be wise to entrust him with this decision. Maybe even trust fate.

My heart pounded. My soul wailed, fearing he would roll away and end this.

But he didn't. His eyes blazed even brighter, and he dipped in for a kiss — a deep, full-contact one. He ran his hand over my back, pressing my torso against his.

Decision made. And the warm feels all over my body promised it was a good one.

Our lips danced. Our hands roamed. Our bodies squeezed together. Kind of a balancing act, given the narrowness of the couch, but hell. The man was a tiger shifter. If anyone could keep their balance, it would be him.

I ran my fingers through his hair and rubbed my cheek against his stubble. I rubbed other parts too, shoving away the tangle of blankets and shawls that dared limit my movement. And all that time, we kissed.

Roux's hand settled comfortably at my waist for a while, then started drifting upward. I arched, aching for more.

Then steps sounded in the hallway, and we froze.

Roux's lips stayed on mine, and his arms closed around me possessively. But his eyes cut away at a sharp angle, in the direction of the hallway.

Please don't let this end, I prayed. *Not before we truly get started.*

It was like standing on a diving board — the high one — only to have someone drain the pool before you had a chance to leap.

And boy, was I itching to leap.

But there came Bene, sauntering down the hallway. I could hear him humming "The Bare Necessities" from *The Jungle Book* — a dead giveaway, along with the noisy yawn.

Roux tensed. I pressed my face against his chest, braced myself for the teasing that was sure to ensue. But Bene turned down the main stairs, heading for the kitchen. Gradually, the hum and footsteps faded, and we both slumped. Whew.

I was sure Roux would disengage, as a military man might put it. But he didn't. If anything, he held me closer, tucking his chin over my head and rocking ever so slightly.

Clearly, I wasn't the only one who didn't want this moment to end.

Eventually, he loosened up, and our eyes met.

"Please—" I started.

He cut me off with a deep, passionate kiss, and I arched against him. In an instant, we were back to where we'd left off, then racing beyond into virgin territory.

Well, not exactly *virgin*, but I'd never been possessed by such a deep, driving need, or by the certainty that this was the real thing.

Too bad daylight was chasing away the darkness. Soon, the others would stir and find us.

Let them, I felt like growling. We had every right to ride this thrilling, runaway train.

But this wasn't just any morning. It was the morning after a horrific murder, and we were scheduled to travel to Paris to investigate an art theft. Two terribly imbalanced things that seemed connected, though I couldn't explain how.

Slowly, we drew apart. Roux gently traced the curve of my cheek with his thumb, as if imprinting the moment into his memory.

"Promise me this isn't the end of this," I whispered.

He gulped — hard — and thought long enough for my hopes to fade.

"I promise I don't want it to be."

Ah, Roux. A principled man who didn't make vows he couldn't keep.

Which made it my turn to gulp as I imagined all the terrible ways fate could intervene.

He wrapped his arms around me, and I was happy to hide against his chest for a while, listening to his heart beat. Then I forced myself to pull away and stand on unsteady feet.

Roux stayed on the couch a moment longer, flooding my mind with a thousand luscious fantasies.

I held out a hand, and he rose in one smooth, rippling moment that hinted at the tiger within.

"All right, then," I said, none too enthusiastically. "Paris, here we come."

Chapter Thirteen

ROUX

"I still don't understand," Mina griped as the five of us made our way down the street along the Canal Saint-Martin.

The wind blew at our backs, toying with loose strands of Gen's hair. My eyes traced each section of her braid, and my fingers itched to comb through it, just to be able to watch her weave them all over again.

"Gordon always took pains not to involve me or Gen," Mina continued. "Now, he specifically wants us to come along?"

"Fucking Gordon," Marius muttered.

I couldn't agree more. Gordon was up to something — as usual.

"Now, now. Not a way to talk about your godfather-in-law," Bene said. "Even if he's on the wrong side of the law."

Gen had stuck by my side throughout our trip from Burgundy to Paris, which I loved. But her stride hitched at Bene's comment. Apparently, she was still clinging to the misconception that Gordon wasn't such a bad guy.

She figured out Clement wasn't worth her time, my tiger decided. *She'll figure out Gordon too.*

Of course she would. I just didn't want that to happen the hard way.

A snarl escaped my throat, and Bene looked over.

"What did you say?"

"*Rien.*" *Nothing,* I grunted, keeping my eyes down.

A huge lie, because I was rattled as hell by last night.

What's wrong with getting a peaceful night's sleep for the first time in years? my tiger grumbled.

Nothing, except for the fact that the vigilant part of my mind had totally shut off.

Nothing wrong with a couple of innocent kisses either, my tiger huffed.

No, except when they were driven by a burning, out-of-control need. If Bene hadn't come along when he had...

My tiger snarled. *Fucking Bene.*

But really, I only had myself to blame. Overwhelmed by wild cravings and inexplicable emotions, I'd gone deaf and blind to the real world. An evil world that targeted innocents like Gen, as Claudette's awful fate proved.

Even now, my mind was hazy, and it took everything I had to focus.

Gordon. Stolen painting. Potential setup, the calculating part of my mind supplied.

Potential setup blinked most prominently on my radar, because laying intricate traps was Gordon's specialty.

"He called us in because he cares about Dad's painting, and he knows we care too," Gen reasoned.

"Gordon only cares about himself," I muttered.

"I hate to say it, but I have the feeling this is another of those *Roux was right* moments we'll look back on," Bene warned. "You know, *after* the shit hits the fan."

"Would you please keep an open mind?" Gen complained.

There was *open*, and there was *Please use me as a doormat.* We all knew Gordon preferred the latter. But Gen didn't, and I wasn't going to be the one to break the news.

Mina shook her head. "Gordon always has an ulterior motive. We have to be careful."

Gen's expression soured, but she didn't say a word as Mina led us to Gordon's building. Henrik approached from the opposite end of the road, and we converged at the door.

Fabian, the bear-shifter doorman, greeted us with a grim look and let us in.

Gen took the back corner of the tiny elevator, and I stood in front of her as everyone else piled in. When she touched my back lightly, my soul drifted into a world of fluffy clouds and rainbows.

I gritted my teeth. We were about to face Gordon. No fluffy clouds and definitely no rainbows. I had to be prepared.

I squeezed her hand, then released it before my mind numbed entirely.

Upstairs, Gordon opened the door and greeted us solemnly.

"Wilhelmina." His tense voice relaxed when he turned to Gen. "Geneviève. So good to see you."

He brushed kisses over both her cheeks, but his stiff grip on her forearms revealed how worked up he was.

Clearly, the warlock was furious. Not with us, for a change, and thank goodness. Even so, it was terrifying.

"Gentlemen," he rumbled at us in an entirely different tone. Then he lightened up again to address his goddaughters. "Come in, come in."

The man was a one-man Jekyll/Hyde, sweet to the women and thunderous to the rest of us.

Did we deserve it? Absolutely.

Was I still suspicious of the overly kind persona he used for Mina and Gen? Yes. That too.

"As you can see..." Gordon gestured to the living room wall.

Several paintings hung off-kilter, and a gap showed where their father's artwork had hung.

"You remember it, of course," Gordon said.

A huge understatement. Both sisters kept entire encyclopedias of art in their minds.

Gen nodded sadly. "*Easter at the Château.*"

"Such a tranquil scene," Mina added. "The château, the lawn, the trees in the background..."

The voices. The click of croquet mallets... slipped out of Gen's head.

Funny how Mina described the sights, while Gen described the sounds. Weird, but I supposed that went with her creative mind.

"Much as I love that painting, I don't understand. Why would anyone steal it instead of that or that?" Mina pointed to a framed Matisse cutout, then what appeared to be a sketch by Paul Klee.

"Because of what it meant to me," Gordon said, choking up.

Gen touched his shoulder in quiet support.

I loved — and hated — that she saw the best in people...including me. But I would rejoice the day she finally accepted the truth about Gordon.

"Who would know that it was important to you?" I asked.

Gordon looked toward the desk, then grumbled, "Celeste."

Everyone fell silent, and I shuffled puzzle pieces around in my mind. Claudette, murdered by a vampire. Gen, attacked by supernaturals. Gordon, targeted through his art.

The common denominator? Celeste.

"We thought the same when—" Gen started, but Mina cut her off.

"When you called," Mina finished quickly.

Gen frowned, clearly wondering why Mina wouldn't mention Claudette.

No details. No confidential information, I whispered into her mind.

How is that confidential? she protested.

I gave her a firm look that said, *I'll explain later.*

"Celeste would know about the painting and how to sneak in here," Mina noted.

Gordon nodded. "Precisely."

"Anyone else?" Marius asked.

Gordon shot him a dark look that said, *You crossed my mind.*

His gaze went to each of us — Henrik, Bene, and me. Lucky for us, we had no motive. But Celeste did.

"What do you want us to do?" I asked before the ugly vibes between Marius and Gordon turned into a full-on electrical storm.

"Find it," Gordon snapped so vehemently, Gen looked stunned.

"Find and extract, or find and report?" I asked. Clipped and clinical worked best when Gordon's emotions ran high. No one needed to see what a warlock that powerful was capable of.

"Find and report, but stand by to act quickly," Gordon growled.

I nodded. "Yes, sir."

"Any other pertinent information?" Henrik asked.

Gordon's face colored, and I pictured him shaking a fist in the vampire's face, yelling, *I'll show you pertinent, dammit!*

Bene and I exchanged wary glances. Gordon never lost his cool. Why was he so close now?

"That is all," Gordon finally said. "As for you..." He pointed sternly at Mina and Gen. "I've called you in because I know you will leave no stone unturned in your search. But Celeste is not to be underestimated. Once the painting is located, you must leave the rest to them."

He means us, the expendable ones, I sighed into my friends' minds.

Marius being the most expendable, Bene added cheerfully.

When Marius growled, Bene shrugged. *That's what you get for banging the boss's goddaughter.*

Marius's eyes shot daggers.

"You must not expose yourself to any danger," Gordon admonished Mina and Gen. "Your father would never forgive me if any harm came your way."

The waver in his voice said he truly meant it. So, maybe Gordon wasn't entirely bad.

Just ninety-nine percent bad, Bene murmured into my mind.

"Why not report this to the authorities?" Gen asked.

Marius snickered into our minds. *Yes. Why not do things legally, Gordon? Got something to hide?*

Gordon jutted his jaw, then answered in a saccharine tone one might use to explain how Santa Claus managed to deliver presents to so many children in a single night.

"It's complicated, sweetheart. And a certain...speed of action is required. Otherwise, I fear the painting may be lost to us forever."

Classic Gordon — changing the topic from his shady methods and working her emotions like a puppeteer.

No more questions, child, his posture commanded as he turned away.

Gen's eyes blazed the way they had when Clement ignored her.

I didn't feel sorry for her, though. I pitied Gordon and Clement, because they were missing the real her.

Underestimating her, my tiger growled. *The way Gordon underestimated Mina.*

I grinned in anticipation of the day Gen proved how wrong Gordon was. But it worried me too, because underestimating her wasn't as risky as underestimating a ruthless warlock.

Good thing she has us to watch over her, my tiger growled.

"Now, then," Gordon continued briskly. "I know Wilhelmina and Geneviève are as motivated as I am to retrieve this family treasure. To make sure the rest of you are equally motived, I offer a €10,000 premium if you find the artwork before it is damaged or destroyed."

Henrik narrowed his eyes. Marius looked at me askance.

"Ten thousand each or ten thousand total?" Bene ventured.

Gordon turned a lethal stare on him, but Mina raised her hand firmly.

"Ten thousand each," she insisted.

Gordon's eyes jumped to her, and I was amazed that she held that killer gaze.

The sweet middle school teacher we'd first met had turned into a formidable negotiator and champion of our rights.

Amazing, isn't she? Marius glowed.

"Do you have so little faith in their motivation?" Gordon challenged.

Mina shook her head. "I have all the faith in the world, but the clock is ticking, and your missions have a history of proving lethal to an unlucky few." She paused, then nailed him with, "I'm sure you value the painting enough to justify such a reward."

Everyone held their breath. Mina was definitely pushing Gordon. But he could hardly say *It's actually not that valuable to me after all.*

"Of course. Ten thousand each," he gritted out.

Bene's eyes sparkled. Marius looked pretty happy too. Henrik wore his usual *I don't give a damn* expression.

But I grew nervous. A desperate warlock was a dangerous warlock. And Gordon was definitely desperate.

"That will be all, then," Gordon announced with a gesture that said, *Shoo*. Then he grimaced. "Must I arrange for accommodations?"

Poor guy. No assistant to do his dirty work since Celeste left, Bene observed.

I begged to disagree. *We* were the ones doing his dirty work. What he lacked was an assistant to deal with the little things.

"We can do it," Bene offered quickly.

"You two are welcome to use my guest apartment, of course." Gordon singled out Gen and Mina.

Marius bared his teeth.

The sisters had probably shared many a sleepover in their lives, but now was not the time. Not with a territorial dragon mated to one of them.

My inner tiger flicked its tail. *Dragons aren't the only territorial ones.*

I inched closer to Gen.

"You're too kind," Mina said. "But I'll stay with Marius."

Gordon gritted his teeth, while Gen's eyes slid to me, then jumped away.

"That's very generous," she replied. "But it would be best if we could find a place big enough to accommodate all of us. You know, for more efficient planning and investigating."

So, whew.

Gordon nodded. "I'll keep you abreast of any new developments."

"We'll do the same," Mina assured him.

"Just a moment, Monsieur Anand," Gordon called as everyone filed out the door.

I froze.

"I'd like a quick word, please." He curled a finger, beckoning me.

Gen's eyes went wide, and Bene shot a not at all helpful *Oh shit* into my mind.

This again? Marius grumbled.

I felt the same. Gordon had a way of cornering me for special favors that only made things worse.

"Yes, sir," I said, more out of habit than respect.

Mina shot Gordon a hard look, but he ignored it.

"Monsieur Anand will catch up with you." He closed the door with a heavy *click*.

I kept my eyes on the gap on the wall, waiting. Wondering. Meanwhile, Gordon walked over to the windows and paced. Not good.

"I have a special request," he finally said.

I braced myself.

"I ask you because you're a man of your word, and I know I can trust your discretion and dedication — unlike the others," Gordon growled.

Oh, this definitely did not sound good.

"Keep Geneviève safe," he announced.

I exhaled. Whew. I would have done that anyway.

I was about to say as much, but he went on.

"She tends to be impulsive and does not yet have Mina's. . . appreciation for the dangers of the supernatural world."

Such a smooth talker. So much wrong with that sentence. Mina *appreciated* the dangers because Gordon had exposed her to them again and again. And the entire supernatural world wasn't dangerous — only the criminal subsection Gordon operated in.

"I will reward you handsomely, with an additional €25,000, to keep my goddaughter safe."

My lips parted in surprise. Did he consider the others so lax or this task so onerous?

"I also don't want her fraternizing with any of the men," he added.

I nearly snorted. Gen would never consider a fling with Henrik. Bene, maybe.

Apparently, he didn't consider me a danger.

Well, you are the dependable one, my tiger grumbled.

Probably true. But I was also the one with an all-consuming desire for her.

"And I don't want her wheedling her way into the operational stage of this mission. Just the research," Gordon barked. "God knows, the girl will try. But you have to stop her, even if you have to throw her over your shoulder and carry her away."

My throat went dry as I pictured how well that would go over with Gen.

"No bonus necessary, sir. I'll keep her safe."

Gordon studied me from head to toe, and the air around me tingled. He was probing my mind for ulterior motives — and boy, did I harbor a few.

I stood perfectly still, trying to think clean thoughts.

"On the contrary — it is necessary," Gordon insisted. "Soon, you will have completed your contract. How long left? Eleven days?"

Twelve days, eight hours, and roughly forty minutes, I knew. But all I uttered was, "Thereabouts."

"It's time to consider your next steps, and a man with your particular skill set... Well..." He trailed off grimly.

My skill set was *military,* but I'd been pushed out of that world by officers who didn't appreciate the lower ranks expressing "opinions" on issues like where interrogation ended and torture began. That left me with narrow options. I could hire out as a mercenary for causes even more vile than Gordon's, or I could work in private security.

The latter wasn't all that inspiring, but at least it didn't make me feel sick.

"You'll want to start your new career with strong references, of course," he said.

I looked over sharply. Was that a threat?

You bet your ass it is, Gordon's smug look said.

"I'll do anything for at least one of my goddaughters not to be corrupted by the likes of your colleagues—"

I clicked my jaw. We might not be angels, but even Henrik's soul was purer than Gordon's.

"—and to keep any harm from befalling her," he finished.

I nearly snorted. If Gordon didn't see fit to use Gen for his own mysterious ends, she wouldn't be in danger at all.

He clapped me on the shoulder and smiled. "Keep Geneviève out of harm's way, Monsieur Anand, and that bonus will be yours."

Which pretty much set me up for disaster, because Gen would not approve.

On the other hand, €25,000 would go a long way in setting me up in something other than mercenary work. And much as I dreamed of more with Gen, that was just a fantasy. Gen was classy. I was... well, me. Ultimately, I was destined to be nothing more than her latest mistake.

My hands curled into fists, and my nails dug into my palms.

"Not a word to her about our arrangement, of course." Gordon flashed a wicked smile.

This was beyond wrong. It was insulting. I didn't need a bribe to protect Gen. I would protect her just because.

I was about to point out that we had no arrangement, because I hadn't actually agreed yet. But Gordon's phone rang, and he gestured me toward the door. "We'll continue this later."

No, we wouldn't.

But over the past ten years, two words had been programmed into my soul, and they slipped out instinctively.

"Yes, sir," I said, making a beeline for the door.

Chapter Fourteen

ROUX

Gen was right about a large enough place for everyone to stay together, to better plan and investigate. But finding that on short notice in Paris was impossible, especially during the week of a huge concert — the reunion of Iron Eclipse, a hard-rock eighties band.

"Iron Eclipse?" Bene laughed. "My parents are huge fans. They have the goofiest pictures of themselves attending concerts about fifty years ago."

"Fifty?" I snorted.

"Okay, maybe thirty."

That was more like it, as I knew. My mother was a fan too.

At the moment, I hated the band, because it was very much in my interest for all of us to stay in one place.

"Maybe we should split up," Marius sighed.

"Not a good idea," I barked, doing my best to keep my eyes off Gen.

"Terrible idea," she agreed.

"There has to be something somewhere," Mina persisted.

An hour later, we'd found exactly two options — the Super Express Motel way out in Saint-Denis or Henrik's apartment. Not that he volunteered it, of course. Mina suggested it, and after much cajoling, he relented. It was in the sixteenth arrondissement, near the Bois de Boulogne.

"Oh. The perfect place to set up an easel and paint," Gen observed as we walked along the edge of the park.

I grimaced. By day, maybe. By night, it made a perfect place for a vampire to stalk prey.

Henrik sullenly led us up seven flights of stairs in a hundred-year-old building that had seen better days. Then he pulled a key hidden behind a heating pipe and opened the door. Everyone peered in, but no one took the first step.

"Not interested? Good. Go elsewhere," Henrik sniffed, stepping inside.

"Definitely interested," Gen murmured, following him.

My tiger snarled at the idea of her entering a vampire's lair, and I practically body-checked Marius out of the way to follow her.

"What's the hurry?" he grumbled.

I kept my lips sealed as my inner beast roared.

Big hurry. She's my mate.

Oh, no, she wasn't. She was just a beguiling woman I'd been semi-obsessed with since the day we'd met. A woman I'd shared a couch with the previous night.

My body heated, and my eyes itched — a sure sign of the glow building within.

I blinked hard, fighting my beast for control.

Gen followed Henrik down a narrow hallway and into the salon, followed by the rest of us.

"Don't touch anything," Henrik snapped, proving himself as generous a host as I'd expected.

"Oh. My," Gen murmured, looking around.

Marius grimaced. "Maybe we should take the Super Express in Saint-Denis."

"What did you expect? IKEA furniture and fairy lights?" Bene asked.

"This is exactly what I expected and why I want out," Marius groused.

I was with him on that. Heavy velvet curtains — burgundy — were pinched back by thick sashes — gold, with tassels — while the room was crowded with ornate furniture fit for a much grander space. The wallpaper featured equally dark, rich colors in a swirly pattern. So many, they almost gave the place a psychedelic vibe.

"It's kind of seventies," Bene observed. "1770s, I mean."

Gen chuckled. "Call it Transylvanian Nouveau."

"Better yet, Neo-Gothic Chic," Bene tried.

Gen giggled. "Wait. I got it. The Undead Urban Loft."

"Parisian Crypt-Conversion," Bene shot back.

They both folded into laughter.

I dropped the small bag I'd packed and got down to business by assigning quarters, starting with the two small bedrooms. "Marius and Mina can take this room. Henrik, I take it that's yours?"

He nodded, blocking the view into his bedroom. All I glimpsed were the heavy blackout curtains.

Meanwhile, Bene and Gen were still at it in the salon.

"I'm serious," he said, anything but. "IKEA should make a line of furniture like this. They could call it Gloomsta."

"Noctornö," Gen tried, running her hand along a coffee table with thick, scrolled legs.

They both hooted away.

"I'm glad someone finds this amusing," Henrik sniffed.

Yes, it was a bit juvenile. But a little laugh went a long way on a crappy day, and today certainly qualified.

Except waking up this morning, my tiger corrected.

I closed my eyes, reliving the feel of Gen's body nestled against mine.

"Sorry, Henrik," she said, fair as ever. "We appreciate getting to stay here, and you get a free pass to make as much fun of my decor as you want."

I had no doubt he would if he ever gained access to her private quarters... something I swore would never happen.

I cleared my throat, covering up my instinctive growl, and finished assigning bunks.

"Will you be all right on the couch?" I asked Gen.

She frowned. "Where will you and Bene sleep?"

"The floor."

"The floor?" she protested.

"We'll be fine, especially if we shift." Bene toed a thick rug. "I call this one."

"I call that one." I pointed to the rug by the couch.

Gen's eyes sparkled. "Um... Sure. The couch would be fine."

Another night of near-yet-so-far might kill me, but I would take what I could get. And maybe when this mission was over...

I hit the brakes on those thoughts, fast.

We discussed the painting and the mission while waiting for a local Vietnamese place to deliver dinner.

"Ten thousand apiece," Bene murmured with dollar signs in his eyes. "What a deal."

"That's not something to celebrate," I warned. "Gordon is desperate."

Marius nodded. "Really desperate."

"The question is, why?" Henrik swirled his red wine.

Gen shrugged. "My dad's work might be amateur, but that painting is priceless to us. Obviously, Gordon feels the same."

"He cares *too* much," Mina cautioned. "As if he has another motive."

Marius made a face. "A safe bet when it comes to Gordon."

"Like what?" Gen demanded.

"My grandmother kept cash in an envelope behind a painting," I offered.

Bene scoffed. "Not sure that would work for Gordon, even if he used five-hundred-euro bills."

"Documents, then," Mina suggested. "Something he wanted to keep away from prying eyes."

Gen frowned. "The backing of Dad's painting was unusually thick..."

Everyone turned. "How thick?"

She held her fingers three-quarters of an inch apart. "About that much. Oh. Wait. I have a picture..."

She forwarded everyone the photo she'd taken on our previous visit. Even so, we soon found ourselves at an impasse.

"What did Gordon want when he kept you back?" Marius asked, changing the subject.

"The usual orders to keep a close eye on the rest of you," I bluffed.

Bene patted my shoulder. "You always were his favorite."

No, I was the one he deemed least likely to make a move on Gen. How ironic, because my tiger was totally fixated on her.

My human side too. I loved her scent...her verve...her upbeat, indomitable spirit.

Dinner arrived, and we ate in silence, each lost in our own thoughts — or fantasies.

"Gordon said, '*your* search,'" Marius observed.

I nodded. "I caught that too. Why doesn't he investigate it himself? He has contacts in all the right places."

"Meaning the *wrong* places," Mina muttered.

"Maybe he doesn't want anyone to know it's missing," Bene tried.

"I'll say. Being robbed by his former assistant isn't a good look," Marius snickered.

I nodded in agreement. "Gordon has many admirers — and an equal number of enemies eager to exploit the smallest vulnerability."

"This could even work in Celeste's favor," Mina said. "If she gets away with this, she'll be another step up the ladder she's so desperate to climb."

"You mean, one step down. Closer to hell," Gen muttered.

"It's a provocation," Henrik decided. "She's provoking Gordon and you." He looked at Gen and Mina.

"I never even met her!" Gen protested.

I touched her shoulder, and *zing!* Sparks zipped through my veins. "Don't take it personally. That's how Celeste operates."

"It also speaks to the idea that this is connected to Claudette," Mina added, thinking it through. "It's not unreasonable for Celeste to hire someone to pressure Claudette into providing intel on us or to hire the thugs who attacked Gen and Roux. Meanwhile, she lashes out at Gordon by stealing something of great value to him — and us."

Gen looked dubious. "Kind of a lot to juggle at one time, don't you think?"

Marius huffed. "Not for Celeste."

"Okay, that's one theory. Shouldn't we consider other possibilities too?" Gen suggested.

For the next hour, we tried, but we kept circling back to Celeste. She had the motive, the means, and a mind twisted enough to conceive of such a plan.

"So much for theorizing," Mina decided. "Now, we need to investigate."

"Now?" Gen pointed to the clock.

Nine p.m. wasn't that late, but late enough for honest souls to settle in for the night.

Criminal minds, on the other hand, would just be starting their shifts.

"Where exactly do we start anyway?" Gen asked.

"I'll begin with my contacts." Henrik stood, headed for the door, then U-turned to snarl, "Allow me to remind you. Do. Not. Touch. Anything."

Bene grinned. "Oh, you mean, leave the dirty dishes where they are? No problem."

Henrik's eyes showed a faint red glow. "You know what I mean."

He threw his coat on with such flair, it looked like a cape. Then he exited and slammed the door behind him. We all listened for the creak of the stairs, but none sounded.

"Creepy as hell," Bene muttered.

"And yet he seems to enjoy our company," Gen observed. "Okay, maybe not *enjoy*. He *needs* company, might be a better way to put it."

I nearly scoffed, but she was right. Henrik had to finish out his contract like the rest of us, but that still left him ample opportunity to do his own thing. And yet, he'd rented a place to stay on the edge of the estate, and he spent most days working at the château.

"I guess eternal life has its downsides," Bene said somberly. "Like boredom."

Gen nodded sadly. "Like forging friendships."

I thought of his mistress, Delphine. She was probably just the latest in a very long line of mortals who'd warmed Henrik's bed — and, with any luck, a little of his heart. But a decade or so was the most that would last. Then he would be on to his next consort and the next...

For the first time ever, I pitied the guy.

Pity yourself, my tiger snarled. *Never getting involved is just as bad.*

I bristled. I didn't make a point of *not* getting involved. I just...um...

I slumped. Okay. I'd been making exactly that point. But relationships could hurt, as I'd learned from my father.

They can feel good too, my tiger murmured. *Look what being with Mina has done for Marius.*

True. Despite maintaining a growly outer persona, the guy practically oozed joy and satisfaction in life. All because of Mina.

We could have that too, my tiger murmured.

My eyes drifted to Gen, then out the window. Maybe we could.

Bene stood and cracked his knuckles. "Well, the night is young, and there's a great bar just down the road from Gordon's." His eyes danced. "Friendly waitresses, decent prices, and more importantly, security cameras that overlook the street. Anyone interested in joining me?"

Marius stood glumly. "Interested, no. But feeling obliged to."

"Dragons," Bene muttered. "So much fun." Then he looked at Mina. "How about you?"

She pulled her laptop from her backpack. "I'd like to check some things online. Not that I expect Celeste to register Dad's painting with Sotheby's, but..."

She and Marius took a long time parting in a scene fit to forever dispel myths of tough, heartless dragons. They kissed, touched, and stepped apart, only to rush back into each other's arms.

Bene tapped his foot impatiently. "You know those operas where they sing goodbye for twenty minutes? This is like that, but worse."

Gen grabbed her coat and headed for the door. "I'll just grab a breath of fresh air."

Mina stuck out a hand. "Not alone, you don't. Could you go with her, Roux? Please?"

Well, if she twisted my arm...

Gen didn't look too put out either.

I joined her at the door, where Bene still waited. "Come on, already, Marius. You're not moving to a different continent. Just heading across town and back."

Marius kissed Mina. And kissed her...

Gen and I beat them out the door. She headed up the stairs, not down.

"What happened to fresh air?" I asked.

She gestured upstairs with a mischievous grin. "Follow me, my dear tiger."

Chapter Fifteen

GENEVIÈVE

As I'd hoped, the stairway opened to the roof, where we found
a deck. My breath swirled as I skipped over to the railing and
looked out.

"Wow. Not a bad view."

Roux stepped up beside me. "Not bad at all."

The treetops of the Bois de Boulogne stretched out before
us, an unmade bed of dark, lumpy blankets. City lights twinkled beyond, all the way out to the sharp lines of La Defénse,
the modern archway that mirrored the Arc de Triomphe. And
if I leaned out to look right—

"Oh! Look!" I caught a glimpse of the Eiffel Tower before
Roux leaned out and blocked the view.

"Oh. Nice," he agreed.

I inhaled his fresh, herbs-of-the-jungle scent. Very nice,
indeed.

Below us, traffic lights changed colors, and cars painted
lines of red or white light. From up here, it all seemed distant,
even peaceful.

"Have you ever lived in Paris?" I asked.

"Only for a few months." He reached out and tapped the
skyline. "Somewhere around...there. See that church spire?"

"No. I see old TV antennas, though."

He stepped behind me and pointed over my shoulder.
"Start from the tall building, go three roofs left..."

"That one?"

He shook his head and leaned closer. "Over there. See that
tall building?"

His chest warmed my back, and I couldn't resist leaning into him.

"Oh, I see it."

"Now go left..."

I raised my hand, and he guided it.

"Oh! I see the church," I said.

"I lived in the next building over." He dropped his arm to the railing but kept the other on my shoulder, boxing me into a nice, cozy space. "On the second floor, with a view of a wall outside the only window." He chuckled. "Have you ever lived in Paris?"

I nodded. "No. Just visits to Gordon. Auberre suits me better. More space, more peace..."

"Suits me better too," he murmured.

Was that a note of yearning in his voice or wishful thinking on my part?

"You don't get bored out there?" he asked.

"No. Not as long as I have good company." Then I blushed. "That sounds like a bad pickup line, but it's true. It doesn't take a lot of people, just the right person. I mean..." I sputtered, embarrassed.

Roux's chuckle warmed my neck. "I know what you mean, Geneviève."

And, oh. There it was again — that three-syllable serenade he sang just for me.

My cheeks warmed, and I rested my hand over his on the railing.

It shouldn't have been a night for tingles and warm feelings, but my synapses pulsed, sending happy signals to every corner of my body.

I'd put that down to static electricity, but now, I knew better. This was sheer, animal attraction — and it had been, all this time.

I swallowed hard, not quite ready to process what that could mean.

On the other hand, I was *very* ready for more contact, so I leaned back and rested my head on his shoulder. He stroked the top of my head with his chin, and I couldn't help picturing one tiger nuzzling another.

I couldn't help picturing a lot of things, but I wasn't sure how to engineer any of them on a cold night on a Paris rooftop.

Roux dipped his head, nuzzling his way from my ear to my cheek.

I held out as long as I could, then twisted just far enough to kiss him. Our timing probably didn't coincide with the sparkly light show at the Eiffel Tower, but it sure felt like it.

Spinning slowly to face him would have been the natural thing to do, but I enjoyed the feeling of a solid wall behind me too much for that. What a relief to feel secure and protected after what felt like days of unknown enemies sneaking up on us from all quarters.

"Not too cold?" Roux slid his hand from my shoulder to my ribs.

I shook my head. "No. You?"

He chuckled. "Feeling pretty warm, actually."

Me too. All over.

I slid my eyes shut as he skimmed his hand over my body, from the hard ridges of my ribs to the softer zone in the middle.

Higher, I nearly begged. *Higher...*

I wasn't normally one to exaggerate my... er, assets, but I found myself curving into an S-shape, nudging my rear toward his groin and my chest forward. Was he getting the message?

Yes, because he slid one hand up and the other down, touching me where I ached for him most. Kneading. Kissing. Whispering...

"You okay with this?"

And how.

I popped the top button of my jeans. "Okay with this too," I murmured, guiding his hand inside.

Seconds later, I moaned and widened my stance, giving him better access.

"Okay?" he whispered.

"Yes. But summer romances definitely have their advantages."

He chuckled. "I think we can make do."

I did my best to facilitate things, reaching back to pop my bra one-handed. And, oh. His hand was warm, and the circles he drew over my skin made my nipples peak.

Our breaths condensed and swirled together before fading into the darkness. My heart rate accelerated, and tiny moans escaped my lips as he worked me with both hands, one down low, the other up high.

Roux went a little breathless too, but I took the prize, especially when he eased one, then two fingers inside.

I gyrated against him. "So good..."

A huge understatement, but I wasn't at my most coherent just then.

He did a fair bit of grinding too, and my mind fast-forwarded to getting it on on all fours with him behind me. When and where we might make that happen, I had no idea. But I added it to a growing list of fantasies.

Normally, fantasies like that were a way to escape reality. Now, they were only a little supplement. Because man, oh man. The things Roux did to me. Like a talented artist, he made a few simple strokes, *et voilà!* A masterpiece.

"Oh...oh..." I cried in time with the thrusting of his fingers.

"*Shh,*" he cautioned.

"You're the one driving me wild," I murmured, not at all upset with him.

He chuckled. "Want me to stop?"

"Don't you dare."

I rested my foot on the lower bar on the balcony railing, setting off another burst of lights in my mind.

"Oh..."

"Shh..."

"Remind me to say that when I get my turn and give you a blow job," I murmured.

He halted, then cracked up. "When you get your turn, huh?"

"Just don't get it in your head to rush this," I ordered, guiding his hand to my other breast.

"Wouldn't dream of it."

That was the last either of us said for a while, which wasn't to say the noise ceased. On the contrary...

"Oh..." I rocked desperately against him. "Yes..."

A wave built inside me, rising, rising...

I gasped and shuddered, racked by a blinding orgasm.

Roux kept up the pressure until I slumped, panting. He held me in my new favorite place — up against him — and went back to nuzzling patiently.

Man. Tiger. Soldier. Friend. I caught glimpses of every side of him, each a different facet of a fascinating gem.

I closed my eyes, savoring the moment. Warm. Cozy. Safe. Satisfied. Would I ever feel this good again?

He tightened his arms around me, promising he'd do his damned best — the only way Roux did anything.

Slowly, I turned and looked up into his eyes.

Wow, I nearly breathed.

He tilted his head. "What?"

His eyes were glowing bright, the color of a harvest moon.

"Eyes that beautiful shouldn't be allowed," I whispered.

He snorted. "Beautiful?"

I nodded. "Beautiful."

And I didn't just mean the color. I meant the soul shining within them.

"I promise I won't tell." I chuckled.

His lips quirked, then closed over mine. And, oh. The man even *tasted* good.

It started out soft and sweet but quickly grew harder and hungrier. I yanked the tail of his shirt out of his pants and ran my hands along his back, eager for more.

But the door squeaked, and someone called up the stairs.

"*Il y a quelqu'un?*" *Is someone there?*

We both froze. I glanced over Roux's shoulder as someone reached for the door. They didn't come all the way up the stairs, thank goodness. They just muttered something about careless neighbors and yanked the door shut.

I listened for a long time after their footsteps faded, then relaxed into a hug.

"Let's just hope that door doesn't lock from the inside. We could be stuck here all night," I joked.

"I can picture worse." Roux chuckled, squeezing me back against his chest. Then he sighed and drew away. "But we might be pushing our luck if we stay."

I groaned and dropped my head against his chest. "I hate it when you're right. Any minute now, my sister is liable to charge up here with a search party."

With a sigh, he released me and helped straighten my clothes.

"How's my hair?" I asked, running my hands through his.

His eyes sparkled. "Perfect."

His lips twitched, and I eased his suffering with a long, hungry kiss. Then I drew a deep breath and took in the view over Paris, wondering how future me would look back on this moment. The first step toward something truly special, or the beginning of another disaster?

Roux brought my hand to his lips and kissed it, erasing those thoughts.

"*Bonne nuit, Paris,*" I whispered.

Roux led me to the door and gingerly tested it.

"Whew. Unlocked."

"Damn," I muttered.

He grinned and led me inside. We descended to the level of Henrik's apartment and kissed outside his door. I held on to that kiss for a long time, cementing it into my mind. Then I cleared my throat, checked my clothes, and stepped inside.

"Is that you, Gen?" Mina called from the bedroom.

"Yep. The roof has a nice deck."

I nearly added, *You should take Marius up there sometime and let him do what Roux did to me. Then we'd both be glowing like a couple of spotlights.*

"Good view?" she asked.

I drew a hand along Roux's cheek, whispering, "The best."

Chapter Sixteen

ROUX

Long after midnight, Bene and Marius returned from their fact-finding trip to the bar.

"How did things go?" I asked, keeping my voice down since Gen and Mina had gone to bed.

I'd scrubbed my hands and changed my clothes, but I still kept as far from Marius and Bene as possible. If they found Gen's scent on me...

What she and I had done was between the two of us, and I really didn't want a lecture on maintaining focus at this critical time. With less than two weeks to the end of our contracts with Gordon, I couldn't afford to blow things — and getting involved with his beloved goddaughter would be the best way to do that.

Can't not *get involved,* my tiger insisted.

True. I normally prided myself on strong self-disciple, but the instinct to hold, to touch, and to claim had been overpowering.

It's destiny, my tiger murmured.

Maybe, but I wished destiny would work on its timing.

"We were able to go through security footage of Gordon's street," Marius said, bringing my mind back to the business at hand.

Video evidence showed Celeste staking out Gordon's apartment days ahead of the break-in. It also showed her making a quick exit the day of the theft and hurrying into a waiting taxi. Unfortunately, the camera angle made it impossible to tell whether she'd been carrying a painting.

"What about things here?" Marius asked. "Everything quiet?"

My blood heated, and I fought to keep my voice steady. "Nothing to report."

Marius disappeared into Mina's bedroom, while Bene and I shifted and settled down on the floor. I started out a good meter away from the couch where Gen slept, but the next morning, I woke up touching her. Or rather, she touched *me*, poking her hand out of the mound of blankets to rest gently between my ears.

The moment she woke, she flexed her fingers and resumed lightly scratching my skull.

I leaned into her hand. Heaven.

When we turned to face each other, her awestruck expression warmed my soul, and I felt a ridiculous rush of pride in being such a fine specimen of a tiger.

"You like that, don't you?" she chuckled, scratching gently.

Hell yes. It might not equal the pleasure I'd given her on the roof, but the moment was special in its own way.

My tail kept tapping in joy, which was tricky, because the place was full of breakable objects. A half-filled wineglass. Framed prints of Prague in the early 1900s. Vases.

I snorted. What the hell did Henrik do with a vase? Fill it with cheery daffodils to brighten up his miserable, eternal existence?

Soon, the others stirred. Bene flopped from side to side for a while, then chuffed, rose to sphinx position, and started meticulously grooming his golden fur. Mina padded from the bedroom to the bathroom, and Gen stood to put on the kettle.

I stood, stretching out one hind leg, then the other, and gave my body a thorough shake. Then I shifted in the hallway and pulled on my clothes.

"I'll fetch breakfast," Gen volunteered.

I practically jumped to follow her. "I'll go with you."

"Me too," Bene added cheerily, spoiling everything.

So, no hand-holding on the way to the convenience store, no stolen kisses at the *boulangerie*. Just a crackling field of sexual energy that followed us everywhere.

We happened across Henrik on the way back to the apartment, and soon after, everyone crowded around his dining table for a breakfast of baked goods, yogurt, and cereal.

"Clement was kind enough to send me a few details," Mina announced, squinting at her phone.

Marius grumbled into my mind. *Kind? The bastard is just trying to curry favor with my woman.*

Gen's expression went hard.

"Apparently, Claudette was keeping notes on our working hours and comings and goings," Mina said grimly.

"Nothing someone couldn't figure out from the outside," I noted.

"Maybe that's why she was killed," Bene said sadly. "The information wasn't sufficient for their purpose."

"Maybe she refused to do more than that, and that's why they killed her," Gen murmured.

"She never did like to do as she was told." Mina's tone was bittersweet.

Gen mustered a tiny smile. "Always a rebel."

"The question is, who killed her?" I asked after a somber moment passed.

Henrik cleared his throat. "I visited the coven Claudette frequented in the past. They were rather bitter about her being wooed away by the vampires of Saint-Germain."

I stirred the air with my hand. "And?"

Henrik shook his head as if I was so, so stupid. "Celeste is known to have worked with members of the Saint-Germain coven in the past."

Members? That was a fraternity of bloodsuckers, not a goddamn country club.

"Still not very solid evidence linking Celeste to Claudette's murder," Mina observed.

Marius made a face. "Not enough evidence to hold up in court, but I'll buy it."

My gut said the same thing, but we needed more.

Eventually, we divvied up jobs, agreeing to regroup at lunchtime. Mina and Marius set off to touch base with a few of his contacts. Henrik headed out to find more of *his* contacts, while Bene and Gen tracked down the taxi captured in the bar's video footage.

Yes, Bene and Gen. I stayed behind in my usual role as coordinator.

Funny how that used to make me feel important. Now, all I wanted was to be out on the streets, getting this case solved so we could all move on to better things.

But I sure as hell wasn't leaving Gen alone in Henrik's place to act as coordinator, nor was I willing to entrust Bene with that responsibility. Hell, not even *Bene* trusted himself to coordinate things.

So I whiled away the next few hours amid Henrik's *Gloomsta* decor, making and taking calls and scrolling through the internet for any hint of Celeste and her associates. As a narcissistic succubus, she couldn't resist social media, though she was careful about what she posted. Still, I found a few leads.

One of France's gossipy newsfeeds had captured her on the arm of a billionaire pharma CEO at a charity dinner for Friends of Notre Dame, for example, and her own feed indicated she hadn't left Paris for the past few weeks.

I researched the pharma CEO as well as Henrik's list of vampires who might have colluded with Celeste. But who? Why? To what end?

Slowly, the hours ticked by. At one thirty, everyone returned to trade notes and eat. Gen took out her sketchbook and drew a mind map, with a spider web of lines intersecting at Claudette, Celeste, and *Dad's painting*.

The taxi driver that Bene and Gen had tracked down remembered Celeste, but not her destination or whether she'd been toting a painting. Clearly, her succubus charms had overwhelmed the poor man's brain.

Otherwise, our investigation had turned up a few tidbits, but nothing that turbocharged our investigation. Not until Mina's phone rang, at least.

Still chewing her sandwich, she pulled out the phone.

"*Allô?*" she said, then switched to English. "Oh hello, Sid. How are you?"

Gen's head whipped around, and my ears perked. Sid, the former art forger and family friend?

Mina nearly choked on her sandwich. "You saw *what*?"

Everyone cocked their heads.

"I'm sending the photo now," she said, tapping into her phone.

"What is it?" Gen whispered.

Mina stuck up her hand, intent on the call.

"Did it come through?" she asked Sid. A short time later, her eyes went wide. "You're sure?"

Gen practically tap-danced in place, dying of curiosity. Me too.

"Yes, please do," Mina continued. "Thank you so much. I'll await your call." Then she hung up, stunned.

"What?" Gen demanded.

Mina stared at her phone, processing what she'd just learned.

"Sid just saw a listing for Dad's painting. It's going up for auction tomorrow evening at a shop in Belleville, in the nineteenth arrondissement."

Gen clasped her hands in hope. "That means it hasn't been destroyed or damaged."

"Hopefully not," Mina said.

"Wait. How would Sid know the painting is missing?" I asked.

Gen rolled her eyes. "You're always so suspicious."

"I prefer *careful*," I emphasized. Something not at all in Gen's nature.

"Sid is always scouring flea markets and auction listings," Mina explained. "It's how he makes a living, along with painting portraits."

That, I remembered. The ex-art forger also painted pet portraits in the style of any grand master a client requested, like bulldogs in classic Napoleon poses. Pretty kitsch, if you asked me, but people with money to throw away on such things were unlikely to ask anyone, let alone a guy like me.

"Can we trust him? This could be a setup," I warned.

Gen rolled her eyes. "Sid was one of my dad's closest friends."

"So was Gordon," I pointed out.

Bene chuckled. "Sid is an art forger. What's not to trust?"

"*Ex*-art forger," Mina emphasized.

As if that made me feel better. But Gen was her usual runaway train, charging down tracks that hadn't yet been laid.

"We need a plan, fast. We need to be there," she insisted.

Even Mina, the more cautious sister, plowed ahead. "Oh, we'll be there, all right."

"Can I suggest you leave this to us?" Marius tried.

Mina's look was uncompromising. "What do you know about art auctions?" She let a pregnant pause tick by, then exchanged sassy looks with Gen. "I say, you leave this to *us*."

I exchanged wary glances with Marius, but neither of us said a word.

Chapter Seventeen

ROUX

"I fear Celeste is baiting you," I warned the sisters the next evening, shortly before the auction in Belleville.

"Well, she's baiting the wrong dragon," Mina declared. Little puffs of smoke escaped her nostrils.

Gen leaned back, wide-eyed. "Whoa. I keep forgetting you can do that."

Marius expelled an angry puff of his own, and Mina shot him a lovey-dovey look. I used to roll my eyes at that, sure Marius was going soft. Now, well…

My eyes drifted to Gen.

Focus, I ordered myself.

We had to track down the painting and expose Celeste for who she was — murderer, thief, and swindler.

But the succubus wasn't making that easy. Sid had made inquiries with the antique shop, which had documents to "prove" the painting was part of a legitimate sale between Celeste and the heirs of a woman named Geraldine Dantou-Beaudetier.

In other words, Mina and Gen. Geraldine was their grandmother.

They'd seethed upon hearing that.

"Now Celeste is forging documents?" Gen had screeched.

"I wouldn't sell that bitch the shit pile around the back of the stables if she begged for it," Mina growled.

"It gets worse," Sid had reported. "The forged documents claim the painting was part of your grandmother's collection, which included other artworks hidden at Château Nocturne since the Second World War, when your grandmother collaborated with the occupying Nazis."

"When she *what?*" Gen had shrieked.

Further evidence that Celeste was baiting them — and possibly setting them up for investigation.

I stroked my chin, trying to figure out what Celeste was up to.

Marius put it best. "Working out the logic of a mind as twisted as Celeste's is beyond me."

"None of this makes sense," Bene agreed. "Why steal a painting, only to sell it? And who's likely to buy a painting by an unknown artist?" He held up his palms in an apologetic gesture. "No offense meant to your father."

Gen sighed. "None taken."

I called to notify Gordon of the new development.

"How would you like us to proceed, sir?"

Gen was beside me, and she leaned in to suggest, "We can attend the auction and buy it back."

My eyes slid shut, and I inhaled her flowery scent. As crazy as the situation was, her presence calmed my soul, pushing away the tense anticipation of the shit about to hit the fan.

"Absolutely not," Gordon barked. "For one thing, I refuse to bid on something stolen from me. Secondly, I don't want Celeste to know we're onto her. That means observing the auction inconspicuously — something you should leave to Monsieur Anand and the other members of my team."

"What if someone buys it?" Gen protested.

"Leave it to Monsieur Anand and his team to follow them. We need to piece together what kind of game Celeste is playing, and with whom," Gordon ordered.

Which was how we found ourselves huddled around a laptop in a café across the street from a modest little antique shop called *Chez Robert — Cabinet des Arts et Objets d'Époque* on the evening of the auction.

Chez Robert might be small, but it was firmly in the twenty-first century, with the auction live streamed to potential bidders who had registered in advance. I'd created an account under an alias, so we were in.

The split screen showed the interior of Chez Robert, with about a dozen people milling around before the auction began. One camera pointed at the crowd from over the auctioneer's shoulder, while another took in the room from the side.

"Recognize anyone?" Marius asked.

We all shook our heads, keeping our eyes on the screen.

My idea of an art auction came from the movies, with a classy venue, neat rows of chairs, and patrons dressed to the nines. This was a more modest affair, both in size and grandeur. The clients, however, fit my stereotype. All looked to be over fifty, artsy, and rich.

"There's Dad's painting," Gen pointed to the screen.

It was propped up on an easel near the front of the room, but no one approached for a closer look.

"And you're sure that's it?" Bene asked.

Gen nodded. "I'm sure."

She and I had visited earlier that day to confirm exactly that. I worried she might snatch it off the easel and run, but she'd kept her cool and pretended to inspect a vase instead.

At one point, I'd noticed her cocking her head with her eyes closed.

What are you doing? I'd whispered.

Shh. I need to listen, was all she'd said.

Listen — to a painting? It made no sense, but Gen moved to the beat of her own drum, and I hadn't asked.

On the live feed, a newcomer entered the room and took a seat near the back.

Henrik perked up, muttering, "Anatole."

"You know him?" I asked. When he nodded, I ventured a guess. "Vampire?"

Forget long fangs. The best way to spot a vampire was to look for a tall, pale, haughty guy with a bored, *Remind me what century we're in* expression.

Henrik nodded, looking concerned. Not a good sign.

"Who's Anatole?" Marius asked.

"A vampire who works for Alexandre Ernaux, the head of the Saint-Germain coven. Even Gordon might choose to back away from him."

Marius and I exchanged wary looks. We were already dealing with an angry warlock and a scheming succubus. Now, fate was throwing a vampire into the mix?

Not fate, Marius grunted. *Celeste.*

An older couple took their places at the auctioneer's table and introduced themselves as Monsieur and Madame Robert.

"Mesdames et Messieurs, please take your seats," Monsieur Robert announced. "We'll begin with lot 471."

Lot 471 was an antique rocking chair set up near the front of the room. The starting price was €750, and it sold for €905.

An assistant moved it aside, opening the view to a bulky dresser that probably weighed more than a minivan.

"Lot 472," Monsieur Robert announced. "Late eighteenth-century oak dresser in the style of Louis the Sixteenth."

A series of feverish bids between two older ladies took it from €2000 to over €3000.

"Sold for €3025," Monsieur Robert said. His wife made a note in her ledger.

It was such a low-key event, he didn't even have a gavel.

The third item was a pair of mirrors set in ugly gilt frames that screamed *Rococo on steroids.* Bids came from two people in the crowd, plus a third bidding remotely, as indicated by a light over a device in front of Madame Robert.

The mirrors went for €1340 — nearly double the list price.

Then came the painting by Gen's father. She leaned forward in anticipation.

"Ladies and gentlemen, lot 474, a charming scene of a countryside château in oil by Thomas Durand."

Gen gripped Mina's hand.

"Bids open at—" The auctioneer looked up, annoyed, at a late arrival.

"Celeste," Mina practically spat.

She was dressed in a shimmery silver gown, all done up like she was on her way to a prime seat at the opera. And hell, maybe she was. She stepped to the middle of the room and looked around like a queen regarding her realm.

"That's her, huh?" Gen muttered.

I nodded with distaste, and Bene sighed. "The one and only."

The auctioneer gestured. "Please take a seat, madame."

Celeste made a show of looking around for a chair until a middle-aged man offered her his, leaving him no option but to stand at the back of the room.

"Typical Celeste," Marius muttered.

She took the seat as if it had been hers all along, barely thanking the man.

"Now, then," the auctioneer said. "Lot 474. Starting at €500. Do I have €500?"

Anatole, the vampire, raised his bid card.

"Interesting," I murmured.

Gen frowned. "A vampire bidding on my father's painting isn't interesting. It's alarming."

"€500... €550... €600." The auctioneer acknowledged as Anatole and an old guy in a three-piece suit traded bids.

"€1000." The vampire jumped ahead, looking to close the deal quickly.

The other bidder shook his head and dropped out.

"I have €1000," the auctioneer said, looking around.

Judging by the previous sales, I didn't expect it to go much higher.

Neither did the vampire, who sat smugly.

Neither did the auctioneer, who picked up a pencil, ready to note the final price.

Then the light over the device displaying remote bids blinked, and Madame Robert read, "€2000 from online bidder 2641."

Eyebrows rose as the bidding continued in thousand-euro increments.

"€3000... €4000... €5000..."

"Who is that?" Mina asked.

"No way of knowing without hacking into the auctioneer's system," I murmured as the light blinked yet again.

"Can you?" Gen asked, a little wide-eyed.

I shook my head. "Not my skill set. But Gordon probably has someone." I pulled out my phone and dialed.

"Or Gordon is the anonymous bidder," Marius mused.

He wasn't, as I established in a call that took less than twenty seconds and ended with Gordon's curt, "I'll get my man on it right now."

Gen stared at my phone while Mina gave her a look that said, *I told you our godfather is a criminal with all kinds of nefarious contacts.*

Bene patted Gen's shoulder.

"€10,000," the wide-eyed auctioneer announced.

"€20,000." The vampire glowered.

A few guests gasped, while others broke out in shocked murmurs.

Celeste's expression went from smug to concerned. Clearly, this was not what she had planned. She glanced back at Anatole, who shot her an angry look.

"Huh. I guess Celeste had some kind of arrangement with the vampire?" Gen observed.

"Then why not sell the painting — or whatever is hidden in it — directly? Why risk an auction?" Mina asked, watching the screen intently.

"Because they want an official transaction that's on the record, but they're doing it at this small establishment to avoid attention," Henrik guessed. "Think of money laundering. It's a similar principle." At Mina's astounded look, he went on. "That's why they forged a bill of sale from you to Celeste. They want to be able to establish the painting's provenance."

"I understand having to trace the history of a Van Gogh to prove it's not a forgery," I said. "But why bother with an amateur painting?"

"I don't know, but whatever's hidden in the painting has to be worth a fortune," Marius said.

"Even more valuable if its origins can be traced," I surmised.

Mina frowned. "We need to identify bidder 2641."

The light blinked again, and Monsieur Robert reported his latest bid.

"€30,000," the vampire countered, giving Celeste the evil eye.

This was definitely not going as they had hoped.

"€35,000," Monsieur Robert read from the screen.

Gasps erupted when the vampire leapfrogged Anonymous's next bid, going straight to €50,000.

"I wonder what the record at Chez Robert is," Bene murmured.

Judging by the auctioneer's expression, they were close to breaking it.

Monsieur Robert dabbed sweat from his shiny forehead as the next bid appeared on his device. "€60,000."

"€75,000," the vampire growled.

Even the auctioneer stared.

My mind spun, spitting out different theories, but Mina and Henrik were ahead of me.

"Okay. So, Celeste brought the painting to this antique shop so Anatole could buy it with an official bill of sale," Mina said.

Henrik nodded. "And not just any antique shop, but an out-of-the-way one. That suggests they wanted it sold cheaply and discreetly."

Bene snorted as bidding hit €80,000. "Well, that's not happening."

He pointed as astonished customers reached for their phones.

Anatole pulled out his phone and typed frantically.

"Looks like he's close to the limit Alexandre Ernaux gave him," Henrik surmised.

Ernaux must have given the go-ahead, because Anatole raised his bid to €85,000.

"€85,000 is a lot of money, but Celeste could have easily stolen more from Gordon," Mina decided. "How is all this worth her trouble?"

"It's probably just a fraction of what she will receive from Alexandre in a separate, private transaction," Henrik said. "But only if things go to plan."

Marius chuckled bitterly. "Well, they aren't."

"For the record, Celeste, I'm not to blame this time," Mina huffed bitterly at the screen.

"She can't hear you," Gen pointed out.

"I wish she could," Mina growled.

The bids continued inching up, surpassing €90,000.

"€91,000," the astonished auctioneer read from his screen.

If a vampire's looks could kill, Celeste would have been facedown in a pool of blood.

"I wouldn't want to be Celeste now," Bene muttered. "Anatole's boss will be furious if this deal doesn't go through."

Gen shivered. "Maybe he'll send her after whoever buys the painting."

Henrik snorted. "More probably, he'll feed her to his coven."

Gen paled. "Would he?"

Henrik gave her an obnoxious look that said, *Sometimes, I marvel that you're still alive.*

He had a point, but I would take Gen's good heart and optimism over his dark, gloomy soul any day.

"€92,000," the auctioneer acknowledged Anatole's bid.

Anonymous countered immediately with €93,000.

"Someone really wants that painting," Bene muttered.

The auctioneer looked at Anatole. "Do I have €94,000?"

Everyone in the room stared, giving him more attention than any self-respecting vampire liked.

Gripping the armrests of his chair tightly, Anatole nodded.

"I have €94,000," Monsieur Robert acknowledged.

Anonymous came back with €95,000.

Anatole paced around the back of the room with his phone at his ear.

"Much as I love to see him sweat, something tells me this will only make things harder for us," Marius muttered.

I had the same sinking feeling. Gordon wanted us to identify who was interested in the painting, assuming there would only be one party. Now, we had a vampire *and* an anonymous bidder to hunt down.

"I say we go to Plan B," Bene said. "Grab the painting and run."

I grabbed my phone and texted Gordon. *Any word on the anonymous bidder?*

He called back, because why miss the opportunity to bark at me personally?

"No word on Anonymous yet. But whatever happens, do not let that painting out of your sight. Do you hear me?" he thundered.

"Benedict suggests Plan B, sir," I said.

Bene gave me a murderous look. I shrugged, waiting.

Gordon took a hell of a long time answering. So long, I had to speak up again.

"Sir, please advise. Do you want us to secure the asset or maintain surveillance?"

Secure the asset, Gen's eyes pleaded.

I felt for her, but I also knew the risks that came with that kind of action. Did she?

"Do I have €96,000?" the auctioneer asked Anatole.

He cupped a hand over his mouth, whispering urgently over the phone.

"Last call, sir," the auctioneer offered. "I have €95,000. Will you bid?"

I held my breath, waiting for Gordon to respond.

Anatole stared at the phone, then stuck it in his pocket and shook his head. *No.* He strode out of the shop, furious, with a very flustered Celeste on his heels.

"Sold to bidder 2641 for €95,000," the auctioneer announced.

I gripped my phone harder, impatient for Gordon's reply. "How would you like to proceed, sir?"

Grab Dad's painting, Gen's expression begged.

Gordon waited a split second longer, then grunted, "Maintain surveillance."

I hung up and stood, exchanging wary looks with Marius.

I don't like this, I muttered into his mind.

He scowled. *Typical Gordon shitshow. What's to like?*

Nothing. Especially knowing how Gen and Mina would react.

Chapter Eighteen

GENEVIÈVE

"Boy, does Anonymous move fast," Bene observed, watching the live stream on our screen.

The moment bids on the painting closed, two men entered the shop and flashed IDs at Monsieur Robert. He typed into the device to interface with Anonymous, then released the painting into their custody.

"That means *we* have to move fast." Roux pointed to Mina and Marius. "You two — follow the painting. Wherever it goes, you go."

They nodded and hurried outside.

"Henrik, follow Anatole," Roux barked, and off went the vampire without so much as an eye roll.

Roux turned to Bene next.

"Stand by inside the antique shop to see if anyone asks questions about Anonymous or shows any unusual interest in that transaction."

"Roger," Bene affirmed, taking off.

I stared, impressed. Starting any task at the château came with a certain amount of foot-dragging and cajoling, or at least a show of resistance. Now, the gang jumped into action like a well-oiled machine.

"What do I do?" I asked.

Roux pointed to the laptop. "Keep your eyes on the auction. I'll stand at the front window to see if anyone follows the painting. Watch for my signal. We might need to move fast."

With that, he strode to the front of the café.

I opened my mouth to ask what the signal was, but it was too late.

He peered out the front window, standing at an angle so as not to be seen. We might have been in a Parisian café, but it was easy to picture him peering around the corner of a bombed-out building in a war zone...or stalking prey in a tangled tropical forest.

For the first time, I realized how out of my depth I was.

The live stream showed two men sliding the painting into a crate, then heading for the door. The painting was the size of a small poster, so one man could carry the crate while the other stood guard. Bene entered the antique shop as they exited, which left him in the absurd position of holding the door open for them.

Destiny was definitely messing with us.

I gulped, trying to think fast. When it came to following vampires or hacking into computer systems, I was useless. But I could do *cunning* when I had to, and I knew that painting better than anyone.

An idea jumped into my mind. I grabbed the laptop, shoved it into my backpack, and hurried to exit the café.

"What the—" Roux started.

"Trust me," I murmured, rushing outside.

Gen! he barked into my mind.

I swear, I will not do anything rash, and I won't get involved, I told him. *I just have to be close enough to listen when they go by.*

Listen to what? he demanded.

Whoa. Where are you going? my sister chimed in, alarmed.

She and Marius waited a few doors away, ready to follow the deliverymen when they emerged.

Trust me, was all I had time to say.

Kind of a stretch, since I didn't trust myself. Still, I was on a roll, and it was too late to quit.

I could sense everyone holding their breath, certain another impulsive decision of mine would ruin everything.

And boy, did that sting.

I hurried onward, determined to prove them all wrong.

I jogged across the street to a shop one door down from Chez Robert. When the two men emerged with the painting, heading toward me, I stopped, pretending to study a vintage map in the shop window.

I closed my eyes, straining to hear past the sound of passing cars and pedestrians. At best, I had a few seconds to listen in as they passed, and I had to make that time count.

And — there! I caught the clack of a croquet mallet and the sound of my mother's laugh. Faint at first, then louder as the men brushed by behind me.

No, not that way, I heard Mina say from the time capsule of the painting. The sound was muffled by the crate but still clear enough. *You have to do the gates in order.*

Then, bingo! I caught the young boy asking his mother how much longer "this" would take.

Maman, maman, ça va encore durer longtemps?

This *what?* I wanted to yell.

The men nearly moved out of range, but I was desperate for more. I drew in my fingers, pulling shadows toward me. My view dimmed — that *looking out through the inside of a bottle* feeling that came with shadow-weaving — as I followed the men closely, listening in.

The risk paid off, because I heard something I'd missed before. The boy's mother telling him they were almost done.

On a presque fini, mon chéri.

Almost done with what?

The men continued into broad sunlight, forcing me to hang back and release the shadows that had concealed me. I burned to chase after the painting, but that was for Mina and Marius to do.

Do not mess this up. Do not mess this up, I ordered myself again and again.

So I didn't follow. I stared at a shop window while my mind spun.

Who was that boy? Who was his mother?

They weren't guests at that Easter depicted in the painting, I was sure. Their manner of speech was a little dated, and their voices emerged from a greater distance.

Or a different layer of the painting, I realized.

I turned and headed back to the café, where Roux waited, staring.

"What was that about?" he demanded.

I sank into a chair, trying to make sense of what I'd heard.

"You just disappeared. How did you do that?" Roux went on, keeping his voice down.

Shadow-weaving. I was amazed that it had actually worked, but my thoughts were elsewhere.

Whatever is hidden in the painting has to be worth a fortune, Marius had said.

Money had been one of our guesses, and *documents* had been another. But neither explained the voices of the boy and his mother.

I ran a finger along the café table, recalling the unusual thickness of the frame.

Gordon is a crook and a liar, and he's used you, Roux had once said.

I stared into the distance, moving the puzzle pieces this way and that.

Then it hit me, and I stared at Roux.

"There's a painting behind the painting."

He stared. "There's what?"

"There's a painting behind my father's painting. That's why the frame is so thick. That's what everyone is after — the hidden painting," I said.

He considered. "Makes sense. But what?"

"Something with a mother and a little boy."

He stared at me. "Did you see it?"

I shook my head.

"Then how do you know?"

∞∞∞

Trust me didn't work that time, so I did my best to explain. Roux listened, intently at first, then skeptically.

"You can hear paintings?"

He didn't believe me. Hell, *I* might not have believed me. It sounded that loopy.

But my family had its own unique take on loopy. As in magic.

"Yes, I can," I insisted. "It's the one small kind of magic I can actually perform."

He crooked an eyebrow. "You can do two kinds of magic, and neither is small — especially melting into the shadows like that."

"Tigers melt into shadows," I countered.

"Using our stripes, not magic."

"Don't change the subject," I chided, trying to do exactly that.

"Fine. Let's focus on what you heard." His voice grew softer. "It's not that I don't believe you, Geneviève. I just don't understand."

God, I loved it when he used my full name. But it sure made focusing difficult.

I glanced at the café walls for something to demonstrate with, but the artworks were all cheap reprints of Gauguin's masterpieces, making them soulless and quiet. But seeing the Tahitian beauties Gauguin had painted for his iconic *Arearea* did give me an idea.

I checked my watch. Seven p.m. A Thursday. I took out my phone.

"What are you doing?" Roux asked.

"Checking the opening hours of the Musée d'Orsay."

He frowned. "They're open late on Thursdays."

A quick search confirmed the museum would be open until nine forty-five.

"Boy, you really do know the place," I muttered.

He shrugged. "There's a discount if you come after six, and it's less crowded."

A man after my own heart.

"How is any of that relevant to this?" he asked.

I thought it over, then answered indirectly. "What will you do when we're done here?"

He sighed. "I have to report to Gordon. Personally."

I bit my lip, not daring to ask. But I had to — for my father's sake, and for Claudette's.

"I'll make you a deal," I said.

No, Roux's expression said outright.

I went ahead anyway.

"I'll go with you to report to Gordon. He'll probably be a little more bearable if I'm there."

Roux snorted. "A little? A lot." Then he frowned. "What's the other part of the deal?"

"We make a quick stop on the way."

He looked lost. "At the Musée d'Orsay?"

I nodded.

He shook his head. "Hardly the time for a detour."

"It's relevant. I promise."

He didn't look so sure, and frankly, neither was I, but I kept my game face on.

Ten minutes later, we were riding the Métro's number eleven line. I closed my eyes.

Roux nudged me. "Everything okay?"

I swallowed hard and weighed up whether to answer with the truth or a lie.

The truth, of course. Roux never shied away from it. Why should I?

"Just pretending for a little while."

"Pretending what?"

"That this is a hot date and not an investigation."

His eyes lit up. "Hot date, huh?"

I blushed. "Considering last night... Yes."

He grinned, then shook his head. "I guarantee you, I would do better than discount night at the museum for a hot date."

I smiled back. "You mean, *all day* at the museum? No discount?"

He wound his fingers through mine. "I'll keep my plans secret for now."

My heart skipped a beat. Did that mean he might make good on this fantasy someday?

I put my hand over his. "Watch out. I might just hold you to that."

He slid an arm over my shoulders, then closed his eyes. His turn to pretend?

I kept my mouth shut and my hand over his.

All too soon, we were in the Musée d'Orsay and back to reality.

Roux checked his watch. "Okay, what now?"

I pulled my scarf from my bag and led him to the elevator to the top level.

"My favorite floor, too," he said as we rode up. "But—"

I shushed him and tied the scarf over my eyes. "This isn't about what's here. It's about what I heard in my father's painting — and in the painting hidden behind it."

A good thing we had the elevator to ourselves. I must have sounded insane.

The elevator pinged, and I groped around for Roux's arm.

"Okay, go," I said. "Lead me to any painting, and I'll tell you what I hear." Then he would have to believe me, I figured.

"*Any* painting?" he asked dubiously, leading me out.

I nodded. "Any painting."

I couldn't see his expression, but his long pause gave me a good idea of what that must be. Then he led me forward, keeping me close at his side.

Walking blindfolded through a busy gallery was a strange feeling, but I'd never felt more secure. At least, when it came to moving around safely. I was, however, terrified of failing at the challenge I had assigned myself.

Roux took a few more steps, turned right, and stopped.

"Okay. That one. What do you hear?"

The sounds of the painting came through clear as a bell.

Ha. Easy. "I hear cows. Munching, stomping, mooing. Cows in a field, maybe?"

Roux went totally still, then leaned in. His body heat enveloped me as he checked the blindfold.

"No peeking," he grunted.

"I'm not. Those are cows, right?"

Without a word, he led me onward, then stopped again.

"Okay, now what do you hear?"

I strained to hear, but there wasn't much. "Something in the distance... maybe a wagon on a road?"

Roux didn't say anything, but I could tell I wasn't far off.

"I hear flies buzzing, like a quiet day in the country..." I went on.

He scoffed. "You're just guessing. That could be any of the landscapes in this gallery."

I stomped my foot. "I am not guessing. It's just a quiet scene. Oh!" I froze as a bell chimed. *Bong... Bong... Bong...*

"I hear bells. Like the church tower in Auberre at three-quarters of an hour."

He went silent, and I waited.

"Well?" I finally asked.

"Van Gogh. *The church at Auvers*," he murmured.

"See? I can hear paintings. Well, paintings made with skill and passion." I turned my head, listening, then pointed. "There are two girls talking in a painting over there. And over there..." I cocked my head. "A horse. A kid. Maybe a wagon?"

"Gypsy caravan," Roux murmured, dumbfounded. "By Van Gogh. And *Deux fillettes — Two Little Girls*." He checked my scarf again, then said, "You've been here before. That's how you know."

"Yes, I have been here before. But no, I didn't memorize every painting in every room. I probably couldn't if I tried."

He led me onward, faster. We passed through one room, then another, where he turned me around three times. Then he took me through another few rooms and repeated the process.

"Okay, now what?" he demanded.

I bit my lip, listening. "Horses, over there."

Silence, then a begrudging reply. "Degas. *Le Défilé*."

"Ah, the racehorses." I nodded. "No wonder they sound so nervous." I turned in a different direction, following my ears. "And over there... Water lapping. A lake, or a slow-moving river, maybe?"

Roux's stunned silence was as good as *Yes*.

I went on. "A church. Big, heavy bells." I cocked my head. "Oh. Big Ben?"

"Monet, *Houses of Parliament*," he confirmed in a stunned voice.

I turned and pointed again. "Silverware and china, like in a kitchen."

"Café," he murmured, clearly impressed.

I could think of two. "The one by Degas or the one by Van Gogh?"

A sharp intake of breath told me he was blown away.

Good, because this was important, dammit.

I continued a few steps, but Roux pulled me to a stop when someone cut in front of us. When they passed, he nudged me onward.

"What about that one?"

I frowned, listening. "I hear rubbing...or scraping... Something heavy being picked up, then put down." I waited. "Am I right?"

I couldn't see him nod, but he could well have, judging by the awe in his voice. "*Raboteurs de parquet*, by Gustave Caillebotte."

The floor scrapers. I could picture it.

"Believe me now?" I asked rather smugly.

"Yes. I'm impressed."

Rare praise, indeed. I nearly raised my arms in triumph.

"Bring me to your favorite piece," I said, flush with success.

He did, but oops. Whatever the painting depicted, it was really, really quiet.

I listened — intently — because this felt especially important.

Then I shook my head. "Crickets. All I hear is crickets. Water lapping in the background..."

Then I slumped. Maybe I wasn't as good at this as I'd hoped.

Roux gently pulled down my blindfold, murmuring, "Well done."

I blinked at a blurry nighttime scene with swirls of light. "Oh."

It was Van Gogh's *Starry Night Over the Rhône*, a scene as peaceful as they came. And a fitting choice for a tiger shifter who liked to prowl around in the dark.

"One of my favorites," he mumbled a little shyly.

I held his hand to my heart and whispered, "I promise not to tell anyone."

His eyes sparkled like Van Gogh's stars, and my soul warmed.

Seconds passed, then a minute, and I lost track of where we were and why. We might as well have been on the banks of the Rhône with Van Gogh that night more than a century ago.

Then someone bumped my shoulder, and the illusion broke.

Roux glared at the man, then cleared his throat. "Okay, I believe you. You can hear paintings. But how do you know the voices you heard aren't coming from your father's painting?"

"No one matching those voices was at that Easter with us. Also, they're fainter, like they're coming from deeper down."

Roux waited, as if I were holding something back, but that was all I had.

"So, what painting?"

I slumped, because that was the million-dollar question.

"I have no idea," I admitted.

He chewed that over, and I braced myself for a critical comment like, *Not very useful magic, is it?*

I hung my head. No. It wasn't.

Instead of pointing out the obvious, Roux wrapped me in a hug, and I just about melted into it.

"Well, it's a start. Now we know what everyone is after. A painting."

I could have stayed in his embrace forever, but an ugly thought struck me, and I slowly peeled away.

"So we know what Gordon was hiding — a painting." I shook my head. "But why? And why would he ask us to go after Dad's painting without mentioning that important detail?"

Roux gave me a long, hard look.

I winced. "Because he's as corrupt as Mina says he is?"

Roux nodded slowly, then checked his watch. "We should get going. But not a word of this to him. You understand?"

Feeling sick, I nodded. "I understand."

Roux motioned toward the exit, and I followed him on leaden feet. The events of the past days suddenly overwhelmed me, and I wished myself back into my old life, designing sets for the Children's Theater of New England.

But then I remembered the other parts of my old life — the bad relationships, the stupid mistakes — and decided I didn't want to go back after all.

So what *did* I want?

A crystal-clear image popped into my mind. I wanted a safe, tranquil, and happy life. I wanted to revive the château. And Roux. I wanted Roux.

I watched him out of the corner of my eye. Was that a hopeless fantasy, or a blueprint for the future?

"*Maman, Maman...*" a young boy called.

I whipped around, yanking Roux to a stop.

"We really need to get goin—" he started, then trailed off.

I barely heard. I was too busy staring. Not at a boy, because there wasn't a single child in the gallery, but at a painting. I stepped closer, then closed my eyes.

Maman, Maman...

Oui, mon chéri? his mother replied. *Yes, my dear?*

I opened my eyes again, stunned.

Roux looked at the painting, then at me, though he didn't speak, letting me think.

The painting showed a woman and a boy strolling through a field of poppies. They appeared twice, in fact — once in the distance, then closer to the artist's vantage point, indicating movement over time.

"The voices. They're exactly the same," I whispered. "That's them."

"Monet. *Coquelicots*," Roux whispered without looking at the plaque.

I nodded. "That's Monet's first wife, Camille, and his son Jean."

Roux cocked his head. "But this painting isn't hidden behind your father's."

"Camille and Jean appear in several different paintings," I pointed out.

The plaque beside the painting listed the name of the piece in French and English — *The Poppy Field near Argenteuil* — and the year, 1873.

Roux went very still. "Are you saying Gordon is hiding a Monet?"

"I don't know what to believe. But I know that's them. That's the woman and the boy I heard."

The rest was a riddle, but that part, I was sure of.

Roux studied me a moment longer, then looked at his watch and grimaced. "We can't keep Gordon waiting any longer."

A chill went down my spine. Maybe accompanying Roux to Gordon's wasn't the best idea. How could I face my godfather without bombarding him with questions?

Then I thought of Claudette — and my father, and his friendship with Gordon. This was a terrifying, tangled web, but I had to unravel it, for their sakes.

Twenty minutes later, Roux and I stood in the elevator to Gordon's apartment. Just before it pinged for the top floor, Roux squeezed my hand. He didn't utter a word, but his eyes said, *Not a word about the museum or the Monet.*

I nodded grimly. For once in my life, I had no problem doing as I was told.

Chapter Nineteen

GENEVIÈVE

Gordon poured himself a brandy and swirled it in a slow, calm movement. His eyes, on the other hand...

I looked away from the tempest in them, glancing at the empty spot on the wall, then the floor.

"Your orders were to maintain surveillance," he growled at Roux.

Not a man who accepted failure gracefully, my godfather.

I would have wilted under the pressure, but Roux's voice remained flat and steady.

"Yes, sir, but we weren't able to follow them into the canals."

Mina had reported that much in a brief text message, though we didn't have the full details yet.

"Then you should have secured the asset," Gordon barked.

Never mind that he'd said the opposite at the time.

"Yes, sir, but I judged the risk too great."

Gordon scoffed. "The risk to yourself or the painting?"

"To your goddaughters, sir," he replied, as level as ever. "The area was surrounded by Alexandre Ernaux's vampires."

I hated being the weak link, but Claudette's death had brought the reality of the situation home to me.

"My goddaughters shouldn't have been there in the first place," Gordon grunted at Roux, like I wasn't responsible for my own actions.

"I was there to confirm it really was Dad's painting," I explained.

Gordon muttered at his brandy.

"I was shocked by how much it sold for," I said. "Why would anyone pay €95,000 for a painting by my father?"

Gordon tensed. Just for a nanosecond, but I was paying close attention.

"To spite me, perhaps," he grumbled.

Did he seriously think I would buy that?

"Who despises you so much that they would spend €95,000 to spite you?" I asked, incredulous.

The air around my head compressed, and my ears rang. Whoa. Was Gordon hitting me with his magic?

That is of no interest to you, a deep voice boomed hypnotically in my mind. *That is of no interest to you.* The message echoed again and again. *No interest to you. . .*

I curled my hands into fists, shocked. Was Gordon trying to brainwash me of my suspicions?

I resisted the urge to chew him out. Better for Gordon to think I wasn't onto him.

But, yeesh. Did he think I was stupid?

"It's complicated," he said, keeping up that pounding pressure.

I forced my facial muscles to relax. "I suppose it must be."

And, whew. The pressure eased.

I wasn't sure whether to cheer or frown. Being taken for an idiot was not a nice feeling.

A good thing Roux interjected, shifting the focus from me.

"I have my team following the painting and the vampires. That could lead us to the anonymous buyer, but tracing them via the online bidding system will be just as important."

"I have my man on it now," Gordon grumbled.

That meant hacking. Amazing, how casually he mentioned a crime.

I jutted my jaw, wondering how many times that casual tone had fooled me in the past. Then there was the matter of *his man.* Was the guy even human? And did he specialize in online crime, or did he double as a hit man?

I bit my lip, thinking of Roux, Henrik, Bene, and Marius. Could Gordon use them as a hit team too?

You need to watch yourself around them, Mina had warned me from day one.

I'd had a hard time taking those warnings seriously, but now...

No one spoke for a time, and I forced myself to think. Gordon might have a hidden agenda, but so did I. Priority number one was bringing Claudette's murderer to justice. Priority number two was recovering my father's painting. Both, I was sure, were related.

At that very moment, my sister and Marius were out stalking a mysterious, millionaire art buyer. Bene and Henrik were following ruthless vampires. That put them all on the front lines of danger, while I sat in my godfather's luxurious apartment. Not exactly fair, but I could still contribute to our cause. Not through strength or stealth, but cunning.

I stood and considered the artworks hanging on the wall.

"As long as I can remember, Dad's painting hung there," I said quietly, pointing. Then I gestured to the other artworks. "I'm sure he would have been honored to know his piece hung in a collection as impressive as this."

"The honor is all mine," Gordon said solemnly.

He sounded like he meant it — truly — but I had given up on trusting my judgment. Instead, I focused on facts, such as the value of Gordon's collection. It didn't include anything as jaw-dropping as one of Monet's water lilies, of course, but many of Gordon's artworks were worth five or six figures, like that Picasso sketch of dancing fauns or one of several *Vue de la fenêtre* by Matisse.

"Did my dad help you find any of these?" I asked, channeling *sweet, clueless goddaughter* instead of *amateur sleuth.*

"Many, yes." He pointed. "The Miró, for example."

"*Constellations,*" I murmured. "That's always been one of my favorites here."

It was also one of only twenty-three in the world. How on earth had Dad found it?

I frowned. Gordon could be lying about that too.

"That one as well, and that one, and that one," Gordon went on in a sentimental tone.

"What about this?" I indicated another of my favorites, an original Alphonse Mucha Art Nouveau theater poster.

"Your father came across it while researching another painting and put me in touch with the previous owner." Gordon chuckled, but there was a sad note in it. "I always told him to invest in some pieces himself, but he said, 'My girls are the only investments I care about.'"

A lump formed in my throat. That fit my father to a T. He was an art historian, amateur painter, and World War II buff fascinated by lost masterpieces, but he'd always put us first.

I caught myself before I lost my sense of direction in the fog of nostalgia.

"What was the greatest masterpiece he ever found?" I asked, not daring to look at Gordon.

He hesitated. I was pushing my luck, but playing it safe would get me nowhere.

"Well, there was that Paul Klee he helped recover..." Gordon said.

I nodded. My mother still had the newspaper clippings about that one.

"And that Albrecht Dürer drawing of a lioness..."

My lips curled, and I nearly said, *Bene would like that.*

"Some consider your father's greatest discovery to be that Linz album," Gordon went on.

"I'm sure you're right," I said.

That album — a catalogue of looted art intended for a grand museum Hitler never built — was now part of the National Archives in Maryland. It had proven critical in tracking down stolen artworks and returning some to their rightful owners.

But even that wouldn't account for a vampire and an anonymous bidder duking it out in an auction just shy of six figures.

I went back to the Mucha theater poster. "I wish I could ask my father about his adventures in the art world. Like how exactly he came across that. Did he tell you?"

Gordon stood and loomed beside me, putting me on edge.

"I'm afraid I don't know more. Perhaps you should ask your mother."

"I'll do that," I said, sidestepping away. Then I gestured, indicating his entire collection. "Were these just investments for you, or did you buy them because you liked them?"

Gordon chuckled. "Most started as investments. I hated that Picasso in the beginning, but I've grown fond of it." He paused momentarily, traipsing down his own private memory lane. Was it littered with tombstones of those who'd stood in his way?

An ugly thought hit me out of nowhere. Could my father's be among them?

The notion shook me to the core, though I instantly dismissed it. Gordon might be guilty of some crimes, but he would never have done anything that heinous.

"Some, I liked from the outset." Gordon gestured with his brandy. "But I must admit, the principal idea was to have a nest egg for my retirement."

His eyes slid to the spot where my father's painting had hung and stayed there.

I swallowed hard, remembering how my father used to say, *Where there's smoke, there's fire.*

And Gordon's apartment reeked of both — enough for an entire wildfire.

∞∞∞∞

"Did I go too far?" I asked Roux on the way to Henrik's apartment.

He scratched his chin. "Close. But you backed off at the right time."

Ha. I'd backed off because I was so shocked at what Gordon had revealed.

"All those paintings together are worth one or two million, max," I said. "That's a lot of money in my book—"

"And mine," Roux added grimly.

"—but hardly enough for Gordon to call a nest egg."

"Whereas a Monet would let him gild his entire nest in gold and diamonds," Roux guessed.

"Exactly. *If* that is what's hidden behind my dad's painting."

We mulled it over all the way to Henrik's, then paused outside his door. My eyes wandered to the rooftop deck, and I sighed.

"Guess two places I'd rather be right now."

He grinned. "At home in Auberre?"

I nodded and jerked a thumb upward. "Or up there with you." I worked up the nerve to face him. "You think we might find time to get up there again soon?"

His eyes heated, and he blew out a long breath. "No place I would rather be."

I was just leaning in for a kiss when Mina and Marius entered the stairwell below.

I could have wailed. Roux looked ready to claw the nearest wall. He brushed a kiss over my knuckles, whispering, "Save that thought for later."

Shortly after, everyone squeezed into Henrik's living room. Bene, Marius, and I sat on the couch, while Mina sat on the floor, leaning against Marius's legs. Henrik took an armchair, and Roux paced the perimeter of the room.

I started things off with the most urgent question.

"What happened? How did you lose track of the painting?"

"We followed the deliverymen as far as the Seine, where they loaded it onto a speedboat," Mina said bitterly. "We found a place to shift and followed from overhead, but we lost them when they entered the network of covered canals."

My stomach churned at the thought of my father's painting being tossed around by strangers — not to mention the risk Mina and Marius had taken by shifting and flying in broad daylight.

"What about Anatole?" Roux asked Henrik.

The vampire leaned back in a plush armchair, sipping red wine.

"Anatole went directly to Alexandre Ernaux," he reported with distaste.

If I could have mustered the energy for humor, I might have found some in the idea of a vampire spying on a vampire who worked for yet another vampire.

"How did Gordon react when you told him Alexandre Ernaux is involved?" Henrik asked.

"That caught him by surprise, but he was more concerned about the mystery buyer."

"Well, I'm concerned too," Mina grumbled.

I knew how she felt. Was our father's painting lost forever?

"How did reporting to Gordon go?" Bene asked.

"Oh, you know," I sighed. "He was his usual sweet, understanding self."

Roux snorted but didn't expand. He didn't really have to. Everyone knew Gordon well enough to fill in the blanks.

"On the plus side," he said, "Gen made a major breakthrough."

My heart fluttered a little. I wasn't one for cheap praise, but boy, was it nice to get a little credit sometimes.

Everyone leaned forward, waiting.

"I know what's hidden behind Dad's painting," I said, then elaborated.

They looked skeptical at first, but the more I explained — about the voices of a mother and son, the matching voices coming from the Monet in the museum, and about Gordon's nest egg — the more seriously they considered my theory.

And no one looked more serious than Mina.

"Mom mentioned Dad trying to track down a missing Monet..." she murmured, typing search terms into her phone.

I scooched over to look with her.

"Well, it's not *Woman with a Parasol*," Roux said, leaning over my shoulder to peer at the results.

Wow. This tiger shifter really knew his Impressionists.

"No. That's in a museum in Washington, DC," Mina agreed.

Bene patted Roux on the shoulder. "Bonus points for knowledge, champ." He yawned and handed his glass to Henrik. "Refill, please."

"Then there's *The Cradle*," Mina said. "But that's not missing either, and Jean would have been too little to do anything but gurgle."

Roux opened a laptop and ran his own search. "There are these too. *In the Garden at Argenteuil.* But one is by Renoir, and another by Manet."

"Monet," Bene corrected him.

Mina shook her head. "No, Manet. He, Monet, and Renoir were all friends, and they all met to paint in Monet's garden."

Bene rolled his eyes. "Manet, Monet... How are you supposed to keep track?"

"Not that difficult," Roux grumbled.

"All of those are in museums," I pointed out. "So we can eliminate them too. We need a missing painting."

"Monet also painted Camille and Jean in the garden..." Mina murmured, still searching.

Bene perked up. "See? Monet. I was right!"

Marius patted his head. "Amazing, Sherlock."

Bene shot him a dark look and pulled out his own phone. "This can't be that difficult."

We ignored him, focusing on the painting Mina indicated.

She cocked her head at the photo. "That one's in a private collection. So it would only be a candidate if it was sold or stolen."

I shook my head. "Surely a stolen Monet would have made the news."

I'd been so sure about what I'd heard, but the longer we searched, the more I started to doubt myself.

For a while, everyone went quiet, even despairing.

"So, what did we discover today?" Mina finally asked, rebooting the conversation.

I gritted my teeth. "That Gordon is a lying, deceitful crook?"

Marius rolled his eyes. "She means something we didn't already know."

I made a face. "Well, we know Gordon hid a painting behind the painting, and that others know about it too — Alexandre whatshisname and the anonymous bidder."

"We also know the hidden painting depicts Monet's wife and son," Roux said.

I shot him a grateful look. The man had more faith in me than I did.

"How about this one?" Bene held out his phone.

I looked, then shook my head at the image of a woman knitting in a garden. "That's his second wife, and his son doesn't appear in it."

"Hopefully, Gordon's guy can hack into the system and identify the buyer," Marius said.

Bene stuck out his phone again, interrupting the conversation. "As if things aren't complicated enough, Monet painted Manet painting in his garden."

I sighed. It was good of him to try, but I couldn't see his search leading anywhere.

Then something in my mind clicked, and I grabbed his phone for a closer look.

"How does Monet painting Manet help?" Marius asked.

My heart pounded as I checked the listing. "Because while Monet painted Manet, Manet was painting Monet's wife and son. So, their voices would be part of the scene, even if they don't appear in the painting."

"What exactly did you hear?" Mina asked, growing excited.

"The boy said, *Maman, ça va encore durer longtemps?*" I recalled. *How long is this going to take?*

"That's what I would say if I had to sit for a portrait," Bene commiserated.

"Then his mother said, *On a presque fini, mon chéri,*" I finished. *We're nearly done, my dear.*

"That fits too," Mina agreed.

"Yes, and it matched Camille's voice in the poppy painting in the Musée d'Orsay. So I'm sure that's them."

"You're saying, we're looking for a painting made by Monet that shows Manet, in which Camille and Jean are off-screen?" Roux asked.

I nodded. "Yes. And this could be it."

"Not if it's hanging in a museum somewhere," Marius pointed out.

I read the listing aloud. "Claude Monet's *Manet painting in Monet's Garden* was owned by the German Jewish artist Max Liebermann and his wife Martha." I skimmed a little, then went on. "The painting has not been seen since it went missing from the Liebermann apartment, which was seized by Nazis in 1943."

The room went quiet as I read and reread the article.

"What's the source of that information?" Mina leaned in. "Is it reliable?"

I handed her the phone, waiting.

Her lips moved as she read the listing. Then her eyes went wide, and she slowly put down the phone.

"Is that it?" Bene asked eagerly.

Mina's throat bobbed. "I think we have our painting."

Chapter Twenty

ROUX

"I can't believe Gordon wouldn't mention this to us," Gen muttered.

"I can," Mina grumbled.

Marius and I exchanged knowing glances, and my inner tiger growled.

Poor Gen. I could relate to her sense of betrayal. But in my case, it was the military that had let me down. Well, not all of it, just commanders who didn't like subordinates asking difficult questions about ethics, boundaries, and limits.

Idiots, my tiger snarled.

But I was an idiot too, because I'd missed my chance to tell Gordon where he could stick that €25,000 bonus he'd offered. I didn't need a reward to protect Gen. I just needed for her to be safe.

"How much would that missing Monet be worth?" Bene asked.

Gen looked at her sister. "Millions?"

Mina nodded. "Hundreds of millions, if it's sold publicly."

Eyebrows shot up, and I, for one, tried to imagine how many zeroes that meant, and what number might appear in front of them.

"What about on the black market?" Marius asked.

"Maybe 'only' tens of millions, like *The Tower of Blue Horses.*" Mina shook her head bitterly.

Gen looked a touch jealous. I could relate, because if I had missed such a rare, once-in-ten-lifetimes opportunity to see a

183

lost painting like that Franz Marc, I would have regretted it forever.

On the other hand, not even a long-lost masterpiece was worth the danger and intrigue we'd survived in London.

"Tens of millions would make a suitable nest egg for someone like Gordon," Henrik observed.

I found myself speculating how much money Henrik had. A vampire his age had had centuries to amass a fortune. He'd probably lost a few fortunes along the way too, but he was smart enough to bounce back from his mistakes.

"So sad," Mina murmured, reading about the painting.

Everyone looked up, and she explained. "Max Liebermann, the German Jewish painter, bought that Monet. When he died, his art collection passed to his wife, Martha. Not long after, the Nazis confiscated her villa and most of her property. She committed suicide on the eve of her deportation to a concentration camp."

A somber hush fell over the room.

"The contents of her apartment in Berlin were seized, and the painting was never seen again," Mina finished, pursing her lips.

"Did Dad ever make a trip to Berlin?" Gen asked quietly.

"I'm not sure. But the painting could have been moving through the black market for years."

I stared off into the distance. So many tragedies tied to one artwork painted in a peaceful garden in another era. What would Monet think about all that?

"So... next steps?" Bene asked.

Claim our mate, my inner beast urged. *That way, we stay with her forever and protect her.*

I swallowed hard. I was all for protecting Gen. And the longer we spent together, the harder it was to deny the *mate* part. But right now...

Focus, dammit! I snapped at my inner tiger. *Her life could depend on it.*

The beast settled down, but it wouldn't stop snarling.

"Well, we need to work out where the painting is now," Mina said.

"And we need to figure out how all this connects to Claudette's murder," Gen added fiercely.

Clearly, we weren't as dissimilar as I'd once thought when it came to principles. But I hoped to hell Gen wouldn't pay a high price for sticking to them, as I had.

Marius stood, yawning. "I say we get a good night's sleep and take a fresh look at things in the morning. With any luck, Gordon will have a lead for us to follow."

I frowned. "I'm not sure a lead would be a good thing, considering how Gordon operates."

The man had a habit of sharing information in fractions, keeping the whole picture to himself.

Henrik stepped to the door. "I'll see what else I might uncover."

We watched him go, then listened for his footsteps, though none came, as usual.

"Creepy as hell," Bene muttered.

"Yes, but you have to admire his persistence," Gen said. "He seems as committed to finding out what happened to Claudette as the rest of us."

"Operative word: *seems*," Marius muttered.

"Oh, come on," she chided. "Can you not give him any credit? Maybe he actually cares."

Bene nodded morosely. "Claudette might have had her issues, but she had a way of making you care."

"I know what you're saying," Marius said more gently. "But vampires are a lot like Gordon. It's always safe to assume they have an ulterior motive."

"Such as?" Gen challenged.

Marius shrugged, heading to the bedroom. "Ask me in the morning."

∞∞∞∞

The night passed much as the previous one had — minus a rooftop foray with Gen, to our mutual frustration. Mina had pulled Gen into the kitchen for a private chat about their father, Gordon, and who knew what else, making a late night even later. Meanwhile, Bene shifted, stretched, and settled down to sleep in lion form, half blocking the hallway, making it hard to sneak out quietly.

Stupid lion, my beast grumbled.

That meant Gen and I had to satisfy ourselves with lying as close as possible, her on the couch, me on the floor beside her in tiger form.

"I can't decide whether I'm in heaven or hell," Gen whispered, gently scratching the sweet spot between my ears.

I leaned into her touch, chuffing in agreement. Just being this close made my heart swell. But wishing for more — much more — had a way of dampening that thrill.

Eventually, I fell asleep. And when I woke in the morning...

Gen leaned down to touch me and whisper, "I slept well, but I'll scream if I don't get to do more than scratch your head soon."

I chuffed, telling her I felt the same way.

For better or worse, Henrik didn't return in the morning. And, for better or worse, Gordon had no news for us.

"I hate to say it, but this feels like the calm before the storm," Bene observed over our breakfast of croissants and coffee.

Marius nodded. "We should enjoy it while we can, because that storm is guaranteed to hit soon."

He was right. The morning dragged by as we tried different lines of investigation, but everything sped into high gear in the afternoon, triggered by a call from Gordon.

"Note down this name and address," he barked into my phone.

No *hello*, no questions about the leads we'd been following. Not even his usual *Don't tell my goddaughters* warning.

Clearly, the warlock was desperate. A very dangerous situation, especially for us, his fall guys.

His hacker had identified Anonymous. Gordon made me repeat the name and address twice, then hollered at how long we were taking to get our asses over there.

"We'll be out the door in five minutes, sir," I said, fighting a losing battle to keep my boss calm.

"Another ten days, and we'll all be free of him," Bene sighed after I hung up.

I jutted my jaw. If we didn't get killed in the process, because the site was a mountainside in Switzerland, and the target was a rival warlock.

Mina and Gen exchanged hard looks. How would they ever untangle their lives from Gordon's?

"The next train to Basel leaves in forty minutes," Marius reported. "We can connect onward from there."

"No private jet this time?" Bene complained.

Gen's eyes jumped up.

Marius shook his head. "Organizing that will take longer than the high-speed train."

"Well, make sure you book first class," Bene said with a mischievous grin. "It's on Gordon's tab, right?"

Good old Bene, making the best of a crappy situation.

In no time, we had our things packed and were out the door. And again, I marveled at what a well-oiled machine we'd become. Mina was a huge asset, as was Gen, especially when it came to thinking outside the box.

A little magic doesn't hurt either, my tiger chuffed proudly.

"Still no Henrik?" Gen asked when we reached the train platform.

"Still no Henrik," Bene practically cheered.

We'd spent the morning trying to contact him, to no avail. At this point, all we could do was leave a message and board the train.

"Maybe he's following a new lead," I tried, though I was worried too.

"Maybe he's tanking up on fresh blood," Marius muttered.

"Or selling us out as we speak," Bene grumbled.

Gen huffed indignantly. "Maybe we should give him a little credit."

Marius rolled his eyes.

I know it's a stretch, but wouldn't it be nice if Gen were right? I tried.

Marius shot me a grim look. *Wouldn't it be nice if optimism doesn't kill her?*

I tensed. He was right. Gen was an asset, but she was too new to our world to recognize the dangers.

When the time comes to move, you'd better be sure to keep her far away from the action, Marius warned as we boarded the train.

His words echoed in my mind throughout the long trip.

"So, what's the plan, boss?" Bene asked. "Other than loading up on chocolate while we're there, I mean."

Gen gave him a thumbs-up. "Dark chocolate Toblerone."

He shook his head. "Classic Toblerone, and those little Cailler pralines."

"Even the plain old Lindt is good and not too expensive," Gen enthused.

Marius snorted. "Those two are a match made in heaven."

I barely bit back a snarl. No, they weren't.

Mina grinned and patted Marius's arm. "*We're* a match made in heaven."

Goofy-eyed looks ensued, and I sighed. So much for a well-oiled machine.

I crossed my arms tightly. "When you're finished messing around, I'd like to start the briefing."

"Yes, *boss.*" Bene rolled his eyes.

I counted to ten. He was the one who'd asked, dammit!

Then something touched my foot, and a warm, easy feeling washed away my frustration.

Sorry, boss, Gen whispered, meeting my eyes from over the table of the cluster of seats we'd taken.

I flashed a smile of thanks and started the briefing, keeping my voice down and my foot against hers.

"Gordon's hacker identified the buyer as Kurt Grepper," I reported. "A warlock currently believed to be at his mountain retreat in Switzerland."

"How do we know the painting is there?" Bene asked.

"We don't, so reconnaissance will be key to this mission," I admitted.

"If I'd just bought a new painting, I would want to enjoy it immediately," Gen offered.

"That only applies if a buyer cares about the painting," Mina said. "Not if he sees it as any other investment, like stocks or real estate."

"Or sees it as a way to thumb his nose at a competitor," Marius grumbled.

Gen gaped. "Who would think that way?"

"You have no idea how this world works," Mina said grimly.

"Do you mean Grepper thumbing his nose at Ernaux?" I asked.

He shrugged. "Or at Gordon."

Mina stared. "I shudder to think what that means."

"In any case, that's what we have to go on for now," I said.

"Pretty nice house," Bene observed, scrolling through the pictures Gordon forwarded.

"Very nice, and very difficult to approach unnoticed," I agreed.

Gen leaned in to look at the pictures with Mina, who sat beside her. "Not exactly a little chalet, is it?"

Grepper's mountainside hideaway was a massive, modern block of steel, cement, and giant glass panes. Bulletproof glass, I would wager.

I briefed the team on everything I had, then fielded questions and suggestions on how we might proceed. The landscape blurred past, and so did my mind after a while. Gen remained across from me throughout the three-hour trip, her foot touching mine, keeping the warmth and comfort coming.

I flashed her a weary smile, hoping those vibes went both ways.

"Still nothing from Henrik?" Gen asked when we changed trains in Basel.

"Just this." I shared the brief message he'd sent, saying he was going undercover in Alexandre Ernaux's coven and would be hard to reach.

"I'm telling you, he could be selling us out," Bene warned.

"Why would he do that?" Gen demanded.

"Because our contracts are about to expire. Henrik will be thinking about next steps — such as making connections that could prove useful. Say, with a powerful vampire like Ernaux. And what better way to connect than tipping off Ernaux to the location of a long-lost Monet?"

I tried to keep the faith, but Bene's theory had merit. Even Gen stared out the window pensively.

Gordon's files occupied us through the next leg of the journey. Eventually, we reached Zurich, rented two cars, and drove another hour south, through the sunset.

"So beautiful," Gen breathed, craning her neck at the mountains around us.

Also a bitch to climb, if that's what we'll be doing to reconnoiter Grepper's place, Marius murmured into my mind.

I nodded warily. Yes, the mountains would be a challenge, especially given the snow blanketing them.

It was dark and quiet when we checked into the Hotel du Lac in a town not far from Lucerne. We took their last available rooms — two doubles and two singles for the six of us, including Henrik, in hopes that he might arrive soon.

Gen plucked a key from Mina's hand. "I call a single room."

"I call the other one," Bene reached in.

I blocked his arm. "Not so fast. Two of us have to share."

He nodded. "You and Henrik."

I shook my head. "*You* and Henrik."

Mina stuck the remaining keys in my hand and walked off with Marius. "You figure it out. See you at dinner."

Gen raised a hand. "I have a suggestion."

Bene waggled his eyebrows. "You and me take the double?"

I shot out a hand, wrapped it around his throat, and squeezed.

Gen jumped back. Bene pulled at my hands. "Just kidding, man."

I squeezed harder. "I'm not."

Bene's eyes went wide, and he glanced between Gen and me.

"Is it so hard to settle things without a fight?" she scolded.

"I'd be all for that," Bene squeaked.

"I take one single," she started again. "You two share a double, and Henrik gets the other single. But since he's not here tonight..."

I released Bene with a little shove. "I get his single tonight."

Gen nodded. "For example."

"You expect me to share with this gorilla tomorrow?" Bene complained, touching his neck gingerly.

"Last I checked, he was a tiger." Gen sauntered away with her key. "See you at dinner."

Bene and I watched her go. "Yeesh," he said when she turned a corner. "She's even worse than her sister."

"I heard that!" Gen called.

Bene winced and raised his voice. "I mean, she's as nice as her sister."

I shoved a key into his hands and made for the stairs since the single room was on the next level. An arrangement that had serious advantages, as I came to realize over dinner, when Gen kept her foot resting comfortably against mine. And not just her foot, but her hand too. She laid it lightly on my thigh, out of sight of the others, under the table.

"Watch your cheese," Marius ordered as Bene dug into the fondue we'd ordered. "Keep stirring."

Bene rolled his eyes. "Rules for everything in this country."

"That's one of the few that makes sense," Marius grumbled.

"What about the rest?" Bene asked.

Marius snorted. "Guess why I prefer France."

Gen chuckled, and I closed my eyes, cementing the sound into my mind.

"More bread?" Mina offered... me? Gen?

I tuned out of the conversation and in to Gen. Her scent. Her voice. Her long, silky hair, glinting in the low lighting of the hotel restaurant.

"Oops." She whipped her hand off my leg to catch the bread falling off her fondue fork.

My hand slipped onto her thigh, all by itself. The color of her cheeks deepened slightly, and she glanced at me before stirring the cheese.

"Nice wine," Mina said, checking the label.

"Very nice," Gen murmured, putting her hand over mine.

She closed her lips over the rim of her glass and sipped. Her throat bobbed when she swallowed, and heat rushed through me.

"What's for dessert?" Bene asked, reaching for the menu.

Gen shot me a heated look, and I nearly choked.

She hid a grin with her napkin.

Stop teasing, I growled into her mind.

You love it, she chuckled. *Maybe even* need *it.*

She was right. It had been much too long since I'd allowed myself to loosen up. But this woman made me want things I'd never even dreamed of.

"*Schwarzwälder Kirschtorte. . .*" Bene read from the menu. "*Bündner Nusstorte. . . Zwetchgenschober. . .*" He put the menu down with a grimace. "German makes everything sound like it should come with a hard hat and a warning label. Not exactly appetizing."

"Black Forest cake. Nut cake. Plum pie," Marius grumbled. "Not so difficult."

Bene gave the menu a second glance, then lit up. "*Tiramisu!* I know what I want."

So do I, Gen murmured into my mind, pushing her leg outward a little.

I fought off the temptation to let my hand drop farther.

Not interested? she pouted.

Very interested. Just trying to be patient, I shot back.

Not my strong suit.

I chuckled. *I noticed.*

"Hm?" Mina asked.

I cleared my throat. "No dessert for me."

Not the kind on this menu anyway.

"Just coffee," I added. "Decaf," I added when the waiter came by. Lord knew I didn't need any additional stimulation.

Dessert and drinks took an eternity, but eventually, we finished our meal and headed to our rooms.

"I'll be at breakfast at six a.m. sharp," I ordered.

Marius snorted before disappearing into his room with Mina. "We'll be there at seven."

Bene chuckled. "Sorry, boss."

I shook my head. "This is my new strategy — calling a meeting an hour before I actually intend it."

Bene laughed. "You're smarter than you look."

I headed for the stairs. "*Bon soir,* Bene. *Bon soir,* Geneviève."

"*Bon soir,*" she fake-yawned, proving herself better at lying than her sister.

Upstairs in my room — well, Henrik's, but mine for the night — I brushed my teeth in record time, ran my hands through my hair, and straightened the bed.

Outside, the stairs creaked, and my pulse spiked. A soft knock sounded at the door. When I opened it, Gen slipped past me, sliding her hand along my torso.

I closed the door as quietly as I could. Then I turned, facing her in a small room charged with enough energy for a power plant.

When Gen opened her mouth, I stuck up a hand and closed the distance between us.

"Any more teasing and you'll kill me." My voice came out all husky.

She wrapped her arms around my neck and drew me closer. "I'll make you a deal." She brushed her lips over mine. "I won't tease if you don't hold back."

She waited, lips poised over mine, heart beating hard against my chest.

"Deal," I said, diving into a deep, smothering kiss.

Chapter Twenty-One

GENEVIÈVE

I pressed my body against Roux's, mumbling between kisses.

"Please believe me when I say I'm not usually this forward."

"All good, Geneviève," Roux replied just as breathlessly.

He slid his hands around my waist, then down my rear, while I traced the hard contours of his shoulders. In tiger form, his most prominent features were the stripes decorating his back. Now, the lines of his ribs were most obvious, along with the muscles slabbed around them.

"Speaking of which..." I pulled up his shirt.

"Speaking of what?" he asked, helping me work it over his head.

Muscles rippled along his torso, accentuating every move.

"Ribs," I said, splaying my fingers over those etched, parallel lines.

"You speak in riddles, woman." Then he flashed a mischievous smile. "Or did you mean these?" He slid his hands under my shirt, touching me the same way.

I hadn't, but I sure as hell wasn't going to interrupt his train of thought if it chugged in that direction.

And, oh. Every touch sent another flurry of sparks through my veins.

In no time, he had my bra and shirt off. Bending to kiss me, he could only reach to about the level of my shoulders without contorting, and that wouldn't do. Not with my nipples peaked and calling desperately for his touch.

He helped me execute a graceful descent to the bed — far more graceful than the flop I would have done on my own — and latched on where I needed him most.

I arched under his touch — and, oops, under my own touch too. The man had me so turned on, I was getting all mixed up.

I skimmed my hands over his back instead, enjoying the contrast of my fairer skin against his.

The glide of big, powerful hands over my body gave me a double thrill — the immediate pleasure *and* the thrill of picturing the other side of him. In tiger form, those hands would be platter-sized paws and armed with claws. The soft lips skimming my skin would be punctuated by dagger-like fangs. And while he was gentle, there was no mistaking the ferocity underneath.

"Oh!" My chest heaved as he moved from one nipple to the other.

His movements were ninety percent controlled, ten percent almost-but-not-quite rough. *Commanding* was more like it.

Well, two could play at that game.

With a firm tug, I guided him back up to my lips. That put the top button of his pants within reach — and reach, I did.

And wow. What a long way to reach. The man was already hard, ready, and... er, at impressive proportions, one might say.

Not that I said anything, other than grunting, "Pants. Off."

His eyes glinted. "I'll do mine if you do yours."

I shook my head. "No, I'll do yours, and you do mine."

An entire light show illuminated the jewels of his eyes.

"Yes, ma'am."

Seconds later, we had that mission accomplished. Which left only one last obstacle in my way.

"I know you love this watch, but..." I trailed off, trying to unclasp the damn thing.

It was huge, with dozens of unnecessary functions. Especially at a time like this.

He removed it using some super-secret method that escaped me. Not that I had the brain space for anything that trivial at the moment.

"Finally," I grumbled, giving Roux a playful shove.

He dropped to his back, and I straddled him, bending low.

"I like this angle," I chuckled.

His cheek twitched. "Enjoy it while it lasts."

A shudder of anticipation went through me. This man could bring me to orgasm with a few words. Or just one — my name.

"Geneviève..." he murmured once I'd worked my way down his body, trailing kisses, stripping away clothes, and rolling my lips over his shaft.

He threaded his fingers through my hair and helped me set a rhythm that suited us both, murmuring my name again and again.

If my mouth hadn't been — er, otherwise occupied, I would have mumbled in the same dreamy tone. Because this was more than exploring his body, as heavenly as that was. This was two souls connecting. Trusting. Sharing.

I brought him as close to exploding as I dared, then backed away.

He groaned. "I might die if you tease."

"I thought Bene was the dramatic one." I chuckled, crawling back over his body. "And I'm not teasing. I'm just desperate to feel you inside me."

"That can be arranged," he rumbled, taking the top in one smooth roll.

The man made everything feel so right. So inevitable.

Destiny, a little voice whispered to me.

He trailed his lips to my breasts, leaving one hand free to pleasure me below.

In no time, I was heaving sharp, achy breaths, blindly extending my hands over my head. It ought to have left me feeling scarily vulnerable, but I'd never felt more secure or in better hands.

Literally. I would have cackled in laughter if I hadn't been moaning in ecstasy.

Speech wasn't possible, but I did manage staccato words between breaths.

"Good. Thing. We're. Upstairs."

He chuckled. "Why do you think I let Bene take the double tonight? It's right next to your sister and Marius."

I snorted. "They would drown us out with their own noise."

Seconds later, I contradicted myself with louder and louder cries.

"Shh," Roux said.

"You try shushing with two fingers inside you," I mumbled, gyrating against his hand.

Two *very* talented fingers, in my defense.

He blushed but didn't stop — a perfect combination, as far as I was concerned.

Moments later, his expression went all serious, and he pulled away. I tried yanking him back, but he guided me into a roll, then tugged my hips, bringing me to all fours.

"Like this." His voice was low and gritty with need.

Oh yes. I practically yowled in anticipation.

He paused just long enough to roll on a condom, but even that took too long for me. I bumped his rear and lowered my head, then moaned when he finally slid in.

Calling it doggy style seemed woefully inadequate. Tiger-style was more like it.

"Okay?" he asked, practically trembling with need.

Gentleman was one word for it. *Soldier of honor* was even better.

"Hell yes," I whispered, bracing myself.

He pushed deeper, making my insides burn in the very best way. Then deeper still, advancing cautiously for my sake.

"Don't hold back," I insisted, butting back for more. And more and more...

A tiny bit more would have been too much, but this was perfect. I didn't want tame or plain. I wanted a high to beat all highs, and that was exactly where we went. Soaring, searing, dancing...

Roux made love the way he did everything else. Ferociously. Honestly. Intensely.

The burn spread through my body, bathing me in heat. I fisted the sheets and buried my face in a pillow before my howls woke everyone in the hotel. Fireworks went off in my mind — the kind with crescendo after crescendo, each outdoing the last.

With a rough gasp, Roux came. I shuddered, then cried out in my own high. Time slowed, and we teetered at the peak of ecstasy for a glorious eternity before tumbling down the other side.

We lay panting for a long time, limp, sweaty, and satisfied. My body felt like rubber, but Roux had enough coordination to dispose of the condom before snuggling up. Locking his arms around me, he held me close enough to lose track of which heartbeats were his and which were mine.

"Paris rooftops are all well and good, but there's a lot to be said for a bed," I mumbled.

He chuckled. "True."

There was also a lot to be said for being able to shadow-weave to reach his room unnoticed, as I was proud to note. Maybe I had some useful magic after all. Being extra motivated had helped too.

"On the other hand, we haven't really put this mattress to the test," I mused.

He rested his chin on my head, keeping me firmly trapped. "Soon."

I chuckled. "Not rushing. Just observing."

He snorted. "Observing, my ass."

I snaked my arm back, feeling around. "As you wish."

And man, oh man. I firmly established his to be an A-plus ass.

He laughed, and I almost wished for paint and canvas to capture the moment. Not the sight — blurred lines and dots would be fine — but the cozy feel, the flickering heat inside me, and the sound of that rare laugh.

I wove my fingers through his. "Were you surprised when I came knocking on your door?"

"Relieved. You could have been Henrik."

I broke out in laughter. "That would put a damper on things, for sure."

"Not sure he likes me that way," he joked.

An actual joke. I hid a smile.

Then I sighed. "I'm not sure he likes *anyone*."

Roux shrugged. "He likes you."

"Yeah, sure. That's why he's so cold, arrogant, and snooty to me."

"To most people, he's cold, arrogant, and downright rude. But okay — maybe, he *respects* you is a better way of putting it. But—"

I sighed, cutting him off. "I know, I know. I have to be careful around him. But I do have that necklace of his. You think he'll respect his promise if I ever need a favor?"

"I think so. I hope you never have to find out, though."

So did I.

"What do you know about the woman he mentioned?" I asked. "Katarina."

"Not much, other than she was his fiancée before he was turned."

"Turned voluntarily or against his will?"

"I'm not sure, but against his will would be my guess."

I ran my fingers over his arm, thinking. "So sad. For them both."

Roux nodded. "I think he truly loved her. Maybe he still does. Hard to tell with him."

Hard to tell with lots of people, I nearly said. Not because I doubted Roux, but because of all the times I'd been fooled or had fooled myself.

I wove my fingers through his. Was I fooling myself now?

Roux ran a hand over my hip, and I rolled in his arms.

"Enough about Henrik. Definitely kills the mood," I said.

A bit of a fib, because even that subject couldn't delay my second wind. I ran my hands over Roux's chest, then lower...lower...

Roux sucked in a breath as I touched him. "No risk of that, I think."

In no time, we were tangled together again. I lay back with my arms over my head, panting and bucking in time with Roux's moves. *Total surrender* wasn't usually my style, but hell. The guy was a tiger shifter, and it showed. Besides, I was too deep in ecstasyland to think about things like image or pride.

Some time later, we sank back into the sheets. Well, I sank into the sheets. Roux sank into me. I locked my arms around his back and kept him there.

Out in the hallway, a cuckoo clock sounded — ten p.m. Not all that late, but we were both wiped out. Roux snoozed off first, and I ran a finger gently over his shoulder, tracing where his tiger stripes would be.

I sucked in a long, contemplative breath. A short time ago, I would have laughed at the idea of myself with Roux. Now, I was painting images of forever in my head.

Be very, very careful, I ordered myself. *Don't get hurt again, and don't hurt him.*

The latter seemed laughable, but I had a feeling tough tigers weren't half as tough inside.

I swallowed hard, knowing full well I had a long history of judging men through rose-tinted glasses. I'd done that with Brandon, Nate, and all my other exes. I'd done the same with Gordon in a way too.

The moral of the story? I needed to look at people for who they were, not for what I wanted them to be.

I traced Roux's eyebrow, then his jaw, replaying every interaction of the past hour, day, and week. But no matter how I hard I looked, I saw the same, good man. No cracks in the facade. No facade at all — just genuine Roux.

I rested my hand over his heart and closed my eyes, hoping I had finally gotten it right.

Chapter Twenty-Two

ROUX

I woke early, nuzzling Gen. But for all the sunshine and butterflies in my soul, an ominous gloom crept into the corners of my mind.

Hell of a way to focus on a mission, I'd complained to Marius when he and Mina had kicked off our heist in Mallorca with a night of sex.

Now, I was the guilty one.

"Mm." Gen opened her eyes with a sleepy smile.

God, she was beautiful. And damn, did this feel so right.

She ran a hand along my ribs and her leg up mine.

"If you're thinking about work, stop," she ordered. "We have another hour before getting ready for breakfast, and I intend to use it well."

I turned for a look at the bedside clock, but she caught my chin and steered it back.

"I have a riddle for you. What starts with a P and ends with -ion?" she asked.

I waited.

"Procrastination. The most effective productivity tool known to man," she declared.

I chuckled. "Not sure that's the way it works."

"That's because you've been brainwashed. I'm here to show you the light. A healthy amount of procrastination is the best way to get things done, because it keeps you focused when the time to really get going arrives. But we're not there yet, so there's no need to rush."

I closed my eyes as her hand wandered along my hip and over to my ass.

"I want this more than anything, but—"

She cut me off. "I also want this more than anything, and as for butts..." She snaked a leg around my hip and tapped my behind. "This is the only kind that counts."

I had to laugh, though she cut it off with a kiss. And since her hands were wandering around, taking an inventory of every spot that drove me wild, I had little choice but to pay her back.

Minutes later, I had her knees hooked over my shoulders, my hips pumping hard, and no clue where my self-discipline had gone. It didn't seem to matter much either. Not as long as Gen fisted her hands in the sheets, barely biting back frenzied cries.

Focus here, my tiger urged me. *Focus on our mate. Our future. Our love.*

So I did focus, and focus hard.

"Roux..." she cried. Then she moaned and shuddered in ecstasy.

I came a split second later, wincing at the burn of pleasure-pain. Then I dropped down over her, panting hard.

Gen locked her arms around my back, keeping me in that small, sensual world. The animal instinct to claim was all-powerful, but even my tiger knew this wasn't the time, so I nuzzled her instead. Stiff tiger whiskers emerged along my jaw, and she giggled.

"Oh. Ah. Ouch."

God, I loved that sound.

"Now if I could just rub those soft tiger ears too..." She sighed, making my inner tiger claw for control.

"I swear, you'll kill me one day," I groaned.

She shook her head. "No. One day, I swear I'll give those tiger ears the massage they deserve. But now..." She reluctantly relaxed her grip to peer at the clock. "Now, even I have to admit this is not the time." She let a beat go by, then flashed a huge grin. "Not if we're going to leave time to shower. And I don't mean the military kind."

∞∞∞

Half an hour later, Gen gathered her clothes, kissed me one last time, and slipped out. I took a second shower — a cold one, with plenty of hard scrubbing to erase the scent of sex. Then I dressed and headed down to breakfast. As usual, I was the first one there, but not by my standard ten-minute margin. Mina and Marius strolled in just as I grabbed the local newspaper and folded it open to page eleven.

Marius gave it one look and rolled his eyes. "One of these days, man, you're going to learn to sleep in."

He had no idea how close I was to the dark side, but I took advantage of my bluff.

"Maybe, but not today," I said, telling myself morning sex didn't count.

Heavenly morning sex, my tiger hummed.

I cleared my throat to cover the sound.

Gen arrived next, making a show of yawning into her hand.

"Morning, everyone." She loaded her plate at the buffet, then sat opposite me with her foot against mine.

Bene appeared ten minutes late, as usual, yawning and scratching his chest.

"Still no sign of Henrik?" he asked.

"No," Mina said.

Bene grinned. "Good."

I froze. *Not* good, because he'd totally slipped my mind.

Slowly, I drew my foot away from Gen's. For both our sakes, I needed to get myself together, and fast.

"No messages from Henrik either," I grumbled, checking my phone. "But, yay. Gordon wrote."

Everyone groaned.

"Apparently, he has evidence to believe Grepper had the painting delivered here," I continued.

"Let's hope he's right," Marius muttered.

"Oh. Clement sent me a message too," Mina said.

"Mr. Fucking Persistent," Marius muttered.

Mina elbowed him. "He wants us to be safe."

Bene hooted. "Clement wants *you* to be safe." He pointed to Mina and Gen. "The rest of us can rot in hell as far as he's concerned — another thing he has in common with Gordon."

Mina opened her mouth to protest, then sighed and changed tacks. "Clem called to report new information on the case. Residents on Claudette's street saw a dark Renault come and go a few days before..." Her face fell as she searched for words. "...before the night she died. The camera at the Pelletier farm gate caught the same vehicle, and Clem was able to trace it to Paris."

"Let me guess," I grunted. "To Alexandre Ernaux or a known associate of his."

Mina nodded. "We're getting closer to establishing a clear link between Claudette's death and this art case."

Marius grimaced. "Now, we just need to haul Celeste in."

Bene pointed out the window, indicating the mountainside where Kurt Grepper's villa stood. "Follow the money, and you'll find Celeste. Or should I say, follow the painting?"

We split up shortly after breakfast and spent the day reconnoitering. Mina and Marius drove to the far side of the mountain, shifted, and spied on Grepper's property from the sky. Bene faked a hurt knee to appear like a skier left behind for the day and poked around town for information and vantage points from which to observe the villa. Gen and I drove up the steep mountain road and set off on foot, following a trail, then detouring through the woods to creep closer to the building.

Gen tramped through the snow in high boots. I ditched my footwear a short time later, along with my clothes, and shifted. My paws were as good as snowshoes, and my fur kept me warm.

"Wow," she breathed as I crept ahead.

I swished my tail, delighted she didn't mind having a tiger around.

The closer we came to Grepper's property, the stealthier we became.

Any chance of you hearing the painting from out here? I asked.

"I doubt it." Still, she cocked her head and listened for a good minute.

I listened too, catching the whisper of the wind, the faint puffs of her breath, and the glimmer of sun in the icicles in the trees. In better circumstances, it would have been magical.

Then I frowned. The less magic we encountered at a warlock's mountain retreat, the better.

Gen shook her head. "I can't hear the painting. It's too far, and those walls are too thick."

We trekked around a while longer, then returned to the trailhead, where Gen waited for me to shift and get dressed. The moment I did, she pegged me with a snowball.

"Hey!" I protested, shaking off the snow.

She grinned. "Couldn't resist."

I chased her down, and she squeaked when I caught her.

"This is what I can't resist," I murmured, kissing her.

That hour we spent together up on the mountain was the highlight of my day. A highlight of my life, actually, which seemed dull and dreary now that I looked back to everything before the past few weeks.

But I grew grimmer with every passing hour.

"Dammit, where is Henrik?" I cursed when Gen and I met Mina and Marius at the hotel.

"He'd better not be double-crossing us," Marius muttered.

Gen rolled her eyes. "Can we focus on enemies instead of friends?"

"According to Gordon's informants, Kurt Grepper is scheduled to attend the meeting of the board of directors of some big-shot corporation on the outskirts of Zurich tonight," I said.

"How well-informed are those informants?" Marius asked.

An excellent question. Too bad I had no answer.

"Grepper doesn't keep any staff at the house, so we could make our move as soon as he departs," I finished. "We'll have to act fast, though, because Alexandre Ernaux is bound to send his coven here as soon as he discovers that Grepper was Anonymous."

I want my goddaughters halfway back to France before you begin, is that clear? Gordon had bellowed before letting me go.

Understood, I'd replied as evenly as I could.

Mina, I knew, would do whatever she wanted. And Gen… I grimaced. I would have to break the news to her soon.

Not long after, Bene phoned from his lookout post in a café along the main road.

"Grepper's Porsche just passed me, headed out of town."

"Are you sure he's in it?" I asked.

"Big guy, gray hair. The plates match," Bene replied.

"Be ready to move in fifteen minutes," I said, then hung up.

We all turned to the windows to watch the road, then swiveled as a classic gray Porsche with Zurich plates raced past.

Marius whistled. "Nice ride."

I nodded. "1950s Porsche 356."

Mina rolled her eyes. Gen chuckled.

"Crime definitely pays," Marius decided.

Mina shook her head. "No, it doesn't."

"I like the Jaguar better," Gen declared.

"Maybe, but the Porsche runs," Marius pointed out.

"So will the Jaguar," Gen said smugly. "Roux's been working on it."

Her faith warmed me even if Marius's skeptical look didn't.

"I'll believe it when I see it."

Mina rapped her knuckles on the table. "Can we focus, please?"

I grimaced. *With great difficulty* was the honest answer, but I did my best.

"We head out in fifteen minutes," I said. "Everyone clear on their jobs?"

Mina nodded. "I fly in and circle north of the villa, waiting for your all clear."

"Same here," Marius said, "but a little farther east."

I nodded briskly. "Bene and I will start at the trailhead and approach the villa on the ground. As soon as we give you the all clear, you move in."

"You mean, you, Bene, and I will approach on the ground," Gen corrected.

My stomach sank, because this was the hard part.

Mina shook her head. "You're staying here."

Gen's jaw dropped, but Mina raised a hand in a *stop* sign.

"We need you to stay here and watch the road for that Porsche."

"You mean, stay here and keep out of the way," Gen said bitterly.

Mina meant *stay here and keep safe.* I knew, because she'd talked to me beforehand.

"No, I don't," Mina insisted. "Keeping an eye out for Grepper *is* important, and we don't know what we're headed into."

Gen crossed her arms. "Good for you for being a mighty dragon shifter with the ability to fly and breathe fire. But I can contribute too."

Mina gave her a long, hard look. "How?"

Ouch. Even Marius winced and nudged Mina.

She pursed her lips, then hit a gentler note. "Look, Gen. There are a million things you're better at than I am. But infiltrating a warlock's mountain hideaway is not one of them."

Gen aimed her stony expression at the floor.

"Also," Mina continued, "any mission involving Gordon — and these guys, much as I love them — has a way of going wrong."

Hey, I nearly protested, taking that personally.

Bene did too, but the other way.

I knew she loved me. He grinned smugly.

"I couldn't live with myself if anything happened to you," Mina swore to Gen.

Gen looked up. "How can I live with myself if something happens to you while I'm hanging around a hotel?"

Marius tapped his watch. "We need to go. Now."

Mina hugged Gen, who kept her hands at her sides, then headed to the car with Marius. I stood, feeling helpless as Gen's eyes pleaded with me.

"No space for baggage on this trip, huh?" she finally said.

"No one's saying you're baggage."

"No one is standing up for me either."

Her betrayed expression cut me to the bone.

"I believe in you, Gen. I really do. But Mina is right. We're trained for this kind of thing. You're not. Besides, do you really want to add *breaking and entering* to your résumé?"

"I want to contribute," she persisted.

"You already have. You're the one who figured out there's a hidden painting."

"I don't care about the Monet. I want my father's painting."

I want to make him proud, I read between the lines.

I swallowed hard, knowing that sentiment all too well. The difference was, my father was a selfish ass who'd never shown any interest in his kids. Still, I'd tried to make him proud, because maybe then he would love me.

But Gen's family was tight-knit, with loving parents who adored their kids. She had to know how proud her father would be.

"What would your father say?" I tried. "Would he want you to go with us?"

Gen's lower lip wobbled, and she whispered, "No."

Come on, already, Marius rumbled in my mind.

I sucked in a long breath, then hugged her. Never mind Mina and Marius looking on from outside. I needed that, and Gen did too.

But no matter how tightly I held her, how gently I kissed her, it wasn't enough.

She put her hands on my ribs and pushed me away.

"Go, already."

She turned and slid back into her seat at the table, turning her back to me.

There was so much I could have — *should* have — said. But the clock was ticking, and Mina was right. The risk was too great.

Never mind that leaving Gen behind might alienate her forever.

I swallowed hard. "I believe in you, Gen. I really do. But Mina is right."

Even to me, the words sounded lame.

∞∞∞∞

I drove, dropping Marius and Mina at their starting point just outside of town, before continuing up to the trailhead, where I parked. The mountains around us took on a blueish hue, while the forest grew dark as night.

"Beautiful sunset," Bene murmured as we bundled our clothes into the car, then shifted.

But if my gonads freeze, it's on you, man, he added, shivering beside me in lion form.

Survival of the fittest, I retorted, giving my thick tiger coat a smug shake.

When I headed off, Bene followed one step behind, complaining the whole way.

Now my whiskers are frozen, he grumbled, walking stiffly to shake snow off his legs after every step. *Probably permanently damaged.*

Whiskers were number three on the list of things male lions took pride in, after manes and gonads.

Truly tragic, I chuffed.

We made our way through the forest, slowly approaching Grepper's villa.

I have a bad feeling about this, my tiger muttered.

Not exactly a news flash. The moment I'd left Gen, everything felt off.

I swear, if an icicle falls off one of these trees and impales me, Bene muttered, *you're going to be the one to break the news to my mother.*

I snorted. *Can I be your pallbearer too?*

Bene growled. *Don't jinx me.*

I flicked my tail, making snow cascade from the nearest tree. The flakes glittered with the colors of sunset before showering onto Bene.

Oops. Sorry.

You're not sorry, he said bitterly — even more bitterly than Gen, who would probably never talk to me again.

My tiger mourned.

I pictured presenting her with her father's painting. Would that make up for it?

No. Not even that, I knew.

We slowed, glimpsing the villa through the trees ahead. It was one of those modern, cement-and-glass monstrosities that were nicer to look out from than to look at.

I stopped, glancing around. Bene plowed ahead, still grumbling to himself like Eeyore to Winnie-the-Pooh.

I can't feel my feet. I can't feel my tail. I can't feel my ears.

Well, I could. The air was tingling. Didn't he feel it?

Apparently not, because he droned on and on. I tuned him out to think.

Something feels wrong, my tiger persisted.

Yes, but what?

I racked my brain, going over every detail of the information we'd gathered.

According to Gordon, Grepper would be out for the evening. He would have set some defenses around his property before leaving, but as Gordon had said...

He's not a very powerful warlock.

Gordon had also assured us we had a day's head start over the vampires. And yet, my gut screamed that this was a trap.

I stopped and chuffed at Bene.

Wait. Stop.

Gen and I had ventured farther than this earlier without encountering any defenses. But the air hadn't been tingling then, and it was now.

Tingling with magic.

Bene, stop! I snarled.

He kept grumbling and plowing through the snow. *Stop. Go. Make up your m—*

Bene! I snarled, but it was too late.

A wall of fire erupted before him, and sparks filled the air. He reared up with an earsplitting roar, then fell back, writhing in agony. I rushed to him, then jumped away before contacting the electrified sparks engulfing him. With a final, agonized cry, he collapsed into the snow, totally limp.

Chapter Twenty-Three

GENEVIÈVE

I stared out the window, sipping my hot chocolate. My feet were warm, my surroundings safe, my soul empty.

I can contribute too, my own words echoed in my mind.

So did Mina's sharp rebuff, and the awkward silence that followed.

How?

A question answered by the cold, hard truth. I couldn't contribute.

Even Mina's well-intended comments offered no solace. *There are a million things you're better at than I am...*

Sure, like decorating theater sets. Getting back on my feet after nasty breakups. Hearing background noises in paintings.

Not exactly a résumé to gloat over. *Mope* was more like it, and over the next half hour, that was what I did.

Then a Mercedes screeched into the hotel parking lot, and Henrik ran in.

I jumped to my feet, waving him over to my corner of the lounge.

"Henrik, what's—"

"Where are the others?" he cut in.

I scowled. Right, the others. The *competent* ones.

I slid back into my seat, even more deflated than before.

"Grepper left, so they headed to the villa," I said, keeping my voice low.

"They what?" Henrik barked.

The receptionist at the hotel desk looked over, then away.

"They're going in for the painting," I whispered. "Wait. What's wrong?"

He snorted. "Where do I begin?"

He went on immediately, flooding me with everything he'd discovered about Alexandre Ernaux's coven.

"We have a day's head start on them," I said, dismissing his warning.

"Says who?"

"Gordon."

Henrik stared at me with pinpoints of red in his eyes. The air around me grew heavy, and a faraway ringing sounded in my ears.

The bastard was trying to enthrall me, wasn't he?

I smacked the table. "Cut that out!"

"The coven is on its way now," he insisted. "You don't believe me?"

I crossed my arms. "I believe people who convince me, not jerks who try to enthrall me."

"I was merely trying to speed things along."

I snorted. "Well, that's the thing about trust, Henrik. It takes time and consistency. Now, if you'll excuse me, I have to watch the road."

I said it all haughtily, as if I'd actually chosen that job.

He ran his hands through his raven-black hair, then thumped them on the table.

"There is no time. The coven is coming. We must warn Roux and the others."

"Fine. Warn him." I mimicked phoning.

"I tried. No connection."

I pulled out my phone and dialed. A recording sounded, confirming what Henrik had said. No connection.

"We have no time," he urged.

I looked out the window. The clear skies had clouded over, and snow was starting to fall.

"Gordon said..." I started.

Henrik shook his head, muttering, "Hope springs eternal."

"Are you saying Gordon is wrong?"

He snorted. "I'm saying the coven is on its way now, and they'll stop at nothing to get that Monet."

My stomach sank. "Only an hour ago, Gordon confirmed we have time."

Henrik huffed. "Let me guess. Gordon also confirmed that you would remain a safe distance from the action."

I grimaced. Did he have to rub it in?

Then I froze. "Are you saying Gordon wants the team to get trapped between a warlock and vampires? That makes no sense. Gordon is desperate for the painting."

Henrik nodded. "So desperate, he's prepared to risk their lives for it. *Their* lives," he emphasized. "Not yours." He gestured impatiently. "Use the brain I know you have, Geneviève."

I grimaced but kept my mouth shut as he went on.

"Gordon wants an extremely valuable artwork, but he's distanced himself from every step of this investigation. He's keeping his distance now. Why would a powerful warlock do that?"

I thought it over. "Because the painting is in the hands of an even more powerful warlock?"

Finally, something like respect shone in Henrik's eyes.

"Exactly. The same applies to Alexandre Ernaux's coven. Gordon won't risk crossing them openly, but he can risk *us*. If we secure the painting, good. If we fail, he still has one consolation — no cleanup required for a group of men who know too much about how he operates."

My stomach churned. "But the Monet..."

"Gordon knows this team has overcome impossible odds before. But this is a last-ditch effort, and he knows it." He touched my arm and leaned in, making me shiver. "I don't care about the painting, and I don't care about Gordon. But I hate the idea of him walking away from this unscathed while the rest of us risk our lives."

My mouth fell open. That wasn't exactly a declaration of undying loyalty to the team, but it sure came close. Maybe Henrik cared more than he let on.

My heart warmed. Boy, had Bene and the others underestimated him — the way they underestimated me.

I jumped to my feet and grabbed my jacket. "Let's go, then."

Henrik smirked. "You don't prefer to stay here, where it's safe?"

Part of me did, yes. And part of me screamed not to get into a car with an unreliable vampire.

Still, it was no contest.

"Don't be such an asshole, Henrik," I barked on the way to the door.

He grinned, proving my point, then raced by to hold the door open for me. Old habits died hard for a man raised in a bygone era.

"Also, I'm driving." I held out my hand for the keys.

He snorted. "Don't push it, Geneviève."

I snapped my fingers, waiting. "On the contrary, Henrik. I'm the one tired of being pushed. So give me the goddamn keys before I take them."

He studied me a moment longer then dropped them into my hand. Seconds later, we were roaring up the narrow, twisting road.

∞∞∞∞

By the time we parked at the trailhead beside Roux's rental car, the light flurry of snow had become a near blizzard. Shivering, I zipped my jacket and flipped up the hood. Then I set off against the biting wind, following the faint trail of pawprints Roux and Bene had left. Snow was rapidly filling them, but I could just make out the telltale depressions. Henrik followed, and we plowed steadily onward.

Ten long minutes later, Henrik grabbed my shoulder and put a finger to his lips.

I froze, listening. Someone — or something — was groaning.

My heart jumped to my throat, and I raced ahead, to where the woods ended and the property's snow-covered lawn started.

A surprised chuff sounded, but I ignored it and fell to my knees beside a pair of felines.

"Bene! Are you all right?"

He lay crumpled in the snow, tawny sides heaving.

Just need a minute to catch my breath, he panted into my mind.

Roux stuck his muzzle over my shoulder and huffed. *He'll need more than that.*

His breath hung in the cold air, but the warmth of his body enveloped me, and I couldn't help running my hand over his muzzle. Tigers didn't have manes, but their fur thickened at the corners of their cheeks, making them just as ferocious.

What are you doing here? he asked, glad yet exasperated.

"The coven is on its way right now," Henrik said. "We have to abort."

No kidding. Bene rolled slowly to sphinx position, then collapsed back to the ground.

How much time do we have? Roux persisted.

Henrik grimaced. "Twenty minutes, if we're lucky."

I looked at the house. Light streamed from the windows on the opposite side of the building, leaving the lawn on this side dim. The snow muffled any sound that might have escaped those thick concrete walls, so the only noise was the eerie wail of the wind.

"What happened?" I whispered.

Not sure. It was like a burst of electricity, Roux said. *Or a burst of magic, I suppose.*

I held out my hand, testing the air. Frowning, I moved a few steps right, running my hand along an invisible wall of energy.

"This is spelled. All of it," I whispered to the others.

I thought you checked this area before, Bene grumbled.

"We did, but it wasn't active then." I moved my hand around, getting a feel for it. "This isn't a standing spell. It's being cast by someone right now."

Roux cursed. *You're saying Grepper is home?*

I nodded, peering down at the house. "He knows we're here."

Which means we're out of here, Roux said, nudging Bene.

Snow stuck to their fur and whiskers, and their breath, like mine, swirled in the cold air.

But we saw him leave, Bene insisted.

"We did, and I kept a strict watch on the road. He must have circled back some other way," I said.

We have to pull back. Now, Roux ordered. *Mina and Marius won't be able to provide aerial support in this snow.*

Henrik gestured angrily. "Pull back where? The coven is nearly upon us."

Roux looked from the house to the road. I did too, weighing our chances against a powerful warlock versus our chances against a gang of bloodthirsty vampires, whom we were sure to encounter on the road.

"Or we retreat that way." Henrik pointed up the mountain, away from the house and the road.

A low snarl built in Roux's throat. *You mean taking the coward's way out?*

Henrik cocked his head in my direction, hinting something like, *We have no other option with her around.*

A switch flipped inside me, unleashing a wave of fury.

Weak link? Coward? Cheap excuse to give up without a fight?

I shook my head furiously. Not me, dammit. Not me.

Exactly two seconds later, I started barking orders.

"Henrik, get Bene back to the car. Find Mina and Marius and stand by. If we're not back when the vampires arrive, drive up the mountain. And you—" I turned to Roux. "Come with me."

I set off without waiting for an answer.

"Geneviève, this is impossible," Henrik hissed.

Roux bumped my hand, telling me the same thing.

"I specialize in the impossible," I muttered stubbornly.

"You'll get hit by the same spell that got Bene," Henrik warned.

I shook my head. We wouldn't, because I could sense the lines of magic that ringed the property, as well as unprotected areas, like the path to the front door.

Gen, Roux warned as we approached the house. *We're no match for him.*

No, we weren't. Not if we tried fighting magic with magic or brute force with force. We needed an entirely different approach. The direct one.

"I have an idea," I assured him.

Better be a good one, he grunted. *What are you planning?*

"Sometimes, the best things in life are unplanned," I tried.

Gen...

"What happened to 'I believe in you'?" I demanded.

He halted in his tracks, then dipped his head.

Lead the way.

He looked skeptical as hell, but he didn't try to stop me. He just prowled along fiercely beside me, backing me up.

My heart swelled, and if I'd had a spare moment to drop to my knees and hug him, I would have.

Instead, I hurried to the front steps, stomped the snow off my boots, and rang the doorbell.

Ding-dong. Those cement walls had to be a foot thick, but my keen ears heard the sound echo inside.

Every hair on Roux's long, striped back stood. *Are you crazy?*

The good kind of crazy, I prayed.

I rang again, stepped back, and did my best to gather my wits about me.

Watch it. This man is a powerful warlock, Roux warned.

So is Gordon, I said, nervously watching the door.

I have the feeling Grepper could kick Gordon's ass, Roux muttered.

The door opened, and a beautiful young woman looked at me. Her judgmental gaze skidded over my body, taking in my hair, my clothes, my boots.

Yeah, well. She should try creeping up to a mountain hideaway sometime.

An older man appeared behind her — an aged, groomed Keanu Reeves, I couldn't help thinking — and I forced a smile.

"Mr. Grepper?"

He nodded. "To whom do I owe the pleasure?"

"Geneviève Durand."

In for a penny, in for a pound, I'd figured.

His graying, collar-length hair swayed when he tilted his head, as if my name struck a chord. When his dark eyes strayed to Roux, they showed no alarm whatsoever.

And why should he be alarmed? I could feel magic pulsing all around him — much, much more than I'd ever observed with Gordon. Maybe that was how he'd slipped back to his house without us spotting him.

He looked away from Roux and spent a long time studying me. In a weird, twisted way, I found that refreshing. Finally, someone took me seriously.

"Let me guess," he finally said. "You're here to rob me of my painting."

My nerves wobbled, but I upped the brilliance of my smile. "I was, but I have a new plan."

He looked amused. "*Talking* me out of my painting, perhaps?"

A burst of wind came howling around the corner of the building, making me shiver.

"May I?" I gestured over the threshold, where an invisible wall of magic crackled, waiting for some fool to try to break through — a barrier many, many times more powerful than the magic at our pavilions at home.

Grepper grinned at me with renewed interest, then flicked his fingers, lowering the barrier.

"Please come in. Explain." His eyes gleamed.

The hot young woman — his plaything, I figured — grimaced like I wasn't worthy, but he dismissed her with another firm flick of his fingers.

"This," he murmured dangerously, "I very much want to hear."

Chapter Twenty-Four

GENEVIÈVE

Roux practically plastered himself to my right leg, daring Grepper to try something as I entered the villa. I ran a hand over the dark, intersecting stripes of his back, trying to keep us both calm.

Grepper closed the door behind us, cutting us off from the blizzard. Burning logs crackled in the living room fireplace — a big, featureless slab of concrete — and though the temperature was balmy, the space was anything but warm. All that polished concrete gave the place an industrial feel, while cool gray and black furnishings reinforced the masculine vibe.

Clearly, Hot Young Thing hadn't had a say in decorating. Otherwise, the place would be all fluffy pillows and pastels. She was younger than me, with triple the bra size, which hinted at the type of services she provided for Grepper.

At his gesture, she scampered away like a well-trained poodle.

"May I offer you a drink?" Grepper asked as if this were a social call and not a rapidly unraveling art heist.

"No, thank you." I stood sideways to the fire, warming my hands while glancing at a wall made entirely of glass. On a clear day, the view over the lake and mountains would be breathtaking. Even now, the sight of snow falling over pines was gorgeous.

He helped himself to a drink, then made himself comfortable on a sleek black leather recliner.

"So, my painting..." he prompted.

I shook my head. "I'm not interested in your painting. I'm interested in *my* painting."

"The one I bought at auction?"

"The one concealing a second painting."

He sipped his drink, then placed it aside. "The artwork was my purchase. Hence, it is my property."

"I'm only interested in the front painting. The one of a château."

He studied me for a moment, keeping his cards close to his chest.

"As I said, it's mine. Do you wish to purchase it from me?"

Roux lashed his tail, reminding me time was ticking.

"It's not worth anything," I pointed out.

"On the contrary. I paid €95,000 for it."

"No, you paid €95,000 for a Monet. Quite a bargain, really."

His eyes danced, congratulating me. Not that he came out and admitted as much. He just stuck up a finger, indicating for me to wait while he stepped into the adjoining study.

Roux chuffed at me in disapproval. *The painting doesn't matter, Gen. We need to get out of here safely.*

"You mean, *this* lovely painting?" Grepper reappeared with my father's canvas in his hands.

Just the canvas, removed from the frame, meaning the Monet was elsewhere.

A lump filled my throat, and I nodded. "My father painted it."

"Thomas Durand." He touched the tiny signature in the bottom corner. "He certainly had some skill."

I frowned at his use of the past tense. Chez Robert had only listed my father's name and the date of the painting. How did Grepper know my father was dead?

"It can't possibly have any value to you, but it has great sentimental value for my family," I said.

"Perhaps, but I've grown fond of it." He rolled it up and placed it aside.

"I propose a trade," I said, making poor Roux tense all over again.

Grepper raised his thick eyebrows. "What kind of trade?"

"My father's painting for information."

"Such as. . . ?"

Roux leaned against my leg, warning me. I ignored him — as well as anyone could ignore a five-hundred-pound tiger.

"Such as the fact that a band of vampires is approaching as we speak, determined to steal your Monet. And I mean *now.*"

Grepper reached casually for his glass. "I'm well equipped to deal with them, as your friends discovered."

He spared us a smirk, but I closed my eyes, feeling more like a failure than ever.

"But perhaps there is something else you can offer me," he mused, circling the rim of his glass with a finger.

Anything, I nearly blurted. But I'd learned a few lessons in the past weeks, so I held that back in favor of, "Such as?"

"Information about a mutual friend."

My stomach dropped, and Roux's tail slapped my leg in warning.

"Why not ask your friend directly?" I tried.

Grepper lifted one shoulder in a lazy shrug. "Unfortunately, our relationship has been strained for some years."

This was probably how things had started for poor Claudette, I realized. An uneasy feeling, a bitter deal. . .

"No deal."

Grepper looked up, surprised. "Don't you want to know who it is?"

I shook my head. "It doesn't matter."

He motioned to the next room. "What if I offered you a look at the other painting?"

I gulped, tempted. "*Manet painting in Monet's Garden,* by Claude Monet?"

He dipped his chin. "Quite. Though I must say, I'm surprised your godfather told you."

I froze. "You know Gordon is my godfather?"

His lips curled. "I know many things."

Two guesses who he wants you to spy on, Roux grumbled.

My eyes went wide. Gordon?

Feeling more unsettled than ever — as in eleven on a scale of ten — I shook my head.

"Gordon didn't tell me. I figured it out myself."

Grepper narrowed his eyes, and my scalp began to itch. Badly.

The warlock was trying to read my mind, wasn't he?

I pulled an image of my father's painting to the front of my mind and focused on one detail after another. The colors of the croquet mallets. The familiar lines of the château. The thick, flat strokes my father had used in a direct homage to Monet.

As suddenly as the itch started, it stopped, and Grepper murmured, "Well done, Miss Durand. Well done."

I stared. Did he mean resisting his mind reading or identifying the hidden painting?

But what really made me reel was what Grepper slipped in next.

"Your father would be proud."

I stared. "You knew my father?"

He nodded, savored another sip of his drink — or some memory — for a long time, then studied me quietly.

Finally, he pointed to the next room. "Would you be so kind as to fetch it for me?"

I gulped. The Monet?

Roux blocked me when I tried to step past him.

Grepper chuckled. "Very protective. You choose your friends well, Miss Durand."

"I'm finally learning," I muttered, slipping past Roux into the next room. Logs in the fireplace burst into flames as I entered, illuminating the space. Another of Grepper's little tricks, no doubt.

Roux prowled in beside me, sniffing for... traps? Explosives?

"It's on the desk," Grepper called casually.

Roux padded over to the sliding doors that opened onto a balcony, where wisps of steam rose from a heated pool, melting snowflakes in midair.

Check if the door is open, he urged.

I shook my head and headed for the desk. *If I'd wanted to run, I would already be far from here.*

Roux sighed, following me back to the living room.

Grepper motioned, and I propped the framed painting up on a side table. Then I stepped back to admire it.

"Beautiful, no?" Grepper murmured.

I nodded dumbly. It was. The golden light, the dappled leaves. The simple lines of Manet's hat and beard.

But that was just a slice of a wider scene that had played out in 1874. I pictured a triangle with Monet at one corner, painting Manet from the side while Manet focused on Camille and Jean, who sat at the third corner of the triangle. *That* was what captivated me — the view that stretched beyond the canvas and the elements I could hear, louder and clearer than ever before.

Birds chirped. Bees buzzed. Water trickled in a stream. And a little boy sighed from somewhere to the right, "off-screen."

Maman, Maman. Ça va encore durer longtemps? little Jean complained, much as I had as a kid. *How much longer will this take?*

Of course, I hadn't been sitting for a portrait done by the Father of Impressionism, as some called Édouard Manet.

"*Je sais que tu ressens, petit,*" I murmured. *I know how you feel, kid.*

Encore un petit moment, mon chéri, the boy's mother replied. *Just a little longer, my dear.*

I stood there, transported from this snowbound warlock's lair to a sun-drenched scene in a different time and place.

"He found it, you know," Grepper murmured.

I blinked, getting my bearings. Who found what?

"Your father found this painting," Grepper said.

I whirled around. "He found it...where?"

Grepper shrugged. "He never told me the details. I only know your father hoped to match the owner with a buyer who would bring the painting back into the public sphere."

I swayed on my feet. My father knew Grepper?

Roux snarled. *He could be lying.*

He could, but a sixth sense told me he wasn't.

"So your father contacted Gordon, and Gordon contacted me." Grepper stared into the fireplace.

It took everything I had not to shake him and scream, *Then what?*

But, yikes. My father, Gordon, and Grepper were buddies?

Finally, I ventured quietly, "And did he find that kind of buyer?"

I meant Grepper, of course — or his younger self.

His fingers tightened around his glass. "He thought so. Your father was on his way with a contract, but..."

I tilted my head when he trailed off.

"But?" I whispered.

"He never arrived." Grepper looked me straight in the eyes, waiting.

My knees buckled, and I would have hit the floor if Roux hadn't darted under my hand to steady me.

"You mean..." I started, but my voice failed me.

Grepper nodded sadly. "The brakes failed. His car went off the road. The contract never arrived."

I bared my teeth. "More significantly, my father died."

Grepper nodded. "Sadly, yes." He waited a few moments, then turned up the wattage in his eyes. "I'm deeply sorry for your loss. But let us focus on the painting for now. As you said, time is short."

The sound of car engines straining up the mountain road reached us, and the hair on the back of my neck prickled.

The vampires are here, Roux warned.

Yes, but I couldn't stop now.

"What happened to the painting after that?" I demanded.

"No one knows but the man who took it."

I clenched my fists, desperate to learn who that might be.

Grepper pointed to the painting, hinting. "The man who took it and kept it hidden for all these years."

Roux growled under his breath, and I wondered why. Then it hit me.

Gordon had had my father's painting on the wall for all these years.

I sank into a chair, staring past my trembling hands.

Roux paced in front of me, rubbing one side of his body against my legs, then the other, showing Grepper his teeth.

The warlock raised his hands in a gesture of innocence. "I merely speak the truth. Gordon, on the other hand..."

...is a crook and a liar, I pictured Mina filling in when Grepper trailed off.

Several cars pulled up outside, and Roux growled.

Fucking vampires...

I rocked a little, telling myself I would not succumb to another all-out meltdown as I had over Claudette. There wasn't time for that.

"Are you saying Gordon killed my father?" I gritted out.

Grepper shrugged. "At the very least, he profited from the circumstances. You must ask Gordon if you wish to learn more."

I shook my head, totally drained. Did I *want* to learn more? And who was I to believe?

"Why are you telling me this?" I demanded.

Grepper stared into the fire for a long time. "Perhaps because you remind me of your father. He was a good man. Too good, perhaps." He shot me a significant look.

A veiled warning that I should stop while I was ahead. Well, duh. I knew that full well, but that didn't stop me.

"So, you have the Monet now. Will you do as you originally intended and make it available to the public?"

My hopes rose on tiny, frail wings. Wouldn't it be nice if a little bit of good came of all this?

Roux's tail tapped me, and I thought of a second good thing. Him and me.

If we make it out of this alive, the back of my mind warned.

"Mr. Grepper. Will you exhibit it?" I demanded.

He flashed a wry smile. "Unfortunately, time has a way of eroding one's principles."

"But you have to! What good is it for one person to admire a masterpiece they keep locked away?"

"One might ask, what good is it to share?"

I was hardly in a position to shame a powerful warlock in his own home, but I didn't care any more.

"Shame on you, Mr. Grepper. Shame on you."

Car doors slammed, and voices sounded outside.

Grepper stared into the fire, unfazed by my words or the vampires. I sank my fingers into Roux's thick fur, wishing we could teleport ourselves to another time and place. A place like Monet's garden, where Roux could rest his head on my lap and snooze while I listened to the birds, the bees, and the trickling stream.

Footsteps sounded outside, along with muttered curses. Only then did Grepper move. He stood, annoyed, then paused to look at me.

"In my line of work, I don't often encounter people of principle. Your father was one. You are another." He leaned in, magic shimmering around his shoulders. "But principles can be dangerous, my dear. They can even kill you."

I gulped but refused to look away.

Remember what you told me about picking your battles? Roux warned.

"I have no designs on the Monet. I have no interest in selling you Gordon's secrets," I insisted. "All I want is my father's painting. Please. It's nothing to you, but very important to me."

Yes, I was pleading. But I didn't have it in me to uphold my principles and my pride at the same time.

He studied me long enough to make my hopes rise, only to dash them again.

"I am a businessman, not a philanthropist."

Ding-dong. The doorbell chimed.

So much for being the one with an original approach.

Roux crouched and gnashed his teeth.

"Strange, isn't it, that such an inhospitable night brings so many uninvited guests," Grepper observed dryly.

I, on the other hand, was ready to wet my pants. Grepper could defend himself against a gang of vampires, but what about me? What about Roux?

The bell chimed again, and Hot Young Thing appeared, looking miffed that whatever series she'd been binge-watching had been interrupted for a second time. Apparently, greeting people at the door was part of her job, along with spreading her legs on demand.

What a miserable skill set.

She stood by the door, waiting for Grepper's signal.

Roux pressed against my legs, nudging me toward the study, while Grepper called casually to the vampires.

"Just a moment, please." He walked across the room and picked up my father's rolled painting.

"Suppose I offered you a choice," he asked me.

My gut sank. Now what?

"Suppose I was gripped by a misguided sense of honor and allowed you to leave here with one thing — and only one. Would you choose the painting or Danielle here?"

Hot Young Thing stared, shocked and betrayed. "Kurt!"

"Silence!" he thundered, and she cowered.

The hair on my arms stood as he turned to me, calm as can be. "Which would it be?"

I shook my head. Was he nuts?

I pointed. "Her, of course."

Grepper's eyes glowed with interest. "You would choose her — a stranger — over your father's painting? Over the memories it captures? Over what it symbolizes?"

I gnashed my teeth. If he went on any longer, I might be tempted, dammit.

"Perhaps it doesn't mean as much to you as you suggest," he grunted.

I glared at him. "That painting means the world to me, but it's just a painting."

The fire blazed higher as Grepper held the painting over it.

I flinched, then shot Hot Young Thing the evil eye. "Promise me you'll do something with your life to make this worth it. Something beyond finding a sugar daddy with a nice villa and questionable morals."

"Last chance," Grepper warned.

I turned my back, bracing myself for the crackling sounds and acrid smell that signaled the demise of my father's painting.

I pictured him standing in the garden, dabbing his brush in his paint, then smiling at me.

Just a painting. Just a painting... I told myself. Memories were more precious than the materials that held them, right?

Every nerve in my body tensed.

But there was no crackle, no burning smell. Just Grepper's low mutter.

"Interesting. Very interesting."

What's so fucking interesting? Roux muttered.

Hot Young Thing kept her eyes trained over my shoulder, watching Grepper.

Steps sounded, coming closer, and I forced myself not to shiver. What was the warlock up to?

Grepper stepped around me, still holding my father's painting. What would his next demand be? My firstborn child?

He tapped the rolled canvas against his palm, thinking.

"Think faster," I grumbled, pointing to the door. "Vampires, remember?"

His lips curled into a smile. "Gordon underestimates me, but he also underestimates you."

"Gordon doesn't know I'm here," I noted bitterly.

Grepper's smile stretched. "I won't be the one to inform him."

The bell chimed again, and someone hammered on the door. "We know you're in there!"

Grepper thought for another few seconds, then smacked the painting into my hands.

"Take it, and take her. That way." He pointed at Hot Young Thing, then down the stairs. "Go to the lowest level, through the garage, and out the rear entrance."

I stared as Grepper stepped toward the front door.

"Go, I say!" he commanded.

I stumbled backward, propelled by his magic. Roux bristled beside me, protective as ever.

"Wait. My things. . ." Hot Young Thing made for the stairs leading to the upper story.

I yanked her back and shoved her toward the basement.

"But my things!" she protested.

Boy, had Kurt picked a winner. But I supposed brains weren't the top criteria for her job.

"You can't be that stupid," I muttered, bustling her onward.

"You will go with them, and you will do as you're told," Grepper ordered her in a frighteningly dark tone. "If you live to see tomorrow, you will forget everything."

Her eyes took on a glassy sheen as she succumbed to his magic. "Yes, sir."

"Take her to the Hotel Seeblick," Grepper told me. "I'll make arrangements for her from there."

How he planned to make arrangements with a coven of vampires knocking on his door, I didn't know. But I sure wasn't going to stick around for the details.

"Go, already!" I barked at her.

Finally, Danielle got into gear. She was woefully underdressed for the weather, but I had a feeling she wouldn't choose anything suitable even with an hour to prepare.

The three of us barely made it around the corner of the first flight of stairs before the front door opened, admitting a burst of frigid air that announced more than winter. It announced *vampires.*

But the voice that greeted Grepper wasn't at all what I expected.

"Why hello, Kurt," a woman crooned, all sweet and sultry.

My step hitched, as did Roux's.

Celeste, he muttered.

I was tempted to U-turn and give the succubus a piece of my mind. Then I remembered the vampires and changed my mind, real fast.

I took off, and even Hot Young Thing had the sense to hurry along.

Faster. Go! Roux hollered into my mind.

A message I didn't need to hear twice. I rushed Hot Young Thing along. Whatever happened next, we needed to be as far from it as possible.

Chapter Twenty-Five

ROUX

I brought up the rear of our little group, cursing Grepper the whole way. He'd acted as though giving Gen her father's painting was such a magnanimous gesture, but I wasn't buying that. He would probably enjoy watching the vampires hunt us down once he'd dealt with Celeste.

Meanwhile, we hurried through that concrete block the warlock called home. The austere hallways felt more like tunnels, an effect enhanced by the slanted walls.

"I bet some architect won a prize for designing this place," Gen muttered, leading the way around another blind corner.

Danielle nodded proudly. "He did. It was on the cover of magazines and everything."

Her tone suggested she somehow shared in the accolades when all she'd done was sleep with the architect's rich client, a man four times her age.

She should count herself lucky that Grepper hadn't offered *me* the choice of Danielle's life or the painting. I would have taken the painting and run, principles be damned.

I scowled. Okay, probably not, but I would have been tempted.

Still, it proved one thing. Gen and I might be opposites in a hundred small ways, but we were on the same page when it came to the important stuff.

A match made in heaven, my tiger hummed.

Yes, but we had to make it out of here alive first. And if we did—

When, not if, my tiger snarled.

— and *when* we did, I vowed to make her mine.

But first, we had to evade those vampires.

Gen pushed through a big steel door, and we jogged through a subterranean garage illuminated by eerie green lights. The place was the temperature of a refrigerator and filled with two perfectly aligned rows of four cars each. I rushed past the first two, then slowed to gape at the next pair. One was the vintage Porsche 356 we'd seen earlier, and the other, a 911 that dated back to the 1960s, judging by the chrome trim and short wheelbase.

"It's like the goddamn Batcave," Gen muttered, rushing on.

"You should see the rest of Kurt's collection in Zurich," Danielle said, chalking up another nonachievement. I ought to have pitied her, but all I felt was contempt.

I did, however, feel a little awed by the cars. Grepper even had a 1950s Porsche Roadster down there — one of only sixteen ever produced, if memory served. I paused to admire the two-piece windshield and hammered aluminum body.

"Roux!" Gen hissed.

I hurried on, chagrined.

Gen peered out the high window in the main garage door, then shook her head. "Dammit. The driveway is full of vampires."

I couldn't see out the windows in tiger form, but I could sense the vampires out there.

"Rear doorway…rear doorway…" Gen searched around. "Where the hell is the rear doorway?"

She looked at Danielle, then scowled. Of course, Grepper's mistress of the month had no clue. So beautiful, yet so damned stupid. I couldn't see the appeal.

"Oh! Here!" Gen called a moment later, pointing to a niche partially concealed by a floor-to-ceiling cabinet that housed Grepper's tools.

I didn't covet Grepper's woman, but those tools…

It took everything I had not to stop for a closer look.

The floor of the next hallway sloped up while the ceiling sloped down, crushing in on us like jaws. Gen paused at the solid steel door at the end, then sniffed the air.

I did too. Nothing.

Slowly, she turned the knob and peeked out. Frigid air sliced through the gap, along with a burst of snow flurries.

"Four vampires," she whispered, easing the door shut. "Searching the yard."

My mind raced. If we waited, would the vampires pass or would more join them?

Gen glanced back toward the garage, then shook her head, and I agreed. No turning back now.

She slid her father's painting into the inside pocket of her jacket, then gripped Danielle by the shoulders. "Okay, listen, and listen good. I need you to stick close to me. Very close. Do not say a word, and do not make any noise. If you do, you're dead. You get that?"

Danielle bit her lip and nodded.

Still, Gen pressed on. "I mean it. If push comes to shove, I won't hesitate to leave you behind — and believe me, death by vampire is not a good way to go."

Danielle paled, nodding again. Rich warlocks might be to her taste, but vampires were definitely not.

Gen turned to me next, whispering, "You stick close too. No heroics."

I let out a low snarl, not at all on board with that plan.

"Trust me," she repeated, so fiercely, I nearly stepped back. "I have a plan, but it will only work if you stick close." Then she grimaced. "And if it doesn't work... *Then* you can try heroics. Not before. Okay?"

Not at all okay, because tigers and proud soldiers led from the front. But we were out of options.

Okay, I agreed. *But if things go south, you need to run.*

While you fight to the death? she retorted.

That was pretty much the plan. And it would be worth it to ensure she survived.

Gen rolled her eyes. *How is death a better plan than "Stay close and don't make noise"?*

Just a backup plan, I promised.

She shook her head. *Believing in me is better.*

I took a deep breath, then nodded. *I believe in you.*

She turned to the door, frighteningly resolute. She listened for a moment, then glanced back at Danielle. "Like I said, stay close, and don't make any noise."

When she nodded, Gen eased the door open and headed out into the blizzard.

Fucking Grepper. Apparently, he could manipulate weather too.

Arctic wind stung my nose, and I squinted into the darkness.

There, there, there, and there. Gen pointed at four vampires fanned out around the yard.

I'd only spotted three. So, wow. Points for *her* night vision. Part of her mixed shifter ancestry, perhaps?

What she did next came from the witchy side of her family, though. I stared as she melted into the shadows by the door. Literally. One minute, she was there, and the next, she was gone. Danielle's front side vanished too. Her back wavered like a mirage, then disappeared as well.

I said, stay close! Gen hissed into my mind.

Stretching my nose as far as I could, I stepped forward. My nose tingled, then my ears and face as I eased through a wall of darkness. And, oh. There was Gen, with Danielle huddled behind her. The space around them was pitch-black, and the world beyond grayer than before, as if we were peering out through a dirty lens.

Closer! Gen urged.

I glanced back. My head and shoulders were within Gen's bubble of darkness, but the rest of my body was in the gray zone that marked the outer world. I pressed forward, making myself as small as possible.

Watch your tail, dammit. Gen gestured.

My tail prickled as I yanked it in.

Slowly, I realized what Gen was doing. She hadn't found a dark area to hide in. She was *casting* it. The air around us warmed and wobbled as she wrapped shadows around us like a cloak.

A very lumpy cloak, she muttered. *Do you have to be so big?*

I hunched, telling myself I was a soldier cramming into a foxhole instead of a guy hiding behind a woman. And Gen was right. *Stay close and don't make noise* was a better plan than taking on four vampires. And as for heroics...a good soldier knew when to lead and when to trust the skill sets of others.

And what a skill it was. Forget camouflage, face paint, and *under the cover of night* tactics. Gen could wrap shadows around herself and around us.

She shuffled forward, paused, then rushed toward a tree. My fur tingled, and the shadows stretched, reaching their breaking point. Another step forward, and the feeling eased again as we reached a thicker pool of shadows under the tree. So, the more natural shadows Gen could draw on, the better.

"Stop. Shh!" One of the vampires whipped around.

We froze.

All four vampires looked in our direction, though none focused on our precise spot. So, whew. Gen was doing a damn good job hiding us.

But she couldn't hide our scent. I steeled every muscle in my body when one of the vampires sniffed the air and stepped closer...closer...

Shit, Gen shouted into my mind.

Hold still, I whispered.

But he's getting closer! she protested.

Danielle, I noted, had her eyes squeezed shut. Not an effective strategy, but at least she didn't scream and give us away.

Hold still, I told Gen. *But be ready to move, fast.* I glanced around. *See that big pine? Go there.*

I said, no heroics, she retorted.

Call it diversionary tactics, I rumbled back.

As the vampire approached, I crouched, then leaped for his throat. Shouts broke out from the others, but surprise was on my side, giving me a head start — something I sorely needed to kill the vampire then retreat into the forest and double back to the shadows of the big pine.

As a tiger, I knew all about blending in. But, whoa. Gen was nowhere to be seen.

In here, Gen called into my mind.

I looked around. *In where?*

Her camouflage was that good.

Three more steps, then turn right.

I did as I was told and — *oof!* — bashed into Danielle.

"Watch ou—" she complained, but Gen slapped a hand over her mouth.

I whirled, checking the vampires. It was uncanny, the switch from the crisp, clear view I'd had "out there" to the washed-out, *view out a dirty window* of Gen's shadow. Not that I was complaining.

The vampires gathered around their fallen comrade. Within seconds, his body turned to ash that was whipped away by the wind.

Good riddance.

"Spread out," one vampire ordered the others. "He can't be far."

I wasn't, but we were upwind now, which meant we could slowly inch away from the villa. It was awkward as hell, moving while mashed up against each other to fit within the shadow Gen cast. But I would take that over being out in the open.

We crept steadily along until Danielle slipped in the snow and yelped. The vampires whipped around, eyes shining blood red.

"Over there." One pointed slightly left of us.

"No, over there," another countered, pointing higher up.

"Wait," one of the vampires called, flaring his nostrils. "I smell someone. Not just that cat. There's a woman too."

Gen froze.

"With very alluring blood," the vampire added a moment later.

The other two whipped around, eyes glowing.

"How alluring?" one asked, coming closer.

Gen dug her fingers into my fur. I nudged for her to keep moving. Slowly.

The first vampire huffed. "Better than that bitch in Auberre who refused to talk."

Gen froze, and I barely bit back a snarl. Did he mean Claudette?

"Where? I don't see anyone," another vampire demanded.

"She's out there," the first confirmed.

I bared my teeth, ready to tear all their throats out and avenge Claudette. But getting Gen to safety was my priority.

Don't even get me started, she barked. *Those bastards killed Claudette!*

It's time to escape, not exact vengeance, I hissed.

Maybe we can do both, Gen shot back, flooding my mind with an entire battle plan. Then she paused. *Can you do that?*

The wind and snow intensified, making the vampires hunch and turn their backs. This was our chance to escape.

Forget revenge, I urged Gen. *We need to get out of here.*

She shook her head fiercely. *They killed Claudette.*

My gut roiled with conflicting emotions, and I finally nodded.

All right. But the minute I call a retreat, you retreat. Understood?

She nodded, practically baring her teeth at the vampires.

Chapter Twenty-Six

ROUX

The nearest vampire brushed the snow from his shoulders and started toward us, following his nose.

Head that way, I told Gen. *Over by those boulders.*

She nodded and led the way slowly forward.

I stuck with her for a few steps, then split off to creep along a hollow. When I was twenty paces away, I called into Gen's mind.

Now!

She threw a snowball at a tree, drawing their attention.

"Over there!" one of the vampires yelled, falling for our ruse.

I doubled back through the hollow, then tackled the nearest vampire. The acrid taste of blood filled my mouth as I tore at his throat. He slashed at my side with needle-sharp fingernails, then gradually went limp. I hated for Gen to witness that gory a spectacle, but she, like I, had Claudette at the forefront of her mind.

Killing a vampire was no easy feat, but I was powered by twice my usual strength, and it was over in an instant. I raced away before the other two could reach me, zigzagging to throw them off. Then I rushed to my rendezvous point with Gen.

Four or five more steps uphill and a little farther left, Gen called urgently.

The vampires dropped back, mired in a snowdrift.

I crept onward, following the tingle of magic to slip into Gen's shadow more gracefully than last time. Still, it was jarring, the way she and Danielle appeared directly in front of my nose.

I flashed Gen a wicked grin.

We make a good team, you and me.

Her eyes lit up, she hummed into my mind. *We do.*

Shouts broke out on the far side of the house, and I pictured Grepper arguing with Celeste and a group of angry vampires.

Move. Quickly! I urged Gen.

The remaining vampires hesitated, torn between us and helping their comrades with Grepper. But they plowed on a moment later, intent on tracking us down.

I'll drop back here. Next rendezvous is that tree stump, I noted, coiling my muscles.

We kept up the guerrilla tactics, covering another hundred-plus meters of ground while looking for opportunities to kill our foes. Still, it was slow going, and I worried that "our" vampires might be joined by more from the main force at Grepper's door.

Gen scowled. *I hate to root for Grepper, but better him than the vampires.*

She continued plucking shadows out of our surroundings and weaving them around us. An eternity later, we reached a steep, rocky area. Gen glanced back, then yelled, pushing Danielle to the ground.

"Get down!"

A massive shadow swept overhead. Flames crackled, illuminating the falling snow, and dragon roars exploded into my ears.

Where the hell are you? Marius thundered into my mind.

I caught a glimpse of his dark form sweeping over the trees before disappearing into the blizzard.

We're just north of you, moving northeast, I reported, nudging Gen along.

Another burst of fire lit the sky as Mina followed him. Mental chaos ensued as her voice joined Marius's and Gen's in my mind.

Just keep distracting the vampires, I told Marius.

My pleasure, he rumbled, looping around for another pass.

He and Mina could barely fly in the snow, let alone target vampires under tree cover, but even random bursts of fire helped.

Keep moving, I urged Gen. *Not far to go now.*

I ambushed and killed another vampire, then ran back to rejoin her.

Run! Just run! I yelled when we reached the trail. It was snowed over, but we could move more quickly here.

The faster we moved, the harder it became for Gen to weave shadows, but Mina and Marius kept the last vampire at bay long enough for us to race toward the trailhead. I spotted Henrik and Bene there, urging us on. But the final vampire was closing in on us, fast.

"Keep going. Quickly!" Henrik ordered, passing me to attack the remaining vampire.

Bene waved us on weakly. "Yes — quickly would be good."

A fierce fight broke out behind us. I spun to protect Gen. Snarls sounded, snow flew, and blood sprayed. Then a piercing cry broke the air, and the vampire fell, killed by Henrik.

A weight lifted from my heart. The vampires who'd murdered Claudette were dead.

Bene studied Danielle. "Who is this?"

"I'll explain later," Gen said, placing her father's painting into the car, then helping Bene in.

I rubbed my muzzle in the snow, disgusted by the bloodstains. Revenge never tasted as good as one imagined.

"Roux, Henrik. Let's go!" Gen yelled.

She jumped behind the wheel of the rental car I had driven up the mountain earlier, with a stunned Danielle in the front seat. Henrik "helped" me into the back seat, though he nearly slammed the door on my tail.

Watch it, I snarled.

He gave me that haughty, *I'm surrounded by heathens* look he did so well, then turned to follow us in the second car with Bene. We raced away just as more vampires appeared on the trail, but long sprays of dragon fire kept them at bay.

I shifted to human form and wrestled on the clothes I'd left behind earlier — no easy task with Gen racing around the tight hairpins in a blizzard. She beeped and swerved as we sped past the cars blocking Grepper's driveway.

"Can you see what's going on?" Gen asked as we raced by.

I squinted toward Grepper's villa, spotting at least half a dozen vampires and a woman in a white fur coat who almost blended in with the snow.

"Celeste," I muttered.

She was pleading with Grepper and the vampires. No one, it seemed, was happy with her.

At a curt gesture from Grepper, Celeste spun away, looking pale but defiant. She raised her hands, ordering the vampires aside in her usual regal manner. Clearly, she was looking to make a quick exit.

But the nearest vampire drew a knife, and her eyes went wide.

Blood splashed in a wide arc. Celeste buckled. The vampires went into a frenzy, sinking their fangs into her body before it even hit the ground.

That was all I saw before the snow closed in — that, and Grepper closing his door in disgust.

My stomach churned, but I didn't have it in me to feel sorry.

"What's going on?" Gen cried, not daring to look away from the treacherous road.

I gulped down the bile in my throat. "They got Celeste," I said quietly. "The vampires, I mean."

Gen's mouth fell open, and her eyes darted to the rearview mirror, but she kept driving.

"Oh my God," she murmured.

You make your bed, you lie in it, Bene rumbled in my mind, telling me he'd seen it too.

I touched Gen's shoulder. "Right now, you have to focus on getting us out of here — all of us." I indicated Danielle.

Her hands tightened around the steering wheel, and she nodded, though she looked sick.

I glanced back. From what I could tell, Henrik hadn't so much as swerved at the gory sight. Either he truly despised Celeste, or he'd had his eyes glued to the road when it happened.

Luckily, I blocked his view, Bene murmured into my mind. *Nothing worse than finding yourself in a car with a blood-thrilled vampire.*

So, Bene had more sense than I thought.

Good move, I told him, surprised to be as relieved as I was. Bene, Marius, Henrik, and I had been thrown together by fate, and we'd all counted down the time until we could be free of Gordon — and one another. But we'd meshed into a surprisingly good team, and the thought of anyone getting hurt — or going their separate ways after our contract concluded — struck deeper into my heart than I thought it would.

Marius. Mina. Everything all right with you? I called into their minds.

Yes, but the sooner we all get out of this blizzard, the better, Marius replied.

Henrik stuck to our rear bumper all the way down the mountain, blinding us with his lights. Still, I appreciated the buffer he provided against any vampires who might pursue us. None did, thanks to Marius and Mina spraying fire over the road behind us.

The snow petered out as we drove, suggesting Grepper was the one driving it. Well, let him keep those vampires snowbound as long as possible. We were making tracks.

When we reached the outskirts of town, Marius and Mina peeled away to land at their starting point behind a barn.

We'll rendezvous on the south end of the village in ten minutes, I told Marius. *Henrik, Gen, Bene, and I will clear our things out of the hotel.*

We'll be there, he confirmed.

What about our passenger? Bene asked.

Leave that to me, Gen said, keeping her lips tightly pursed.

The only two hotels in town were the Hotel du Lac, where we'd stayed, and the Seeblick. Gen dropped Danielle off at the latter with firm orders.

"Like Grepper said, you'll do as you're told," Gen barked.

"I'll do as I'm told." Danielle nodded, looking blank and hazy. Grepper's spell was holding, it seemed.

"Go inside. Charge the room to Grepper. He'll contact you in the morning," Gen said.

He wouldn't — not directly. But he would make arrangements, I was sure.

Arrangements, as in bumping her off? Gen asked, alarmed.

I shook my head. *That will raise too many questions. He'll get her safely off to some place far away. Probably wherever he met her with a big gap in her memory.*

Gen grimaced, then nodded to Danielle. "Okay?"

"Okay." Danielle moved robotically to the hotel door.

We waited until she stepped inside, then took off for our hotel.

Ten minutes later, the six of us were reunited and roaring down the road to Lucerne.

I sat beside Gen, who drove, while Bene stretched across the back seat, still recovering from the shock inflicted by Grepper's magic. Mina, Marius, and Henrik followed in a second vehicle.

When we'd informed Mina and Marius of Celeste's demise, their reactions had been predictably grim.

Celeste deserved the worst, and she got it, Marius had huffed.

I can't believe I'm saying this, but I agree, Mina had said glumly.

No one would shed tears for Celeste, but the reality would take some time to really sink in.

"What do you think is happening back at Grepper's now?" Gen asked, glancing over her shoulder.

I shrugged. "It looked to me like Grepper had the upper hand there. I wouldn't be surprised if he's back in his study now, sipping brandy and admiring his Monet."

Gen grimaced. "And...Celeste?"

It's truly over for her, Bene snorted into my mind.

"The vampires will leave as soon as they...um..."

Drink their fill came to mind, but that was a little graphic.

"As soon as they finish with Celeste," I finished. "They'll dispose of the body — or leave that for Grepper."

"Either way, the vampires will hit the road soon," Bene warned.

Gen pressed down on the accelerator.

I reached across the seats to squeeze Gen's hand, grazing her father's painting in the process.

"We got what we came for," I said. "That's all that matters now. That, and getting home. We can figure out the rest there."

I shot her a significant look, because *the rest* meant a hell of a lot more than Grepper, Celeste, and the vampires. I meant us too.

Gen looked back again, then squeezed my hand.

"Home sounds good."

Chapter Twenty-Seven

ROUX

"Good morning," I mumbled, finding Bene in the château kitchen the next morning.

We'd returned only a few hours earlier, and everyone had fallen directly into bed. Gen and I had curled up together in her bed without bothering to change or undress, and we'd fallen asleep after barely a kiss.

Well, maybe one or two.

We'd snuck in a few more when we forced ourselves awake at seven a.m., but there was no time for more. Not with so much still unresolved.

I showered, dressed, and lumbered to the kitchen, not far ahead of Gen.

Bene looked up from the bacon he was frying. As tired and disheveled as he looked, he still managed a teasing smile.

"Good morning? Maybe for the guy who didn't sleep in his own bed last night."

So, he'd noticed. Impressive, given that he was still getting the last of Grepper's magic out of his system.

Ignoring him, I loaded a tray with plates, silverware, jam, and other breakfast supplies. The sooner we started this meeting, the better.

I lifted the tray and stepped toward the dining room, then stopped and closed my eyes.

This had been Claudette's job.

I swallowed hard. She and I hadn't been close, but that didn't lessen the tragedy.

Aside from the sound of sizzling bacon, the kitchen went quiet. Bene put a hand on my shoulder.

"I know how you feel, man," he said in a husky voice. "I know how you feel."

We stood for a long minute, thinking. Remembering. Wishing. Bene, especially, I guessed, since he'd been friendly with Claudette. *Too* friendly, I'd thought at the time, but now, I was more forgiving. Honest, good-hearted friends had been a rarity in Claudette's life, and Bene had been one of the few.

"Small consolation, but you did get the bastards who killed her," he added a moment later. "Celeste got what she deserved too."

Then he cursed and turned back to the stove.

"You're making me burn the bacon, man," he complained, not too convincingly.

I let that one slide and carried the tray to the dining room.

Marius entered, stretching his arms high in a yawn. Mina slid in beside him, and his arm came to rest on her shoulders. They smiled and kissed, and instead of the usual stab of jealousy, my mood lifted. There was a lot of bad in the world, but a lot of good too. And if those two could defy the odds to get together, so could other couples.

One, in particular.

Gen entered the dining room next, and my soul soared at the sight of her.

Mate, my inner tiger rumbled.

Yes. Yes, she was. And the minute we wrapped up this mission, we would be discussing that.

She smiled and whispered into my mind. *We'll do more than just discuss, I hope.*

I grinned, and for the briefest of instants, my surroundings faded away.

Or maybe not just an instant, because the next time I blinked, Bene was shouldering me out of the way, muttering, "Just what we needed. Another set of lovebirds."

"Another set of what?" Marius grumbled cluelessly.

Mina nudged him in the ribs, hiding a grin. "Get the milk, please."

Henrik appeared, and for once, I was glad for the distraction.

"*Bonjour*," he said, giving Mina and Gen one of those old-fashioned bows he executed whenever he forgot what century he was in.

He stood by his chair, polite enough to wait for the rest of us, but not polite enough to disguise his impatience.

"All right, everyone," Bene announced a moment later. "Dig in."

We did, and a few minutes passed in quiet munching, slurping, and requests to pass butter, salt, or the toast platter.

Gen didn't eat much. No surprise, considering everything she'd been through — not least of all, what Grepper had said.

Are you saying Gordon killed my father? she'd asked.

At the very least, he profited from the circumstances.

Even I had been shocked to hear that, despite my already low opinion of Gordon. Poor Gen had to be reeling.

You must ask Gordon if you wish to learn more, Grepper had added.

Would Gen dare? Would I if I were in her shoes?

Mina stood. "Coffee refill, anyone?"

Bene raised his mug with a smug smile. "Yes, because it's excellent coffee, thanks to me."

"Thanks to our Breville Barista Pro X380," Mina teased while pouring.

"*My* Breville Barista Pro," he emphasized. "That beauty is the number one improvement we've made here at the château."

I snorted. "I'd rank renovating the stables higher."

Bene shook his head. "That earns spot number two, tops." He sipped his coffee, then kissed his fingertips and flicked them outward. "Definitely top of the list."

"Mina's painting of *The Tower of Blue Horses* in the west wing is a bigger improvement than that coffee machine," Marius countered.

"Ha. Says the guy who moved *out* of the west wing," Bene shot back. Then he grinned and looked at me. "Speaking of people who've started sleeping in the east wing—"

He howled when I kicked him under the table. "Hey!"

I swiftly changed the subject. "Time to begin this debrief."

Bene pushed his chair out of kicking range and rubbed his shin while muttering into my mind. *I did not deserve that.*

You totally deserved that, I shot back, then turned to Henrik. "First, I believe thanks are in order. If you hadn't arrived to warn us about the vampires, things could have ended very differently."

Henrik straightened his collar, exuding snobby, *I told you so* vibes.

"I have to say, you had us worried for a while there," Marius admitted.

Henrik's frown said, *How on earth could anyone ever be worried about a vampire as wonderful and pleasant as me?*

"What are you suggesting?" he snipped.

"Come on, Henrik," Mina said. "You didn't respond to any of our messages. Even you can appreciate that seemed suspicious at the time."

"By which she means, even more suspicious than usual," Bene threw in, not all too helpfully.

I cut in, trying to defuse things before Henrik's fangs extended.

"The point is, we're grateful. So, well done and thank you."

Bene pointed to Gen. "For the record, she believed in you the whole time."

Henrik rewarded her with a slight nod. So, not exactly oozing gratitude, but not quite as snooty as usual.

"Now, what else can you tell us about those vampires?" I asked. "Such as, what kind of fallout might result from all this?"

Mina nodded solemnly. "Most importantly, should we expect Alexandre Ernaux and his coven to pay us a visit?"

"Let them try," Marius growled, inching closer to his mate.

Henrik jerked his head in a no. "Alexandre's sole interest was the Monet."

"And?" Gen asked.

"According to my contacts, Grepper made it clear that Alexandre's issue was with Celeste, not him. Now that she is dead, the matter is settled."

Mina looked doubtful. "How settled?"

"Grepper's considerable power convinced the coven to back down. Unless Alexandre Ernaux offers to buy the Monet, it will remain in Grepper's hands."

"Won't Gordon be pleased," Marius muttered vindictively.

"Do you think Grepper will exhibit it?" Mina asked.

Gen grimaced. "I doubt it."

She didn't bring up what Grepper had insinuated about Gordon. I supposed we would find out soon enough, though I didn't relish the encounter.

"What about the vampires we killed — the ones who murdered Claudette?" I asked. "Ernaux won't be angry about that?"

Henrik shook his head. "He was furious that they contracted out to Celeste without his permission. He offered them a chance to redeem themselves in Switzerland, and they botched it. Ernaux has no reason to come after you."

"You mean, to come after *us*," Mina corrected.

He gave her a cold look. "Our association ends when my contract with Gordon ends. Which is..." He made a show of checking his watch. "Let me see... Oh yes. Next week. But, no. None of us has reason to fear retribution from Alexandre Ernaux."

Silence prevailed as everyone processed the fact that we were finally rid of Celeste — and safe from Ernaux.

"What else did you discover?" I asked.

Henrik rolled a hard-boiled egg over the table, cracking the shell agonizingly slowly. "We were right — Celeste hired vampires to pressure Claudette for information on us. My informants also confirmed that Celeste hired the nagas who attacked Roux and Geneviève that night."

"The night I came to the rescue." Bene patted his own chest.

"We both did," Henrik snipped.

"For which I'm eternally grateful," Gen said, placating them both. *But even more grateful to you,* she whispered into my mind.

I flashed her a tiny smile. *My pleasure.*

"I guess that means everything is all right on the vampire front," Bene concluded.

Gen grimaced, though she refrained from saying, *As right as things can be when it comes to vampires.*

"Which brings us to the painting," I said, trying to move things along.

Gen stood and carefully unrolled her father's painting, holding it up for us.

"So good to have Dad's painting back," Mina murmured.

"Thanks to Gen's quick thinking," I said.

I'd nearly flipped out when she'd marched up to Grepper's door, but her crazy plan had worked.

"Her quick thinking *and* her magic," I added. "We wouldn't have escaped without her shadow-weaving."

Mina nodded proudly at her sister, and even Marius grinned.

"More magic left in this family than you thought, eh?"

Bene groaned. "Don't encourage them. They'll start sneaking up on us, just for the fun of it." He faked a shiver. "Like, sneaking up on me in the shower."

Mina groaned, and Gen shook her head. "Nothing there we need to see."

Marius snickered, and Bene put a hand over his heart, showing how wounded he was.

Henrik shook his head, nailing the *oh, how I suffer* look perfectly.

Mina laughed. "Just wait. Dora is scheduled to arrive soon. Then there will be three of us practicing magic around here."

I'd met the cousin briefly, and she was nice enough. Still, I wasn't so sure about yet another change at the château. Then again, it had already changed with Marius becoming part of the family, thanks to Mina. So, that was a done deal. But would Bene stick around after his contract ended?

I glanced at Gen. Would I? Could I?

Please, I nearly pleaded.

She nudged my foot with hers, assuring me she didn't need convincing.

So, change was definitely in the wind. A huge life change, not just a change of scenery.

I couldn't wait, but one worry nagged at me. Was I cut out for a settled life and a serious relationship?

My tiger hummed happily. *Try me.*

Marius pointed at the painting. "As good as it is to have your father's painting back, something tells me Gordon won't be as happy about it. Not without the Monet."

My phone rang, and everyone groaned.

"Let me guess," Bene muttered. "It's Gordon."

I checked the display, nodding wearily. "He'll want a few words, for sure."

"Oh, I have a few words for him," Marius growled.

I was about to take the call when Gen put a hand on my arm. "Wait. What are you going to tell him?"

Exactly what I'd been wondering. What to tell Gordon and what to withhold.

"I'll summarize," I finally said.

Gen squeezed my arm, shaking her head urgently.

The phone rang and rang.

"Just silence the damn thing," Marius grunted. "Let him wait."

I considered for a long minute. It was one thing to be selective in what I shared with Gordon. But openly defying him while still under contract... It just wasn't in my DNA.

Gen snatched the phone out of my hands and silenced it. Even without the noise, my nerves remained taut.

"I have an idea," she declared.

I stirred the air with my hand, hurrying her up.

"Possibly a brilliant one," she added.

Bene grinned. "You mean, another idea that sounds crazy but somehow works out in the end?"

She gave him a thumbs-up. "Exactly."

I waited, not all too convinced.

Finally, she came out with it. While everyone looked skeptical at first, we soon leaned in, absorbing every detail.

"Wow. Bold plan," Bene murmured when she finished. "The question is, will it work?"

Mina chewed that over for a moment, then nodded. "Gen's right. We need to take charge instead of defaulting to Gordon."

"But he has to think he's in charge," Gen added quickly.

Bene chuckled into my mind. *These sisters are more devious than they look.*

I preferred *clever*. But, yes. Gen's plan could work.

She handed me my phone. I took a deep breath, reviewed what I wanted to say, and turned the sound back on, waiting.

"He'll call back," Mina said. "I guarantee it."

She'd barely uttered the words when Gordon did exactly that. This time, I answered.

"Yes, it's me." I winced and held the phone away from my ear at his reply. "Sorry I couldn't get to the phone in time. Good to have you on the line now, though."

Bene rolled his eyes, but I knew it wasn't in my interest to antagonize Gordon. He would be antagonized enough as things stood.

"Yes, sir. Mission accomplished. We have the painting. No, sir. No trouble. Grepper wasn't at home, and there was no sign of those vampires," I lied.

Silence fell over the line. A long, stunned one.

"No trouble at all?" Gordon finally asked, loud enough for his voice to carry to the others.

Marius snorted. "He sounds so hopeful."

Mina shushed him while I replied. "No, sir. An easy in-and-out operation."

Bene made a face, rubbing his sore shoulder, while Marius grimaced. *I doubt Celeste would see it that way.*

Well, she was dead, though I wasn't going to be the one to spill the beans to Gordon.

"Yes, sir. I'll deliver it to you later today. Or perhaps you'd prefer Gen and Mina to."

Gordon practically tripped over his own tongue to answer. "Not necessary."

Gen frowned at Mina, who shrugged back.

"I want you and that painting on the first train to Paris," Gordon ordered.

Gen held up her phone, having already pulled up the train schedule.

I nearly said *The next train leaves in an hour,* but Bene tilted his empty mug toward me.

"The next train leaves in two hours, sir," I reported.

Bene grinned and passed me a croissant.

"Yes, sir," I continued to Gordon. "That will get me to Paris by noon."

Us. That will get us *to Paris by noon,* Gen whispered into my mind.

Yes, that was the plan. But Gordon didn't need to know that.

Gordon didn't need to know a lot of things.

Chapter Twenty-Eight

GENEVIÈVE

"Geneviève," Gordon stammered when I appeared at his door with Roux. "I wasn't expecting you."

"She insisted on coming," Roux said in reply to Gordon's dark look.

I was a set designer, not an actress, but I'd picked up enough from years in theaters to muster a convincing smile. "I couldn't bring myself to let the painting out of my sight."

I also couldn't bring myself to part with Roux, but Gordon didn't need to know that.

If I hadn't spent the entire trip to Paris steeling myself for this visit, I might have recoiled when Gordon hugged me. But I kept up the act and hugged him back, no matter how my stomach churned.

Grepper hadn't come out and accused Gordon of playing a role in my father's death, but he did say Gordon had profited from it. If that was true — a big if — I had to know what that role was.

I took a deep breath, trying to settle my heaving emotions.

"Well, I'm delighted to see you," Gordon said, releasing me. "And delighted that you were able to recover the painting."

Roux nodded. "Like I said, sir. An easy in-and-out operation."

Gordon looked around expectantly, practically rubbing his hands together.

I unslung a storage tube from my shoulders and carefully removed the painting.

"Here it is. Unharmed, thank goodness." I unrolled it and held it up, peeking over the top edge to watch my godfather's reaction.

He stared, confused. "Where's the rest?"

"The rest?" I echoed, innocent as a lamb.

"Yes. The frame."

"That's how we found it, sir," Roux said. "No frame. That is the correct painting, isn't it?"

The man was a master of the poker face. Normally, so was Gordon, but his cheeks went from pink to red.

I interjected before Gordon exploded. "*Of course* it's the right painting. I know my father's work when I see it."

Gordon opened and closed his mouth like a fish gulping for water. "But the frame..."

I shrugged cheerfully. "We can replace the frame. But we can't replace Dad's painting."

"Yes, but..." He clenched his fists, then glared at Roux. "Your orders were—"

"Our orders were to retrieve the painting, sir," Roux interjected.

Electricity filled the air, reflecting Gordon's ire.

"When I say, *get my car,* I don't have to specify four tires and a bumper, do I?" he snarled.

Roux and I had agreed to keep mind-speak to a minimum in case Gordon picked up on it, but I was sure Roux was thinking something along the lines of, *I don't know. I'm not your fucking driver.*

He didn't deign to reply, though.

"What. Happened. To. The. Frame?" Gordon gritted out.

"Like Roux said, this is how we found it," I said.

Gordon's eyes bugged out. "We? You were there?" He turned to Roux, thundering, "Did I not make myself clear when I said my goddaughters were not to be part of the operation?"

Roux replied in the same flat tone. "You did, sir. But she insisted."

I nodded cheerily. "I did."

"And since we had a comfortable window in which to execute operations, according to the intelligence you supplied..." Roux said.

Comfortable, my ass, I nearly snorted. And as for *intelligence*, Gordon's information had been way off. By design, I feared.

The room tingled with magic, and I sensed Gordon reaching into Roux's mind. Mine, too, but I was ready this time, serving up images of snowy Swiss landscapes and my father's rolled-up, unframed painting on Grepper's desk.

Gordon started pacing. Briefly, he came to a halt, opened his mouth — then shut it and went back to pacing.

It would have been comical if the situation weren't so damn twisted. He couldn't come out and ask about the Monet because he'd lied about that from the start. He'd lied to Roux, and he'd lied to me.

My gut roiled. Mina had been right about Gordon all along. But his crimes might run even deeper than she suspected, if Grepper were to be believed.

I thought of my father. My mother. All the years they'd missed out on sharing together, and all that he'd missed with Mina and me.

My cheeks colored as I faced Gordon, and I longed to confront him directly. But what would that accomplish when he would vehemently deny any involvement?

No. My best course of action was to learn what I could by operating as deviously as Gordon did.

"I don't know why, but the painting was removed from the frame when we found it," I said, ashamed at how easily the lies rolled off my tongue. "Whether Celeste or Grepper did that, we couldn't tell."

That was the beauty of the situation. Gordon couldn't accuse us of hiding the Monet from him, because our story was perfectly plausible.

"If my informants are to be believed, Celeste is dead," Gordon growled.

I did my best to look shocked.

"Oh my gosh. That's terrible." I said, skirting around a more direct, *Good riddance.* "What happened?"

Gordon looked out the window. "My contact didn't elaborate. But it seems Celeste chose to associate with the wrong people."

I swallowed hard. Claudette had chosen to associate with the wrong people too. Had my father also made that mistake in his friendship with Gordon?

We all fell silent, lost in our own thoughts.

"Tell me again," Gordon demanded moments later. "This was exactly how you found it?"

I nodded quickly. "Rolled up, like this."

"No frame?"

"No frame," Roux echoed in his usual, flat tone. Boy, did that come in handy for lying.

I made a mental note, then erased it. I'd already shaved enough around the edges of my morals. I couldn't afford to trim any more.

I tilted my head, imitating the old, gullible me. "I didn't realize you were so interested in the frame. Was there something important about it?"

"Yes! I mean, no." His eyes darkened, and he glared at Roux.

I touched Gordon's arm, keeping his focus on me. Safer for everyone that way.

"Gordon," I said as gently as I could. "Is there something you're not telling me?"

My heart hammered, because this was it. His last chance to convince me he was the good-hearted man I'd always taken him for.

Silence stretched... and stretched, like a balloon filled past its limits. A vein in his forehead pulsed, and beads of sweat glistened on his brow.

"Of course not," he said gruffly.

Boom! The imaginary balloon burst, taking my loyalty to Gordon with it.

"It's just..." He cast around for a moment before going on. "I suppose I grew fond of it as it was. It looks some-how...different this way."

Wow. A blatant lie. To my face.

If it weren't for Roux signaling for me to remain cool, I would have lost it.

"Well, we have the painting, and that's what counts," I forced myself to say.

Gordon's expression told me how off the mark I was. Then he turned to Roux.

"What else do you have to report? No sign of Grepper on the way in or out? No sign of Alexandre Ernaux's men?"

Roux's gaze was perfectly level. "Nothing, sir."

Gordon still didn't look satisfied, but he never would be, short of Roux pulling that Monet out of one of his cargo pockets and saying, *Oh yes. I almost forgot about this priceless artwork you never mentioned.*

"Still, I think it would have been better to work through the authorities," I said.

"And risk your father's painting?" Gordon shot back. "It could have been destroyed by the time the authorities took action."

"Well, I'm sure Dad would agree it's not worth me — or you — gaining a criminal record for breaking and entering, or worse."

Much, much worse, in your case, I almost added.

Roux held up his oversized, multifunctional wristwatch. "We need to get going if we're to catch the train we booked for the trip back."

Good old Roux — always pulling me back from the brink.

I checked the antique clock on the mantelpiece and won-dered if that had been stolen too. Then I rammed a steel rod down my backbone and faced Gordon.

"He's right," I murmured. "We really ought to go. Unless you have any more questions?"

Gordon's eyes bored into mine, and for the first time, I saw suspicion there.

Well, that beat seeing me as gullible, I decided.

The tap on my skull grew unbearable as he tried to spy on my thoughts. Then he frowned and looked away again.

"No. That will be all," he grumbled, then threw in a belated "Thank you" to keep from sounding too harsh.

So, maybe he really loved me.

Maybe that could be useful also flitted through my mind. Another concerning sign of how devious I was becoming.

I headed for the door before Gordon corrupted me any further. But a calendar on a side table caught my eye — one of those small, triangular ones that stood on its own. We had one at the château too, but ours was a freebie from the nearest car shop that featured grainy photos of local scenery. Gordon's came from a bank, judging by the fancy styling and discreet sponsorship label, and it featured famous artworks.

It was open to November, and the picture showed Monet's *Meules* — Haystacks.

Opportunity wasn't knocking — it was banging on the door to my mind. So, I grabbed it. Literally, by picking up the calendar and studying the image.

"Monet," I mused. "So beautiful."

Gordon shrugged. "Yes, but popularity has made some of his pieces almost ordinary."

"You're right. It is nice to come across lesser-known pieces," I said.

Roux shot me the same look he'd used when I'd charged up the stairs at Grepper's. Yes, I was treading on thin ice. But I had to know, for my father's sake.

"Mom said Dad was trying to track down a couple of lost paintings when he died," I went on.

My mother had said no such thing, but that was a safe enough thing to say since my father had always been working on one such project or another.

"One was a Monet, I think," I continued. "Did he ever tell you about it?"

Gordon's gaze went out the windows, but he didn't focus on the view of the canal below or Montmartre in the distance.

"I remember your father gathering information about a missing Monet, but not the timing," he finally said.

The tic by his eye said otherwise.

It took everything I had not to shake him, because along with the lie, I sensed profound sorrow. Why? What did Gordon know that I didn't?

"Mom never talks about his accident," I said quietly.

My voice went a little scratchy, and I joined Gordon in gazing off into the distance.

"But I've always wondered," I added truthfully. "What can you tell me about it?"

Gordon looked at me sharply, but I kept my eyes on the windows.

"The police said it was brake failure," he said, choosing his words carefully.

That was what the police reported. Did Gordon think otherwise? Did he *know* otherwise?

"Did the car have a current inspection?"

Gordon shrugged. "I'm not sure. It was your grandmother's. But, sweetheart..."

My shoulders tensed. If he chose this moment to hug me, I might vomit.

"...sometimes it doesn't help to wonder."

Ha. Didn't help me or didn't help him, especially if I suspected murder?

"I know, but it hurts not to know," I said. No need to hide a lie that time.

Gordon nodded gravely. "I understand, but why not remember the good instead of the bad?"

In any other context, I might have agreed. But not when it came to hiding an ugly truth.

Roux cleared his throat. "Forty-five minutes left to catch the train."

Factoring in the walk to the station, that meant we had to get moving soon.

Part of me longed to keep up the amateur sleuthing. But probing any deeper would arouse Gordon's suspicions. I hadn't voiced my concerns to Mina before, but I was ready to now. The moment I got home, I would talk to her.

Then I corrected myself. The moment I got home, I would shag Roux senseless. *Then* I would talk to Mina.

Still, I was ready to push Gordon on one last topic.

"Oh!" I exclaimed, turning to Roux. "Didn't Gordon promise a premium for finding the artwork before it was damaged or destroyed?"

Gordon's eyes just about bugged out of his head.

"€10,000 each, right?" I went on.

Roux's eyes told me not to push my luck.

"And really, the whole team made it possible," I threw in. "Henrik, Marius, and Bene too."

"You said it was an easy in-and-out operation," Gordon growled at Roux.

Roux scratched his cheek, clearly torn.

Well, I wasn't. "*That* part was easy. Gathering information and tracking down the painting took a *lot* of work," I said.

A hurricane raged in Gordon's eyes, and Roux shook his head to defuse things.

"Not necessary, sir."

Earlier, Roux had told me that Gordon had offered him €25,000 to keep me safe and that he had no intention of cashing in on the reward.

Whatever I did, I did for you, not for Gordon, he'd practically snarled.

Typical Roux — too principled for his own good.

Well, I, for one, would be happy to squeeze a bonus out of Gordon.

So, squeeze I did. Mercilessly.

"Of course it's necessary," I insisted. "Gordon is a man of his word. Aren't you?" I smiled up at him sweetly.

The room vibrated with magical energy, and he gritted his teeth.

"Of course, but—"

"Really not necessary," Roux murmured, meeting my eyes.

I refuse to have that hanging over us, he whispered into my mind.

Well, I wouldn't mind having that much cash to hang *anywhere.* Still, I had to respect his point.

I thought quickly, then stuck up a finger. "Oh! Wait. I have an idea."

Roux looked at me in alarm. *Another one?*

"Doesn't your contract end soon?" I asked him.

He had the grace not to rattle off the exact number of days, minutes, and hours, as Bene would. He just nodded. "Next week."

"What about terminating those contracts immediately? Instead of a cash reward, I mean." I looked at Gordon. "I know better than anyone how generous Gordon can be, but maybe that's a simpler solution."

Bene would grouse about letting €10,000 slip away, but I doubted Gordon would pay out anyway. Terminating their contracts, on the other hand, wouldn't cost him a cent, and I had the feeling he looked forward to being rid of the guys as much as they looked forward to being rid of him. So, a win-win for everyone.

Especially me, because I would get a tiger shifter all to myself for a well-deserved break — and a much-needed heart-to-heart.

"Not a bad idea," Roux admitted.

Gordon's eyes blazed stubbornly, but a moment later, he relented.

"Fine. I'll send the paperwork through later today." He scowled and looked around, remembering he no longer had an assistant to help with such things.

"I'll ask Mina to draft an addendum," I said. "She's good at that kind of thing."

Mina hated me volunteering her for anything, but I figured she wouldn't mind in this particular case.

Gordon's expression remained sour, but he nodded. "That would be helpful."

Roux tapped his watch.

"Oh — the train," I said cheerily. "We should get going."

I hugged Gordon, a gesture made more palatable by my little victory with the contracts. Then I scooted out the door, right behind Roux.

Just when I thought we were home free, Gordon called out sharply.

"Wait!"

I gulped and turned slowly, bracing myself for an onslaught of magic. Would Gordon probe my mind as he had before? Would he try to wipe my memory, as Grepper had done to his Hot Young Thing?

"Yes?" My voice wavered.

Gordon's eyes pierced mine. Then he cleared his throat and murmured, "Just a moment."

When he disappeared into the study, Roux squeezed my hand and whispered, "If he tries something, run for the stairs."

God, I hoped that wouldn't be necessary.

Gordon returned, carefully rolling my father's painting. He slid it carefully into the storage tube, then handed it to me.

"You take it. My gift to you and your sister. I love you all, you know. Your whole family."

He said it so gruffly, so genuinely, that a corner of my heart melted. No matter how I searched for a hint of a lie, I couldn't find one. Just sincere, bottomless sorrow.

Which made me more conflicted than ever. What did it all mean?

I found myself hugging him again. "Thank you, Gordon. For everything."

Then I peeled away and walked out the door, waving good-bye.

Chapter Twenty-Nine

GENEVIÈVE

We arrived back home late. Extra-late, in fact, since Roux and I had stopped for dinner before making the final leg of the journey to the château.

How did it go? Mina had texted me earlier to ask.

Surprisingly well. Details tomorrow, I'd promised.

The hair on the back of my neck stood when we drove past the turnoff to Claudette's home and the police station in Auberre.

Roux took a hand off the steering wheel to squeeze mine.

I closed my eyes, going from melancholy to grateful. We'd been through so much together, and he'd always stuck by my side.

He did the same when we made the turn for home, near the spot where we'd been attacked, and again when we passed the chapel. I pulled his hand to my lips for a quick kiss, then released it to let him park.

He turned off the engine, but I didn't move. I just sat, gazing at the château. Only a few weeks ago, I'd arrived here, clueless and reeling from another bad breakup. Now, that felt like a lifetime ago. I felt wiser. Tougher. Even more loved — not just by family members, but by a special someone.

A *very* special someone with stripes and a tail. I grinned at the wall before me.

"Everything okay?" Roux asked softly.

I smiled at him. "Sorry. All good."

We exited the car and ascended the stairs to the massive front doors. I looked up, thinking of all the different times and circumstances I'd faced those doors, from skipping through as a child, to greeting guests at one of my grandmother's huge parties, to entering, crying, after my father's funeral, and more recently, my grandmother's. But the good times outweighed the bad, such as the wedding we'd recently "staged" for Mina and Marius.

So much had changed over the years, but the sense of connection was stronger than ever. To my past, and to all the people we'd welcomed here over the years. And a profound sense of connection to the man I entered with now.

I gripped Roux's hand and stepped through the doors.

Habit made him steer for the right-hand stairs, but I tugged him toward the hallway behind the left-side stairs — the one leading to the lower story of the east wing, where I lived.

"Do you need anything from your room?" I asked, praying he would say no.

He shook his head, following me.

"Anything from the kitchen?" I asked as we passed it.

Another shake of the head.

A voice called out, and I winced. Damn.

"Well, hello," Bene said, stepping out of the kitchen with a bowl in his hands.

"Hello, Bene. All good here?" I asked.

He nodded, tilting the bowl at me. "Madame Picard made crème brûlée. You want some?"

"No, thanks. See you in the morning," I said, towing Roux on.

"Let me guess," he teased. "You have your own stash of crème brûlée in your room?"

I laughed. "Something even more tempting."

"There's only one thing more tempting than crème brûlée," Bene observed.

"Don't encourage him," Roux muttered, but it was too fun to resist.

"Two things," I shot back. "Chocolate mousse is one."

"And sex is the other," Bene filled in without missing a beat. "But not when it's with Roux. That ranks down under crème brûlée. Way down with asparagus soufflé."

Roux shot him the finger.

"You're speaking from experience?" I challenged.

"Hell no," Bene said. "But I'm sure asparagus fits. You know, all soft and floppy..."

Roux growled under his breath, while I laughed outright.

"Good night, Bene. Enjoy your crème brûlée."

He sighed and retreated to the kitchen. "Enjoy your asparagus."

Oh, I planned to. But the hallway stretched on and on, and my room was all the way at the end.

"What?" I asked in response to Roux's quiet grumble.

"I'll show him fucking asparagus..."

I stopped and slid my arms around his neck. "I prefer you show *me*."

He grumbled, slowly pinning me against the wall. "You know what I mean."

I did, and he proceeded to debunk Bene's theory in record time. Before I knew it, I'd wrapped both legs around his waist and was grinding shamelessly against him.

I opened my mouth for a joke, but Roux smothered my words with a kiss. His arms flexed, easily holding me up, and his tongue stroked over mine.

Tigers did not mess around when it came to sex.

I jutted my elbow toward my room.

"Much as I like — er, *love* this — we should get moving before Bene shows up with more asparagus jokes."

"Screw Bene," Roux grumbled, kissing my neck.

I chuckled. "I'd rather screw you. Soon."

When he scraped his teeth over my skin, I nearly yowled. Suddenly, sex in the semi-public place didn't seem like an issue.

But Roux pulled away and slowly lowered me. I grabbed his hand and raced toward my door. We burst through and slammed it behind us.

The lower story of the east wing was its own little apartment of four big rooms, arranged in a square. An old couch and a coffee table stood by the fireplace in the first room. My queen bed took up a fraction of the second room, facing the windows and kitty-corner to another fireplace. Mina's apartment above mirrored mine, though her bedroom faced the back while mine faced the front. A good thing, because sound carried, even with walls as thick as these.

Usually, that helped reduce the noise I was subjected to from upstairs. Tonight, it was likely to be the other way around.

I stopped, pushing back Roux's jacket, then tossing it on the couch. He threw mine on top of it, and more layers quickly followed.

It was cold as hell, and I quickly led him to my bedroom.

"Should I light a fire?"

His eyes glowed as he shook his head. "Later. Right now…"

He trailed off, running his hands over my body. Kissing muffled my squeaks of pleasure, but when we finally rid ourselves of our last layers and slid into bed—

"Oh!" I gripped the carved posts of the headboard as Roux kissed his way down to my core.

I'd left on a lamp in the living room, and a slice of dim light spilled into the bedroom. Just enough to make out a comical hump under the blankets. Well, it might *appear* comical. The sensations were heavenly, and my cries rose in pitch. Roux wrapped his arms around my thighs, drawing me to his mouth. It was raw. Greedy. And so, so satisfying.

No more sneaking off secretly. No more keeping quiet. This man was mine, and I was his.

And boy, did I let the world know it when he brought me to the first shattering orgasm of the night.

"Shh." He chuckled, climbing back up my body as I lay panting in the sheets.

"You want Bene to joke about asparagus all week?" I scolded.

"Pretty sure we've eliminated that possibility."

A lock of hair fell over his eyes, giving him a roguish look. Nice to see my straitlaced military guy loosen up for a change.

I grinned up at him, trying very, very hard not to crack more asparagus jokes.

Don't you dare, he grumbled.

I changed tack, patting the mattress. "What do you think? Comfortable enough?"

"Didn't really notice. But, yes." He ran a hand over it. "Seems pretty comfortable."

I cupped his cheek, growing serious. "Comfortable enough for you to use for a long, long time?"

Sparkles flashed in his amber eyes. "Are you asking me to commit to a mattress?"

I play-smacked him. "I'm asking you to stay. With me. For..." My tongue tangled there. *Forever* crossed my mind, but I didn't want to scare him off. "For a while, at least."

He shook his head. "Not for a while. Forever. Tigers know *forever* when they find it." He took a breath, then went on. "Geneviève, you could live in a shack and sleep on the floor, and I would be there with you."

He paused, searching my eyes. Half afraid, I sensed, that I might say no.

As if.

I wrapped my arms around him as my soul soared off to cloud nine.

"I'm all for forever — as long as it's with you. If you can take me for that long, I mean."

When he shook his head, his chin scrubbed my shoulder, making my blood heat. "More like, if you can take *me*."

I chuckled. "My dirty mind is listing all the ways I can take you. Starting with this..."

I ran my leg along his and bent my knee outward.

He sniffed along my neck, then growled in my ear. "I like the way you think."

"I am a genius sometimes."

His snort tickled my ear. "When you're not trying to get yourself killed."

"Other than those times, yes. But let's not get sidetracked, please."

"Wouldn't dare," he murmured, covering my lips.

We briefly considered, then discarded, the idea of a condom. We both had supernatural immune systems, and the remote possibility of being joined by an adorable baby tiger shifter nine months down the line didn't qualify as a huge risk in my book.

Soon, I was wrapped around Roux as tightly as the ivy on the stable walls, breathing hard, and very much enjoying digging my fingers into his muscled ass. But missionary position was a little too tame for my mood, and soon, I found myself curling upright.

"Suppose I suggest we switch to all fours?" I panted.

His eyes flashed, and he reared back, making space for me to roll. I came to my knees and wiggled my ass.

He made a choked sound and slid up behind me. "And here I am, trying to be patient."

I butted against him, spreading my knees. "You might be, but I'm a lost cause."

"Never," he swore, and he meant it.

I added that to the long list of things I loved about him.

He crept forward, gripping my hips. I held my breath, my heart revving in anticipation.

When he pushed in — and in, and in — I gasped at the slow, sweet burn.

He paused. "Breathe, Geneviève."

I shook my head. "Oxygen is overrated."

He rocked forward, then paused. I lowered my head and rocked back. If he thought I needed time, he was wrong.

No one would ever accuse you of playing for time, he chuckled in my mind, though his voice was strained.

"You can be the patient one in this relationship," I murmured, then gasped again.

He eased away, then pushed forward. Once...twice...

I waited, tuning in, because sex was like jump rope, double-Dutch style. You had to catch the rhythm before jumping in.

And boy did I jump. We rocked together again and again. Slowly at first, then harder and faster.

My hair swayed in front of my face. The blankets slipped away. Warm, sharp breaths tickled my back. I leaned right, making my hair sway to one side. Roux made a hungry sound and ran his teeth along the side of my neck.

I shivered in anticipation. Those weren't regular, human teeth. They were elongated, like a tiger's.

"Yes," I mumbled, angling my head to give him more space.

He ran his teeth back up, and I begged for more.

"Yes. . . please. . ."

I wasn't actually sure what I was begging for, only that I needed it badly.

"Are you sure?" Roux rasped in my ear.

Of course I was sure, though I couldn't name what I was starving for.

"It's forever, Gen," he warned.

I nodded stupidly. We'd already given *forever* a thumbs-up. So, what was the holdup?

Then I realized what he meant. A mating bite.

The notion ought to have filled me with fear, but it didn't.

Roux scraped his teeth along my neck again, breathing harder than ever. Then he tensed, muttered to himself, and kissed me instead.

"Not tonight."

"Who says?" I protested.

"Believe me, I want it too. But we ought to wait."

I shook my head. "Waiting is also overrated."

He kissed the light scratches on my neck.

"Picture how good it will be when we're not exhausted. When we've had a good day. When things are settled."

I could have screamed, but then I remembered all the times he'd saved me from myself. Was this another one?

"In case you haven't noticed, delayed gratification is not my thing."

He chuckled. "Oh, I noticed. But we don't have to wait a long time. Just for the *right* time."

I slumped. "I hate it when you're right."

Then I pictured a moonlight walk. A slow dance. Candles. Clean sheets. A fire crackling in the fireplace.

Maybe waiting wouldn't be so bad after all.

"I'll make it up to you. I promise." He snuck a hand along my ribs to cup my breast. "Now, where were we?"

I bumped back against him.

"Right... about... here," I squeaked when he pushed back into me.

That was the last thing I said for a long time, and the only sound was the quiet creak of the bed as we worked our way back into a steady rhythm. No talking, just panting. Touching. Needing.

"Yes..." I moaned as an inferno raged inside me.

Roux slammed into me again and again, and I rocked back, amplifying every thrust. Our steady rhythm faltered, then went completely haywire.

Roux hammered several more times, then exploded inside me with a strangled cry. I opened my mouth in a silent howl of ecstasy, and my vision blurred.

When it slowly came back into focus, I was in a different place and time. In place of wrinkled sheets before me, I saw a tangled forest stabbed with long shafts of light. I smelled damp leaves, and I felt dirt under my paws.

Wait. Paws?

Roux exhaled and lowered his hands from my hips to the mattress. I sensed it, but I saw something different — a blur of orange, black, and white stripes gliding along at my side as I trotted through that forest. Together, we passed through bands of light and the dark shadows in between. Light, shadow. Light, shadow...

I spotted triangular ears flecked with white but tipped in black, and a long whip of a tail where orange and black squeezed into orderly bands. Above all, I saw glowing, amber eyes.

You're stunning, the me in my vision breathed to her mate.

He chuffed and whispered back. *You're the stunning one, my mate.*

I looked down, going wide-eyed. My chest was furry and white, wrapped with thin lines of black. My legs were long, lean, and orange, my nose creased by thick black stripes.

All that, I knew because I saw myself through Roux's eyes.

Then that vision faded, and I was back in bed, staring at the sheets. Slowly, I crumpled to my stomach. Roux pressed over me, equally exhausted.

He found my hands and wove his fingers through mine. His quick breaths stirred a few strands of my hair, but otherwise, we didn't move.

I'd never felt so warm. So wanted. So connected.

Eventually, we cleaned up, rearranged the blankets, and spooned together, with Roux's front to my back and his thick arm resting over my chest.

I closed my eyes and hummed in satisfaction. That vision would soon be reality. And, wow. Then I could control some types of magic and shift too. A dream come true.

"Thank you," I whispered. "For everything."

He shook his head. "Thank *you.*"

I snorted. "What do you have to thank me for? Other than great sex, I mean."

He chuckled. "I love it when you're modest."

"I'm so bad at so many things, I like to give myself credit for the things I'm actually good at."

He shook his head. "Not true. You're good at magic…"

I snorted.

"You're good at diplomacy too."

"Diplomacy?"

He nodded firmly. "When it comes to dealing with us and with Gordon."

I groaned. "I'm giving myself the rest of the night off from bad things."

"Good. Think about the future."

I perked up and curled my fingers around his. "Like, a mating bite?"

He snickered. "And they say men are obsessed with sex."

"It's your fault."

He sighed. "Now you sound like Bene."

I laughed, then stroked his chest, thinking. "You realize that if we take that step—"

"When," he corrected me.

I smiled. "*When* we take that step, it will make Marius your brother-in-law. Can you handle that?"

He grimaced, then shrugged. "Could be worse. Could be Henrik."

I gagged. "Please, no. Don't even joke about it."

He grinned. "Well, I think your mother will like me better than Marius," he said a little smugly. "I know more about art."

He knew a hell of a lot, as I'd learned — and loved. Still, that wasn't what worried me.

"Seriously," I went on. "Do you think you can live under the same roof with Marius? I mean, not when you're assigned to work together, but doing it by choice."

He gestured up. "Luckily, it's a big roof."

He had a point there.

I glanced around, rearranging the space in my imagination. I hadn't had time to spruce things up and make the apartment homey, but it would be great when I did. Not just this room or my sitting room, but the other two rooms too. Kids' rooms, maybe?

Roux's eyes went wide when he caught the gist of my thoughts, and I bit my lip.

"Sorry. I'm getting a little ahead of myself."

He pulled me closer. "Always good to have a visionary on the team."

"As well as someone with their feet on the ground." I pointed at him.

His amber eyes glowed. "Not on the ground. More like cloud nine."

I snuggled back into a spooned position, and we lay quietly, growing drowsy. It had been a hell of a day, but for once, we could look forward to sleeping in the next morning.

"About that mating bite..." I whispered.

He groaned. "I've created a monster."

I chuckled. "You really don't mind waiting?"

He shook his head. "Like I said, tigers are patient. And we know a good thing when we find it." Then he kissed my shoulder and pulled the blanket a little higher over our shoulders. "Good night, Geneviève."

"Good night," I whispered, then smiled. "The best in a long, long time."

He nuzzled me with his chin. "The first of many."

Chapter Thirty

ROUX

We had all morning to sleep in, and for once, my inner alarm clock didn't go off at five a.m. I slept until six, then spent a full hour basking in bed. Bene had always claimed that counted as an activity, and I'd always scoffed. But now...

Well, maybe lions weren't as stupid as I'd thought.

I basked and basked, thinking about the past life-changing weeks. I even glanced around, deciding where to put my few belongings. When I slipped out of bed, it was only for a quick trip to the toilet and to light a fire in the fireplace.

When I turned back to the bed, I found Gen peeking at me. She patted my ass as I slid back into bed.

"Sorry. Couldn't help admiring my favorite view."

I wrapped my hands around hers and locked them at my chest. "This is my favorite."

She smiled, gazing into my eyes. "Sleep well?"

I nodded. "So well, I slept in."

"Seven does not count as sleeping in," she declared, pulling me back under the covers.

We spent a good hour there, and only a few seconds of that were devoted to talking.

Eventually, we forced ourselves out of bed, taking advantage of the last warmth of the fire to dash to the bathroom for a shower.

Gen held a hand under the water, testing the temperature. "Sorry. It takes forever to run warm here."

"Not as long as it takes upstairs in the west wing," I observed.

Gen grinned. "Number one reason to move in with me down here?"

I shook my head. "Like I said, you could live in a shack with no bed or running water, and I would be there with you, loving every minute." Then I smiled. "But, yes. Warm water has its advantages."

An advantage we made full use of, showering for much longer than my usual three minutes.

"What?" Gen asked, picking up on my thoughts when we toweled off.

I shot her a weak smile. "Sleeping in, then taking a long shower. I'm definitely getting soft."

She play-smacked my stomach. "Nothing soft there, mister." Then she glanced down and winked. "No asparagus effects either."

I caught her in my towel. "If this relationship is going to work, we're going to have to ban Bene's bad jokes from the bedroom."

"We're in the bathr—" she started, all snarky.

I cut her off with a kiss, then mumbled, "Bathroom too."

It was only meant to be a quick kiss, but one led to another and another, and we would have landed back in bed if the in-house bell system hadn't ring just then — the only part of the château's 1930s wiring in that still worked reliably.

I groaned. "If that's Bene ruining a perfectly good morning with a call to breakfast, I'll kill him."

Gen patted her stomach. "I could eat, though." Then she grimaced. "But I'm not looking forward to the teasing."

"Let them tease," I declared, grabbing my clothing.

And tease they did, especially Bene.

He cracked a huge, theatrical yawn when Gen and I entered the dining room, then made a show of checking the clock.

"Oh, look who's last to breakfast," he announced. "And who's coming to breakfast with whom."

"Oh, leave them alone, Bene." Mina chided.

"He's just jealous," Gen said, making a show of kissing me.

Bene shook his head sadly. "It's true. I've been secretly lusting after Roux for years, and now I'm heartbroken."

"So heartbroken, you've eaten almost all the bacon?" Mina challenged.

"I'm drowning my sorrows," he declared.

I sat in my usual place and poured myself a cup of coffee. I was going to need it with this gang.

"You need to add an item to your job list," Marius told Mina. "Better sound insulation for the east wing."

Gen blushed but shot back, "Finally, you noticed."

Mina pointed to Marius. "Any noise we make is his fault."

He flashed her a wolfish grin, not at all repentant. "Your fault."

I buttered my toast, channeling all the Zen I could muster.

"You should add better noise insulation for the benefit of us in the west wing too," Bene threw in.

"Which you have all to yourself now," Mina pointed out.

Bene waggled his eyebrows. "Lots of space for company."

Henrik looked up from reading the newspaper in his usual corner, disgusted by the level of conversation. The paper was probably a week old, but *current events* had a different meaning when a guy lived for centuries.

A pang of sorrow hit me — a rare thing to feel for Henrik. To live that long without ever finding your true love, or worse — finding and losing her... No wonder the guy was permanently downcast.

I put a hand on Gen's thigh, resolving to treasure every moment we had together.

Bene studied Gen and me. "Wait. How serious is this? Don't tell me I'll have to share the woods with two tigers instead of one."

"All 120 acres," Mina muttered. "Poor baby."

"Once our contract ends, you can leave any time you want." Marius pointed out.

"I will, believe me," Bene retorted.

"You can't leave, Bene!" Mina admonished.

"Not with that coffee machine, at least," Marius grumbled, unmoved.

"That beauty is mine, buddy," Bene growled.

"Bene can't leave. He's like family." Gen sided with Mina.

"Yes, like a really annoying younger brother," I muttered.

Henrik nodded silently, then gazed out the window, and I wondered about the family he must have outlived by several centuries.

Another argument against eternal life, if you asked me.

"Just wait. I'll leave a hole in your lives when I'm gone," Bene declared, then gestured to me. "Pass the eggs, *brother*."

I passed the platter without comment.

"You have another week of my fine company," Bene said through open-mouth chewing. "Then I'll be out of here."

"And how terribly we'll miss you," Henrik deadpanned.

Mina shot Gen an alarmed look that said, *Please tell me Henrik isn't staying.*

Gen frowned back, and I sensed her thinking of the pendant he'd given her. As long as she had that, she and Mina could feel relatively safe, if not free of his company.

My inner tiger snarled. *Relatively safe?*

Well, I would be around to make that a one-hundred-percent guarantee.

"And what are your plans, Henrik?" Mina asked, picking her words carefully.

He barely looked up from the newspaper. "Time will tell."

The thing was, she couldn't evict him. Henrik had rented the caretaker's cottage on the edge of the château grounds — a place that had been sold decades earlier and was now in the hands of an absentee landlord. It had been empty for years, but Henrik seemed comfortable enough there to stay for a while. Not an idea any of us relished, even if he had saved our asses in Switzerland by alerting us to the vampires' arrival.

"And your plans, Roux?" Mina asked in a more encouraging tone.

I looked at Gen, who blushed.

Stay. The longer, the better, she whispered into my mind.

"Better watch out," Bene warned. "When a cat settles in, it's hard to get rid of him."

"Who says I want to get rid of him?" Gen retorted. "Or, wait. Are you talking about yourself?"

Bene wagged a finger at her. "Oh, I see through you, lady. You're just after my coffee machine."

I sipped from my mug, then nodded. So did Marius.

Bene snorted. "You know you'll miss me when I'm gone."

"We'll try to," Marius muttered.

Mina kept her eyes on me, reminding me of her question.

"Um, I'd like to stay a while," I said as evenly as I could. *Forever,* I added, saving that part for Gen's mind only.

She flashed me a radiant smile, and Mina grinned knowingly.

"So this *is* a long-term thing," she observed.

"Of course it is," Bene filled in. "I could see it coming from miles away. But I see advantages in this for all of us."

"Advantages?" I growled.

Bene nodded cheerily. "Like you relaxing a little, champ. Maybe even letting the rest of us sleep in occasionally." He laughed at Gen's expression. "If he does, you get full credit. If he doesn't, we'll blame it on him."

"How is everything always my fault?" I protested.

Bene smirked. "Because you're in charge, buddy. But not for long, so enjoy it while you can."

Gen's eyes sparkled. "You want to tell them, or should I?"

"Tell us what?" Mina asked.

Everyone looked over.

I finished my toast, drawing out the suspense.

"Tell us what?" Bene insisted.

I flicked the crumbs from my fingers and took another sip of coffee.

"He's torturing us on purpose," Bene muttered.

"Payback for all the bad jokes," Marius commented.

Absolutely. I dragged it out a little longer, then came out with the news.

"Gen talked Gordon into ending our contracts immediately."

Bene looked delighted. Henrik, indifferent. Marius, suspicious.

"How?"

I shrugged. "She's just that brilliant."

"I am — sometimes," she agreed. Then she turned to Mina. "Oh. I told Gordon you'd help draw up an addendum to that effect. You know, since he lost his assistant," she added snidely.

"Fucking Celeste..." Marius muttered.

Gen gave him a sharp look. "Don't speak ill of the dead."

"Well, rest in peace and all that," Bene muttered, not too sincerely. "Now, back to our contracts... How did you convince Gordon?"

"Gen could convince the Pope to convert," Mina assured him.

Gen laughed. "I don't know about that. And as for Gordon... He wasn't too pleased to get Dad's painting back without the frame, though he wouldn't admit what he was really after. So I called it *mission accomplished* and reminded him about that bonus he offered. I even argued that everyone deserved ten thousand each..."

"*I* definitely did." Bene patted his chest.

Marius snorted. "Do you mean the moment you got zapped by the magic spell or the time you got hauled away in the back seat of a car?"

Bene frowned. "Okay, not my best moment. But that magic *hurt,* man."

Gen patted his shoulder. "I'm sure it did."

"Couldn't you have negotiated to split €10,000 between us?" Bene persisted.

Marius shook his head. "No way would Gordon pay up."

Gen nodded. "That's what I figured. This way, you get a clean break without him dragging things out indefinitely."

Mina walked over to where she'd left her laptop. "I'll send him the addendum right now."

Gen joined her, making suggestions. After typing away for a few minutes, Mina showed the results to Marius, then me. We both nodded.

"What about me?" Bene complained.

She started turning the screen around, but he waved a hand. "Nah, all good. I trust you."

"Henrik?" Gen asked.

The vampire locked eyes with her, then nodded. "I trust you."

High praise from a vampire, indeed.

Mina sent off the addendum, and everyone picked quietly at the remaining food. Minutes later, my phone pinged with an incoming message, echoed by more pings around the room. We all grabbed our phones.

"Wow. That was fast," Marius observed.

"I guess Gordon is that desperate to get rid of us," I said dryly.

"The feeling is mutual," Henrik chimed in.

Everyone checked the fine print — even Bene — then signed and returned their contracts before Gordon changed his mind. The moment I did, a weight lifted from my shoulders.

For months now, we'd been beholden to the whims of a ruthless warlock, doing work so fraught with danger that we didn't dare dream of the future.

But now, we were free. Really free — to go anywhere, do anything...

Or go nowhere at all, my tiger hummed happily.

I leaned over and kissed Gen.

Marius rolled his eyes. "It begins."

Bene snickered. "Says the guy who mooned over Mina from day one."

"I did not moon," Marius growled. Then he looked at Mina and broke into a goofy, lovestruck smile.

"I rest my case," Bene muttered.

Our phones pinged with Gordon's countersignature, and I reread the contract three times, not quite believing my eyes.

Bene checked his, then gave Gen a high five. "Bonus aside, you are a goddamn genius. And I have to say, you're more devious than you look."

She sighed. "Not sure *devious* is something to be proud of."

Mina patted her shoulder. "Around Gordon, it's necessary."

Gen gulped, and I knew she was thinking about her father.

Mina tilted her head in question, but Gen forced a smile. "I'll tell you later. For now, let's celebrate. Is it too early for champagne?"

"It's never too early for champagne." Bene jumped to his feet, heading for the wine cellar.

Mina tapped her lips while we waited. "It will be a relief to divest ourselves of Gordon. But the money he paid us to host you here sure didn't hurt."

"We'll all work doubly hard," I said immediately.

Henrik gave me a frosty, *speak for yourself* look.

Gen's phone rang, and we all tensed. Was that Gordon?

Her eyes went wide as she answered in French. "Oh, *bonjour*, Monsieur Delmont. Yes, yes. So nice of Lily to have spoken to you."

Marius looked lost, but Mina perked up and mouthed, *The electrician I've been trying to get for ages.*

Gen put the phone on speaker in time for us to hear the electrician's reply.

"My future daughter-in-law tells me your electrical work is a matter of the utmost urgency." He sighed. "So I've found a time slot for you — and only one, between February and the end of March."

My eyes went wide. That was much sooner than anyone had anticipated.

Mina nudged Gen, who nodded and relayed the unspoken question. "Just to check, you're aware of the scale of the project?"

"Yes, I'm familiar with the place, and I'm confident we can do it in that time frame," Delmont assured her. "But I'll need to visit to calculate an estimate. How would tomorrow be?"

Mina's mouth hung open. The man hadn't replied to multiple queries over the past months. Now, he was offering to drop in tomorrow.

Gen did a fist pump. "Tomorrow would be fine. Thank you."

He suggested nine a.m., and my tiger side grimaced.

What about basking with our mate?

I shushed the beast. Nine a.m. left plenty of time for basking, and we had a lifetime of mornings to enjoy afterward.

"Lily mentioned a classic car..." Delmont hinted.

Gen grinned. "Absolutely. I'll show it to you at the end of our tour of the buildings. See you at nine o'clock." Gen hung up, then gave her sister a high five. Everyone hugged — apart from Henrik, though he did look impressed — and I patted Gen's shoulder.

"She specializes in the impossible." I grinned proudly.

Gen's eyes sparkled. "Now I just need to come through for you with that Wiggly carburetor."

"Wrigley," I corrected her, one hundred percent sure she would manage that — as well as assuring Delmont he would get a free ride... eventually.

Bene reappeared with a bottle of champagne, and we all raised our glasses in a toast.

"First, to Claudette," Mina said somberly.

She didn't add, *To ridding the world of the monsters who killed her*, but I guessed everyone thought that. I definitely did.

"To Claudette." Everyone touched glasses, and a long, quiet minute went by.

"I feel like we have to do something in her honor," Gen finally said.

"Like planting a tree or a rosebush, maybe?" Mina suggested.

Gen shook her head. "I was thinking something really special. Like... hosting a summer camp here or something. Something that offers kids a safe place and good opportunities."

Two things poor Claudette had never had the "luxury" of, I figured.

"I like that idea, but it will take time until we can offer something like that," Mina cautioned. "We'll need power, plumbing, and a roof that doesn't leak."

Gen nodded. "Extra motivation for us to work hard."

Typical Gen. All heart, all forward momentum.

Weeks ago, I might have thought Gen was biting off more than she could chew. Now, I had no doubt she would pull it off — and sooner than anyone expected.

I, for one, was ready to work my ass off to make her vision a reality.

"You know, that would be worth me and my coffee machine sticking around a while longer," Bene decided.

"Anyway... I think Claudette wouldn't mind if we asked Bene for a joke to lighten things up," Gen said.

"I agree." Mina turned to him expectantly.

He cleared his throat — twice, hinting at hidden grief.

"Let's see... Okay, here's a joke. Two sisters and their cousin inherit a chateau, but the catch is, they have to put up four strangers. A lion, a dragon, a tiger, and a vampire."

Mina rubbed her hands together. "This, I have to hear."

Even Henrik was hooked.

"And?" Marius prompted when Bene hesitated.

The lion shifter grinned. "The straitlaced sister gets the wildest guy, and the wilder sister gets the straitlaced guy."

Mina laughed outright, while Gen protested. "Wild?"

"In the best possible way," Bene assured her. "Which leaves the vampire and the lion." He let a beat go by, then blew Henrik a kiss. "I guess you and me get to live happily ever after, dude."

Everyone laughed, except Henrik, who flashed his fangs.

Bene chuckled. "Seriously, man. You've got a choice of me or Clement."

Marius hooted. "That, I have to see."

"I guarantee you won't," Henrik snipped.

I wondered if Delphine, the prostitute, crossed his mind. But how would that work? Delphine was human. He was a vampire.

"All right, all right," Mina cut in. "Enough of that, before you fight and threaten my grandmother's china — again."

"To our credit, we haven't had a good fight in *weeks*," Bene pointed out. "I feel like we're due one."

Mina shook her head firmly. "Not before we finish our toast." She raised her glass again and nodded to Henrik.

"To the end of our contracts," he said, as pleased as I'd ever seen him.

"And new beginnings." Gen touched her glass to mine.

We clinked, getting lost in each other's eyes before the others nudged us to clink with them too.

"See? Hopeless." Marius shook his head at us.

I ignored him, kissing Gen. Her lips tasted like champagne, and the joy in her eyes made my heart flip.

"To new beginnings," I whispered, letting everything but her fade from my vision.

Chapter Thirty-One

ROUX

One week later. . .

It was one of those rare fall days in Paris — sky a brilliant blue, air crisp, sun shining. Perfect for that date I'd been promising Gen.

We walked hand in hand along the Seine, a new experience for me. Not the Paris part, but walking hand in hand like a couple of happy lovers. Which I supposed we were.

Mates, my tiger growled. *Even better.*

We hadn't made it official with a bite yet, but that wasn't far off. And in the meantime. . .

"Wow. A whole day, just to enjoy ourselves," Gen murmured, tilting her face toward the sun as we walked.

"Two days," I reminded her.

"True, but yesterday felt a little more like work."

"If that's work, I'm happy to put in overtime," I declared.

We'd spent the previous day rearranging her — er, our — apartment in the château and moving my things in, followed by a long afternoon walk through the surrounding fields, woods, and vineyards. A perfect day, as far as I was concerned.

The others had finally eased up on their teasing, and Bene had even helped me move my few things over to Gen's.

The faster you move out, the sooner I get the west wing to myself, he'd said. *The entire west wing, baby.*

Don't get too comfortable, Gen warned. *We'll be renting those rooms soon.*

He shrugged. *I'll cross that bridge when I get to it. And in the meantime, my own little kingdom.*

Bene definitely cultivated a short-term mind-set. But I, for one, wondered what the future held for him.

I've decided not to decide until the new year, he'd announced in typical Bene fashion.

That long? Marius had grumbled.

Mina elbowed him.

I mean, only *that long?* he'd corrected himself glumly.

It was all an act, though — Marius being grouchy, Bene unable to commit. We'd all grown into what felt more and more like a family — even Henrik, bizarrely — and it was hard to imagine the château without everyone there. Living together-but-apart in our own little apartment within the grander place was a perfect arrangement as far as I was concerned.

"Things will change when Dora arrives," Gen mused as we walked along.

Her cousin — the third co-owner of the château, together with Gen and Mina — was due to arrive in about one month, just in time for Christmas.

I squeezed Gen's hand. "Things changed when you arrived — for the better."

"I just wonder how long Dora will stay. She's been pretty noncommittal about it so far."

I chuckled. "I thought I was coming for a few months, and now, I never want to leave. Maybe the same thing will happen to her."

Gen laughed outright. "You mean, finding the perfect person and falling in love?"

I shrugged. "Why not?"

Gen snorted. "Her options are Henrik and Bene. I can't see either happening."

"Don't forget Officer Dulaire."

She snorted. "Clem is not her type."

Surprisingly, I felt sorry for the guy. He'd lost Mina and passed up his chance with Gen. If I were him, I would regret that for the rest of my life.

I held her hand a little more tightly, grateful things had worked out as they had.

We walked in silence, gazing at the Louvre on the opposite bank.

"That's where those thieves got in to steal the crown jewels," I murmured, pointing to an upper balcony on the middle floor.

"Bastards," she grumbled. Then she held up a finger. "Oh! I know what they could do to increase security at the Louvre."

"Bring in vampires and warlocks to cast spells?" I guessed.

She nodded. "Can you imagine? Thieves would think twice."

I shrugged. "They didn't stop you."

She made a face. "I only did it for my dad's painting. Also, we got lucky."

I snorted. "Not luck. You were brilliant."

"Maybe just a little." She grinned.

We walked on in silence. A short time later, she pointed to another architectural landmark.

"Oh — the Orangerie!"

I patted my pocket. "Got our tickets right here. Six p.m."

"And I have my sketchbook right here." She patted her backpack. "I can't wait."

She'd decided on a theme to paint on the ballroom walls — water lilies in the style of Monet. Everyone loved the idea, so we weren't just visiting the museum to enjoy the paintings. We were researching too.

Gen grinned and slid her arm around my waist. "For the record, this is already the best date ever. Brunch was delicious too."

We'd detoured to my favorite place in the Latin Quarter on the way over, but that was just a warm-up to what I had planned.

"Not the best date yet, but it will be," I promised. "We're nearly there."

I'd tried to create a little suspense about our next destination, and while it had to be obvious, Gen clapped and cheered when we arrived.

"The Musée d'Orsay!"

I nodded. "For pleasure, not work. And not just the cheap ticket. We have all day." I patted her backpack, then my pockets. "We have your sketchbook, drinks, and a reservation for the Café Campana at three."

Her eyes went wide. "The one that looks out through the face of the clock?"

I nodded, fairly proud of myself. "I got us the best table for two, with the best view."

"How did you manage that?"

"Marius knows a guy who knows a guy... I didn't ask too many questions, though."

She tsked. "Monsieur Anand, are you letting your principles slip?"

I shook my head. "Principles are for big things. Other things, you can let slide."

She laughed. "I'm corrupting you."

I kissed her hand. "Just a little."

I'd prebooked tickets — full price for the first time in my life, but it was worth every penny — so there was no waiting in line. We started with the sculptures on the lower levels, formerly platforms in the converted train station. Gen already had her sketchbook open, ready to choose a subject.

"How about Rodin?" I asked, pointing to *The Gates of Hell*.

Gen whisked right by it. "Are you kidding? Total mood-killer."

She spent a minute contemplating the dynamic lines of Bourdelle's *Hercules Slaying the Stymphalian Bird*, depicting the demigod as an archer, then moved on.

Avoiding the crowd at Degas's *La Petite Danseuse*, we continued our search, eventually working our way up one level.

"If only he did tigers," I murmured when we reached François Pompon's *Ours blanc*, a smooth, minimalist polar bear in marble.

Gen chuckled, and I thought she might sketch it. But she walked straight on to Bugatti's *Walking Panther*.

"This one," she said firmly.

I scratched my chin. "Not a tiger, but close."

"I'll make him into a tiger for you," she declared and proceeded to do just that from a nearby bench.

I sat beside her, my arm propped behind her, my thigh touching hers.

Heaven, my tiger hummed.

A day in one of my favorite places with the woman I loved? Yes — the best. I focused on Gen as much as the artworks around us, mesmerized by her quick, confident pencil strokes. When she paused to smooth back a stray lock of hair, my soul sighed. That small, simple movement held so much grace and serenity, it swept me away.

Truly heaven. And I could look forward to weeks of the same, because we'd soon be painting the ballroom, among other jobs at the château.

Home, my tiger hummed happily.

I touched Gen's back and watched as she made the panther — now a tiger — practically leap off the page.

She stopped to contemplate her work, then the sculpture. "Bugatti... Like the car maker?"

"Brother to the car maker."

She chuckled. "Of course you would know that. Pretty artistic family, huh?"

"They don't hold a candle to yours."

She laughed, bumping my shoulder. "Maybe in some ways. But we'll leave the cars to you."

Visions of handing me tools and sketching me at work on the Jaguar danced through her mind, and I hid a grin. The equivalent of me watching her sketch, I supposed.

Twenty minutes later, we stood and explored other artworks on that level. Then we indulged in cake and coffee at the café, right by the massive clockface with its iconic views over Paris.

Gen reached across the table to wipe a crumb off my cheek. I licked it off her finger, and *whoosh!* My inner temperature soared, and my tiger grew dangerously hungry.

Gen licked her lips, which only made things worse.

"There's got to be a broom closet we could disappear into around here," she murmured.

I thought she was joking, but no. After a few dead-ends, she found one by sneaking down a narrow hall of administrative rooms.

"Oh my gosh. I really am a genius," she whispered, running her hands down my rear in the darkness of that small space.

"You are," I agreed, helping her shed a few layers and hoisting her up.

We might not have scored points for *grace* or *elegance*, but we did manage *quiet*.

The important thing is to score, Gen chuckled into my mind.

Then she choked back a moan and hung on.

So, whew. I hadn't exactly planned on that little interlude, but it was like Gen said. Sometimes the best things in life were unplanned.

Afterward, we held each other, panting hard. Then, when we caught our breath, we doubled over in chuckles at what we'd just done.

"Shh. Shh," I urged, trying to muffle my own laugh.

"Talk about an artistic movement," Gen chuckled.

"An interactive installation," I threw in.

We both cracked up. I'd never laughed so hard — the silent kind where you heaved for breath and held your sides.

"Now you've truly corrupted me," Gen said when we finally got ourselves together.

"You, Mademoiselle Durand, are the one corrupting *me*," I insisted.

She listened at the door, then nodded. "The coast is clear."

We snuck out as stealthily as we'd snuck in. Then we split up at the restrooms to clean up as best we could. I splashed my face with water and ran my hands through my hair, undoing the bedroom look Gen had given me.

A twentysomething guy at the next sink glanced over, wide-eyed.

"*Euh… tu profites bien des expos, toi?*" he deadpanned. *Enjoying the exhibits, huh?*

I grinned. "*Inoubliable.*" *Unforgettable.*

Then I found my way back to Gen, who whispered in my ear. "I'm almost tempted to ditch the museum and head to Henrik's place. Now that we know where he hides the key and all..."

I steered her firmly to the last hall we intended to cover — the Impressionists.

"I'm chock-full of impressions for today," Gen grumbled.

"Indulge me," I whispered, tugging her gently along.

Something in me thirsted for a full-circle moment, having been here with Gen in bad circumstances and now in good.

I put my hand over her eyes, whispering, "Take me to my favorite."

"You still don't believe me?"

"Oh, I believe you. But it's like seeing a masterpiece — you want to see it again and again."

She grinned and held my hand, keeping her eyes closed. "Okay. Just keep me from knocking into furniture. I can only hear paintings."

And off she went, identifying the artworks we passed by sound.

"Gustave Caillebotte — *The Floor Scrapers*. Gypsy caravan. A church."

I nodded. "*L'église d'Auvers-sur-Oise*." The woman was amazing.

"*Bong, bong*," she joked, pointing to Monet's *Houses of Parliament*.

I chuckled. "Yes, Big Ben."

And yes, her eyes were still closed. I would have sworn it was impossible, but hey. That was Gen's specialty. I grinned so wide, a woman gave me a side-eyed glance that said, *These paintings aren't that amazing.*

Maybe not, but Gen was.

"There." Gen pointed. "Your favorite."

She opened her eyes, and we admired Van Gogh's *Starry Night Over the Rhône* for a while.

"My turn for a request. Ready?" she asked.

I didn't reply right away, too busy imprinting the moment in my memory. How many times had I stood in exactly the same spot, but alone, not even imagining the turn my life would take?

"All good?" Gen asked quietly.

I squeezed her hand. "Great."

Better than I ever thought life could get, in fact.

Yes, we faced a huge challenge in terms of saving the château. And yes, we would probably encounter more nasty supernaturals in the future. But as long as we stuck together — all of us, not just Gen and I — we could surmount those obstacles. We could thrive beyond our wildest dreams.

My chest swelled as I smiled at her. "Lead the way."

She set off, backtracking through until we reached Monet's *Poppy Field.*

"This is where you figured it all out," I said, more in awe of Gen than the painting.

"Thanks to your help," she whispered.

I let my eyes wander over the painting, noting the prominent elements. Camille's blue parasol... The red stripe in Jean's hat, matching the color of the waist-high flowers... The slight V of the landscape farther back...

Gen did the same with her eyes closed. Was she listening to little Jean call to his mother? The whisper of wind over the fields?

A smile played on her lips, then faded away as she tuned in to something else. Seconds ticked by. Then she lurched and blinked, gazing around.

I grabbed her arm, going on red alert. Had she sensed danger? Intruders? Yet another painting?

God, I hoped not.

I searched her eyes. "What is it?"

"Nothing. Sorry. I mean..." She leaned in and whispered. "I saw it. Monet's painting of Manet in his garden."

I nodded dumbly. "We both saw it."

She shook her head. "No, I mean, I had a vision of it. In a big frame on a wall in a different gallery." She closed her eyes again, recalling the vision. "There were people there... cocktails... Like opening day at a new exhibit."

Her eyes popped open, and she grabbed my arm. "A gallery. Grepper is going to show it."

My eyes went wide. She could see the future too?

"I guess I can't be sure. But it felt so real — the same way I saw you and me as tigers."

Now *that* vision, I liked.

"And now, this," she murmured.

Her eyes shone, and she clasped my hands. "Maybe we did it. Maybe we convinced Grepper to exhibit the painting."

"If he does, it's thanks to you."

"Wouldn't that be something?" Her eyes shone with excitement.

I drew her in for a kiss. Whether Grepper exhibited the painting or not didn't matter much to me. But it mattered to her. And, hell. If anyone could talk a greedy warlock into doing the right thing, it would be Gen.

"*You're* something, Geneviève," I said, letting her name roll off my tongue. "Truly."

She grinned up at me. "If so, then it's you bringing out the best in me."

Sneak Peek: Touched by Starlight

A missing masterpiece. A magical inheritance. A temptation that's impossible to resist. All Pandora "Dora" Ross wants is to help her cousins renovate the château they inherited, finish her thesis, and quickly move on to a stellar new career. Instead, she finds herself reluctantly playing sleuth and taking on shifters, vampires, and a long-lost masterpiece...

Books by Anna Lowe

Château Nocturne

Brushed by Moonlight (Book 1)

Marked by Moonlight (Book 2)

Touched by Magic (Book 3)

Touched by Starlight (Book 4)

Bound by Midnight (Book 5)

Spellbound in Sedona

Wind Whisperer (Book 1)

Fire Dancer (Book 2)

Dream Weaver (Book 3)

Sherwood Forest Shifters

Tempting the Sheriff (Book 1)

Tempting the Outlaw (Book 2)

Tempting the Maiden (Book 3)

Lure of the Dragon (Book 1)

Lure of the Wolf (Book 2)

Lure of the Bear (Book 3)

Lure of the Tiger (Book 4)

Love of the Dragon (Book 5)

Lure of the Fox (Book 6)

Aloha Shifters - Pearls of Desire

Rebel Dragon (Book 1)

Rebel Bear (Book 2)

Rebel Lion (Book 3)

Rebel Wolf (Book 4)

Rebel Heart (A prequel to Book 5)

Rebel Alpha (Book 5)

Fire Maidens - Billionaires & Bodyguards

Fire Maidens: Paris (Book 1)

Fire Maidens: London (Book 2)

Fire Maidens: Rome (Book 3)

Fire Maidens: Portugal (Book 4)

Fire Maidens: Ireland (Book 5)

Fire Maidens: Scotland (Book 6)

Fire Maidens: Venice (Book 7)

Fire Maidens: Greece (Book 8)

Fire Maidens: Switzerland (Book 9)

The Wolves of Twin Moon Ranch

Desert Hunt (the Prequel)

Desert Moon (Book 1)

Desert Blood (Book 2)

Desert Fate (Book 3)

Desert Heart (Book 4)

Desert Rose (Book 5)

Desert Roots (Book 6)

Desert Destiny (Book 7)

Sasquatch Surprise (Book 8)

Desert Yule (a short story)

Desert Wolf: Complete Collection (Four short stories)

Blue Moon Saloon

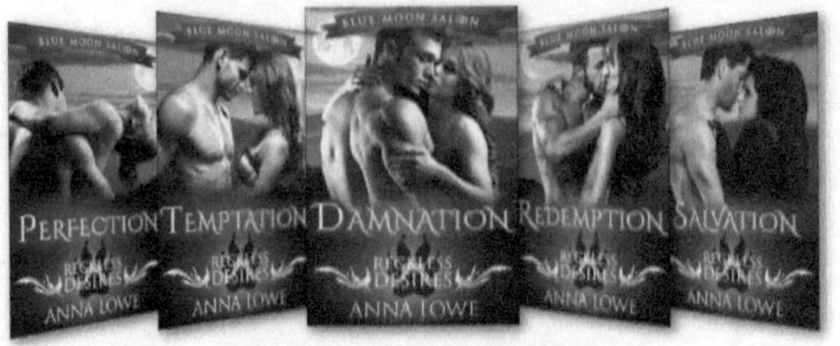

Perfection (a short story prequel)

Damnation (Book 1)

Temptation (Book 2)

Redemption (Book 3)

Salvation (Book 4)

Deception (Book 5)

Celebration (a holiday treat)

Shifters in Vegas

Paranormal romance with a zany twist

Gambling on Trouble

Gambling on Her Dragon

Gambling on Her Bear

Gambling on Her Panther

Serendipity Adventure Romance

Off the Charts

Uncharted

Entangled

Windswept

Adrift

Travel Romance

Veiled Fantasies

Island Fantasies

www.annalowebooks.com

About the Author

USA Today and Amazon bestselling author Anna Lowe loves putting the "hero" back into heroine and letting location ignite a passionate romance. She likes a heroine who is independent, intelligent, and imperfect – a woman who is doing just fine on her own. But give the heroine a good man – not to mention a chance to overcome her own inhibitions – and she'll never turn down the chance for adventure, nor shy away from danger.

Anna loves dogs, sports, and travel – and letting those inspire her fiction. On any given weekend, you might find her hiking in the mountains or hunched over her laptop, working on her latest story. Either way, the day will end with a chunk of dark chocolate and a good read.

Visit AnnaLoweBooks.com